To Kathy

From The Savino Sisters Mystery Series

Enjoy!

(Book 3) Not Worth Dying For

Loretta Giacoletto

Loretta Giacoletto

Copyright © 2018 Loretta Giacoletto

All rights reserved.

ISBN: 1986698920
ISBN-13: 978-1986698924
Library of Congress Control Number: 2018904159

Cover

Elizabeth Mackey
Graphic Design

ACKNOWLEDGMENTS

My thanks to Bob Lambert, Diane Giacoletto Lambert, Heather Giacoletto, Judy Hendricks, Elizabeth Lambert, Nick Giacoletto, Paul Giacoletto, Chris Giacoletto, Peg Bohnenstiehl, Steve Giacoletto, Michelle Giacoletto, Captain Guy Means of the St. Louis County Police Department, and to Dominic Giacoletto for his patience and continuing support.

1

East of the Arch

Blessed are those brief moments of uninterrupted peace—that unsuspecting pre-dawn before the stench of death brings with it an abomination yet to be discovered.

In St. Louis on any given riverfront morning, a 630-foot steel monument known as the Gateway Arch keeps its vigilant watch over the downtown cityscape: a conglomerate of modest skyscrapers; convention hotels; street-level retail shops and eateries; warehouses from the nineteenth century, and Busch Stadium, home of the Baseball Cardinals. The panoramic view from the Arch extends westward into the sprawling St. Louis County suburbs and across the Mississippi River eastward into Illinois, a once-over of East St. Louis before skirting past the man-made mounds of landfill visible from Interstate 70 and beyond that landfill, Horseshoe Lake State Park.

The subtle pride of Southern Illinois offers a number of recreational conveniences, with its haven for wildlife interspersed with picnicking, fishing, quiet boating, and seasonal duck hunting. Plus those havens less desirable—a welcomed solitude for suicide, illegal drug dealings, and eyebrow-raising sexual encounters. Not to mention the unceremonious disposal of dead bodies.

Loretta Giacoletto

On the pre-dawn Monday of August 12, 2013, in an area bordering the park's 2,400-acre lake, an unsettling calm had crept into a bank of trees, its shadowed glory of leaves in their prime hovering over the body of a well-toned man of average height stretched out on his side. His closely cropped gray hair covered a head turned to one side. The astonished look on his face reflected a point of no return, where swarms of flies buzzed over two gunshot wounds—one to the heart with blood staining his stripped shirt, another to the space between vacant eyes that once attracted an enviable number of women.

2

Home Again

"It's time the two of you came home." Those were Nonnie Clarita's words to Margo and me during the last of many phone calls we'd made to her during our 2013 Italian holiday. Really? After several unpredictable glitches we'd extended our vacation by several weeks yet to be used, and home for all concerned meant St. Louis. "Your mom hasn't been around whenever you called for good reason," Nonnie went on to say. "She's got herself mixed up in a heap of trouble."

"Our mom," Margo and I replied as one. "You've got to be kidding."

"Would I kid about a thing like murder? Come on, by now you ought to know me better than that."

We certainly did, especially since Nonnie had recently opened her heart and soul to us about the love of her life, an ill-fated teenage romance from long ago, one that resulted in three mysterious deaths during the Second World War, life-altering events so traumatic and heartbreaking they eventually triggered her immigration to America.

Now Margo and I were back, having started our day at Malpensa Airport in Milan, and from there to Newark before arriving in St. Louis at nine-thirty in the evening. It had been an uneventful yet grueling journey that covered over twenty-four hours of travel with bloodshot eyes wide open and begging for closure. We Savino sisters—Margo and myself, Ellen—parted company at Lambert Airport, each taking a taxi to our individual suburban condos—hers in upscale Clayton, mine in the more affordable Brentwood. By the time I'd unpacked and gone through my mail, I did nothing else other than shower, slip into soft PJs, and snuggle into bed, feeling no pangs of guilt whatsoever. After all, had I still been in Italy, it would've been six in the morning after a sleepless night, so in St. Louis time I had some serious catching up ahead of me.

Somewhat refreshed by eight o'clock the next morning, I drove over to the Holly Hills house of my youth, a comfortable brick bungalow that my mother and her mother still shared. As was the custom of all inhabitants, former and current plus the closest of friends, I entered through the back door, stepping into an enviable mudroom equipped with a durable door mat meant for wiping any trace of dirt from the soles of dust-laden shoes before crossing the threshold into the temple of cleanliness. On seeing Mom, her back turned to me as she wiped down the kitchen sink, I felt an immediate sense of relief, given Nonnie Clarita's cryptic telephone comment about her only child involved in a heap of murderous trouble.

"Mom," I said. "Is everything okay?"

She turned, dishcloth in hand and ready to resume cleaning on a moment's notice. One look at me made her burst into tears before blurting out, "I thought you decided to stay another week or so. Where's Margo?"

"Uh … I guess at home sleeping. Our plane didn't get in until late last night."

When Mom wiped her runny nose with the dishcloth and then flipped it into the sink, I knew Margo and I indeed had a problem. Enter Nonnie Clarita, with one task in mind, putting on the morning coffee. As soon as the coffee maker showed signs of doing its thing, Nonnie patted the arm of her only child, handed her a tissue, and offered a few comforting words. "New day. It can only get better, right?"

Talk about awkward, I cleared my throat. "*Buongiorno*, oops I mean good morning."

At the sound of my voice Nonnie jumped a good two inches off of the ceramic tiled floor. "What the ... oh, it's you, Ellen. Such a scare you gave me." She opened her arms and wiggled her fingers. "Get over here and give your nonna a hug. Your ma, too."

I covered the short distance in five easy steps and we three generations engaged in a group squeeze, the kind requiring no spoken words. When our embrace ran out of steam, Nonnie repeated Mom's earlier question. "Where's Margo?"

Before I could answer, she pulled me aside and gave her interpretation of a whisper in my ear. "Don't tell me your sister met somebody on the plane, one of those mile-high bathroom disgraces?"

"I heard that," Mom said, folding her arms. "Really, Mama, must you be so crass?"

"Nothing happened," I assured both of them, at least not in a plane.

Mom stepped back, looking me up and down before she said, "Not bad. How many?"

"Twenty, give or take." I was, of course, referring to my recent weight loss.

"Whatever you did, don't stop."

"Looks like Ellen maybe got herself a boyfriend," Nonnie said with a wink in my direction.

"Nothing serious," I added, returning Nonnie's wink with a glare. "A holiday fling that's already over."

"Sit," Mom said, pointing to the kitchen chair I'd used since my teenage years. "We'll talk about this fling after coffee."

"There's nothing to talk about. I've moved on, so has he."

"He has a name," Mom said.

"Not one I care to repeat." Nor one she'd have recognized so what would've been the point.

Having set three cups and matching saucers on the table—one at each end for Mom and Nonnie, mine on the side—I poured steaming coffee into the cups while Nonnie took flavored creamer from the fridge and almond biscotti from the cookie drawer. After we sat down, the next few minutes were devoted to our simple breakfast, with me taking an occasional glance in Mom's direction.

Whatever the current problems, they'd played havoc with Toni Riva Savino's face, creating dark circles under puffing eyes and frown lines in the corners of her mouth that hadn't been there before Margo and I left for Italy less than two months before. As for Nonnie, she hadn't changed one comforting iota. In fact, she may've looked even better than the last time I saw her. Confession is supposedly good for the soul, or so I'd been taught, and while Margo and I had been abroad communicating via cell phones with Nonnie, she had unloaded the sins of her past on us. In details so graphic and passionate I could not imagine Nonnie ever revealing them to her daughter, our oh-so-uptight Mom.

While in Italy we'd also found out a few tidbits about our mom at eighteen, her age of rebellion when she summered in the same village where Margo and I had spent a week or so unearthing family skeletons. I tried picturing Mom as the mama-mia, defiant teenager my surprise Italian relative had recently described: long dark hair, pink lips, and blue eyes with amber specks. The amber specks still defined her blue eyes but in today's world she'd allowed her cropped hair to do its own thing—a mass of uncontrolled dark curls streaked with salon-made nutmeg and the occasional strands of natural gray.

What once had been no longer was. We three generations were living in the now, a time to deal with whatever skeletons had recently surfaced in the fifty-something's life.

"So, what's going on?" I dared to ask. Silence was the only answer Mom gave me so I pressed a bit further. "Nonnie mentioned something about a murder."

"You told her?" Mom said, directing her question to Nonnie.

"I might've said something," Nonnie replied with her usual shrug. "But I didn't go into any details. Those I leave to you."

"This had better be good. Margo and I cut our trip short to hurry back and do whatever daughters are supposed to do when their mother is accused of murder."

"What?" Mom tapped her breast. "Not me."

"Not yet but the damn thing's in the works," Nonnie said. "Just give it some time."

I stuck out my defiant arms, showed Mom and Nonnie my upright hands. "Stop right there. Whatever this particular *it* is, just give *it* to me straight, okay? From the beginning, if that's even possible."

"Anything is possible, if you believe hard enough and wave your magic wand," said a voice from the doorway. Without a doubt, the words and their tone of delivery could only be described as cynical. I didn't have to turn my head to know they came from my only sister, my traveling companion during most of our sometimes-adventurous-but-never-boring Italian getaway."

"Well, it's about time you showed up," said our mother, her prickly attitude far more tolerable to the tear-jerker one she'd foisted on me earlier.

"Good seeing you too." Margo moved with her usual grace, hugging Mom and then Nonnie while I remained seated so as not to facilitate another Kumbaya moment. After helping herself to coffee, Margo rattled the pot, letting me know we needed more.

Yes, I could've told Margo to make it herself, but after all these years of independent living she still hadn't mastered the proper ratio of coffee to water. Cold water, that is. How many times did I have to tell her? Of course, had I waited long enough, Nonnie would've hopped up and put on a fresh brew. Or Mom would have. Instead, I pushed back my chair and did

7

my duty while Margo presented a rapid-fire rundown of our vacation. Make that the highlights. Nice, her rendition saved me from having to re-hash the heartbreak of my first love, an international affair so short-lived I'm not sure it even happened, had it not been for the ache still pestering my heart. As for Nonnie's first love, further details would have to wait until we heard about the murder that brought us home prematurely.

"Uh, excuse me," I said, waving the nearest dishcloth before realizing it was the same one Mom had used to wipe her runny nose.

"*Zitto*, everybody quiet," Nonnie said with a gesture of crisscrossed hands. "Ellen's got something she wants to say."

"It's about this murder that Mom's supposed to be involved in. Could you please tell us what's going on so I can get on with my own life." Ugh, did those words come from my mouth? They seemed so … self-centered. For a convent dropout, that is, which may explain why I chose not to take my final vows.

"The telling ain't that easy," Nonnie said. "But go ahead, Toni. From the beginning."

Mom sighed, deep and with more emotion than she usually expressed, other than with the death of my dad. "You may recall Val Corrigan."

"That two-timing jerk Kat has been dating, even though she should've known better," Margo said, referring to Kat Dorchester, Mom's best friend since their Catholic high school days in the Central West End of St. Louis.

The color drained from Mom's face. She hesitated before speaking in a low voice. "Er … that would be … would've been Val."

"So, what are you saying?" I asked, stirring two cubes of sugar into my unacceptable lukewarm coffee. "That Val finally got caught cheating on some woman who truly believed he loved her and now he's dead?"

"Or maybe a married one whose husband wasn't so forgiving and now he's still dead?" Margo added. "Not that I should be casting the first stone."

"Tell us something we don't already know," Nonnie said, her first

8

comment on the topic.

"Mama, please," Mom said. "We aren't talking about Margo, not this time anyway."

"You got that right," Nonnie said. "So, Toni, don't keep your girls guessing any longer."

Mom blew her nose into the crumpled tissue she dug out of her pocket. "Just hear me out. And please, no smarmy comments."

"El, more coffee please," Margo said with a snap of her fingers.

Telling Margo to get her on damn coffee would've ruined whatever momentum had just begun. Instead I headed toward the sink to empty my cup and grab the pot of freshly brewed coffee. "Go ahead, Mom."

"Go ahead, Toni," Nonnie said.

"That's what I've been trying to do." She took a deep breath and let it out with her next words. "As you all know, Kat and I have been best friends since our freshman year at Rosati-Kain."

"Don't tell me you cheated on Auntie Kat." Margo made her point by sticking one middle finger in each ear. "How could you, Mom? Replacing your best friend forever is practically as bad as cheating on your hair stylist. Say it isn't so; I don't have the heart to hear it."

Nonnie got up and yanked Margo's fingers from her ears. "Show some compassion. This ain't easy for your ma."

"Sorry, Mom. Please go on. I won't say another word until you're finished."

"That's what scares me," Mom said. "Your silence speaks louder than any of those sarcastic comments you feel compelled to dish out."

"Get on with it, Toni. Or I'll tell the girls what I know, which may be a different version from what you want them to hear."

"Er ... right. Well, as you may recall, last year around Christmas, Kat suffered a horrific attack of colitis and wound up in the hospital between the holidays—a terrible time what with most of the medical staff taking off to celebrate with their families. Anyway, Val being a free-spirited kind of guy started dating this woman and that woman. I couldn't bring myself to tell Kat that I'd allowed myself to become one of those women."

Our mother hadn't looked at another man in the five years since Dad died, not to my knowledge anyway. I opened my mouth but quickly closed it, honoring my promise not to interrupt.

"On the other hand," Mom continued, "keeping quiet about my betrayal—which I did—only made things worse, knowing it would ruin our friendship when Kat eventually found out. What I should've done, and now regret that I didn't do, was to end my relationship with Val. Easier said than done.

"After five lonely years, I just wanted someone to care about me, to pull out my chair before I sat down, to take me to fine restaurants, and the latest movies without me having to wait for the films to go video. Although Kat eventually regained her health, Val kept calling me and taking me to even nicer places—live theater and the symphony. Of course, I didn't tell Kat since she'd admitted to falling in love with Val, against her better judgment. The woman was no fool. How utterly stupid of me, involved with a man I wasn't sure I even liked. Given enough time, I might've loved Val but first I had to trust him. That was the hard part, since I no longer trusted myself to do the right thing.

"It's all history now. Kat and I never had the discussion we should've had, a shameful *come-to-Jesus* moment with me asking her forgiveness. Nor will Val ever be able to ask Kat's forgiveness since he experienced his own *come-to-Jesus*, literally. His body was found over in Illinois, not far from downtown St. Louis. Now Kat's on the verge of being arrested for his murder, which I don't *think* she committed—long story. A possible lovers' triangle, police are calling it, given Val's fondness for the ladies, myself included." She paused, taking a deep breath before proceeding. "As I said before, I don't think Kat could've done such a terrible thing. Above all else, one thing is for certain: I did not kill Val Corrigan."

Mom finally stopped talking, giving me a chance to speak up. "So-o,

Not Worth Dying For

how do you know Kat didn't kill Val Corrigan?"

She gave me her look of exasperation, one perfected over the years. "Because, Ellen, at the approximate time of Val's death, Kat and I were together. We spent the entire night at her place. Just the two of us. And now, wouldn't you know: the police consider Kat's alibi more than a little suspicious, making me a prime suspect along with her."

3

Lawyering Up

Antonia Riva Savino, our ultra-sensible and ultra-obstinate mom, who as a young mother had ruled El and me with an iron fist and a tongue sharper than Nonnie Clarita's, said a shitload about both of them. Whatever could our mom have been thinking in the here and now? At fifty-eight, no less, having an affair with her best friend's main squeeze, a guy juggling more than one woman simultaneously. Never had I seen Mom so shook up. But then, never had she come close to being arrested for a crime she claimed not to have committed. Or helped Kat Dorchester commit. On the other hand, I could see Mom helping to cover up a crime Kat might've committed. Crimes of passion often begin with a simple romp in the sheets before descending into a more hellish type of unbridled passion, which Kat often said epitomized her mixed lineage of Black, White, and Asian.

Time for me to exit the family home. El, too; she almost knocked me over while scrambling to the door and from there, the backyard and alley. We parted in the driveway, leaving Mom behind to tend the real estate appraisal business she operated from home and Nonnie to restore order in the always spotless kitchen while El and I resumed the life we'd left behind two months before our Italian holiday, one that had evolved into an adventure of more than one crime, more than one passion, and more than one discovery of family skeletons.

Although I'd taken an extended leave from my paralegal position and wasn't due back for another two weeks, I really needed a sit-down with my boss, who at forty-six was one of the top personal injury lawyers in St. Louis. And happily married to the love of his life who'd given him three well-mannered kids, making him off-limits to me. All-American to the core, Blake Harrington was an attorney whose opinion other attorneys respected. With a wave of the hand I breezed past his gatekeeper Evangeline and entered the inner sanctum of his private office.

There sat Blake, leaning back in his ergonomic swivel chair, his size twelve Cole Hahn loafers propped on the desk cluttered with life-altering printed matter. He shifted his feet to the floor, squared his shoulders against the back of the chair, and with half a smile, snarled a stream of accusatory questions. "What? Why the early return after asking for more time off? No ring on your finger? No permanent move to Italy? You couldn't stay away any longer?"

"Could've. Would've. Should've. Unfortunately, a family emergency came up."

He leaned forward, resting his forearms on the desk. "Don't tell me the almost-nun sister of yours got herself pregnant."

"Not exactly … well, no … although El did meet someone."

"And you?"

"Met, connected, and split, thank God," I said with a snap of fingers. "The story of my life, one I don't regret in the least. But I'm here on another matter."

He sat back again and with a wave of one hand gestured for me to continue. I relayed the story Mom had told El and me, practically verbatim knowing she would be horrified about my sharing such stupidity with Blake Harrington, a man who respected her as much as she did him. While I explained her predicament, Blake sniffed and cleared his throat. He blew his nose, a testament to the hay fever harassing a sizable chunk of the St. Louis area population until the first freeze would kill the offending pollen, a welcomed relief that usually occurred in early November.

"Fred Montgomery," Blake said with a nod. "I'll make the phone call."

"For my mom and her friend Kat Dorchester?" I asked, already knowing the obvious.

"Hell, no. Don't go sentimental on me, Margo. The friend—and possible perpetrator—needs her own attorney. No way is this Dorchester woman bringing down your mother."

"Then you think Mom is innocent?"

"Just what is it you've been sniffing this early in the day? Have you learned nothing from me these past seven years? Of course your mother's innocent, especially with Montgomery representing her."

"But what about Kat?"

He twisted his mouth to one side and contemplated my question, taking longer than necessary to come up with a response I could live with. "Have her call me. Only then will I initiate a contact on her behalf. With a different attorney, one almost as good as Montgomery but not quite. In the meantime, your mother should stay away from the Dorchester woman."

∞∞∞∞

Monday morning, ten o'clock, found Mom and me sitting across the desk from Fred Montgomery. He was … how should I say this without coming across as petty, unkind, and shamefully shallow. With great difficulty, yes, because those words describe me to a perfect T. While Fred listened to Mom repeat the same story she already told El and me, I searched his face and overall appearance, trying to imagine him as a brilliant man whose wisdom had come with age—his in the neighborhood of mid-sixties. Those thick lips, hooded eyes, and portly mid-section did nothing to project such wisdom. Nor did the lack of a wedding ring on his third finger, which made me think there'd never been a ring to get in his way.

No need to worry about this attorney-client relationship going beyond that of strictly professional, even though I'd now seen a side of my mother

I never expected, one capable of betraying her best friend to enjoy the pleasures of modern dating and guilt-free sex with no strings attached. In other words, my life as an uninhibited thirty-something.

"Do you need the explicit details?" I heard Mom ask him. Please, cringe-worthy details did not become Toni Savino. Cringe-worthy details better defined my modus operandi.

Fred Montgomery honked into his rumpled handkerchief, a sharp contrast to the inconspicuous manner in which Blake Harrington had cleared his nose. "That won't be necessary," he said. "At least not for now. What can you tell me about your friend Kat Dorchester and the deceased?"

"You mean Val Corrigan," Mom said.

"Unless there's more than one victim, yes."

"Maybe start with Kat," I said, patting Mom's arm, a gesture her old self would've shaking off.

Fred showed me his chunky palm, distancing himself in a way that made me think of him more as Montgomery than Fred. "I'd like to hear from your mother, unless you're also a prime suspect or involved in a potential cover-up."

"Margo was in Italy when Val died," Mom said with a lift of her chin. "As was her sister Ellen, who would've been here today had she not gone back to educating today's youth. Ellen is a middle school librarian and teacher of literature. Adored by her students; or so I've ... been ... told." Her voice trailed off before she continued, "None of which interests you at the moment, judging from the look on your face."

Montgomery checked his watch and stifled a yawn. "On the contrary, Mrs. Savino, it's your nickel we're talking on."

More like an obscene amount of dollars if this investigation wound up with her going to trial. "Talk fast Mom. Mr. Montgomery charges by the billable hour."

"Like your mother, I too can speak for myself." Montgomery turned to her. "In the event you are charged with a crime, we will discuss my retainer fee at that time. Otherwise, my fee for holding your hand during police interviews will be within reason. Now, please continue."

Mom shuffled in a chair not nearly as comfortable as what Blake Harrington provided his clients. "Kat and I have been friends since high school," she said. "Best friends, I should add."

"And yet, by your own admission, you chose to betray that friendship."

"In a moment or two of weakness, I'm not proud of this, Mr. Montgomery."

"Please, call me Fred."

"I prefer Mr. Montgomery, unless you insist otherwise."

"The only thing I insist on is honesty, Mrs. Savino. On that I cannot, nor will I, bend."

Mom heaved a deep sigh. "First and foremost, I am not a liar. What I say to you will be the truth as I see it."

"And as you would have me see it," he said.

"Of course. As I told you before, I appraise real estate, high-end commercial and upscale residential." She reached into the outer pocket of her handbag, pulled out one of her business cards, and handed it to him.

"I'm neither buying nor selling, Mrs. Savino."

"One never knows, Mr. Montgomery. But there is a point to my card. That's how I first met Val Corrigan through his uncle, Horace Corrigan." She tilted her head to gaze at the ceiling while tapping the row of fingers on her right hand. "That would've been around 2003 when I appraised a property the Corrigans later bought—the Creole Exchange. You've heard of it?"

"Who hasn't," he said. "At one time I considered moving there but decided the urban scene didn't appeal to the country boy in me."

Not Worth Dying For

"It does take a certain mindset. Anyway, Val had moved back to St. Louis to partner with his uncle in some real estate ventures, mostly in what once was the downtown Garment District, including the Creole. Their partnership went well, even years later with Horace dealing with cancer. What kind, I don't know. His cancer had been in remission, but then several years ago, the poor man expired when the cancer metastasized to the brain. Or so the story went." She looked at the lawyer, his chin propped up by one beefy fist. "You're familiar with the medical term?"

Montgomery nodded with his eyelids. "My father was an oncologist."

"Oh, that must've been quite rewarding."

"On the contrary, it was quite depressing. For the most part he treated those who were beyond help."

Mom blinked, sending a single tear down her face. I dabbed my eyes when she said, "Prostate cancer took my husband five years ago."

"You have my belated sympathy, Mrs. Savino. Please continue."

"Some years later, after the uncle succumbed … died, that is, I received a phone call from Val. He asked me to appraise certain properties Horace had left to him—a six-unit apartment house in Clayton, a brick ranch in Town and Country, and some acreage in High Ridge. All in all, the total value appraised in the neighborhood of six million. Val in turn contacted Kat Dorchester to act as his real estate broker. Within a year she sold all three properties, netting Val a substantial increase on the six million and a tidy commission for herself. To celebrate, Val took both of us out to dinner at Alfredo's downtown. You know the restaurant?"

"I eat there every Thursday evening," he said. "*Fred Recommends*—you may have seen it on the specials menu."

"I tend to avoid restaurant *Specials*. Often they're … disappointing."

"Unspecial you mean. Please continue."

Mom went on to explain how Val had fawned over Kat Dorchester, a woman not easily impressed, having suffered through several divorces and one affair ending on a low note. "Several days after Alfredo's, Kat agreed to a single date with Val, one that turned out to be a weekend in the Bahamas. The next weekend Val took her to New York where they attended two theatrical productions and drove through Central Park in a horse-drawn carriage. Corny, according to Kat, but in a way she found irresistible. They soon became a couple, or so Kat and I thought. But then I ran into Val at the Fox Theatre with an attractive woman who had her arm linked with his. Romaine Sloane, he introduced her as. The following week I saw him having dinner at the Ritz with a blonde, younger and prettier than Kat. Zoe something, didn't catch the last name. In both instances Val saw me before I saw him and went out of his way to show off his lady friends. Then there was that evening at the Marriott when I stepped off the elevator as he was getting on with yet another woman, one I recognized as Jet Gregson, a former appraiser and property manager before switching to real estate broker. We'd never actually met nor did Val introduce us. Instead he acknowledged me with nothing more than a simple nod.

"I shared none of this with Kat. She'd been having some health issues that eventually sent her to the hospital so one more aggravation the woman did not need."

Montgomery asked where Mom fit into this, a simple question that made her blush.

"One afternoon while I was visiting Kat in the hospital, who should walk in but Val, his arms filled with peach-colored roses. When Kat noticed the attached card was addressed to someone other than herself, she threw a bedridden hissy-fit, in spite of Val blaming the florist for the mix-up. Kat also threw a pitcher of water in Val's direction. He ducked, leaving me to take the icy bath meant for him. I mean, literally. We backed out of Kat's room and into the hallway where Val patted my face dry with his monogrammed handkerchief.

On our way to the parking garage, he mentioned having tickets to the symphony, center aisle, four rows from the front, and said it would be a shame for them not to be enjoyed. A pick-up line that blatant hardly deserved a response, but Val had been an asset to my appraisal business, recommending me to several bankers during a time when the economy was suffering as were a number of major real estate deals. I all but batted my eyes and said, 'Surely you have a friend who would appreciate sitting next to you.'

"No surprise, the friend turned out to be me. Our evening began with steak and lobster at Rick's on the Riverfront, followed by strawberries and champagne, and then the symphony. We ended with a friendly peck on the cheek, leaving me feel fulfilled but not in the least bit guilt-ridden. I did not expect to hear from Val again, other than business related to his various real estate developments. But after several days passed, he called and asked if I'd seen Kat.

"My most recent visit had been the day before. That infection of hers had me worried, although the doctor said in time it should clear up. I agreed to visit Kat with Val that evening. Lengthy hospital stays tend to bring out the worst in patients confined to bed with contagious infections and Kat was no exception. We stayed long enough to sympathize with her. On our way down the elevator, Val said he was starving, a bit clichéd for even me to swallow. And yet, having nothing better to do, I played along. We wound up at his place, where he insisted on making Western omelets. You know— ham and cheese, onions and peppers all diced up and added to a thin layer of eggs starting to bubble in the skillet. Not as good as Mama's, nor mine, not that I'm bragging. Of course, I didn't go into that with him."

"Nor should you with me." Montgomery waved his hand for her to continue.

"Sorry, my intent was not to bore you," Mom said. "Now here's where it gets … how should I say … not one word from you, Margo … rather personal."

"You went to bed with Mr. Corrigan," Montgomery said.

To which I coughed, having attempted without success to clear my throat. I winced and squeaked out an apology. Not good enough, Mom suggested I excuse myself from the lawyer-client interview. "Please, how bad … or good … can this be," I countered. "It's not like I've been living in my own bubble all these years."

"My point exactly," Mom said. "I'd set higher standards for myself, only to fail miserably with Satan's first temptation."

Loretta Giacoletto

For one brief moment she bowed her head, a simple gesture making me glad to be part of the Millennial Generation instead of her Baby Boomers.

"Ladies, please. Let's move beyond the bedroom for now," Montgomery said. "Tell me about that night you spent with Kat, the night Val met his unfortunate demise."

Having regained her composure, Mom crossed her arms in a defiant manner. "Just so you know, there was no kinky stuff going on between Kat and me. Nor has there ever been. I only swing in one direction. As for Kat, don't get me started."

"Mother!"

"Just testing your shockability, Margo. Now about that night, Kat was back to her old self. Healthy, sassy, and negotiating high end real estate banking no other broker seemed capable of closing, given the current economy. She'd invited me to spend the night—a sleepover after celebrating our fortieth-class reunion from Rosati-Kahn. Do you attend high school reunions, Mr. Montgomery?"

He honked into a second handkerchief and dabbed his eyes, "Nasty affairs I try to avoid. I went to Country Day."

"Ah, that explains a lot."

"Hardly, thanks to a scholarship obtained through generous benefactors, I was one of the few Catholic boys attending Country Day."

Mom raised her brow and shot me a knowing glance. Where St. Louisans attended high school revealed their social and economic status and often their religious affiliation, in particular, that of their parents.

"Can't say I lived up to the school's image of power, polish, and prestige," he said, stifling a yawn. "But to this day when Country Day alums and their kids get into serious trouble, it's me, the unremarkable Fred Montgomery, they come running to for help."

"No need to explain or to justify," Mom said. "I can name any number—"

20

Not Worth Dying For

"Enough," I told her. "You're getting off topic again."

"Not intentionally," she said, sending me a look of reprimand. "In any case, after the reunion ended, Kat and I stopped for drinks with several classmates before heading back to her place."

Montgomery slid a pad and pencil across his desk. "Their names, please, and where you stopped that evening. Also site of the reunion." Mom leaned over the desk and with her best penmanship, wrote down three names and the name of a bar I recognized from the Central West End. As soon as she slid the pad and pen back to Montgomery, he gestured for her to continue.

"We arrived at Kat's around eleven-thirty."

"Address?" Montgomery said, pen poised in his hand resting on the pad. He added the information as Mom gave it to him. Having been to Kat's condo a number of times, I conjured up the image of ultra-modern and ultra-messy, a far cry from Mom's ultra-traditional and ultra-orderly. And yet, when these two best friends with opposing traits were together, they turned into the school girls of long ago, accepting each other's quirks and petty annoyances.

Montgomery sneezed, a reminder as to what had brought us to his office. I tuned back into Mom's monologue, noting her words seemed more than a tad rehearsed.

"Kat and I drank some wine and chatted for another thirty minutes before calling it a night," she said. "I slept in the guest room by myself. Incidentally, I've already had this discussion with detectives from the Major Case Squad. Right down to where we all went to high school."

"I'd be more surprised if you hadn't," Montgomery said. "After all, this is St. Louis. As for Kat Dorchester, you're sure she went to bed? Alone? You saw her go into her room."

Mom hesitated before answering. "Kat had changed into an oversized t-shirt and baggy PJ bottoms. When I last saw her, she was sitting on the sofa, her bare feet propped on the coffee table."

21

Loretta Giacoletto

"Is there anything else you want to tell me, Mrs. Savino?"

"Nothing I can think of, Mr. Montgomery."

"Then I have a question for you." He leaned forward, forearms on the desk ala Blake Harrington, and hands clasped.

"Of course I'll answer it to the best of my ability."

"That evening, the evening in question, did Kat Dorchester know about the affair between you and the deceased Val Corrigan?"

Mom blushed, a reaction I'd expected earlier in the exchange. "Not to my knowledge. If Kat knew, she didn't say."

"Had she known and said nothing, would that have been unusual?"

"Kat could be secretive but usually not with me."

"Usually? I don't understand," he said.

"Kat could also be vindictive but never with me."

"Again, the best friend thing. I suggest you avoid Ms. Dorchester until some of these issues get resolved." He stood up, his cue for Mom and me to do the same.

"Do you foresee any problems with the police?" I asked.

"As of now, maybe so, maybe not. It will depend on what the Major Case Squad discovers and what it decides to pursue. Above all, do not underestimate the tenacity of these detectives. A crime such as this begs to be solved."

4

Kat

Talk about ambivalence, I didn't know what to think when we left Fred Montgomery's office, what with a police investigation that could go in any number of directions. My only concern was any direction leading to my mother.

"I'm worried about Kat," Mom said as I pulled out of the parking lot and onto Clayton Road. "Perhaps we should stop by her place."

"Not a good idea," I said, easing into the busy traffic. "Fred Montgomery thought you should stay away from Kat, at least for a while. So, did Blake."

"You discussed the details of my situation with Blake Harrington? Is nothing sacred, Margo?"

"Not when it comes to proving your innocence. Granted, Blake's area of expertise may be personal injury but he has connections throughout St. Louis and the Metro East. His influence and common-sense approach to a variety of legalities have made him a well-respected attorney."

"Nevertheless, I want to speak with Kat. Now, in person. If this offends your legal instincts, that's too damn bad."

"Did I just hear what I thought I heard?" First things first, which meant slamming on my brakes to avoid rear-ending the car in front of me that had stopped for a red light. "You said *damn*. You never say *damn*. Or *damned*. Or any other cuss word."

"Cuss words be damned." She showed me her right hand, forefinger and thumb a millimeter away from touching. "Not when I'm this close to being accused of a crime I did not commit. So are you with me?"

"You should call first. Make sure Kat is home."

"She'll be there. We already talked this morning, before Fred Montgomery."

"Speaking of Fred, what did you think of him?"

"Rather pompous and full of himself, thank God. Aren't these the characteristics of a good lawyer?"

∞∞∞∞

The aroma of freshly brewed coffee welcomed Mom and me, as did Kat when she greeted us at the door wearing nothing more than a matching set of bra and panties. With a wave of long fingers toward the kitchen coffee station, she told us to help ourselves, and then hurried into her bedroom to finish dressing. Designer clothes were scattered throughout the living room, making me wish for an extra two inches added to my height and another twenty pounds to my weight. Okay, forget the extra weight but Kat's hand-me-downs would've been welcomed in the closet of any five-feet-ten-inch-fashion-conscious female. After sidestepping Kat's exercise ball, I stumbled over a stray Nike sports shoe and heard my ankle pop. "Shit," was the best I could manage, knowing Mom's aversion to anything more explicit.

"Watch your mouth," she said anyway. "And don't remind me of my earlier slip."

"My lips are sealed," I said before pursing them. If only my brain could've erased all thoughts of my mother's remarkable fall from grace.

Not Worth Dying For

She'd terrorized El and me when we were kids, always demanding perfection. For El, it was all about brainpower; for me, projecting a hot babe image. But without the sex, please. Jeez, a throwback to the fifties and Nonnie's era of look-but-don't-touch. As for the here and now, my fallen mother was flirting with possible exposure as a murderer or aiding a murderer or covering-up after the fact.

"Hey, girl … and girlie." This from Kat, who still considered me a thirty-something going on naughty nineteen. She was standing in the bedroom doorway, a vision of sexually charged cougarism showing off her African-inspired kaftan and bejeweled flip-flops. Mom came out from the kitchen where she'd been wiping the countertops and I hopped up from the oversized white leather sectional eclipsing an otherwise ordinary living room. Group hug, of course, which made me think of El, who, had she been there, would've participated but only to avoid a searing reprimand from our mother.

Kat stepped back, hands squeezing my shoulders tighter than needed. "Margo, sweet Margo, Italy has done wonders for your complexion." She winked and for my eyes only, mouthed a two-word question. *Any sex?*

"Same old same old," I replied, "only younger."

"Careful, darling. Better yet, choose wisely and hopefully, only once."

"I hear you, Auntie Kat." Loud and clear. She'd been preaching those pearls of wisdom to El and me for years.

"Enough, you two," Mom said. "We're here to support Kat in her hour of need."

"Support me? I don't think so." Kat belted out a laugh tinged with sarcasm. Or perhaps hysteria, hard to tell which. "I'm no more a murderer than you are, Toni. We must stick together; get through this together."

"Uh, not according to Blake Harrington," I said, cringing from within as I sat down again. "He's already referred Mom to a criminal defense lawyer."

"Well, thanks for nothing." Kat faked a sniff, similar to the kind she

25

once taught me. Except she did hers better.

Mom stopped sipping her coffee and threw Kat an obligatory bone. "Blake said if you call him, he'll give you the name of a different lawyer."

"As good as yours, Toni?" Kat asked with a raised eyebrow.

"Why not. After all, it's not like there's only one top lawyer in all of St. Louis."

"So-o, after I get my lawyer, how 'bout we trade," Kat suggested.

"Sorry, I'm keeping mine."

"Hmm, what did you say his name is?"

"I didn't. And what makes you think my lawyer's a *he*?"

At the rate this conversation was heading, it would not end well. I tried a more flattering approach. "Come on, Auntie Kat. With your powers of persuasion you can sell yourself as easily as any piece of real estate."

She put one hand on her hip. "Holy Bejesus, girl. Are you telling me you think I killed Val? The man was positively crazy about me. He showered me with gifts and pricey entertainment and far-away weekends. Why would I want to kill a super generous sweetheart like Val? Right, Toni?"

Rather than answer Kat's question, Mom asked one of her own. "Have you heard back from the Major Case Squad?"

"A phone call from Detective Winchester, again confirming answers I've already given him. How many times must he ask about my relationship with Val, the reunion he didn't attend with me, our drinks with the girls afterwards?" Kat plopped down beside me and stretched out her long legs to rest her feet on the teak coffee table. After wiggling her toes, she looked at Mom with the same intensity as a cat eyeing its prey. "What about you, Toni?"

Mom swallowed a gulp so big it must've been lodged in her throat. "Nothing yet."

"Maybe you'll get the other guy," Kat said. "Doughboy, the white dude."

"Sam Reardan, CBC," Mom said, referring to an elite catholic high school. "Five daughters, Rosati-Kahn."

"Figures. Winchester, single," Kat said. "Basketball star, Vashon. Did you tell Reardan we went to Rosati too?"

"Enough," I said. "Can we move beyond the basic *what high school did you attend?*"

Kat gave a playful slap to my knee. "You bet, Mogo. Whatever you want to talk about, I'm game."

Mogo, I hadn't heard that goofy nickname in ages. Good thing El wasn't around to be reminded of her version of my name, one she created as a three-year-old to honor me, her big sis at five.

While I was thinking of a topic more upbeat to introduce, Mom stood up and started inching toward the door. "We should go, Margo. I have paperwork for an appraisal that needs my attention."

"Anything I should know about?" Kat asked.

"At this point, no," Mom said.

Kat didn't push the issue, making me think she was as happy to see us go as we were to leave. A walk to the door and a quick brush of the cheeks was all it took to send Mom and me on our way.

After we were settled in my car, I turned to Mom and said, "You know Kat better than anyone else. Do you think she found out about you and Val?"

Mom didn't hesitate before answering. "If she didn't, she's a better actress than I am. Kat knows and at some point she will make me pay, of that I have no doubt. Right now she hates me and I don't blame her."

∞∞∞

Loretta Giacoletto

As soon as we walked into the kitchen, Nonnie greeted us with a worried look on her face and a note that she passed on to Mom. "He wants you to call him, the nosy detective who stopped by and stayed too long."

"Sam Reardan?" Mom asked.

"No, the other one. The smooth talker."

"That would be Guy Winchester." After glancing at the note, Mom crumbled it in her hand. "I hate this whole charade. I hate Guy Winchester."

"Make the phone call," I told her. "Delaying won't make the problem go away."

"Give me that." Nonnie pried opened Mom's fingers. She removed the note, straightened out the wrinkles, and shoved the paper back in Mom's hand. "Here, make the damn call."

The dreaded phone call took no more than a minute to complete, time enough to deepen the frown lines furrowing a forehead that used to be wrinkle-free. "The detectives will be here tomorrow at four," Mom said. "Winchester and Reardan, they're out to get me. If nothing else, to ruin my reputation. I can feel it in my bones."

"Maybe El can arrange to be here," I said.

"Meaning you can't, not that I need you."

I put on my sorry face and explained I'd promised to help Blake with a special project, the annual St. Louis Kids Auction he was chairing. Canceling out would've been unthinkable, considering the unbillable time he'd given me on Mom's behalf.

"What about Fred Montgomery?" she asked.

"Too soon. He said not to call unless you're invited to interview at the police station."

"Invited, humph," Nonnie said. "More like ordered, just like the *Tedeschi* did during the war. The *Tedeschi*—Germans ... Nazis ... take your

28

pick—came knocking at the doors of *i nostri paesani*, ordinary villagers my battle-scarred papa had known his whole life. Like lambs being led to slaughter, they went with the *Tedeschi* and never came home."

"Please, Mama. No war stories, not now."

"Whatever you say. Forget about the *Tedeschi*. Forget about the lawyer. Forget about anybody who can't be bothered. God willing, you can count on me. And Ellen, she won't fail you."

Talk about the ultimate guilt trip; Nonnie knew how to twist the blade without drawing a drop of blood.

5

El on Board

"It's your turn, El," Margo said in the Big Sis phone voice she still used on certain occasions, those that left no room for compromise. "Tomorrow afternoon, Mom's house, four o'clock—on second thought, no later than three forty-five. Put on your best convent face and bring your rosary. And wear that postulant outfit—if it still fits."

"I have no clue what you're talking about," I said, knowing whatever *it* was would not set well with me. Or with the rebellious stomach talking back to me, a not-so-gentle reminder of the school cafeteria lunch that had gone down without a blip the first time. Oh yeah, Margo had me with *it's your turn*, but not in a good way. Had I been a smoker, this would've been the time to light up. An Oreo or three might've worked but I'd sworn off them since Italy.

Instead I listened to her rat-a-tat delivery that went from Blake Harrington to Fred Montgomery and from Kat Dorchester to the detectives who'd already struck fear and resentment into our mother who always seemed in control. When Margo ran out of verbal steam, I dared to ask, "And what will my role in this on-going investigation entail?"

"For God's sake, El, you have to ask? Do you have any idea what I've been doing for the past two days? No, I don't suppose you do. Let me spell it out. L-i-s-t-e-n. You listen to Mom. A-s-s-u-r-e. You assure Mom. S-u-p-p-o-r-t. You support Mom. Never ever let those detectives get the upper hand where Mom is concerned. Do I make myself clear?"

"Loud and louder. Now, what about Kat?"

"Were you not listening when I told you Mom's pretty sure Kat knows about her and Val Corrigan, even though Kat has done nothing to confirm this?"

"In other words, keep Mom and Kat away from each other."

"Exactly. Mom won't give you any grief on that. As of now, she's miserable, contrite, and almost malleable. So, I can count on you?"

"Was there ever any doubt?"

∞∞∞∞∞

By three forty-five the next afternoon I was seated at the family kitchen table, having followed Mom's lead by passing on Nonnie's offer of wine.

"Since when?" Nonnie asked while pouring a glass for herself.

"Since the detectives decided to visit again," Mom said. "That's all we need, them sniffing around and declaring us drunk."

"Us?" I asked, immediately regretting my poor choice of the single word.

"If being here makes you uncomfortable, feel free to leave," Mom said. "Now, before the detectives start pounding on the door."

"They pounded the first time?" I asked.

"Not exactly, but they did make my heart pound."

"Mine too," Nonnie said, having drained the wine from her glass. "You had to be here, Ellen. Except you weren't. You and Margo were gallivanting around Italy, poking your noses where they didn't belong."

31

Loretta Giacoletto

"Details of which we will discuss later," I said.

Nonnie shushed me with a forefinger to her lips as soon as Mom was otherwise distracted, unfortunately, by the doorbell chiming. Its distinctive sound of a mantle clock reminded me of the day my dad installed the system, as a surprise for Mom. Oh, how he loved surprising her, almost as much as she loved his surprises.

I headed toward the sound along with Mom and Nonnie, the three of us creating a bottleneck in the kitchen doorway. Taking charge with my best librarian voice, I said, "One at a time please. I'll get the door after the third ring. Mom, you and Nonnie take your favorite seats in the living room."

I took a deep breath, counted to ten, and opened the door to see two men wiping their feet on the mat. How considerate. Mom must've set them straight on their first visit.

"Detectives," I said, "come in, please."

They did and introduced themselves as Sam Reardan and Guy Winchester. I held out my hand and shook theirs, at the same time explaining my relationship to Antonia Savino.

Reardan, a dumpy sandy-haired guy in his early fifties, wore a snarky frown and rumpled suit with baggy trousers. The muggy St. Louis morning had prompted a line of perspiration on the shirt collar pinching his neck, one that begged for an extra inch of cotton material. The big, black, and bold Winchester wore his clothes with the assurance of a Nordstrom mannequin, reminding me of Nicco Rizzi, the dashing but oh-so ambiguous detective I'd encountered in Italy during several murder investigations.

"Your mother is expecting us," Winchester said.

"Yes, she's waiting in the living room."

"Her mother too?" Reardan asked.

I smiled to avoid a snicker. "It's the Italian way."

"I suppose you'll be there as well," Winchester said.

32

Not Worth Dying For

"Will that be a problem? If so, I'm sure our lawyer will drop everything and come over."

"That won't be necessary," Reardan said. "At least not for now."

After the initial greeting and comments about the warm September day, the detectives sat down, positioning themselves in chairs facing each other with Mom and Nonnie hugging either end of the sofa. I pulled up a straight chair across from the coffee table, creating a square area with Reardan to my left, Winchester to my right.

"Coffee, anybody?" Nonnie asked.

The detectives shook their heads.

"Wine then, straight from Italy although I got it on The Hill," Nonnie said, referring to the Italian section of St. Louis that boasted a variety of eateries ranging from affordable to the ultra-pricey as well as several grocery stores specializing in Italian imports. She scooted her behind—what she called her *dietro*—to the cushion's edge, bracing herself to get up.

"Negative," Reardan said. "But thanks anyway. Now, a few more questions, just to clarify some issues."

Nonnie scooted back, disappointment registering on her face. "Just so you know, my daughter would never kill anybody. Or anything, not even a spider. We keep this big one in the basement. It gets rid of annoying insects, as if there were any other kind."

"I can speak for myself, Mama."

"Good," Winchester said. "So as not to prolong this discussion, we will ask Mrs. Savino the questions and only Mrs. Savino will answer them. Are we all in agreement?" He opened the little black notebook he pulled from his jacket pocket and flipped to a page partially filled with tiny cursive. "Mrs. Riva?"

Nonnie threw up her hands. "I'm not here to make trouble, even in my own house."

He looked at me with a raised brow, unable to recall my name.

33

"Ellen Savino," I said. "Yes, I agree."

"Thank you, ladies," Winchester said. "So, Mrs. Savino, tell us about this affair with the deceased, Val Corrigan."

Nonnie sucked in her breath. She opened her mouth, then snapped it shut, allowing nothing more than a single gasp to escape.

The audible gesture, of course, perturbed Mom enough to speak up. "Really, Mama, if this makes you uncomfortable, feel free to leave."

"Only if your mama being here makes you uncomfortable."

"As a matter of fact, it does."

"Okay, I'm going. I'm going." Nonnie had already extracted herself from the sofa when she turned to me. "How about you, Ellen?"

"I'm staying." Only because I'd never have heard the end of it from Margo if I took the coward's way out. The last thing I wanted on that pre-autumn day was a blow-by-blow, pardon my pun, description of my mother's cheating affair with her best friend's lover. Nevertheless, I settled my forearms onto the arms of the chair, gripped the polished wood trim with my sweaty palms, and listened to details of the romance that had developed between Toni Riva Savino and Val Corrigan.

Toni leaned back, lowered her hands to her lap and interlocked eight fingers, palm side up. She turned her hands inward, all the better to observe them, and wiggled her fingers to control their shaking. Only then did she speak. "To be perfectly honest, I don't know what more I can add to what I've already said. Business led to friendship. Friendship *eventually* led to drinks and dinner, which soon led to more elaborate entertainment."

"None of which Kat Dorchester was privy to." Reardan stuck one hand into his coat pocket. He pulled out a packet of man-size tissues, removed a single tissue, and evacuated his bulbous nose, its nostrils red, the skin cracked and irritated. "Allergies," he offered as a one-word explanation.

Toni responded with a drop of her eyelids that lasted but a few seconds. "As I told you before, to my knowledge Kat was not aware of the growing friendship. Between Val and me, I mean. After all, I'd known him for a number of years, as had Kat."

"At what point did the friendship become sexual?" Winchester asked. "By that I mean the first-time date or approximate date, the circumstances leading to said act, and the actual place said act occurred."

Toni felt herself blush, from neck to cheekbones. She shifted her derriere into a more comfortable position while wishing Ellen had walked out on Mama. Too late now; she'd make the best of an awkward situation. "Do you want to know the length and breadth of *said occurrence?*" she asked. "The minute details of *said occurrence,* and the amount of pleasure, if any, derived from *said occurrence?*"

Reardan yawned and through bloodshot eyes glanced at his wristwatch. Perhaps a gift from his wife; otherwise he would've referred to his cellphone. "Go on, Mrs. Savino. Detective Winchester or I will let you know when the details fail to interest us."

"I should think more like fail to arouse, Detective."

"It's all subjective but most likely, nothing we haven't heard before. If we don't get what we're looking for today, there's always tomorrow—at the police station. Our interview room is quite comfortable though small. No whips or chains, I promise. We'll even make room for one other person … most likely your lawyer although that's your call."

Toni replied with a lift of her chin. "After today I doubt the two of you will have further reason to see me. Or I, either of you."

"That will, of course, depend on what you tell us and how much of it can be corroborated," Winchester said while looking at his cell phone. "Don't waste our time, Mrs. Savino. It's now or tomorrow at the station."

"Oh very well," she said, unable to hide her annoyance. "My first sexual encounter with Val occurred at his place, or rather his uncle's condo. Deceased uncle, Horace Corrigan."

"Before Kat Dorchester moved into the romantic column," Reardan said.

35

"Well, yes or no, not exactly, but—"

"That doesn't mesh with your original statement, how you and Val didn't start your secret dating until Kat was recovering from …" Winchester flipped through his notes, "a nasty case of colitis."

"It's not like I was keeping a journal, Detective Winchester. Although I suppose some people do."

"Women more so than men," Reardan said.

"I beg to differ," Toni said. "Val kept a record of such things. Not on his iPad but in a small black notebook." She shifted her attention to Reardan's partner. "Similar to yours, Detective Winchester. I'm surprised you didn't find it while searching his apartment. You did make a thorough search?"

"There was a notebook, yes," Reardan said. "But nothing about female companionship."

"Perhaps he used a special code. Or had more than one notebook. Not that I cared one way or the other."

Winchester jotted something down in his notebook. "Now back to that first time."

"July of last year," she said. "I think … hmm, yes … mid-July. Hot and muggy, just like today. I met Val at his late uncle's condo and he escorted me around the place. When we got to the master bedroom, I checked out the walk-in closet, not realizing he'd followed me inside. He said something in a low voice and when I turned and asked him to repeat it, he kissed me, very long and very hard, at the same time backing me into a row of his uncle's suits—hand-tailored as I recall, perhaps light-weight wool or a silk blend. What happened next, I'm not quite sure—I certainly wasn't drugged—but to my surprise Val and I wound up on the closet floor, along with at least two of the uncle's suits. My skirt went up; his pants went down. And then we had sex."

"To your surprise?" Reardan asked. "You're saying you had no idea where this was going when you walked into the closet with Val Corrigan

Not Worth Dying For

following close behind."

"I'm a real estate appraiser, Detective Reardan. A cautious one at that, which means I do not allow myself to be put in vulnerable positions."

"You don't consider the walk-in closet as vulnerable," Reardan said.

"Under certain circumstances, of course. But I'd known Val for some years."

"Four," Winchester said. "Last time you told us you'd known him for four years."

"Well ... I meant to say more than four years, closer to seven or thereabouts. Maybe ten or so, but don't ask me the exact date because my memory's not as good as it once was."

"And why is that?" Winchester asked. "Perhaps a stroke or other medical condition?"

Toni leaned back, right hand patting her heart, a passive-aggressive ploy she'd picked up from her mama. "Good grief, no. Too many other things on my mind, I suppose. The walk-in closet had been a one-time encounter, that is, until more recently."

"And you were seeing other men in the meantime," Reardan said.

"No, I was not. And even if I had been, why would that be of interest to you?"

"Because you're a person of interest, Mrs. Savino."

She put one hand over her mouth and muffled a yawn. "Will that be all for today, Detectives? I have a dreadful headache."

"I know the feeling," Reardan said. "My headaches come from tossing and turning at night, which comes from too many details clogging my overcharged brain. Are you worried about something, Mrs. Savino?"

"Such as a guilty conscience? Certainly not. But I do have this appraisal business that gives my brain a constant workout."

37

"In what way," Winchester said. "Appraising property should be fairly cut and dried. You have a formula. You follow that formula. You arrive at a fair price. Period."

"If that were the case, anybody could be an appraiser. No board exams to pass, no license to procure, no obligation to the client or to the mortgage lender." She stood up and edged toward the entryway. "Sorry, detectives, but duty calls and I don't have any time left to ignore my clients. If you'll excuse me, please."

"Until next time," Winchester said as he followed her. "At the station, so as not to further impose on your hospitality."

She turned, looked him directly in the eye, and replied with a catch in her voice. "It's no imposition on my part, truly."

"Nor would it be on our home turf," Reardan said. "Have a good rest of the day, Mrs. Savino. And don't work too hard.".

6

Guilt by Association

"Who the hell do those two jerks think they are," Nonnie said. She stood at one of the side windows flanking the front door with me at the other, both of us watching Reardan and Winchester get into the plain-wrapper police car.

"They're only doing their job." I turned at the sound of Mom's footsteps heading up the stairs, her shoulders slumped with the burden of what was yet to come.

"Didn't I tell you about your mom being in a heap of trouble," Nonnie said in a low voice. "Was I right or was I right?"

"Surely you don't believe she killed Val Corrigan."

"Guilt by association, Ellen. Kat or this Val or God only knows who. Toni ain't been herself for weeks. Maybe if you'd talk to her, without me around to make her feel the shame of her actions. Not that I'm one to be, you know ... pointing the finger."

"No need for any finger pointing. After all, not one of us is perfect."

"But some are closer than others, which makes this whole mess all the tougher on your ma since she's always had a high opinion of herself."

Arm in arm we returned to the living room where I helped Nonnie plump up the throw pillows and straighten the arm rest covers, housekeeping details Mom routinely performed as soon as guests went out the front door. Except Reardan and Winchester didn't qualify as guests. More like unwelcomed visitors.

With the room back in order, I expected Nonnie to head for the kitchen. Instead, she plopped down on the sofa; and patting the cushion next to her, ordered me to sit, which I did.

"Talk to me, Ellen. And don't ask what about."

Who could resist an invitation such as that? Not me. "Well, I have been wondering about our phone conversations while Margo and I were in Italy. Did you ever tell Mom the whole story about you and Stefano Rosina? Why you left Italy and never went back, how much you and Stefano had loved each other?"

"Humph. I tried, more than once. But Toni only listened with half an ear and only heard what she wanted to hear—what's that you call it?"

"Selective hearing."

"Yeah, that's it, selective hearing. Which is why you should be the one she turns to, what with your religious calling, even though you chickened out before the wedding. Leaving Jesus stranded at the altar took a lot of guts on your part."

"Hardly an accurate assessment ... I mean—"

"Yeah, I know what you mean. Same as you know what I mean. And don't tell me your mom should unload on Margo. You know I love your sister, but for this your mom needs someone with a shitload of compassion and common sense."

Shitload, one of Margo's favorite terms. Not sure who first brought it into the Savino household although Margo's language tended to be more colorful than Nonnie's. "Please, don't start in again about my beautiful mind," I said.

Not Worth Dying For

"Nor Margo's beautiful face; *basta*, I get it." She picked up the remote from the coffee table and clicked on the TV. "Now, if you'll excuse me, I got this movie recorded I've been wanting to watch for days. Not that I'm telling you what to do, but this would be a good time to have that talk with your mom."

∞∞∞

After knocking on Mom's bedroom door, I waited a minute or so and then knocked again. It took the third knock before she told me to come in. The room she once shared with my dad hadn't changed much in the last five years since I'd been there. Same pale green walls, same carpet with its darker shade of green. The Twilight Zone, my parents had called their special place. I never thought to ask why.

The light of a fading afternoon had cast its pallor over the room, except for the area where Mom was sitting upright in one of two recliners. She motioned for me to take the other. I couldn't help but wonder if anyone had sat there since Dad left this world for what she had insisted would be a better one, given all the suffering he'd endured those last months of his life. Mom too, although neither of them had complained, at least not in front of me.

"Do you want to talk about it?" I asked.

"Only if you want to listen."

Her response was so Margo, answering a question by tossing it back in my lap. Not that her response came as a surprise. Margo was so Mom, except for Mom adhering to the Catholicism with an unquestionable faith that far exceeded mine, even during those years I spent isolated in the convent. And now this ... this messy triangle—so unlike my self-righteous mother.

Mom cleared her throat and began where I knew she would, talking about Dad and how much she missed him. They'd always done everything together, even when Margo and I were kids, which we thought very romantic, just like the movies they watched while holding hands in the theater or at home on the sofa.

Loretta Giacoletto

"When your dad died, a part of me died too." She turned her head and looked out the window, as if to find his image settled in the clouds of early autumn.

I missed my dad too; but losing a parent was different from losing a mate, a soul mate. That I could never be to Mom. Or Mom to me. And now this. Somehow she'd managed to weave a tangled web, or gotten herself caught up in a web already weaved, and I felt obliged to help untangle it. Margo would've been better at this. Margo thrived on drama and intrigue, more so since encountering both in Italy. But this was our mom, our life in St. Louis; and if I didn't make the most of this moment, there'd be hell to pay from Margo and Nonnie.

"About this thing with Val," I said with some hesitation. "Was there more to it than … the sex?"

She leaned over to the small table separating our recliners, opened the drawer, and pulled out a folder. After flipping through several photographs, she settled on one and handed it to me. "Meet Val Corrigan."

"The late Val Corrigan," I corrected her. She sniffed, making me wish I'd kept my mouth shut. He appeared to be average height, slender with sandy-colored hair, and was leaning against a fence with his arms folded and legs crossed at the ankle. The background looked familiar, Big Cat Country at The Saint Louis Zoo, making me think of Kat Dorchester. As much as I loved Kat, she was capable of first pouncing and later feeling no remorse whatsoever, especially when it came to the cut-throat world of real estate brokers. "Val doesn't look anything like Dad."

"Give me some credit," Mom snapped. "I wasn't chasing a ghost or trying to relive my past—or maybe I was without realizing it. The man exuded … charm, and not just in the physical sense. He knew how to make love with words, the kind that stayed with me through the night and until we met again." Her voice trailed off only to resume with a touch of embarrassment. Odd, considering her recent revelations. "Oh, dear. Excuse my lack of propriety, what with you still … you know, still a virgin."

"Not since Italy," I said, immediately regretting my matter-of-fact acknowledgment.

42

"Ellen! I'm more than a little surprised. How could you?"

"You do realize I'll never see thirty again. At my age you were married and mothering Margo and me."

"Married being the key word. Please don't tell me you came home from Italy pregnant."

"No, I came home early because you were in trouble."

She scoffed, just as Nonnie had done when we last spoke. "Nothing I can't handle on my own."

"Nor should you, not with Margo and me to provide support—emotional and otherwise. As for Val Corrigan and his powers of seduction, what about Auntie Kat?"

"I suppose he had the same effect on her."

"Obviously that's one tidbit you never shared with her."

"Of course not. Were you not listening to my conversation with the detectives?"

"Yes, but it's not like they were waterboarding you into a confession. Or that you'd sworn to tell the whole truth and nothing but. Although, listening to your cat and mouse game with Reardan and Winchester I did wonder who was playing whom."

"Well, now that you mention it, about that overnight with Kat, I may've misspoken."

"Misspoken as in lied?"

"Must you always be so precise?"

"And you're not." God forbid, was I turning into my mother? Something I promised myself would never happen. I reached over, touched her hand, and told her to continue.

First things first. She sniffed, blew her nose, and then spoke in the rehearsed tone she'd used with the detectives. "That night—the night in

43

question—I told Kat goodnight and went into her spare room. While saying my prayers, I heard the front door close and figured she went out but this I can't say for sure since I didn't leave the room. Nor did I bring it up to Kat later."

"Do you think Kat is capable of killing Val?"

Lifting her shoulders, she opened her palms, a *how-should-I-know* gesture Nonnie often used. "Once when Kat was in her early twenties, she walked in on her then-boyfriend, found him in bed with a girl they'd both met at a party the night before. Kat broke a vase over the boyfriend's head. If that wasn't bad enough, she used one of the shards to cut the girl's face, other places too."

"Rumors and gossip," I said with a shake of my head. "They do have a way of growing out of control."

"Not in this case," Mom said. "During the mayhem I was parking the car and only saw the aftermath, a bloody scene Kat admitted to having created. The boyfriend was staggering about in a daze; the girl in a state of hysteria. Not that I blame her, considering the deep gash across one cheek and blood seeping through the shoulder of her T-shirt. We—Kat and I— dumped the two of them at Barnes Emergency and drove off without giving our names. Not one of my finest moments I must confess, although the ER was at my insistence. Kat wanted to let the girl bleed out. Good thing I met your dad shortly thereafter. Joe was so grounded."

"Amen to that. About the boyfriend and the girl Kat assaulted …."

"The girl came from money. No charges were ever pressed."

"What about her face?"

"As I've already said, the girl came from money. Hard to believe the two of them got married."

"How romantic," I said with more than a touch of sarcasm. "The cheating guy married the girl Kat disfigured."

"Pay attention, Ellen. That's not what I said … or what I meant to say.

Kat and the cheater got married. It didn't last but a year or so, way before Margo came along."

Add another failed marriage to Kat's resume. I couldn't imagine her ever being so out of control. Nor could I imagine the Toni Riva that Mom just described as her *Then Self*, a loyal enabler of the *Wild Kat*.

Nor the sassy teenage version that Franco Rosina had described to Margo and me during our recent trip to Northern Italy. He'd met our mom in 1973 at the train station in Pont Canavese, an awestruck teen encountering his first American girl. 'Dark hair fell below Antonia's shoulders and was secured by a headband across her forehead,' Franco told us. 'She wore flared pants low on the curve of her hips and a yellow tee shirt. Her lips were painted a soft pink. Amber specks marked her blue eyes.'

Even now as Mom and I spoke, I could see those amber specks visible in her expressive eyes—all that remained of the girl who'd made her mark on Nonnie's village. We leaned back in the recliners, each in our own world of contemplative silence.

"Can I ask you something, Mom?"

"You can ask but that doesn't mean I have to answer."

That was the mom I knew best. "Never mind," I said.

"If Margo were here, she'd ask."

"Not only is Margo beautiful," I said, "she's also courageous." I stopped short of playing the poor me card.

"Quit fishing for bullshit compliments, Ellen. Ask your question."

My mom resorting to another expression of vulgarity, would wonders never cease. I took a deep breath and gave my mouth free rein. "At what point in your life did you become such a holier-than-thou, self-righteous …."

"I suppose the word you're looking for is—"

"Madonna, that's the word."

"My, how you flatter me. I rather doubt the Madonna reference but for now I'll give you an A for diplomacy. As for your question, I wanted more from you and your sister than I had growing up. Don't get me wrong. I had an admirable upbringing. Nonnie gave me the freedom to be myself, to make mistakes, and to learn from those mistakes. But I set the bar even higher for my girls and for myself as a parent. If I've failed either you or Margo, I take full responsibility for any pain I caused over the years."

I cringed whenever Mom took the high road of blame, but felt compelled to say something to soothe her aching spirit. "It was me who let you down when I left the convent."

"And I behaved like an unrealistic spoiled brat—slapping you for following your heart instead of my mine." This time she reached across the gap separating the two recliners and squeezed my hand. "I am sorry."

"Me too, for disappointing you."

"I'd be lying if I denied my feelings at the time. But look at you now— doing what you love, at least I hope you are."

"For now, yes. But not forever. I want my own children, to love and to teach and to watch them grow."

"Don't wait too long, Ellen."

"I won't but first things first, finding someone to grow old with."

"Not the man you met in Italy?"

"Bad timing," I said, surprising myself by adding, "Mr. Right was right for me but I wasn't right for him."

"In other words, Ellen, you were not his top priority, the most important person in his life."

"Not at that moment in time."

"Don't count on bumping into another Mr. Right. Make the good life happen instead of waiting for it to happen."

7

Devil in the Details

Toni Savino rarely showed her vulnerable side, if indeed she even possessed one. But, of course, she must have, otherwise she never would have allowed herself to get mixed up with Val Corrigan. Easy enough to blame her downfall on the loneliness of widowhood; but truth be told, the unlikely affair with Val had given her an excuse to escape into a world of romantic fantasy. Not too shabby for a woman of her age. Middle-age, indeed, too young for the social security her mother relied on; too old for the assorted men Margo couldn't resist. Too sensible to be taken in by the unattainable as had the ever-sensible Ellen.

Val Corrigan had introduced Toni to his world if only for a brief time. Truth be known, to no one but herself, she did feel bogged down with guilt. Not for his actual demise, the horrific fear he must've felt in those final moments, if indeed he'd had any warning; but rather the lack of grief on her part. The lack of any feeling whatsoever, other than how Val's death had affected her personally and business-wise, more to the point, her reputation as an ethical appraiser who avoided any hint of shady dealings.

Ellen finally left without being asked to, or told. Thank God, at least she hadn't lost her sense of optimal timing. Toni moved from her recliner

47

to the carpeted floor where she assumed a lotus position. Drifting into peaceful meditation was her primary objective, a ritual she began when dealing with the loss of her beloved Joe. Always in the privacy of her bedroom since her mother would've thought the ritual a waste of productive time, the only time that really mattered. Not that Toni needed her mother's approval for anything; but after a lifetime of sharing the same home, she'd learned to skirt conflict whenever possible. Except when those conflicts tilted into Toni's comfort zone and then she didn't hesitate to speak her mind. Nor did her mother.

Conflict in the workplace presented a different matter, one not so easily dismissed since it involved the success of her business, her reputation as one of the best commercial real estate appraisers in the St. Louis area. And now this … this murder investigation, the humiliation of having to reveal herself as one of many women Val Corrigan had bedded before someone ended his life with one bullet between the eyes and another to his heart. Damn his Don Juan heart. Her prayers for his soul had ended after the first week of his death. One rosary a day, that's more than he would've given her had the tables been turned. Enough with the pity party. Or the pretentious indignation. She'd willed herself to stay in control by disregarding any emotional conflict involving Val Corrigan.

As for those despicable detectives, she relegated Reardan and Winchester to the back burner, not out of sight or of mind but not so obvious as to present a constant distraction. At least not for now. She also promised herself to avoid unnecessary contact with her dear friend Kat Dorchester. As in not answering Kat's phone calls or returning Kat's messages. Enough was more than enough. As usual, Kat had compromised her own credibility, and Toni had vowed not to allow Kat to commit the same offense against hers, what with those two bloodhounds sniffing around for any morsel that might bring her down. So much for meditation. She'd try again before bedtime. Perhaps a few decades of the rosary, if not the entire five. For her beloved Joe.

After taking a leisurely soak in the tub, she did her daughterly duty by going downstairs to spend the evening with her mother. Boring, yes, but in times such as this, boring had certain advantages, a blessing not to be underrated. Together, the two of them decided on a pay-for-view movie,

Not Worth Dying For

one Toni hoped would keep her mind off that annoying back burner.

∞∞∞

True to her self-imposed moratorium, Toni avoided all contact with Kat Dorchester for the next three days, going as far as to erase Kat's messages before listening to them, an affront against her best friend she would never have considered in the past. But her past with Kat did not involve a murder investigation. To keep such matters relegated to the back burner, Toni inspected three commercial properties, wrote appraisals on two others that had been pending, and went to lunch with a private lender who was considering her for future appraisals. All in all, a good week so far, that is, until Detective Winchester called, requesting her presence at the Fourth Precinct in South County.

"Two o'clock tomorrow afternoon works for Detective Reardan and me," Winchester said.

"Do I need a ... er, my lawyer?" Toni said in a low voice so as not to betray the fear welling in her throat. She heard her mother gasp but avoided making eye contact with her.

"It's within your rights to have an attorney present," Winchester replied. "If tomorrow afternoon is a problem, get back to me. Otherwise, we'll see you and your attorney then." He cleared his throat. "As a reminder, Mrs. Savino, the interview room must've been designed by a minimalist who didn't allow for more than four individuals—you and your lawyer, Detective Reardan and me."

"Understood, Detective Winchester. I'm quite capable of answering questions without help from my mother or my daughters."

"There's more than one?"

"Indeed. But neither daughter meets your criteria as a person of interest. They were vacationing in Italy when Val Corrigan died."

∞∞∞

Fred Montgomery had agreed to the two o'clock appointment without

49

Loretta Giacoletto

bringing up his fee. Nor did Toni ask, although she did carry a healthy balance in her checking account plus a decent portfolio of investments. If only her mother hadn't continued pacing back and forth on the front porch. If only her mother hadn't resorted to that old adage, "A mother is only as happy as her saddest child."

"So, as the only child of an only child, what does that make me?" Toni asked. "A barometer for your happiness index?"

"As if you never worried about your own daughters," Clarita said. She sat down, next to Toni on the porch glider. "So far, so good. Neither of them have been accused of killing a cheating lover."

"Nor have I, so knock it off. And please stop referring to Val Corrigan as my lover."

"How should I refer to him? How about this: the lover my daughter shared with her best friend, among others. Sweet Mother of Jesus! Middle-aged children ... tell me again, what're they called?"

"The sandwich generation."

"Yeah, panini would've been easier to remember. This ain't the way life works, missy. Panini kids are supposed to take care of their dying parents, not the other way around."

"Neither of us is dying anytime soon unless you know something I don't."

"That'll be the day, the way you run me to the doctor every time I sneeze or wheeze or forget to eat those damn prunes you insist I can't do without. You should be so good to yourself. I hope you got yourself tested for one of those ... whatchamacallit ... sex diseases."

"I will not dignify that comment with a response."

"Which tells me you haven't."

"Give me some credit. The STD tests came back negative. You know—crabs, syphilis, and so forth."

50

"Ugh! Why didn't you say so right away instead of wearing me down with worry?" Clarita closed her eyes and squeezed them tight. "Pardon me while I erase the whole sordid sex picture from my brain. That's not how I raised my daughter."

It was an argument Toni could not win, nor have the last word. Thankfully, it ended with Margo and Ellen showing up, their faces bordering on near hysteria. Toni glared at her mother while the girls pulled up two porch chairs and sat across from her and their nonnie.

"Okay, so I called them," Clarita said. "What did you expect?"

"Nothing less than our absolute support," Margo said. "Of course I'll take off work early."

"And I'll come as soon as school lets out," Ellen said.

"You'll do no such thing. Neither of you. I'm perfectly capable of handling this myself. Well, with help from Fred Montgomery."

"A good man," Margo said. "At least from my first impression."

"But nothing to look at," Ma said. "I saw his picture in the yellow pages."

"Really, Ma. What does Fred's appearance have to do with his representing me?"

"Plenty and in a good way. I don't want you getting distracted … again."

Margo held up her palm. "Enough, both of you. Now, Mom, tell me, word for word: what did that creepy detective say when he called."

Toni repeated the Winchester conversation, her voice reflecting undeniable fatigue.

"That's it?" Ellen asked. "A simple invitation to the Fourth Precinct and nothing more? How are you supposed to prepare yourself?"

"She ain't. Don't you get it? Those detectives are out to destroy my Toni."

"Ma, please. As for you, Ellen, need I refresh your memory? You were here for the home interview with Detectives Reardan and Winchester. And you, Margo, accompanied me to Fred Montgomery's office. The two of you know as much as I do."

"No, Mom. We only know as much as you want us to know," Margo said. "There's a huge gap in-between."

"Good luck with getting your ma to fill in the gap," Clarita said. "And when she gets to the station, don't be surprised if we get a phone call about those detectives deciding to hold her overnight."

"Can they do that?" El asked.

"They're the police," Clarita said. "They can do whatever they want."

"Not when I have my lawyer. Right, Margo?"

Margo cleared her throat. "For the most part that's correct."

"What about the other part?" Ellen asked. "Worst case scenario?"

"Working for a lawyer doesn't make me one."

"But you do know something about the law."

"When it comes to personal injury, yes; but Blake doesn't handle criminal cases."

"Margo, don't toy with me," Toni said. "Just say what you think, keeping in mind, I did not kill Val Corrigan."

"What about Kat? I'm just saying: if the case against her is sufficient enough to press charges, you could get hit by the fallout and possibly be held over for obstruction of justice."

∞∞∞∞

The drive from Holly Hills to the Fourth Precinct took Toni Savino no more than twenty minutes, but those twenty minutes of contemplating the unknown soon escalated into sheer agony. What more could the detectives ask of her that hadn't already been asked and answered to the best of her ability. Guilt wore many hats, none of which fit her, at least not at the moment, in her time of reflection. Get real, who was she kidding? Margo and Ellen, perhaps. Her mother, certainly not. Scary, yes, that a mother such as Clarita should know her daughter better than the daughter knew herself.

The necessity of having to call Fred Montgomery only added to Toni's anxiety. Given this new wrinkle in the investigation, she fully expected to write off any plans for next year's vacation after paying the lawyer whatever he decided an appropriate fee. She parked her Chrysler sedan in the open lot, got out, and to her relief, saw Montgomery exit his vehicle, an older model Mercedes-Benz.

She shook his hand, its coarseness not what she expected from a lawyer. "Nice car," she told him.

"Bought and paid for years ago. Although I live rather conservatively, I don't hesitate to assume a bulldog approach when it comes to protecting my clients."

"Then I take it you've been here before."

Montgomery responded with a snort that did nothing to endear him to her. "This precinct and all the others, plus those on the Illinois side. Shall we get on with this?"

After entering Precinct Four, they found Winchester waiting in the lobby. He initiated a round of perfunctory handshakes and thanked them for arriving on time. "Follow me," he added. "We'll chat in the interview room—Detective Reardan and me."

"Interview, is that the same as interrogation?" Toni asked, to which Montgomery cupped one hand under her elbow and administered a comforting squeeze.

"What's in a name," he whispered.

"Not much," she murmured. "A rose by any other name would smell as sweet unless it's a sweat-soaked Rose being interviewed during the Spanish Inquisition."

"Here in St. Louis we're far more civilized," Winchester said, opening the door and gesturing for Toni and her lawyer to enter. "Be assured, no whips or chains, just straight-forward Q and A."

More handshakes. Reardan's palm was sweatier than Winchester's. Beefier too; Winchester's hand matched his physic, with fingers long and slender like the high school basketball player he'd described from a former life. He backed out of the room and closed the door, leaving Toni and Montgomery with Reardan, who directed her to a small table facing a large window. No doubt a two-way, she figured, having watched her share of crime shows on TV. By now Winchester and his team players would've parked themselves in the adjoining room, on the other side of the window, watching her every move, looking for any sign of sweat beads forming on her upper lip. Whips and chains, indeed. What about mental torture, the anguish of not knowing what the next few minutes would bring.

Fred Montgomery took the chair beside her, a welcomed disruption to the various scenarios she'd been imagining. He smelled of wine and men's cologne, the kind permeating sample cards that sales clerks distribute at Macy's, along with discount coupons she often used when Joe was still with her. If only God hadn't taken him, she wouldn't have gotten herself mixed up with Val Corrigan, other than for the purpose of business and even that had taken an unexpected ugly turn.

Reardan cleared his throat and took the seat diagonal to hers. Like Winchester before him, the doughboy detective thanked her for coming, as if she had any choice. The door opened, to her surprise Winchester again, this time with a manila folder and four bottles of water, one of which he offered to her. She shook her head, showed her palm. Water invariably equated to an obsessive desire to relieve herself, one more distraction she didn't need. Winchester placed the water bottles in the middle of the table. He settled his long frame across from Reardan and shoved the folder in his direction.

Toni stifled a yawn, reminding her of the restless night she'd endured. Five hours of sleep did not make for a person of interest capable of deflecting the toughest of questions. What was the phrase Margo had tossed her way? Obstruction of justice, would that make her an obstructionist? Only if she'd done something wrong. Better yet, if the

Not Worth Dying For

detectives could prove she'd done something wrong. She glanced at her wristwatch, an anniversary gift from Joe she wore every day, a reminder of what once was. She wanted to go there again, that once-was place with Joe, if only for a moment or two, but what ... who was that? Montgomery, his shoulder nudging hers, the nerve of him. He asked Reardan to repeat the question, obviously one she hadn't heard the first time.

"That night you stayed over at Kat Dorchester's," Reardan said. "What time did you go to bed?"

She sighed. "As I told you before, Kat and I got to her place around eleven-thirty, and after some wine, we went to bed—in separate rooms."

Winchester referred to his little black notebook. "Yes, that was your original statement, verbatim."

"So you didn't go out again that night?" Reardan asked.

"At midnight, hardly. It's not my style. Besides, at that hour where would I have gone?"

Reardan raised his brow; Winchester shuffled in his chair. Out with it, Toni thought, just say what's on your mind. She didn't want to be kept dangling on a hook like some fish struggling to escape.

Reardan took the lead. "What about Kat Dorchester? Did she go out again?"

"You'd have to ask her, Detective Reardan."

"We have, Mrs. Savino." The expression on Reardan's face remained as impassive as Winchester's. "Kat Dorchester has admitted that she lied to us during previous interviews, to be more specific, after viewing a video photo of her exiting the condo garage at twelve-fifteen the night in question. A passenger was sitting in the front seat, again recorded on the video. Security cameras sure do come in handy. In fact, those cameras give a more accurate account than that of any eye witness."

Toni felt her jaw drop, an automatic reflex not anticipated. She opened her mouth, only to feel the lawyer's hand covering hers, squeezing it to the

55

point of pain. She hoped Kat had secured a good lawyer, one who found her worthy of Blake Harrington's referral.

"Not one word, Mrs. Savino," Montgomery was saying, without looking in her direction. Instead he directed his comment to Reardan. "I'd like to see that video or a photograph, Detective Reardan."

"Not a problem." Reardan removed a photo from the manila folder Winchester had brought into the room.

The garage video photo with its stamped time and day didn't lie, at least about Kat leaving fifteen minutes after midnight. And, yes, the passenger side indicated a second person wearing a Cardinal baseball cap, head lowered so as not to reveal face or gender.

"It would appear Kat Dorchester concealed pertinent information about the night in question," Montgomery said. "But the passenger in this photo could've been anyone."

"This is true," Winchester admitted. "At least for now, although the photo does send up a number of red flags, some of which are blowing in your direction, Mrs. Savino."

Again Montgomery squeezed her hand, his way of silencing her. "Until you have something more significant than suppositions, do not attempt to harass my client." Montgomery scooted his chair back and placed one hand over Toni's, expecting her to follow his lead. She hesitated.

"Not so fast," Reardan said. "We have more questions for Mrs. Savino."

"Whatever I can do to help, Detective Reardan." Toni pulled her hand away from Montgomery's. She leaned back with squared shoulders and Montgomery abandoned his effort to get up.

"Well, here's the thing." While running one hand through his sandy hair, Reardan paused long enough to dig his fingernails into an area above the right ear.

"Have you seen a dermatologist?" Toni asked. "I know an excellent one."

Reardan stopped scratching and without looking at his persistent fingers, wedged them between one solid thigh and the wooden seat. Having regained his composure, he continued. "You've been a commercial real estate appraiser for how long?"

"Seventeen years, give or take."

"And before then?"

"A real estate agent."

"Same as Kat Dorchester," Reardan said.

"Not quite, she's a broker. In today's market many agents also arrange financing for the properties they sell, combining their duties under a single title, that of broker. May I go now?"

"Only if you'd rather come back tomorrow. We've just begun, Mrs. Savino."

While Toni was trading barbs with Reardan, Winchester had been flipping through his notebook. He stopped, set the notebook on the table, and went back several pages to one punctuated with bulleted phrases.

"So, in the event you would've appraised ... hmm, a run-down building on Washington Avenue ..."

"Not too many of those left," Toni said.

Winchester stopped further comment with the show of his palm. "Please, let me finish. I'll let you know when it's your turn. Now, where was I?" Using a forefinger, he scrolled down the page, every inch covered with words written in miniature, as if the paper came at a premium price.

"By any chance were you taught by the nuns?" she asked.

"Grade school, John the Baptist," he said without looking up. "It closed years ago. About that run-down property ..."

"On Washington Avenue," Toni said. "Sorry, please continue."

"Right, and you've been appraising commercial real estate for

57

seventeen or so years. So, in say ... 2003 you might've been appraising properties on Washington Avenue."

"I suppose that's possible. It's been so long ago. I'd have to go back and check my records."

"You do keep meticulous records," Winchester said. "Correct me, only if I'm wrong."

Toni opened her mouth, changed her mind, and then responded with a nod.

Winchester set his notebook aside and reached for the manila folder. "Praise be to the miracle of digital research," he said, shuffling through papers until his fingers landed on one particular item. "Says here, that in the year 2003 Antonia Riva Savino appraised a certain piece of property in the eleven hundred block of Washington Avenue, otherwise known as the Garment District, for $3,000,000, as in $12 per square foot on 250,000 square feet. Correct?"

"May I see the official document?" Toni asked.

Winchester slid it across the table. She glanced at the address, her printed name and her cursive signature, as did Montgomery. "This seems in order, although after ten or so years I don't recall the specifics of this particular property."

"Now that's where things get really interesting," Reardan chimed in. "Turns out, the real estate developer who bought said property was none other than HC and Associates."

Toni swallowed the lump forming in her throat and pressed her knees together to keep them from knocking. "Any bank considering a property loan such as this would've hired me, or someone in a similar position, to do an in-depth appraisal. That's the way it's usually done."

"Which bank and who was the individual in charge?" Reardan asked.

"You mean the commercial lender," Toni said. "Without checking my records, I can't say for sure. Perhaps it's on the document."

58

Not Worth Dying For

Reardan took charge of the document and ran one sausage finger down it. "Here we go. Central Alliance Bancshares. You worked with Del Durante."

"If you say so."

"Just confirming what I see before me. So you never had any direct contact with the developer, HC and Associates?"

"Not that I recall."

"Are you even aware of HC and Associates, its principle in 2003, and its most recent principle in 2013?"

Toni's throat had gone dry, making it too parched to speak. She paused, holding up one forefinger before opening the closest bottle of water. Potty break be damned. After one delicate sip, she indulged herself with several unladylike gulps. "Sorry, where were we? Oh, yes, HC and Associates. Off hand, I don't recall. As I said earlier, I deal with so many companies and individuals."

Winchester and his damn notebook. He flipped to another page. "HC and Associates was formed in 1999 by Horace Corrigan. Does that ring a bell?"

She blotted her lips with two delicate fingertips. "Of course, thank you for the clarification. Horace was Val Corrigan's uncle and partner in the company. Val took complete control after Horace passed away."

"From a long bout with cancer," Winchester said. "Do you recall the year?"

"I don't know the particulars. It's not like Horace Corrigan and I were good friends."

"Not as good as you and Val Corrigan. Correct me if I'm wrong."

Montgomery spoke up, finally. "No need to sling arrows, Detective Reardan."

"Just answer the question. Did you know Horace Corrigan?"

59

Loretta Giacoletto

"Yes, I knew Horace."

"And over the years you did have other business dealings with Horace Corrigan."

"From time to time, yes."

"But you didn't see fit to inform us of this during our previous conversations," Winchester said.

Toni swiveled her head from Reardan to Winchester. "Frankly, no. At the time, my prior interactions with Horace Corrigan didn't seem relevant to the death of Val Corrigan."

"Even though Val Corrigan had taken over HC and Associates after his uncle died?"

"I fail to see the connection, Detective. Now, unless there's something else …."

After exchanging a brief glance with Winchester, Reardan said, "Nothing more at this time, Mrs. Savino. However, please be advised that you still remain a person of interest in this case. Do not leave the area without checking in with us first."

"Not likely, considering the legal fees I'm incurring as we speak, Detective Reardan."

"That'll do, Mrs. Savino." Fred Montgomery stood, this time taking her with him.

"Wait. I have a question," she said, shaking off Montgomery's firm grip. "What about Kat Dorchester?"

"Ms. Dorchester still remains a person of interest," Winchester said. "Unless you have evidence that would place her at the scene of the crime, in which case …"

"Of course I don't. Kat wouldn't have killed Val."

Winchester cleared his throat. "Somebody did, Mrs. Savino, in a brutal

60

way the media did not describe in detail. If not your friend Kat, then who?"

"I have no idea, Detective Winchester. I hardly knew any of Val's acquaintances."

"What about the other women—intimate friends besides you and Kat Dorchester?"

"Isn't that your job? After all, it's not like I'm a private investigator."

8

The Creole Exchange

Since returning from Italy, El and I had spent more waking hours at our childhood residence than at our own grown-up places. There we sat in the Holly Hills living room, listening to our mother recount her afternoon with Detectives Reardan and Winchester while Nonnie Clarita watched Vanna White turn letters on *Wheel of Fortune*. A minor distraction at best since Nonnie had turned down the volume and activated the closed captions, one of the few TV options she'd mastered on her own.

"Don't mind me," Nonnie said with eyes focused on the TV screen. "There's only so many times I can hear about the police badgering your ma."

"And yet, here I am, back at home without a single bruise or bloody nose." Mom forced a smile that didn't fool any of us. "And with my reputation as an ethical appraiser still intact."

Those dark circles under our mother's eyes said more than any half-truths spilling from her mouth. Having spent the past eight years working for a personal injury attorney, I possessed a better understanding of certain legal issues than the average lay person. Premises liability, for example.

62

Not Worth Dying For

Suppose an adventurous adolescent wandered into a building undergoing renovations and fell through a hole in the floor. In the rare event of no liability insurance, who would pay for the broken leg? Good luck getting the developer to show some compassion, unless the kid's parents were smart enough to hire my boss. Blake Harrington knew all the angles and then some, which made him the top P.I. lawyer in St. Louis.

"It's complicated," Mom added as an afterthought.

At which point my mouth fell open. After closing it, I managed to say, "Whoa, stop right there. Please don't tell me that you used the irreparable C word during this afternoon's inquisition. In my world of layman versus legal terminology, the word *complicated* invariably sends up a red flag."

"Give me some credit, Margo. It was all I could do to keep my head on straight; but in retrospect, I don't think the dreaded C word came into play."

"Evidently not, or the detectives would never have let it pass."

El, who must've been in her own little world, finally spoke up. "Calm down, both of you. Now that we've cleared the complicated air, tell us about your business dealings with Horace Corrigan and what, if any, of those dealings extended to his nephew Val."

"And if any of these dealings might've been devious enough to justify his murder," I said.

Nonnie held out the remote, freezing Vanna White on the TV screen. "Hold on, Missy Margo. Are you suggesting your ma had anything to do with her lover's murder?"

"Ma, please. We agreed you would refrain from referring to Val Corrigan as my lover."

"You suggested; I did not agree."

"Now, now, Nonnie," El said in the voice she used for her middle school students. "Don't be upsetting Mom."

"Okay, no more lover talk—unless your ma pisses me off."

63

Or Nonnie pissed off Mom, given the speed at which Mom hopped up. She made a quick exit, leaving El and me open mouthed and Nonnie unpausing the TV and turning up the volume. Who was I to argue— Nonnie's house and Mom's, Nonnie's rules—although she did have the decency to lower the volume when Mom returned, one hand gripping an official document.

"My appraisal of the Washington Avenue property," Mom said, passing the report to El, who skimmed over the single page before handing it to me. At first glance nothing seemed unusual since over the years El and I had occasionally helped with Mom's paperwork and were somewhat familiar with documents such as this.

"Perhaps if you'd start from the beginning," I said, assuming my role as a Blake Harrington protégé. "Just stick to the basics."

Mom cleared her throat, a sign for El and me to prepare for a shitload of unnecessary details, just as I would've done. Yes, in some ways, though not all, I am my mother's daughter.

"I first met Horace Corrigan during my initial inspection of the Creole Exchange," Mom said. "An unplanned meeting, I might add, since appraisers usually work alone and for good reason—to avoid the appearance of collusion or undue influence with potential developers and investors. What's more, this particular Garment District assignment was my first through Central Alliance Bancshares and I desperately wanted to establish a good relationship with Del Durante, the bank's top commercial lender. Nevertheless, Horace insisted on accompanying me through the property, and after considerable discussion, I finally agreed."

"Don't tell me you also played rub-a-dub-dub with Horace's you-know-what."

Jeez, Nonnie, give the poor woman a break, I so wanted to say but held my tongue. Mom, however, had run out of patience with the generational bullying that supposedly passed for concerned parenting. She lifted her chin and spoke through gritted teeth. "Isn't it past your bedtime, Mama?"

"So we're back to Mama. Just get to the point. The girls ain't got all night."

Not Worth Dying For

"It's all right," El said in a soothing way. "We're here for as long as it takes."

Mom shot a few daggers in Nonnie's direction before continuing. "As I was about to explain, the Creole Exchange building had been standing for over a hundred years and in its heyday was the pride of Washington Avenue. But when the Garment District faded, so did the Creole Exchange, along with similar buildings in the area. This particular property, the Creole, had deteriorated into a state of disrepair, rat-invested and unfit for any type of occupancy. To make matters worse, a dozen or so indigent people had left their meager belongings on the second level, making me grateful during the inspection to have Horace accompany me from one floor to another. The old-fashioned way, I might add, through a series of stairwells that included all levels since the elevators were no longer operational. At least the owner had sense enough to leave the electricity turned on. For that alone, the homeless should've been grateful, having a warm place to sleep at night. Instead, they took out their frustrations on Horace and me after we left the building, hurling insults in our direction, along with some rather disgusting trash. Thank God, the police came along and sent them away."

"The nerve of some people," Nonnie said. "Did you give the riffraff a helping hand, as in greenbacks?"

"Not that it matters; but yes, I did."

"Good, it matters to me. What about this Horace guy?"

"More generous than I was, in particular with one of the Creole campers who complained about the quality of air in the building, as if he planned on buying a place there. Anyway, the more Horace and I talked that day, the more I realized he wanted more of me than I was capable of giving without compromising my growing reputation as a reliable appraiser. In other words, he wanted me to appraise at a low price, thereby insuring the bank would be more inclined to lend at a favorable interest rate."

"Which you, of course, refused to do," said El, who never would have considered doing otherwise.

Whereas I, who would've been open to an agreeable arrangement— provided it was legal—had the audacity to ask, "What about the banker?"

65

"Del Durante, did I mention Kat introduced me to him?" Mom said. "No, I don't suppose I did. Kat was representing the seller, who'd bought the property at a ridiculously low price back in the eighties when most investors didn't have the foresight to consider the potential of trendy urbanites actually living downtown. After inspecting the Creole Exchange, I was researching comparable properties when who should invite me to lunch but Del Durante."

"To a pricey place, I hope," Nonnie said. "As long as you were about to sell your soul …"

"I should ignore your snide comment; but if you must know, the affordable Anthony's downtown."

"That bit of dining trivia you recall after all these years," I said, immediately regretting another detour, one I should've anticipated. Out in the hallway, *Vecchio*, our ancient grandfather clock chimed eight times. At the rate Mom was going, El and I wouldn't be making our getaway before ten. Mom must've been reading my mind, so much like hers it scared me. El, on the other hand, had drifted into her personal utopia. No doubt, saying her rosary during Mom-inspired lulls such as this.

"Not that it matters but I had the house salad; Del, a gourmet burger. You, of all people, Margo, should know that Anthony's is where everyone who's anyone goes to see and be seen. In my case, being seen with someone as powerful as Del Durante would've elevated my fledgling appraisal business to a new level with the wheelers and dealers of St. Louis. During our power lunch, Del wasted no time in explaining how he'd collaborated with Horace Corrigan in past dealings and was open to a compromise of sorts with the Creole Exchange."

"Hold on," I said, in a voice sharp enough that it snapped El to attention. "Are you telling us this Del Durante offered you a bribe, one that you, of all people, actually accepted?"

Mom closed her eyes with the panache of an aristocrat sentenced to the guillotine. She opened them to a display of welling tears that touched my soul. "Give me some credit, Margo. You too, Ellen. No money exchanged hands, although at the time I could've used a helping hand, what

Not Worth Dying For

with the diagnosis of prostate cancer looming over your dad and me."

"I'm sorry, Mom. My comment was cruel and unforgiveable."

She waved me off. "What Del Durante offered was a constant flow of appraisals, many of which involved additional properties along the Washington Avenue corridor as well as other sites around the downtown area. A win-win for all concerned, one that started with the Creole Exchange. Let me hasten to add, that particular property was the only one I ever undervalued."

"And did that low-ball appraisal come back to haunt you?" I asked.

Mom teared up. "To my everlasting regret, yes, dammit, yes. Kat made a nice commission on the Creole when Horace bought it. Horace secured a decent loan that should've covered the renovation. Unfortunately, it took longer than expected, what with moving out the homeless, plus hazardous waste and structural issues, plus increased construction costs. Horace ran out of money and had to apply for a second loan after Del Durante turned him down. That's when Centennial Mid-America came into play and needed a new appraisal before agreeing to the loan. Pierce Rendley by-passed me in favor of another appraiser, which really hurt at the time. But then I wound up doing a third appraisal toward the end of completion so I guess I redeemed myself."

"What about Horace's nephew Val?" I asked. "When did you really meet him?"

She sighed. "Shortly after I met Horace."

"Mother of Mary," Nonnie said. "Don't tell me you and Val had a thing back then."

Mom straightened up, ruffled feathers sending a don't-even-think-about-going-there in all directions. "Certainly not. I was faithful to Joe throughout our marriage. And after he died, dedicated to the memory of our life together. That is, until this past year."

67

9

Is Good, Si?

Think positive I told myself. No news could only mean good news. Neither Margo nor I had heard from Mom for a good week. Nor from Nonnie. Not that I was complaining. They had their lives; we had ours. God was good, all was good in the Savino family. At least for the moment.

Unless the phone happened to ring after nine in the evening. Never a good sign unless the caller happened to be a romantic interest, which did not apply to me in my current state of having no one cluttering my life. This particular call, however, registered on my cell as an odd string of numbers I recognized as originating from Italy. Using my sophisticated voice reserved for special people, I answered on the third ring, prompting a melodious response from the other end, *"Buonasera, Elena."*

I responded in kind, still unsure of my caller who used the Italian version of Ellen, its emphasis on the first syllable—EL-e-na. "Uh, who is this?"

"Mi dispiace," came an apology from the tenor voice. "It is me ... I, Franco Rosina."

"Franco! Good grief, why are you calling at this hour? It must be five in the morning Italy time."

68

"Our time is your time, Elena."

Which made no sense to me, even though his English was better than my Italian. Still, I carried on. "Oh dear, I hope you aren't calling with bad news. Is it your papa?"

"Papa is good. I am good. We—papa and me—are here in St. Louis. At the *aeroporto*."

"In St. Louis! Oh my God, I had no idea. Where are you staying? No, of course you'll stay with me … or Margo … or Mom. Stay right where you are. I'll meet you at the airport baggage claim. You know what I mean?"

"Si, we know the baggage place," Franco said. "But staying with you not necessary. St. Louis has many hotel beds, does it not?"

"Please, Franco. I insist. Nonnie Clarita would never forgive me if I sent you to a hotel."

Okay, so I lied about Nonnie. But had she not been so wrapped-up in Mom's problems, she might've agreed to my welcoming the surprise family from Italy. Or not. Most likely not.

After one phone message followed by a text message to Margo, I headed out the door and on to Lambert Airport, a fifteen-minute drive from my condo in Brentwood. How intuitive of me, having cleaned my cozy place the evening before without realizing I'd be having company so soon. Company from Italy, not even remotely on my radar although Margo and I had both issued invitations for our newly discovered relatives to visit us in America. A sincere, well-intentioned invitation, yes, with no strings attached. Unless, that is, we were to count fulfilling our curiosity as to Nonnie's reaction on coming face-to-face with Stefano Rosina, her first love … make that Second World War teenage lover. To make matters worse, Stefano was the unacknowledged father of our straight-laced mother, a once defiant teenager who'd met him during a visit to Italy that did not go well, and was now up to her tilted chin in a potential charge of murder—worst case scenario—or the lesser charge of aiding and abetting.

Once inside the airport I hurried to the baggage carousels and spotted the Rosina men leaning against a convenient post, arms crossed and feet

69

buried in luggage. The 7,500-mile journey from Italy had left its mark on tired faces that showed their years in ways I hadn't noticed while in Italy. At fifty-seven and a stranger to Margo and me, Franco Rosina had invited us into his Pont Canavese home. Not only did he share the food he prepared and the full-bodied wine he made, but the details of his summer of 1973, how he'd entertained our All-American Mom when the two of them were teenagers.

Franco's father Stefano had reached eighty-four years, two more than Nonnie. Him I sort of knew, but mostly through her eyes, memories from sixty years past. A grandfather and uncle—half uncle—Margo and I had never heard of until our Italian holiday. How weird for all of us. Our own dad had been dead for five years, an only child whose parents had died too young, before Margo and I were born.

I greeted these new relatives with a subdued version of the Italian way. Much like we'd greeted each other in Italy—a gentle hug and light brush of kisses to both cheeks. "Welcome to America," I said, knowing Stefano had been here at least once before. My greeting seemed rather inadequate, perhaps because Margo wasn't with me to exude enough charm for both of us. Still, I gave it my best shot with the addition of a sincere, "Welcome to St. Louis."

Stefano spoke his first words, far gentler than when we first met a few months before. "Grazie, Elena. You are too kind."

I reached for one of the suitcases, only to have the handle snatched away. Stefano took charge of his own luggage as did Franco, well-worn suitcases on rollers and shoulder bags slung over their shoulders. They followed me a short distance to the airport garage where due to the late hour, I'd secured a convenient parking slot on the same level. Stefano opted for the back seat, leaving Franco to sit up front with me. We drove in silence for a few minutes, the only sound coming from Stefano drifting into a light sleep.

Please don't snore, I thought. But if you can't help yourself, no snorting or smacking your lips or doing other weird things you'll later deny. Don't make me report anything negative about you to Clarita Fantino Riva. Your coming here is awkward beyond words. And for God's sake, do not … not … not … suffer a heart attack and die before we get this incredible

Not Worth Dying For

family scramble straightened out.

I'd almost forgotten about Franco until I noticed his chin bouncing against his chest. "You must be very tired," I said. "Just hang on a while longer. We're almost to Brentwood—that's where I live."

Franco straightened up and looked at me without the smile I'd come to expect. "Your nonna and your mama," he said, "do they know we have come to St. Louis?"

I shook my head. "I tried calling Margo but she didn't answer so I left two messages. I hope you don't mind sharing a room with your papa tonight. It's quite comfortable, twin beds and a private bath."

"The same as a hotel room but without *la famiglia* connections. Grazie, Elena, is most generous of you. I am curious though. What did Toni—your mama—say when you told her about meeting Papa and me in Italy?"

"Well, actually, I haven't told her yet."

"Oh, I see." He sat back, shoulders slumped.

"It's not what you think, Franco. Mom has been pre-occupied."

"Ah-h, she has a gentleman friend?"

"Did have one. Sort of, that is, not a match made in heaven."

"You believe in such things?" he asked.

"Not in this case. Unfortunately, the man died under mysterious circumstances. He was murdered."

Franco crossed himself. "May his killer burn in hell."

"Careful what you wish for. The police consider my mother a prime suspect."

"Merda!" Stefano grumbled from the backseat. He spoke in Italian to Franco, who answered in a like manner, relaying my brief explanation of Mom's predicament.

71

"And what about Clarita," Stefano said, surprising me with the length of time it had taken him to bring up Nonnie's name, the woman he claimed to have thought about every day since they last parted.

"Sassy as ever," I said and then paused, preparing myself to massage the truth with my next statement. "Margo and I haven't talked to Nonnie about you since we came home, not with my mother always around."

"What? You cannot talk about me in front of Antonia?"

"Uh, it's complicated. Mom has enough on her plate already."

"Antonia has stopped eating?" Stefano asked. "This is not good."

"No, no. Enough on her plate—it's just an expression. Too much to think about, si?"

"Ah-h," Franco said. "That one I will have to remember."

"And Clarita, what does she say about Antonia's plate?" Stefano asked.

"Hmm, well ... she listens more than she talks."

"Clarita? I do not think this is the Clarita I once knew. When we meet again, she will have plenty to say. As will I."

Time sure drags when there's nothing but negativity to report; but after what seemed like an eternity, I pulled into the Brentwood Gardens complex and made my way through the winding streets before stopping at the garage attached to my condo. After pressing the remote, I watched the door slide upward, and then eased into the opening. Another click closed it and a third from my car opened the trunk. Soon after, we were settled inside, along with my guests' luggage, now deposited in the spare bedroom.

A quick tour of my compact home ended in the kitchen with Stefano propped on a bar stool while I explained the basics of my new espresso coffeemaker to Franco. He nodded with feigned interest.

"You already know this, right?" I said to the guy who cooked like a trained chef.

Not Worth Dying For

"Si, but is good hearing you explain in English. Mine I need to practice." Franco tried to hold back a yawn but the yawn had its own agenda.

"Sleep as late as you like," I said, bringing the evening to an end. "I leave for work early and won't return until four in the afternoon. After that my weekend belongs to both of you. Knowing Margo, she'll stop by at some point tomorrow. And maybe Mom—depending on her schedule."

"And Clarita?" Stefano asked.

Franco patted his hand. "Patience, Papa."

"Patience, bah. Don't talk to me about patience." He slid off the stool and stretched his arms overhead, a gesture Franco repeated.

"*Buonanotte,*" we said as a mutual good night and exchanged kisses again. Just as we would've in Italy.

Back in the hallway I hesitated at the guestroom door and said to Franco, "Before you go to bed, I have a question that doesn't have to be answered this evening."

"You want to know what to call Papa and me. Is only right you should ask. Tomorrow you explain the American way."

∞∞∞∞

The next morning on my drive to work the phone rang, and the Bluetooth took over. Margo, who else. "Sorry I didn't get back to you last night," she said. "I was … otherwise engaged."

"New guy?"

"A real hunk—curly blond hair and six-pack abs. Nothing serious, a one-night stand at best."

"Not that I'm telling you what to do—"

"Then don't. So what's this about the Italians coming over? When?"

"Now. They're already here, at my place."

73

Loretta Giacoletto

"You're kidding, right? No, I guess you wouldn't kid about the family skeletons. Of course, my place is bigger."

"And better, but where would you … otherwise engage?"

"You're such a dear. Who else but you would sympathize with my unfulfilled needs."

"Hmm, I could think of a few guys."

"Gotta go, little sis. I'll swing by your place during my lunch break. *Ciao*!"

Ciao, the Italian fever was contagious.

At noon Margo's text message to me read: *Italians gone but luggage still here. Guess that means they'll be back. Call when you get home.*

Gone, as in gone for a walk? Well, it wasn't like they needed my permission to explore the neighborhood. Or the nearby malls, some of which were accessible by foot, just not my two. Unless, that is, said feet were encased in serious Nikes and taking a walk that matched the mileage I'd put them through while in Italy.

But on this St. Louis afternoon when I pulled into my driveway, a second car had already taken up the extra space. Unsure of what to expect, I walked into the kitchen and found my guests sitting at the counter, each nursing a goblet of wine. Both men slid off the stools and greeted me in the usual way. I couldn't help wonder how many times that greeting would occur over the next … however long they planned on staying. Surely not the max of a ninety-day visa, but what did I know about two men I'd spent maybe a max of six hours getting to know. Of course Franco and Stefano hadn't met up with the uninformed St. Louis she-devils as yet. Just thinking about the unpredictability of that scenario made me cringe.

I had to admit the appearance of my guests had improved considerably in the nineteen hours since picking them up from the airport. The lack-of-sleep puffiness had dissolved into chiseled faces that defied their years. Steel gray hair flared back from Stefano's face, accentuating his bronze complexion. His dark blue eyes did not seem as brooding as when we first met. For an Italian he was rather tall, maybe an inch or two under six feet, as was Franco. But Franco's skin was fairer; his hair, reddish brown; his eyes as blue as Stefano's. Other than height, general build, and eye color, very little linked them as father and son, at least from my perspective.

Franco had already poured wine into a third goblet, which he handed to me. After a simple click of glasses, we allowed ourselves the pleasure of a sparkling Moscato. One sip led to another and then a third. I held up my glass and observed the dancing bubbles. "You brought this from Italy?"

To which Stefano grinned and said, "In Asti, where else. Is better than you buy here. *Tre bianchi* from Franco, *tre rossi* from me. Three each—what your U.S. Customs allows."

"About the car in my driveway ..."

"*La macchina?* A rental," Franco said with a shrug. "There is room in your garage, si?"

"Of course, but how did you know where to go? I mean to rent the car and how to get there."

"Is no different than when you visit Italy," Franco said, lifting his glass to me. "Papa and me and the Internet, we figure things out."

Having underestimated my guests, I felt my face heat up and changed the subject. "Margo stopped by earlier when you were gone. I'm sure she'll be back soon."

"Tell Margo to call first," Franco said. "To make sure we are here, instead of there.

"There?" I asked.

"Si, Papa wants—"

"I want to visit Clarita," Stefano said. "Surprise her. Antonia too."

"We should call first."

75

Loretta Giacoletto

"No, no, no," Stefano said, wagging his finger sideways. "We surprise Clarita."

"Please," Franco said with pleading eyes. "Let Papa do this his way."

"Okay, if you insist; but I will text Margo to meet us there."

"This surprise-before-the-surprise I do not understand."

"You will when we get there."

"Humph," came a guttural sound from Stefano's throat. "I think it is you who may be surprised, Elena."

"Hold that thought," I said.

"What? Where? You think me a magician?" Stefano said.

While Franco was enlightening Stefano, I hurried to my bedroom and opened the box of Nonnie's treasures, items she'd left behind in her parents' house when she immigrated to America, the same house Franco now owned. Having selected the gray folder, I returned to the living room and passed it on to Stefano.

He glanced inside and nodded. "Si, is only right I should return these to Clarita."

"You think she will remember?" Franco asked.

To which Stefano replied with another, "Humph."

Memo to self:

1. *Stay out of Nonnie Clarita's love life.*
2. *Drink more wine.*
3. *Refrain from using American slang.*
4. *Do not argue with know-it-all Italians.*
5. *Drink more wine.*

10

Not on My Watch

Rather than taking my car, Franco insisted on driving the compact SUV he'd rented, which I didn't challenge since it would allow me to observe his capability in navigating our St. Louis streets. While I carefully enunciated every number and letter of our family home address, he entered the information into the Italian version of the Mazda's GPS and relied on those instructions instead of my quicker route that would've made more sense.

"For those times Papa and I go without you," he explained so as not to offend me.

Right, as if he fully expected Nonnie Clarita to welcome her long-ago lover with open arms. Only time would tell and very soon. As expected, the GPS route took longer than my shortcut version; but Franco handled the traffic with no problem, a breeze compared to what I'd experienced in Italy where controlled havoc ruled, even in the remote villages.

I told Franco to turn into the alley behind our family home; and to my relief, when we pulled into the asphalt parking area, Margo was getting out of her car. As soon as we exited ours, I waited for the usual hugs and kisses to pass, yet hoping they would go on and on, whatever it took to delay our entering into the den of unknown horrors. During the second round of greetings, Margo caught my eye from over Stefano's shoulder and gave me a confident thumbs-up. Already I felt better, knowing her relaxed attitude would take the edge off mine on the verge of panic.

Stefano was already walking toward the back door, meaning I'd have to do a quick sprint in order to catch up with him. Instead, Franco pulled me back with a firm grip to my arm. "Let this be Papa's time," he said. "And Clarita's."

"He's right," Margo said. "Regardless of the outcome, we will be here to soothe any shattered egos."

We stood our ground midway along the sidewalk, with Nonnie's flourishing vegetable garden to our right; her fragrant rose garden to the left. Stefano had come bearing gifts—a bouquet of peach-colored roses in one hand, in the other a gift bag appropriate for liquor, and under his arm the folder I'd given him before we left my place. He found the backdoor buzzer, hesitated but a moment, and then held his finger to the button.

"*Basta*, Papa," Franco said in a voice too low for his father to hear. "Basta."

Margo touched Franco's forearm. "It'll be okay; you'll see."

Or not. The sound of Nonnie's outside voice erupted with the force of a dragon, sending virtual flames through the closed door and into the yard. "All right, dammit. I'm coming. I'm coming."

Stefano lifted his finger from the button just as the door flew open. As did Nonnie's eyes. Never had I seen those expressive eyes so wide. Nor did I expect the door to close as quickly as it had opened. Almost close, that is, had it not been for Stefano's foot blocking the threshold. "*Merda*," I heard Franco mutter from behind, followed by Margo's American version, "Shit!"

The door opened again, bringing a collective sigh from the three of us.

Nonnie was not smiling when she said, "What the … oh my God … it can't be. Is that you, Stefano?"

"Si, Clarita." After that, a flood of Italian words spilled forth, too fast for me to understand.

Or for Margo whose knowledge of the Italian language far surpassed mine. After another minute she said, "I think he's begging her forgiveness."

"No, no, Papa is talking about times past," Franco said. "The rest would not be right for me to tell you. Is too ... how you say?"

"Personal," Margo said. "Damn, I didn't believe the old gal still had it in her."

"Nor my papa. Look at them. The more he talks the softer he makes her face."

Italian charm, I couldn't help but think. I'd experienced it firsthand while in Cinque Terre. Damn fate for not letting things go my way.

"Perhaps we should leave them alone," Franco said. "In Italy this would be a good time to go for some wine."

Which we were preparing to do until Mom pulled up and parked her car in the space next to Margo's.

She got out and walked over to where Margo and I were standing with Franco. To him she gave a polite nod, obviously not recognizing the man she'd known years ago when both were teenagers. To Margo and me she asked with her usual air of authority, "What's going on?"

"We're on our way to Rudy's" Margo said. "Come with us."

"At this hour?" Mom said, again glancing in Franco's direction.

He stepped forward, bowed slightly, and then straightened up, a look of uncertainty crossing his face. "*Ciao*, Toni. It has been a long time. Do you remember me? Franco Rosina."

She forced a half-smile, the Mona Lisa one with pursed lips. "Yes, of course. So nice to see you, Franco." He moved one foot closer and placed his hands on her shoulders. She allowed him a kiss to each cheek but did not return the greeting. "What brings you to St. Louis?"

"My papa," he said. "I brought him to see your mama."

"You what?!" Mom stepped back, making no effort to hide the stunned look on a face growing redder with each word she repeated. "No, no, no, no, no!" She stomped her foot onto a weed creeping through the cracked asphalt and using the ball of her foot, twisted the weed into obliteration. "You should've checked with me first."

After she released an imperious humph, Franco opened his hands and said, "Papa was afraid you'd try to keep him from her."

"As well I would have. I'm sure you meant well but my mother is getting on in years. As is your papa, who's even older and has no business gallivanting half way across the world to relive an ill-fated romance that's kaput … you know what I mean?"

Franco nodded. "*Si, fini* … but not in the mind of my papa. Nor in his heart."

"No offense, but for all we know, your papa could be senile. Whatever was once between him and my mother is no more. Although knowing the extent of that *whatever*, I'm sure it served at least one good purpose fifty-nine years ago."

Looking from one daughter to the other, she spoke like the mother of our teenage years. "Margo. Ellen. What were you thinking? And why didn't you warn me? Mama must never know Stefano Rosina came to St. Louis. Never, never, never. Do I make myself clear?"

"Sorry, Mom," Margo said, her voice betraying the nervousness that would've matched mine if I'd mustered the courage to speak first. "You're too late. Stefano already came a-knocking and Nonnie Clarita let him in."

Mom's face went from its current state of disemboweled red to a putrid shade of green. She bent over, clutching her stomach. "Dear God, I think I'm going to be sick."

"No, you're not," I said, having found my voice. "Nonnie can take care of herself. If she doesn't want Stefano bothering her, she'll tell him to leave."

Not Worth Dying For

"And go where?" Mom asked.

"Toni, please," Franco said, reaching out to her, only to withdraw his hand when she recoiled from it. "You should have seen your mama's face as she listened to my papa's words. So *bella* I almost wept. Do not deny them this time together after almost a lifetime apart."

"Keep out of this, Franco. My mother is none of your business."

"Ah but my papa is. And you need to stay out of his business and your mama's."

Margo put one hand on Mom's arm and squeezed ever so lightly. "This isn't easy for you. Hell, it's not easy for any of us, which explains why we were on our way to Rudi's when you pulled up."

11

Hearing the Words

As soon as Stefano walked into the mudroom, Clarita closed the door and without saying a word, accepted the gifts he presented to her. Having placed his offerings on the utility counter, she fell into his waiting arms, still strong and confident for a man in his eighties. The touch of him brought back memories of their last time together, a hotel room in downtown St. Louis when she was twenty-three to his twenty-five, as well as their first time together, two teenagers in Italy making love in the cellar of her home.

This afternoon she caught the fragrance of his day thus far—a combination of after-shave lotion, red wine, and pungent garlic. "You came back," she said in their *Piemontese* dialect. "I knew you would, someday."

"I should not have waited so long," he replied in measured English. "Forgive me, I beg of you."

"What's to forgive," she said with her usual shrug and then stepped back, breaking the physical hold he had on her. "Now that I think about it, plenty, I guess."

She searched his face, looking for any semblance to the younger one she'd known so well and still saw many a night, in dreams that ended too

82

soon when she awoke in tears. His hair had turned from a rich dark brown to shades of silver streaked with tarnished strands. The hair brushed his collar and flared back from his face in a stylish European cut she'd seen in magazines and on TV. His eyes hadn't changed, still midnight blue and brooding although the outer corners were etched with wrinkles acquired over a lifetime. Deep lines creased the hollow of his cheeks, giving them what Toni would've referred to as character. Toni, dear God, would she ever accept Stefano as anything more than the disgruntled man whose seed had given her life.

Unsure of her next move, Clarita picked up the gift bag and without looking inside, she asked, "What did you bring me?"

"Genepi. I made it myself."

"Yeah, I figured as much." Genepi made from Artemisia flower heads, Clarita hadn't sipped the herbal liqueur since leaving Italy. Her papa used to make Genepi, as did many of his *paesani.* Him, she thought of often. Her mama, not so often. Not a day passed that she did not think of Stefano ... if for no reason other than to punish herself.

Stefano also brought her roses. Nice, but not as nice as those she grew in her own garden. He followed her into the kitchen and stood over her while she ran tap water into a vase and added the flowers.

"Grazie," she said, centering the vase on the table. "I suppose you ought to come with me."

"To bed?" he asked, turning his mouth into a crooked smile.

Inwardly, she stifled the giggle of the girl she'd left behind in that damp cellar from long ago. Hands to hips, she now glared at him. "After fifty-nine years? No, dammit ... there's this and that to talk about."

"This and that, hell." He cupped her chin in the palm of his hand. "After fifty-nine years, why wait one minute longer."

"What I mean is: not before we get re-acquainted which should take longer than a minute."

83

"My life I measure in minutes, Clarita." He snapped the thumb and forefinger of his left hand. "Here today; gone tomorrow."

"As if I need reminding. I just thought we'd be more comfortable sitting down. My knees ain't what they used to be."

"Mine are. So's everything else."

"*Spaccone*," she called him.

"Not if I speak the truth."

She cast a downward glance to the crotch of his pants, put a hand to her lips, and muffled a chuckle. "So you do. Then I take back what I said. Some things never change."

He tapped a row of fingers to his chest. "With Stefano Rosina they only get better."

"You always had a bullshit way with words. But just because you're here, don't expect me to rush into anything." She led the way, taking him through the claustrophobic hall and from there into the sunny living room where the TV blared. She clicked it off and with the remote still in her hand, motioned him to the sofa. He sat on the middle cushion, pulling her down beside him. The ticking clock grew louder, reminding her not to waste precious minutes.

"About the forgiveness," she said, "there's too much to forgive. Let's just move on from all those painful yesterdays."

He shook his head. "No, I did not come all this way for a quick *amen*. Please, just this once," he said. "Let me hear the words. I *need* to hear them, to ease my own guilt. I *need* to say them, to ease yours."

The words, how often had she thought of them? And as time passed, changed them to accommodate the consequences of his actions or of hers. "Okay, me first."

She leaned into his ear, sunk her teeth into the lobe until he flinched, and then kissed the raised spot. "I forgive you, Stefano Rosina, for making me love you and no one else. I forgive you, Stefano Rosina, for making me

84

think we were married when we weren't. I forgive you, Stefano Rosina, for waiting so long to follow me to America the first time. I forgive you, Stefano Rosina, for leaving America with your seed already planted inside me, even though you didn't know it. I forgive you, Stefano Rosina, for giving me my beautiful, self-righteous Antonia, who reminds me every day of you. I forgive you, Stefano Rosina, for making a second child with someone other than me. I forgive you, Stefano Rosina, for making me hate you as much as I once loved you, even though it was what I wanted at the time."

Tears ran down her cheek as she said, "Your turn. I *need* to hear the words, to ease my guilt."

He took her left hand, opened the palm, and kissed the naked base of her ring finger. "I forgive you, Clarita Fantino Rosina, for making me love you above all else. I forgive you, Clarita Fantino Rosina, for feeding me poisoned mushrooms so you could escape to America and never return to Italy. I forgive you, Clarita Fantino Rosina, for denying me the pleasure of watching our daughter grow up, for sending her to Italy as a young woman, only to break my heart with the cruelty of her tongue. I forgive you, Clarita Fantino Rosina, for not letting me love the second woman I married as much as I always loved you. I forgive you, Clarita Fantino Rosina, for making my son Franco question my love for him over my love for you."

He took a deep breath. She waited for him to exhale before pressing her forefinger to his lips. "All is forgiven, Stefano Rosina. Past, present, and future—however long that may be."

"Dear God, you're still as *bella* as the last time we met." He moved closer, his lips a breath away from hers.

She pulled away, leaned back and laughed, for the first time since he walked into her life again. "Do you remember that day at the Jefferson Hotel here in St. Louis?" she asked. "How we made love as soon as you came into my room?"

"A scene I have relived many times over the years."

"Not with your other wife, I hope."

"Relived in my heart, I meant to say."

"I know what you meant, Stefano."

"She was a good woman, Clarita. You, she would have liked."

"I would've hated her."

He thought about this for a moment. "Si, you would have."

"Did you ever speak of me to her?"

"No," he said with a slow shake of his head. "I did not trust myself to do such a thing. Besides, what good would it have done? She got pregnant on our wedding night."

"By herself?"

"No, a poor choice of words. I *got* her pregnant."

Clarita closed her eyes. "Spare me the details."

Stefano leaned over and kissed her eyes. She opened them, looking into his until they both pulled away.

"What about John Riva?" he asked. "Did you tell him about me?"

"Not a word. John died thinking the baby inside me came from him."

"A good way to die," Stefano said.

"Not really. He crashed his car on the way to work; there was an explosion."

"Jesus, I am sorry." Stefano brought her hand to his lips and kissed it again.

"Just so you know, to this day I still carry his name. Here in America, I am Clarita Fantino Riva." She rarely thought about John Riva, even when the monthly returns on his investments showed up in her checking account.

"If only I had—"

86

She pressed two fingers to his lips. "What's done is done. All is forgiven, right?"

He nodded and kissed the fingers lingering on his lips. She pulled her hand away, tracing those fingers over the hollow of his nearest cheek and down to his jawbone.

"Don't stop there," he said.

"I ain't through talking. About Toni, when the two of you met in Italy, she knew about you and me but not about you coming to America, not about you being her papa. That is, until Lucca Sasso told her."

"Lucca meant well. He was trying to protect me. And you."

"Yeah, I figured as much. But I sure had a lot of explaining to do when Toni came home. Never have I seen her so upset."

"Did you tell Antonia how much you hated me?" he asked.

"She didn't give me a chance to talk about you—one way or the other. And what about your son?"

He paused, running his tongue over his lips. "Do you think, would it be possible ...?"

"Si, the Genepi. Stay here and I'll get it."

Minutes later she returned with the opened bottle, two small goblets, and a dozen Oreos sitting on a plate. "Toni buys these. Some people dunk them but not me. They're very American." Stefano picked up one cookie and examined it from all angles before popping the entire thing into his mouth. "Welcome to my—our—daughter's world," she said. "And don't you dare spit it out."

Instead, he took another and ate it too, washing down the remains of both with the Genepi she'd poured.

"Tell me about your son," Clarita said.

"Franco came to America with me. Him, I know you will like."

Loretta Giacoletto

She lifted her brow. "Is he anything like you?"

"I do not think so. Franco is his own person."

"As is our daughter. She's nothing like me."

"Si. This I know from when Antonia and I first met. She hated me then."

Clarita scoffed at this. "Give it time, depending on how long you plan to stay. And don't tell me that will depend on me."

"No need for me to say what you already know," he said. "Here is what I know. It was a good thing you did those many years ago, selling your family home to Franco."

"More selfish than good. I wanted you to think of me every time you went there."

"I did, Clarita. Shortly after Franco moved in, I went upstairs to the room that had been yours. I lay down on the bed you'd slept in, closed my eyes, and took myself back to the night we made love there. Had my wife still been alive, this—my lust for you—would have counted as adultery against her. But she was already dead, so I pleasured myself, all the while thinking of you."

"Don't get me started," she said. "I know the feeling."

"*Permesso* to kiss you now?"

She did not look at him when she gave her answer. "One time, no more."

Nor did he look at her when he asked, "And if you enjoy the one time?"

"Those words, you remembered them from our first time."

"So did you. How old were we then?"

"More like how young. Me, a mere fifteen. You, a grown-up seventeen. Damn, if that had been my Toni ... as a teenager ... I would've—"

88

"Shh, this about you and me and now."

What started with his lips caressing her cheek moved to her trembling lips and a push of his tongue into her mouth, giving her a taste of the Genepi and Oreos combined with the wine and garlic she smelled on encountering him in the mudroom moments before. "Just like our first time," she said, licking her lips after the kiss had ended.

"Is there a chance we could relive that time again? Not on the ledge of your papa's cellar but in a comfortable bed, the one you sleep in each night. Do you still dream of me?"

"Only when I want to punish myself," she said. "Just so you know, I ain't the girl I used to be. Some parts have shifted here and there; but thank God, I still got my own teeth."

"All the better to bite me with." He leaned over and nipped her earlobe, his teasing gesture another reminder of their earlier years. "*Permesso* to make love with you now?"

Ever so lightly, she tapped two fingertips to the hollow of his cheek. "Better we should take this slow and easy."

"Si, the first time," he said, pressing those same fingertips to his lips. "After that, you will have to hold me back."

"Still the bad boy, Stefano. Is that what you've been trying to tell me?"

"Something like that."

She straightened up. "Well, I'm smarter now than I was at fifteen. Smarter than at twenty-three too. And don't be telling me your time is running out 'cause I don't need a reminder that mine is too."

"Does this mean you want me to go?" he asked.

"No, I want you to stay so we can get to know each other again."

She waited for him to entice her with more words. Instead, he got up and stepped away from the sofa.

89

"You're leaving?" Opening one hand, she snapped two fingers. "Just like that."

Stefano motioned for her to stay seated and with one forefinger, indicated he'd be right back. He quickly returned with the folder he'd left on the mudroom counter and handed it to her. "You must've forgotten this all those years ago when you came to America," he said, "along with other keepsakes from our time together. Franco found them stored in a box when he bought the house."

She picked up the folder, already knowing what it contained. "I didn't forget. My life with you I left behind, for Mama to see with her own eyes how things had been between us. Oh, how I wanted to punish her, just as she had punished me."

"What little I knew of Bruna Fantino, I doubt the woman would've given you the satisfaction of looking inside."

"Yeah, dammit. Otherwise, she would've burned everything and smashed the box into a thousand pieces, which is what I wanted her to do. Of all times for her to respect my privacy."

"As did Franco. He passed your secret box of treasures on to Margo and Elena. It was your *nipote*—"

"*Our nipote*," she corrected him. "They have your blood as well as mine."

"Si, it was *our nipote* who showed Franco and me the contents. That's when he found out about you and me. And about Toni—the American he befriended in Pont Canavese, not knowing they shared the same papa. Franco's main concern was for his beloved mama, the mama who adored him and he loved with all his heart, the mama whose memory I uphold and respect. Still, when Franco asked about you, I could not lie to him, Clarita. He knows you were and will always be the love of my life."

"Do you think his mama knew about me?"

"She never asked."

Not Worth Dying For

"Some answers women already know without having to ask."

At last Clarita opened the folder. "How well I remember that day," she said, picking up a charcoal drawing of two dark-haired and dreamy-eyed adolescents. Side-by-side profiles of them gazing somewhere beyond the artist's rendition. A second drawing sat under the first, this of the couple kneeling face-to-face. Not a stitch of clothes on either one and wrapped in a tight embrace, they were kissing with an unbridled passion the artist had managed to capture.

"You were so beautiful, Clarita. I did not think it possible to love anyone as much as I loved you. There are other items that Elena and Margo brought back, things they thought you meant to take but forgot. Elena called them your treasures. Of course they had no way of knowing you left them to punish your mama. Or me." He reached in his shirt pocket, pulled out a small, tissue-wrapped package, and opened it. "Even this?" he asked, showing her a gold wedding band nestled in the palm of his hand.

With that, she choked back a sob, the first of many than began to flow like a dam that had finally burst.

He took her left hand, slid the ring over her fourth finger and kissed the no longer naked base. "Look," he said, showing her a second ring. "I still have mine too." He slipped the ring on his little finger, shrugged, and said, "Arthritis."

She kissed the base of his ring finger, not wanting to let go. When she did, it was to meet the gaze in his eyes.

"Now?" he asked. "Can I make love to you now?"

"Yes, please, before time runs out."

12

Rudi's

While I'd been busy convincing Mom not to interfere with the aging lovebirds getting re-acquainted, Franco and El had assumed their positions in the rental—Franco behind the wheel and El riding shotgun, my usual position when she was driving. Not so this time. I was trapped in the back with a very pouting Toni Savino who was used to getting her own way. We headed toward Rudi's, a popular bar located less than a mile from our family house, an easy and expected walk when in Italy; but we were back in St. Louis and four—make that three—people from the neighborhood about to engage in a heated exchange made better sense in the privacy of a car than on the sidewalk.

"I don't like this, not one bit," Mom said.

"Really," I replied rather weakly. "It's not like Nonnie's a teenager about to have her heart broken for the first time."

"The woman is too old for this kind of nonsense."

"And you weren't?" I said, referring to the recently deceased Val Corrigan. Nonsense, most definitely; heartbreak, highly unlikely.

92

"My interaction with Val was totally different and you know it." She sat back, arms folded and jaw set.

"Keep it up and your face will freeze like a sour grape." Yes, a throwback to my time as a teeny-bopper and hers as the confrontational mother.

"This is nothing but a game for you, Margo."

"Not really but until this *Stefano Rosina and Clarita Riva thing* becomes a problem for her, or for him, I refuse to make it my problem. Nor should you."

"I will not have that man overnighting in my house."

"May I remind you: the mortgage-free house of which you speak is as much Nonnie's as it is yours. After all, she did help pay for it. To say nothing of the fact that Stefano is your—"

"Don't even *think* about going there, Margo."

"Okay, I won't. But if Stefano making Nonnie happy offends you that much, he can spend his nights elsewhere. Right, El?"

El jerked forward but didn't turn to face Mom or me. "Uh … sorry, I wasn't paying attention. Too busy helping Franco navigate."

"Liar, liar, pants on fire," I countered, knowing full well her head had been tilted in my direction seconds before.

Not to be outdone, El managed to change the topic with a quick gesture to her right. "Is this our lucky day or what? There's Rudi's and a parking space on the street."

Franco's parallel parking put mine to shame, which made perfect sense considering the minuscule spaces allotted for street parking in Italy. Not so in St. Louis. We got out and started walking toward the bar, two by two with El leading the way and Franco beside her. Rudi's was sending out its customary mix of mouth-watering scents—burgers, fries, onions, toasted ravioli, beer and wine.

"And where are the Italians currently staying?" Mom asked as if

Loretta Giacoletto

Franco wasn't within earshot of us.

"With Elena," he said from over his shoulder. "And will continue to do so. That is, if Elena will have Papa and me."

"I wouldn't have it any other way," El said, to my relief.

The late afternoon crowd had gathered inside Rudi's, a few customers having parked themselves at the long, inviting bar, a choice neither El nor Mom would've considered appropriate for unescorted females, Franco notwithstanding. I zeroed in on a corner table, away from prying ears since depending on the circumstances, Mom had been cursed, or blessed, with the annoying habit of raising her voice when she wanted to make a point.

El passed the beverage list to me and I ordered a bottle of California red wine, not expecting it to match the quality of what we'd gotten in Italy. It turned out decent enough, given the awkward situation the four of us had found ourselves.

After a few moments of silence, Franco asked Mom if she remember Filippo.

"That would be Fil the worry wart who tried to pass me on to you. He had the jealous girlfriend."

"Si, Nora," he said. "They married and have one son—Amadeo."

Both El and I perked up, any excuse to enter a conversation centered on something other than the elephant at our table. "Margo and I met Filippo and Amadeo during our stay in Pont Canavese," El said. "Amadeo is a detective with the Torino police … I mean Turin."

"No need to translate, Ellen, I've been to Italy." Mom looked from El to me and back to El.

"Amadeo was a friend," I said. Whatever it took to erase the new worry line creasing Mom's forehead.

"Why would I think otherwise?" she asked. "So, the two of you were

Not Worth Dying For

in some kind of trouble over there."

"But you just said—"

"Nothing we started," El chimed in. "Although Margo was knocked unconscious—sort of by accident."

"Sort of, my ass," I said under my breath. I could've added the two bodily assaults while in Cinque Terre but Mom had already narrowed her eyes in my direction.

"And why haven't I heard about this before now?" she asked.

"You had to be there," I said. "In spite of the pain and humiliation I suffered, that particular incident falls under the category of minor. A mere blip on the radar screen that ultimately resolved some unexplained issues."

"There were other incidents?" she asked.

"None worth repeating." I drummed my fingers on the table. "Let's see. Who else did we meet that you would've known from your visit in the seventies? El, help me out."

"Donata Bartolini," El said.

"Ah, yes," Mom said. "Donata had a daughter near my age. I think the daughter died."

"That's right," I said. "We met her son Pio—Donata's grandson. But really, it was Amadeo we knew best."

"Oh dear, I hope the two of you didn't fight over this Amadeo."

"Mother, please!" El said. "Not in front of Franco. And no, Margo and I did not fight over Amadeo."

Franco grinned, his only response to the discussion he'd started. While he was pouring more wine, a woman who'd been sitting at the bar, swiveled off her stool and walked over to our table. More like strutted, with long legs meant for a chorus line in her younger days. Which is not to say she wasn't still attractive. Quite the contrary, full lips painted a glossy red and almost

95

too-black hair pulled into a bun at the base of her neck. I glanced at Franco, thinking he might've done something to encourage the stranger while Mom had been interrogating El and me. Instead she headed directly toward Mom.

"Toni?" She held out a limp hand of long fingers and scarlet nails. "Romaine Sloane. We met some time ago at the Fox Theatre. Sorry, that particular performance escapes me. But what can one expect from a less-than-stellar theater company touring the Midwest."

Having been a huge fan of the Fox, as was El, I could've argued the point but didn't think it worth my effort.

Mom shook the woman's hand with about as much enthusiasm as had been offered. "Oh, yes, now I remember. Val Corrigan introduced us."

"That's right. What a pity about him dying so suddenly. We must get together for a nice but somewhat morbid chat. I recently moved and then went to China so I haven't had a chance to catch up on all the details."

"You were in China?" I said, moving the conversation in a more upbeat direction. "How perfectly marvelous."

With that, Franco got up, grabbed a chair from the next table, and we made room for Romaine to join us. Franco ordered a second bottle of the earlier wine and we exchanged names with the woman I now recalled as Mom having described earlier as one of Val Corrigan's lady friends.

Mom interrupted our discussion with a loud clearing of her throat. "About Val," she said, "You do know he was murdered."

As if on cue Romaine Sloane squeezed out a splash of tears while Mom explained the horrific circumstances of Val Corrigan's death, leaving out her connection as well as Kat's. "Just hearing the details breaks my heart," Romaine said, mopping her wet cheeks with a paper napkin. "No doubt the killer was one of those misguided females who pursued Val. Ours, on the other hand, was a special relationship—more platonic than physical."

Platonic, what a joke. Rather than risk an undisguised snicker, I drained the wine from my glass.

Not Worth Dying For

El, on the other hand, took a more direct approach. "If you haven't already done so, you … uh, might want to check in with the police. I mean regarding that special relationship."

Romaine lifted a pair of arched eyebrows matched to perfection. "And why would I want to open myself to such scrutiny. Surely, the police aren't talking to every Jan, Jill, and Julie who ever knew Val Corrigan. That exercise in obsessive futility could take forever."

"Then do nothing and let the detectives find you," Mom said with a flick of her hand. "Those investigators have a way of narrowing their field down to a very few—"

"What," Romaine said, "bitches hungry for the attention of any man?"

"No-o, more like *persons of interest*, in the vernacular of law enforcement."

"Excuse me," Romaine said as she pushed her chair back, only to be stopped by Franco's soothing words.

"Please, do not go, at least not yet," Franco said in an endearing manner similar to what I used on certain occasions.

Romaine projected a smile, far more sincere than the one she'd foisted on us earlier. "That's awfully sweet of you … er—"

"Franco, Franco Rosina from Italy."

"How utterly charming, Franco from Italy." Romaine took a pen from her purse, scribbled something on a stray paper napkin, and handed it to him. "Call or text me for a get-together. I'd love to talk about Italy." She stood up and directed her next comment to Mom. "Now, much as I dislike repeating myself, if you'll excuse me, I have things to do."

After Romaine's hurried departure, Franco elaborated on a concern that had already crossed my mind. "I don't know about the rest of you; but I think the lady knew this Val Corrigan better than she wants us to think. Toni, perhaps you should make a friend of her. Find out what she's not telling you."

97

"How perceptive of you and of my feelings. Better yet, perhaps *you* should make a friend of her, Franco." Mom placed one hand on his forearm. "Forgive me for my earlier rudeness. I suppose it was the shock of your father and my mother."

"It is I who should apologize," Franco said, "for … *how you say* … for Papa and I … blindsiding you."

Her mouth twitched before settling into an unsure smile. "A perfect choice of words, I could not have said it better myself."

"Uh," I started out with a single toe, intending to test the virtual water's temperature. "I was … that is, El and I … were wondering how we should refer to you, Franco, considering we are … sort of … related."

"Not sort of," El said. "There's no getting around this. We are blood relatives."

"In Italy is not such a problem," Franco said with a lift of his shoulders. "Nor would I think it would be here in America. But to answer your question, I am the brother of Toni Savino—half-brother to be more precise. Okay with you, Toni?"

She thought about this, longer than most people who'd grown up without siblings would have. "Si … yes, I suppose so. But you do realize I am older than you."

He held up one hand and wiggled the fingers. "Si, I think by several months." He made a fist, then spread his fingers to expose his open palm.

"Awkward, to say the least," Mom said.

"Only when discussing actual dates of birth," I countered.

"Either way, it makes me *lo zio*—the uncle—to you, Margo. And to you, Elena."

"Uncle Franco," El said with a broad show of teeth. "Sounds good to me."

"Me too," I said, matching her grin. Just like that, our self-contained

Not Worth Dying For

family had grown by two more.

"Not to be a wet blanket," Mom said. "But for now, let's keep this in the family."

"Is not for me to decide," Franco said. "I—Papa and me—we are the outsiders."

"Speaking of ... what about Stefano?" I asked, kicking El under the table. Three pair of eyes focused on Mom, waiting for her input.

"I'm not ready for Stefano yet," she said.

"He's not going away," I said. "At least not for a while."

"No need to remind me. But must everything be decided here and now?"

13

Then and Now

Clarita braced the length of her back against the wall, giving Stefano enough space to adjust his arm behind the down pillow she'd brought from home. They lay facing each other, naked under a single top sheet, its cotton fibers absorbing the sweat of their damp bodies. His more so than hers, just as she recalled from long ago. She closed her eyes, trying to recapture a moment from their past, only to give up when she felt the brush of Stefano's lips, first on one eye and then the other. She opened her eyes to his, to what mattered more than anything else—the two of them living in the here and now.

"You sure Elena won't mind?" Stefano asked. "You and me making love here, I mean."

"What's to mind? Ellen expects you to make yourself at home, which means this bed is your bed," Clarita said, referring to one of two single beds occupying the guest room. "As for me being sure, I'd have to say: no surer than I was the first time we made love. And no surer than when I thought we got married in Ceresole Reale."

"One of my many regrets, Clarita." He rolled onto his back, leaving her

100

Not Worth Dying For

with less room than before. "If only I had known the marriage was not legal, that you had to be eighteen to marry without your mama's permission."

"Yeah, that's what we get for paying that phony-baloney Serina to perform the ceremony."

"Serina may've been gypsy—"

"Not by birth, she deserted her husband and babies to run off with a caravan passing through Pont Canavese."

"True gypsy or not, the woman was a damn good artist. She made you and me come to life in her drawings."

"Tell me about it." She lay her head on his chest, its damp hair tickling her nose. "We were quite the pair, you and me, so proud of our young bodies, so sure of our love. That wedding fiasco turned out to be a real heartbreaker for both of us, at least then. But time passed, and if you hadn't followed me to America, there'd be no Antonia now."

"And if I had not gone back to Italy, there would be no Franco now. My son is my strength. He means everything to me."

"It's the same with me and Toni. Too bad she hasn't warmed up to you yet."

Stefano lifted the sheet, fanning himself and Clarita before letting it drop back to serve as a cover. "Who needs air conditioning in this hellhole called St. Louis? One look from Antonia is enough to freeze my balls."

"Speaking of ..." Clarita reached down and stroked his precious jewels. Not too long, just a tease for what was yet to come. "You'd think we were a couple of kids, Toni never leaving us alone in the house, always watching our every move."

"Just as your mama would've done."

"Humph. You got that right."

He leaned over, and nibbled on the lobe of her ear until she let out a soft moan. "You like?" he asked.

101

Loretta Giacoletto

"No, but don't stop now."

"Give Antonia time," he said, lips pressed to her ear. "How long have I been in America? Less than a week. How many days since you last took me into your bed? Four."

"And here we are now, making *l'amore* in the afternoon, for God's sake."

"All the better to see you, Clarita."

"And you. With no place to hide our wrinkles and bulges and battle scars."

"What's to hide?" Stefano lay back. He pulled off his part of the sheet and rubbed his right side. "This zipper I wear with pride. Without it, I would not be here."

Clarita moved down, eyed the appendectomy scar he'd been rubbing, and pressed her lips to it. "Same goes for my caesarean. Without it, I might've survived, but not Toni."

"Let me see," Stefano said.

She lay back and pushed the sheet aside. He bent over, traced the faded scar with one finger and then kissed it, just as Clarita had done with his. He moved his hand further down until Clarita stopped him with hers. Wiggling out from under him, she said, "Not so fast. You need a time out."

"Time out? This I do not understand."

"Give the playboy a rest, Stefano."

"Ah-h, so what I make good, will be even better the next time. That I get."

She kissed the palm of his hand and held it to her breast. "Talk to me some more, about then and now."

"With pleasure." He moved a few inches away from her, one foot on the floor to keep from sliding off the bed. "I wish I could have seen you then, so full of life with our baby still inside you. Shameful I know, me with

Not Worth Dying For

another baby growing inside my legal wife. But at the time I did not know about you, Clarita. Nor did I find out until much later when your mama told me you were recently widowed with a new baby. She even told me the baby's birth date. That's how I knew Antonia had to be ours—yours and mine. At that point what was I to do? The honorable thing became my only choice."

"Nor would I have expected otherwise. How I wish we could've taken our time growing old together and thanked God for the privilege of watching our bodies change with the years, even though those changes weren't for the better."

"Your body is as beautiful as the first time I saw it by candlelight in the stable. Dear God, you made my heart pound at seventeen and you still make my heart pound at eighty-four. So hard I thought it would jump through my chest—then and now."

"Even now? Maybe we shouldn't press our luck. I'd hate having to explain how you died on top of me. Or underneath me." Clarita giggled. "Toni would be mortified. Although ... come to think of it, maybe not. She's no longer the clone of Mother Teresa she once was."

"This I do not understand."

"Our daughter fell from grace last year. It was not pretty."

"Ah-h, with the best friend's lover, who has since died at the hand of another. Elena told me and Franco on the night of our arrival."

"Ellen told you? So much for covering up family secrets."

"But I am family, si? The father of an only daughter who barely acknowledges my presence. Antonia Riva Savino, dear God, how I wish I could've given her my name."

"The name Riva has served her well. I'm talking about the insurance settlement."

"Always the money with you *Americani.*"

"Don't go there, Stefano. That kind of talk is what sent you back to Italy the first time."

103

Loretta Giacoletto

He kissed her, long and hard. "Forgive me. This mistake I will not make again."

After a lazy stretch, she changed positions and leaned on one elbow. "Speaking of … how long do you plan on staying?"

"Is too soon to decide but my papers allow ninety days. We should not waste a single day or hour arguing over what might've been, what could've been. Then or now."

"Nor should we waste another minute of this afternoon." She glanced at the clock. "Ellen won't be home for another hour. What about Franco?"

"He promised not before four o'clock."

"How's your heart," she asked, tracing one finger around it.

"Pounding, just thinking about the things we will do before they return."

∞∞∞

I came home from work around four-fifteen and had just pulled into the garage when Franco turned into the driveway. Before going into the house, we brushed our lips against each other's cheeks, making me grateful to have a relative in my life that made this possible.

"Your day at school was good?" he asked.

"Uneventful," I replied, still unable to call him uncle or just plain Franco without feeling a bit uncomfortable. "Couldn't ask for anything better. Shall we see what the lovebirds are up to?"

"Whatever it is, I pray they have finished."

Franco followed me into the kitchen where we found Nonnie and Stefano seated at the counter. A bottle of red wine had been uncorked and four goblets were waiting to be filled. But first a round of greetings, more out of respect for our guests since Nonnie had never introduced the kissing custom in our Holly Hills home.

104

I wasn't sure whose face was more flushed—Nonnie's or Stefano's—but judging from their upbeat demeanor, they must've been engaging in what Nonnie referred to as *you-know-what* over an extended period of time.

"What shall we do this evening?" I asked, to which Nonnie and Stefano exchanged glances.

"You had something in mind?" she asked.

"Not exactly," I said, hoping to prop my feet up and vegetate on the sofa—alone. Shameful, yes, considering our current state of affairs, but over the years I'd come to value my private time, those precious moments when I didn't have to make small talk with friends or extended family, no matter how close they were. I thought about the man I'd left behind in Italy after a brief but meaningful affair. My first love, unfortunately, was still attached to his first love, with no plans of detaching himself in the foreseeable future.

"I have plans," Franco said, as if catching a trace of my thoughts. "With Romaine—already I forgot her last name."

"Romaine from Rudi's?" Nonnie asked. "Around your Mom's age, give or take. Moves like a cat, dark hair pulled back?"

"Really, Nonnie, is there anyone you don't know?" I asked.

"Not in the neighborhood. This is what retired people on a fixed income do, keep an eye on the comings and goings of everybody else, which explains why I'm glad Margo lives miles from my place so as not to embarrass the family." She looked at me, a slight smile crossing her face. "You, I ain't so worried about, at least for the time being. And now with Stefano here, he's been hanging out at Rudi's with me. Both hands on the table and all that stuff. What the hell, you know what a stickler your mom can be when it comes to propriety. Or used to be, not that I'm judging."

"This Romaine talks to everybody," Stefano said. "Even me."

"Imagine that," Clarita said. "She thinks he's cute."

"Cute," Stefano said. "This I do not like. Cute is for *il bambini*."

Loretta Giacoletto

"Maybe in Italy but not in America," I said with a laugh. "Consider *cute* a compliment. As for Romaine Sloane, she knew the recently deceased Val Corrigan. And is *sort of* acquainted with Mom. We met Romaine last week at Rudi's. She'd just returned from China and although she knew Val had died, she didn't know the horrific circumstances until Mom told her."

"Not the Romaine I know," Nonnie said. "This Romaine's been an off-and-on regular at Rudi's for some time. I don't think she has a regular job—more power to her."

"Hmm, not to worry. I, Franco Rosina, will find out all I can about Romaine."

"At Rudi's?" I asked.

"No, no. I invited Romaine to take dinner here, one I will prepare with my own hands. You do not mind, Elena? Perhaps you could take Mama Clarita and Papa somewhere for a few hours, si?"

Mama Clarita? I couldn't help wondering who came up with that term of respect. Perhaps Papa Stefano would work for Franco's papa.

"Is all right?" Franco asked. "I promise not to waste an evening such as this on what you call silly stuff."

"No problem, Franco." *Whatever makes you happy, Franco.*

Memo to self:

1. *Reclaim my privacy*
2. *Convince Mom to make room for Daddy*
3. *Or, convince Nonnie to make room for Stefano.*
4. *Ease Franco out of my life and into Margo's.*
5. *Introduce Franco to someone nicer than Romaine Sloane.*

14

Make Room for Papa

I answered the phone, already knowing what to expect at seven-thirty on a Saturday morning, one designed for leisure activities to improve my overall lifestyle.

"It's your turn," El told me in a low voice laced with undeniable menace. "I've been putting up with the houseguests and Nonnie all week. Not that I don't sort of love the Italians and would do anything for Nonnie, but this enough is more than enough."

"What happened?" I asked. "Don't tell me Mom threw Nonnie out of her own house."

"Indirectly, yes. She won't give Nonnie and Stefano any alone-time. Consequently, they're at my place all day, every day."

"When you're at work."

"And still here when I get home. Correction, when Franco and I get home. Laid back or not, that man is one busy tourist, on the prowl all day, exploring what he calls our amazing zoo and the museums, which he insists are as good as any in Italy, only different. As if one could compare

107

Loretta Giacoletto

Botticelli, Michelangelo, and di Vinci with the artists in our museum."

"Excuse me, we have—"

"Please, no lecture on art history, it's not your forte. Nor am I in the mood for trivia. What's more, Franco has taken to entertaining lady friends in the evening. Here, in my kitchen, which means the rest of us have to get lost so he can show off his culinary skills. Would you believe he cooked twice for that Romaine from Rudi's and last night for another woman whose name I've already forgotten."

"Romaine from Rudi's? You've got to be kidding."

"Don't change the subject, Margo. To repeat, I am not in the mood."

"Okay, I get it. So, what do you want from me."

"The whole weekend to myself. Stefano and Franco can sleep here at night but during the day I want them gone. Just so you know, wherever Stefano goes, so goes Nonnie. Not only are they inseparable, they cannot get through a single day without making whoopee, and not always in the bedroom. As soon as I come home, I can smell it in the air, see it on their smug faces."

Images I was not prepared to conjure up. Nor could I imagine a time when I would be. "Whoopee, you say. That's so ... archaic and sweet."

"Only if it's in someone else's home. I'm counting on you, Margo."

"Okay, give me some time. I'll think of something."

"Make it good and make it quick."

∞∞∞∞

Ninety minutes later found me in Nonnie's kitchen, seated at the kitchen table with the Italians, drinking endless cups of Frangelico-laced American coffee. "You're sure you don't want breakfast?" Nonnie asked, skillet in hand, to which she was shown a collective negative response of three upright palms.

108

The back door rattled. The room went silent, a rush of tension vibrating through the air as Mom walked in, a bag of groceries clasped in each hand. Franco and Stefano both stood up, a gesture of civility Mom either ignored or failed to notice. Instead, she wiggled the bags toward me, my cue to deal with her purchases, a job I would've foisted on El had she been there. What a chicken baby El had been, unable to deal with two foreign houseguests we'd only recently met, to say nothing of our aging Nonnie entangled in a romantic tryst with one of them—her first love, our newly discovered grandpa. And until recently, unacknowledged papa to our mother who refused to accept any part of Stefano Rosina other than the genes he'd unintentionally passed on to her.

Margo to the rescue, you bet. I'd stepped into shoes as practical as those El swore by and intended to get a few things resolved, regardless of how long it took or how many tears might get shed to accomplish my goal. Stefano and Franco were still standing, waiting for Mom to make the next move.

"*Buongiorno*, Antonia," Stefano belted out as if his daughter suffered from a hearing malfunction.

"*Buongiorno*, Toni," Franco added in a slight whisper.

Mom nodded with the enthusiasm of an airport TSA guard. After gesturing for the men to take their seats, Nonnie set about making a fresh pot of coffee while I arranged the groceries on their appropriate shelves. Mom took off like a bird in flight, heading toward the hallway when Nonnie grabbed her arm.

"Excuse me," Mom said, shaking loose from Nonnie's grip. "Nature is calling."

"Ten minutes, missy, and then I expect you back here."

Missy. It was one thing for Nonnie to use that word in that tone on El or me, but when she referred to our mother as missy, the word took on a whole new dimension from an era long gone.

Scary, yes, but nevertheless effective since Mom did return in the allotted time. She helped herself to the coffee and Frangelico before sitting down at the far end of the table, only to find herself suddenly flanked on

109

either side by the Italians. Stefano extended one hand and covered hers with his. When she made an effort to pull away, he wouldn't let her.

"I begged your mama's forgiveness and she gave it to me," he said. "I now beg forgiveness from you."

She yanked harder and he released her hand. "There's nothing to forgive. Mama said you didn't find out about me until you were back in Italy, married to another woman you'd also impregnated."

"This is true."

"And a shock for me," Franco said in a cheerful manner. "I only found out about Papa's first love when Margo and Elena came to visit us."

"Nice try, Franco, but hardly a fair comparison," Mom said. "After all, you grew up with a mother and father, surrounded by family and loved ones. Here in America, it was just Mama and me."

Nonnie made a noise under her breath before spewing out a few choice words. "Just Mama and me? Thanks for nothing. I gave you a good life, Toni. Or so I thought. Did you ever want for anything?"

"Other than a father, no. What a dunce I was, worshipping John Riva, a man I never knew, one who turned out to be nothing more than a paper transaction."

Stefano had been drumming his fingers on the table, only to stop on hearing Franco's translation of the dunce comment. "*Idiota* you call yourself." He leveled a forefinger in Mom's direction. "The *man you never knew, the paper transaction,* gave you his name, gave you financial security. For that you can thank him and your mama. But the papa who gave you *la vita* sits before you now." He paused, patting a row of fingers to his heart. "Here I am, Antonia, ready to give you the love and attention I held back these many years. For as long as Clarita and my visa allow me to stay, I will be the papa you only *dreamed* of having. And after I go back to Italy, I will continue to be that papa for as long as I live."

Nice promise until Stefano got to the end, giving me a knee jerk reaction. I narrowed my eyes, hands gripping the table edge. "Hold on

Stefano, I don't like the sound of this, the part about *as long as you live*. Please don't tell me you're dealing with an incurable disease."

He shrugged, his gesture reminding me of the first time we'd met in Italy. "Other than old age, not to my knowledge. Nor that of my *dottore*. Still, every day I wake up seeing the green side of the grass is a day I treasure as a gift from God."

"Is the same for me," Franco said, pouring Frangelico into his empty cup. He lifted the cup as a salute to Mom. "I have always wanted a brother or a sister, Toni. I hope you will let me be the brother you never had."

"Never *knew* I had," Mom corrected him. She turned to Stefano. "I'm open to a non-combative relationship."

"Non-combative?" he said. "You agree not to fight? What kind of papa do you take me for?"

"I told you this wouldn't be easy," Nonnie said. "You can do better than that, Toni."

"Let me rephrase my comment. I am open to a civilized relationship."

"She means no name-calling or insulting comments," I explained.

"Exactly," Mom said with a look that told me she'd gotten away with more than she first anticipated. "To clarify, could we please dispense with all *familial* references. By that I mean, no daughter or sister, no papa or dad or father or brother."

A look of disbelief crossed Stefano's face. "After all these years you want this blood we share to remain a secret within the family?"

The wheels in Mom's head were working overtime. "Well, I wouldn't go quite that far."

"Right, missy. You take care of your appraisal business. Leave the family business to me."

"But the neighbors—"

Loretta Giacoletto

"The neighbors, get real. Take a look around. We're the last family on this block free of scandal. And that ain't for long. As for Stefano and me, we are husband and wife, married in Italy years ago and now reunited. The exact wedding date, who cares, especially since nobody around here knew John Riva anyway."

"Mama, how could you!"

"Toni, how could you?"

"Stop, both of you," I said.

"Si, no more arguing, no name-calling," Stefano said, slamming the side of his fist on the table. "Me, I am Stefano Rosina, husband of Clarita Fantino Riva Rosina. Or Rosina Riva, whichever Clarita prefers."

"And I am Franco Rosina. Or Frank if you prefer. No zio, no uncle. No embarrassing the St. Louis family."

"Whatever comes out of my mouth at any given time works for me," I said. "I'll pass the word to El."

"For now could we at least have some vino?" Stefano asked.

"At this hour?" Mom said. "It's mid-morning."

"Not in Italy. There, is late afternoon. My dottore advises me to drink at least two glasses of vino each day."

The sound of a chair pushing back to scrape across the tile brought an immediate reaction from me. "Stay where you are, Nonnie," I said before she went any further.

Mom hadn't moved either, which came as no surprise. Civility was one thing; cordiality quite another. Again, Margo to the rescue, this time in the name of hospitality, however strained. Having answered my call to duty, I set the bottle of dry red and a corkscrew in front of Franco and told him to do the honors. While he uncorked, I gathered the goblets and paper napkins. After the pouring we lifted our glasses in a simultaneous, "Salute!"

To which I added, "Welcome to America and to our family."

112

Wine drinkers tend to have a routine for the first sip. Or, in the case of Stefano and Franco, first gulp, followed by a hand across the mouth. Although father and son shared very few physical features, there was no denying their mannerisms. I glanced at Mom, hoping to find some gesture that would identify her as Stefano's daughter but saw nothing. For sure not the prim and proper demeanor she'd nurtured over her adult life.

"About the sleeping arrangements," Nonnie said, tracing one finger around the rim of her goblet, a cleansing habit I'd picked up from her. "Stefano stays here."

"In the guest room," Mom said.

"That's where his suitcase goes, where he hangs his clothes in the closet. Where he sleeps is none of your business."

The breath I'd been holding expelled with Nonnie's commanding words, giving me the courage to add, "Well, that wasn't so bad, was it?"

"It's a start," Nonnie said. "As for your mom's current predicament, she still needs all the help she can get. This Val Corrigan investigation ain't going away."

Franco nodded. "Si, I spoke to Romaine Sloane about him."

"You what?" This from Mom and Nonnie, both speaking as one.

Wine quickly disappeared from the glasses and Franco poured another round while he shared his Romaine experience with us. "I think Romaine Sloane likes me—more than I like her. I know she liked the first meal I prepared for her—the sweet onions and red and yellow pepper strips sautéed in olive oil, the veal cutlets topped with a generous amount of lemon zest. The second meal was even better."

"Stop it, Franco," I said with a groan. "You're making me hungry."

"How else can I explain Romaine? The woman has the appetite of a mountain climber, to say nothing of those incredible legs. *Mama mia*, that's all I got to say. She once danced for a living, or so she told me."

"Did she say anything about China?" Mom asked.

113

"Only that she came back some weeks ago. She already knew how Val Corrigan died before you told her, Toni."

"Lying bitch," Mom said. "Sorry, as a rule I don't resort to such vulgarity."

Really, since when? Had I been sitting closer to her, I'd have patted her hand. Instead, Stefano did. Franco waited for the moment to pass before continuing.

"Romaine also mentioned another lady friend of Val Corrigan. I wrote the name down as soon as Romaine left. Otherwise I would not have remembered it." Having removed a slip of paper from his rear pocket, he squinted to read it. "Ah, si, here she is. Jet Gregson."

Stefano plucked the note from Franco's hand. He squinted at the paper, too, before slipping on the specs tucked in his shirt pocket. "Jet Gregson ... Jet Gregson. Who would give their daughter such a name?"

"In America anything is possible," Nonnie said. "And not everyone gets named after a saint."

"Is the same in today's Italy," Franco said.

"So, do we talk about unusual names or the people who carry such names?" Mom asked. "Either way, the Jet you're referring to is actually Jeanette."

"Now that we've resolved that much, do go on," I said. "What did Romaine say about Jet Gregson?"

"That Jet loved Val and he loved her. Or so he told her. Once upon a time he also loved Romaine. Or maybe he made love to her without loving her. With Romaine is not always easy to understand her words, especially with her mouth spraying food everywhere. What doesn't spray, she washes down with wine. More wine than I drink, which makes me even more in awe of her."

Hmm, I was beginning to feel a *la famiglia* connection with Franco, like maybe the two of us had something in common—sex but, of course, not

114

with each other. "Don't tell me you … er, showed Romaine your bedroom."

Franco rocked one hand. "Is something I considered but did not think Elena would approve. Besides, the bed is not made for two, although this we could've figured out. 'Is not rocket science,' as the *Americani* say." He looked from Stefano to Nonnie and back to Stefano.

"Bravo for your restrain, my son."

"Go back to Romaine Sloane," Mom said, not bothering to hide the disapproval clouding her face. "Did she say anything else about Jet Gregson?"

"Let me think. Very jealous, considered suicide two times, threatened to cut off Val's balls—but only once. No, nothing out of the ordinary … for lovers in Italy. Perhaps is different here in America."

"Threats are one thing," Mom said. "Acting on them quite another."

"Well, if that's all you got to report, how about helping your papa move his things in." Nonnie turned to Stefano. "That is, if you'd rather stay here than there. Me, I'm not pushing you one way or the other."

"I like when you push," he said, getting up from the table. "Let's go, Franco, before Antonia changes her mind."

"Call me Toni," she said. "Everyone does."

"But not everyone is your papa. If you do not mind, I will call you Antonia or I will call you Toni, whichever rolls off my tongue first."

"Whatever, but don't make an issue of the daughter thing unless people ask, okay?"

"You would rather have people think I am the boyfriend of your mama instead of her husband?"

"Undocumented husband," Nonnie said. "There is a difference."

"One less complicated," I said. "That's for sure."

115

15

Jet

"You need to hang out with Romaine and Franco," Margo told me while we were working out. Let me rephrase that, *ordered me*. Same as she'd *ordered me* to join her gym and continue the accidental makeover I'd begun in Italy, the result of walking instead of driving everywhere and satisfying my appetite with smaller portions of better quality food. "You know what I mean," Margo went on. "Break bread with the two of them—actually, Romaine—the next time Franco cooks for her."

"And why … would I …want to do … that?" I asked through a huff and a puff, while trying to match her pedaling speed. She'd synchronized our individual videos to Kelly Clarkson singing "What doesn't kill you makes you stronger," a title that best exemplified me at Forever Fit. Side-by-side with Margo, riding stationary bikes and not feeling any love whatsoever.

"Romaine knows more about Val Corrigan than she's letting on," Margo said. "All you need to do is let the woman talk herself silly while feasting on Franco's fantastic food."

"Absolutely not. Fantastic is highly overrated." A single, emphatic shake of my head sent a spray of perspiration into the pungent air. Slowing

116

Not Worth Dying For

my pace, I lifted one cramped hand to my forehead and jiggled the headband up and down, hoping to absorb beads of sweat creeping toward my eyebrows.

"Don't stop now," Margo said. "Surely you can talk and pedal at the same time."

Just what I needed, an excuse to stop altogether, which I did since what I had to say was more important than the pedaling making me stronger. "Look, Margo. Things are bad enough already, what with me feeling like a stranger in my own home."

"Don't be such a pussy. Your house, your rules ... to a point ... that is."

"Hmm, point taken and carefully considered. As I think about this, with Stefano having moved in with Nonnie, perhaps Franco should be given the pleasure of *your* company for a while."

"El! Don't be ridiculous." Margo's pedaling came to an abrupt stop. "How would it look? Me inviting my current squeeze—"

"Since when and who?"

"Doesn't matter and don't interrupt. Hypothetically speaking, if I were to invite a certain squeeze to sleep over, how could I explain Uncle Franco occupying the spare room?"

"Uncle Franco, really. I thought you were adamant about playing down the kinship angle."

"I was and still am." Margo snapped her fingers and we started pedaling again, me at the pace of a slug who drank too much beer. "Uncle Franco will remain an open secret between you and me."

Coughing into my hand, I mumbled a response.

"Speak up, El. I can't hear you," Margo all but shouted over Carley Rae Jebsen wanting some guy to maybe call her.

Raising my voice several decibels, I managed to say, "Our secret for two has been expanded to include my condo neighbors who know me too well. The simple truth made more sense than a May-December romance that no one bought."

"Whatever blows your skirt up, little sis." With a lift of her chin, Margo the big sister show-off pedaled herself into a standing position. If that wasn't bad enough, she had to stick it to me. Or, in her preferred terminology—my sorry ass. "Faster, El. Faster."

Faster did not make me stronger. Nor did standing to pedal. I kept up with Margo for a minute or so, then let my butt find its rightful seat and uttered a few breathless words. "About this new squeeze in your life …."

"No one in particular; but you know me—always be prepared."

"Not buying the scout thing, Margo."

She hunched over the handlebars, cycling faster than before. "Franco's always talking about how much he loves your place. Says it's cozy and comfortable."

"Just wait until he sees yours, that queen-size bed in the spare room. I've had my Franco turn; now it's up to you."

"Have I ever said how much I hate you, El?"

"Over and over, it's the sister-tie that binds us."

∞∞∞∞

After surviving a weight-lifting session I hated more than the biking, Margo announced we were through for the evening. My sorry ass and I followed her into the brightly colored locker room crowded with assorted females, none of whom looked as bedraggled as I felt. "Straighten up," Margo whispered while drilling one finger into my spine, a reminder of just how spineless I'd become. "I will not have you embarrassing me."

"Can't help myself, Margo."

"Yes you can. It's one thing to be a wuss, another to look like one."

Rather than waste any more energy defending myself, I sat down on the nearest bench and let Margo retrieve our gym bags from the locker we shared. She sat beside me, both of us fanning ourselves with hand towels when we heard a voice called out, "Hey, Jet, what are you doing here?"

A rather attractive fiftyish female had been heading toward the exit but stopped before reaching it. She backed up, sought out the woman who'd called her name, and the two of them began chatting.

Margo poked me, an overkill gesture since my hearing is every bit as good as hers. "How many Jets can there be?" she whispered.

Only one to my knowledge, a name I'd recently heard from Franco who heard it from Romaine who, according to Franco, seemed to know more about the Corrigans than she'd let on when we first met her.

"Quick, do something." Margo and her demands, would there ever come a time when I didn't have Big Sis hovering over me, pushing me to do whatever it was I didn't want to do because she didn't want to either. Before I could come up with an immediate solution for *doing something*, Margo grabbed my hand and squeezed tightly while giving me a wink. With her left eye, no less. *Lo sinistro* ... as in sinister ... what Nonnie would've referred to as *up to no good*. Typically Margo, I thought, until she slumped to the tiled floor, eyes rolled back with nothing but the whites showing.

I knelt beside her and projected a voice bordering on hysteria, "Help me, somebody!" Margo fake or Margo real, I didn't know for sure and wasn't taking any chances. I'd seen her like this once before: this past summer in Monterosso, Italy, after someone had attacked her in a dark alley.

The female known as Jet swung around. To her credit, she hurried over to where I was tending Margo and asked what had happened.

"I ... I don't know. One minute she was fine ... the next, this."

"Maybe a seizure," this Jet said. Highly unlikely but with Margo on stage or off, anything was possible.

"Have Abby call 911," yelled someone from the gathering crowd.

119

"Who's Abby?" I asked.

Jet showed me her Bette Davis eyes, round as marbles and with a seductive bulge. "Abby works the front desk. Abby knows everything."

"No ... no, that won't be necessary." Margo's pulse seemed normal. Having laid my hand against her cheek, I resisted the urge to haul off and slap it. Instead, her hand flew up, landed on my wrist, and pinched the underside, causing me to let out a little yelp and Jet to scrunch up one eyebrow. Blonde, making me think it probably matched the hair tucked under her Cardinal baseball cap. "Uh ... it's possible my sister might be dehydrated."

"An easy fix." Jet reached into her gym bag, brought out a water bottle, and unscrewed the lid. Rather than pass the bottle to me, she rained its contents onto Margo's face.

Margo coughed and sputtered. She opened one eye, thankfully revealing the iris back where it belonged. By then, I'd helped myself to Jet's bottle and was holding the bit of remaining water to Margo's mouth. "Here, Sis. Take a sip; you'll feel better."

For better or worse, Margo went through the motions of gasping and gulping while I thanked Jet profusely and offered her my extended hand. She leaned over to shake it, giving me a chance to introduce myself.

"Jet Gregson," she replied and straightened up. "Do I know you from somewhere?"

"Gosh, that's hard to say. This is my first time at the gym ... this gym." I nudged Margo. "Feeling better, Sis?"

Instead of answering, Margo rolled to her knees and from there, her feet, leaving me to do the same. After a series of spasmodic coughs into her towel, she exchanged names with Jet Gregson and thanked her with more enthusiasm than I'd expressed, an impressive feat I vowed to imitate at my first opportunity.

"It was nothing, really," Jet Gregson told Margo before directing her next words to me. "If you're sure everything's under control, I'll be on my way."

"Er … uh … maybe we could get together sometime," Margo said, only then eyeing Jet's trim form in all its glory. "For a water or maybe yogurt … Greek yogurt, non-fat."

Jet laughed, showing off a mouthful of remarkable teeth. She placed one hand on Margo's shoulder, a gesture the more cynical me would've construed as disingenuous; worse yet, condescending. "No need to go overboard. You'd have done the same for anyone in trouble."

"That's for sure," I told Margo. "We shouldn't keep Ms. Gregson any longer."

Margo clung to my arm for support as she spoke her next words. "Oh-h, I am so sorry. It's just that ever since my bout with——"

"Perhaps a run through Forest Park," Jet said, "sometime when you're feeling up to it."

Just like that, Margo perked up, in what would've been considered an amazing recovery for anyone else. "Saturday morning, eight o'clock works for me," she said in a raspy voice brought on by all the coughing. "How about you, El?"

"Darn!" I slammed one palm against my forehead. "Wouldn't you know? I have a previous commitment. But don't let that stop the two of you."

Jet turned to leave and spoke from over her shoulder as she again headed toward the exit. "Seven works better for me. That way we'll beat the heat."

∞∞∞∞

"Since when did you get back into running?" I asked Margo while we drove home from Forever Fit.

"Since not hearing you come up with a better idea." She motioned for me to pick up the speed, an impossibility in city traffic as both of us knew.

121

Loretta Giacoletto

"How else did you think we'd get a handle on Jet Gregson's explosive relationship with Val Corrigan?"

"Let's see," I mused, tapping one finger to my chin. "You could've used that private investigator who works for your boss."

"Give me a break. Do you have any idea what a P.I. charges per hour?"

"Didn't you say something about him owing you a favor or two?"

"I did and he does, but I prefer holding on to those chips until there's a serious need. In the meantime I expect you to do some research on Jet Gregson before I sacrifice my tender feet to the running gods on Saturday."

"Bless you, Margo. You'll do much better in Forest Park than I would have. After all, you're always telling me I have two left feet, hardly ideal for running. Although ... those feet worked just fine at that Italian dance hall in Castellamonte."

"No need to thank me for those years I yanked you kicking and screaming through the awkward stage of your early teens."

"Thanks, I needed that."

"My pleasure," she said with an endearing smile I seldom trusted. "Sacrifices such as these are what bind sisters together. We're about family and you did the family proud in Italy—I mean Nonnie's village—the way you managed to hold your own with that deplorable Hells Angel, Pio Gavello."

"He drove a Vespa, Margo. As did your guy, Amadeo Sasso."

"Whatever. Have you heard from Pio since we got back?"

"Nope, nor do I expect to. Which reminds me, what about Pio's devious grandma. I wonder if Stefano has found the courage to tell Nonnie about his *special* friendship with Donata Abba."

"Well, Nonnie could hardly expect Stefano to deny himself female companionship all these years, considering his highly charged libido."

Not Worth Dying For

"Or so we've been led to believe," I said.

"Still, there's something kind of weird about people of a certain age indulging their sexual appetites so blatantly."

"In particular, those weird people related to us—is that what you're trying to tell me?"

"Only passing on what Mom told me," Margo said. "It seems Stefano gets rather boisterous—Mom's description, not mine."

"Kind of romantic, I'd say. Stefano making up for lost time with Nonnie. All those years apart."

"Not sure I buy your rationale. Maybe he's punishing our mother for being such a snot. You know, treating them like criminals."

"As if either of them would let that happen. Think, Margo. Here we have Nonnie's former best friend Donata making octogenarian whoopee with Stefano, the guy Donata wanted for herself when all three of them were teenagers, even though Stefano only had eyes for Nonnie and vice versa when they eloped. Or whatever it's called in Italy."

"An undocumented wedding," I reminded her.

"A matter of semantics," Margo countered, "but at the time so very real to Nonnie and Stefano.

"Do you think they'll make it legal this time?" I asked.

"Blake Harrington is working on it."

"Your boss, no kidding. Don't tell me the personal injury business has slowed down."

"Hardly. He's looking into the wedding possibility as a favor to me. Of course, I haven't said anything to Nonnie. But just in case …."

"Why Margo, I never pictured you as a traditionalist, a romantic one at that. Perhaps I should talk to Father Timothy on behalf of Nonnie and Stefano."

"Why El, I never pictured you as a practical romantic. Oh, wait a minute, let me rephrase that. A more accurate picture of you would be that of a devout romantic."

Talk about one-upmanship on the verge of getting nasty. Our discussion ended with me crossing myself.

16

Romaine

By Friday afternoon I was more than ready for a weekend break from my students and most likely they felt the same about me, in particular two boys who'd gone head-to-head over the merits of keeping or abolishing the death penalty. After separating the boys, literally, without resorting to help from the principal, I left school with my head held high, looking forward to the reports I assigned them to complete by Monday. God bless their free thinking and right to disagree.

Home, all I wanted was the sweet solace of my personal space. Perhaps the chance to revisit my time in Cinque Terre, an indulgence I hadn't allowed myself since leaving the Ligurian coast of Italy. I couldn't help but wonder if *he* ever thought about me. *Lorenzo Gentile*, there, I said his name. Out loud, for my ears only. Not nearly as painful as the anticipation preceding my action. My first love, it wasn't supposed to end so abruptly. Not after I'd given him my body and my soul. No strings attached, at least from the perspective of a man already attached to his first love. Unfortunately, not me.

On arriving at the personal space I now shared with Franco, I learned he'd made plans for entertaining Romaine Sloane in a few hours. I already

125

knew the routine, one destined to start in the kitchen, eventually lead to the living room, and from there to his room with the twin beds.

"You too," Franco told me. "Is only right you should share our evening meal and interesting conversation."

"No, no. I wouldn't dream of imposing."

"Is no imposition. Besides, Romaine desires to make friends with you. This I heard from Romaine's own mouth when I invited her. Please, Elena, for me I ask this. Otherwise, I take Romaine to one of the fancy *ristoranti* on The Hill," he said, referring to the St. Louis neighborhood known for its Italian eateries, bakeries, and imported groceries.

"She might like that," I said, noting the disappointment clouding Franco's face. "Of course, none of the food served on The Hill compares to what you would prepare here."

"My thinking exactly. Then you'll spend the evening with Romaine and me, si?"

"But I have things to do ... in my room."

"No problem, sweet Elena." He kissed my cheek. "You do your things. I do mine. When Romaine arrives, I will knock down your door."

"One knock will be fine, Franco."

∞∞∞∞

Time in my room, I planned on making every minute of Jet research count, hopefully gathering enough information to satisfy Margo. After changing into casual wear, I opened my laptop and went to work.

A thorough search on the Internet, at least from my limited perspective, provided some background on Jeanette "Jet" Gregson. Based on the Facebook people she identified as high school friends, Jet recently celebrated her thirty-fifth class reunion, putting her age around fifty-three. She grew up in the desirable suburb of Kirkwood, All-American to the core. A graduate of Fontbonne College, she listed her current occupation as real estate broker and currently lived in the Central West End of St. Louis, a stone's throw from

Not Worth Dying For

the venerable Forest Park. Long ago divorced and having reverted to her maiden name, she made no mention of children but had posted several photos of two teenage nieces.

Google displayed a photo of the pale blonde Jet Gregson decked out in sequins and lace, her ankle-length skirt revealing one slender leg attached to a spike-heeled foot. Her escort, an average height, unidentified male wore a tuxedo that fit too well to have been anything but tailor-made. They were attending a charity auction at The Ritz-Carlton with Jackson and Saradell Littlejohn—names I recognized as movers and shakers in the St. Louis community. Jet's date could've been Val Corrigan. He certainly resembled Mom's photo of Val at the zoo. I considered forwarding the photo to her, a risky damned-if-I-do; damned-if-I-don't, what with her thoughts preoccupied with the on-going Nonnie and Stefano saga rather than with proving she had nothing to do with the on-going Val Corrigan mystery. Instead, I Googled Val Corrigan and read the article on his murder, which included a studio photograph that confirmed him as the same man pictured with Jet Gregson.

Mission accomplished I told myself after the productive laptop session. Margo would be ever so impressed. Before I could connect with her, a light tap on my door postponed the interaction. "Elena, are you there?"

Good thing he didn't knock down my door. When I stepped into the hallway, the aroma of garlic, basil, and tomatoes sautéing in olive oil greeted me. Add to that, the enticement of an opened bottle of red wine, breathing on the bar that separated the kitchen from my living room. Franco was performing his culinary magic at the kitchen counter, making me glad he'd insisted his party of two should be increased to an uneven three. I mouthed a sincere *grazie*. In return he blew a kiss my way and resumed his duties with more love than I'd ever shown my kitchen.

Perched on a barstool, Romaine Sloane wiggled a set of manicured fingernails in my direction. She crossed her long legs, allowing a flip flop sandal to dangle off the end of one foot displaying painted toenails sprinkled with glitter, a reminder of Margo's salon-spa pedicures. Romaine's plaid sundress accommodated the 90-degree weather defining September in St. Louis as typically unreliable. She'd pulled her dark hair back in a ponytail that made her appear younger than the sophisticated bun I recalled from our first meeting.

"So nice of you." She held out a hand as limp as the one I shook at Rudi's.

"Any friend of Franco's ..." I said, not bothering to end my welcome with the obvious cliché. Nor was it fair to blame Franco's guest for the headache I'd acquired from staring at my laptop screen too long.

Romaine slid off the stool and picked up three dinner plates sitting on the counter. While Franco continued his meal prepping, she helped me set the dining table. From there we moved to the living room with our filled goblets of wine, a nice red she'd brought that elevated her a few levels in my estimation. With a wave of my hand I motioned her to sit. She did, choosing the one chair I considered my favorite.

Get over it, I told the potential forever-single lurking within my vulnerable psyche. What next? A cat to keep me company. Perhaps a second cat to keep the first one company. Never mind, I'd forgotten about cats inducing me to sneeze. Perhaps a goldfish. Never! I wanted ... better yet, needed the kind of love that required something of me in return. Perhaps a dog. One that would greet me whenever I walked through the front door. First things first, getting through this evening.

I sat in my second favorite chair and smiled at Romaine.

"Franco is such a hoot," she said, again crossing her legs.

To which I smiled again. "And a wonderful cook."

"Amen to that." She opened her arms into a wide swoop and then let them fall to the slight bulge of her stomach, patting it with affection. "I'm such an unredeemable foodie."

"Aren't we all," I said, relieved that Margo wasn't around to voice her disapproval.

Romaine cocked her head, all the better to observe me. "Now how are you and Franco related?"

128

"He's my uncle. My mother's half-brother."

"Oh, yeah. I do remember Franco explaining the relationship. Rather odd, but aren't we all in one way or another."

I could've argued the point but didn't think it worth the effort. Instead I crossed my legs, ladylike at the ankles. Mom would've been proud.

Romaine lifted her head and called out to Franco, "You okay in there, chef?"

Without turning from his range duties, he gave a thumbs up. "No problem. Tell Elena what we did yesterday."

"Yes, do tell." I leaned forward with feigned interest. Sorry for the hypocrisy, Jesus.

"Well, first we went to the top of The Arch. Right Franco?"

"Nice," he said, giving another thumbs up.

"Then Franco wanted to cross the river so we took the Poplar Bridge into Illinois, and from there drove around Horseshoe Lake. You know, scene of the Val Corrigan horrific crime."

"What was it like?"

"Ghastly, I suppose. Not that I was there to witness it."

"Er ... I meant Horseshoe Lake. What did you think of the park?"

"Oh, the park, of course. Lots of water, a road around the water, and trees between the road and highway."

"Romaine showed me where the man's body was found," Franco called out from the kitchen.

On hearing this I straightened up. "You knew the exact location?"

"Just like anybody else, from a map in the Post-Dispatch. Two fatal gunshot wounds according to the newspaper. Dear, sweet Val. Such a tragedy."

129

"Then you were well acquainted with the victim," I said, hoping for more.

"Better than I let on when you and I first met."

"How well acquainted, if you don't mind my asking."

"Not if you don't mind my telling what some might consider too personal." Holding the forefinger and middle finger of her right hand to her lips, she raised her brow as if asking my permission to smoke. Denied, I indicated with a shake of my head and prayed she wouldn't retaliate by refusing to elaborate on the *too personal*. Romaine heaved a deep sigh but did not disappoint me.

"I knew Val better than most, inside and out, from appetite to asshole, as my dear old mum used to say. He had this ugly carbuncle scar, an emergency operation by some quack in the boonies. Val wasn't sure the woman was even a real doctor but she did save his sweet ass. At least that's the story he gave me. With Val, I never knew the factual from the fantasy."

Leaning over, she extracted a tissue from a nearby box.

I waited for her to finish a rather nauseous evacuation before asking my next question. "What was he like? The real Val, I mean."

A convenient tear sprang from one eye and she wiped it away. "A charmer and a bastard, a charming bastard, yes, that would best describe Val. Not one ounce of scruples did the man possess; yet he managed to charm the panties off any woman who could do him some good. Can you believe? At one point the man was servicing four women. Not one of them, except me, aware of the other, or so Val told me. Humph. No female in this day and age can be that stupid.'"

"You wouldn't think," I said, my mind wandering to Kat Dorchester who seemed way too sophisticated to have fallen for any man's bullshit. Not to mention my own mother, who knew what she was getting into and yet became a willing participant.

"And how did you know Val?" Romaine asked. "No way was he romancing someone as young as you."

130

"No, not me."

"Your sister then, whatshername."

"Margo, certainly not. We only knew about Val Corrigan through others."

"*Others* would have to include Kat Dorchester. From what I've heard, she's the number one suspect."

"Then you've spoken to the police," I said.

"Reardan and Winchester, ugh, as if I had a choice. Next time, if ever there is, be assured I will bring my lawyer. Not that I need one, you understand, but better safe than sorry. These detectives, they've interviewed your mother or so I've been told."

"Yes, but only as a possible material witness."

Romaine half-belched, half-snorted a sound of annoyance. "Aren't we all?"

"Then you already knew the specifics of his murder when my mother told you."

"How did you … she …" A look of surprise mixed with anger crossed her face, making me regret giving away information Romaine had shared with Franco.

She leaned forward and spoke in a low voice. "If your tattle-tale uncle wasn't as great in bed as he is in the kitchen, I'd make him pay, big time. For now, however, I'm hungrier than all the demons in hell so he gets a temporary pass." With that she stuck out her tongue and wiggled it in Franco's direction, to be precise his back while he busied himself at the stove. "What else do you already know?" Romaine asked, having returned to her less aggressive position. "That I saw Val hours before he took his last breath."

"Really? What time was that?"

She thought a minute. "Before midnight, eleven or so. Val stopped by my place for his usual nightcap. Something he did several times a week."

"Was he a straight scotch guy or beer from a bottle?"

"Neither. Val's idea of a night cap was far more imaginative than liquor. As was mine." Whatever expression crossed my face erupted on its own and without malice although it did prompt Romaine to level a forefinger at me. "Hey girl, don't knock what you haven't tried."

Wouldn't dream of it, even though I did conjure up an image of Romaine enjoying one of those nightcaps with Franco. No wonder he'd been whistling while he worked.

"Mangiamo!" he called out with a wave of his napkin. "Come!"

My image of him and Romaine dissolved on entering the dining area. Franco had outdone himself, starting with an appetizer of carpaccio—finely chopped raw veal mixed with olive oil and topped with fresh lemon slices. Romaine outdid herself as well, relishing each bite with a vocalization of orgasmic delight that turned Franco's ears as red as my face felt.

"Please pass the bread," I said, anything to distract Romaine from her sexual food fantasy. "From The Hill?" I asked, referring to the crusty slice I selected from the wicker basket.

"Where else," Romaine said with heavy eyelids and a mouthful of macerated meat. "I introduced Franco to the head baker at ... at ... dammit, Franco, help me out here."

"Primo," Franco said. He got up, collected our empty plates, and within minutes he returned with an assortment of figs and cantaloupe wedges wrapped with thin slices of prosciutto. He sat down, our cue to dig in. I picked up the salad fork he'd thoughtfully provided with our individual servings and speared one of the figs. Romaine, on the other hand, opted to use her fingers, licking and smacking each one until no trace of food remained.

Franco's next course consisted of *tagliatelle*, fresh pasta he'd made from scratch thirty minutes before, along with the tomato sauce I'd smelled simmering on the stove.

"*I pomadori* from a farm in Illinois," he explained, rubbing the fingers of his right hand together. "The soil is how you say ... richer."

"The Illinois side," I explained, "the Mississippi River bottom."

"Is not the same river bottom in Missouri?" he asked. "Don't tell me this, too, is complicated."

"For dinner talk, yes," Romaine said. "Remind me not to share any more secrets with you."

"What did I say?" Franco opened his hands.

"Too much or too little," Romaine said. "That first time we met at Rudi's, I mentioned not knowing the details of Val's dreadful murder but I may have misspoke ... sort of."

Liar, liar, pants on fire, Margo would've said, and before her, Nonnie. I, on the other hand, misspoke with a face so straight I almost believed my lie. "Please don't blame Franco. It might've been Detective Winchester who told my mother."

"Damn!" Romaine slammed her hand on the table, shaking her goblet until wine spilled from it. "Is nothing sacred anymore?"

"Not when it comes to a murder investigation," I said. "What's for dessert, Franco?"

He held up one forefinger. "First, *insalata mista*. To aid in the digestion."

Of course, how very American, and un-Italian, of me to have thought otherwise. Franco hopped up from the table, leaving me to gather the plates and utensils from our finished course while Romaine poured herself another glass of wine.

There's something to be said for the proper execution of a basic salad. These bite-size greens were cold and crisp; the ratio of olive oil to lemon juice, spot on. Franco knew his stuff, that's for sure. Romaine knew her stuff too. A simple roll of her tongue across those red lips spoke volumes, sending a message to Franco even I understood.

"Ah-h, the *dolce*," he said. "*Scusami*, please."

More wine for Romaine. Her third since we sat down to eat, plus the two we'd had before. I thought she might be coming unglued. Hopefully, her mouth if nothing else. Margo would've liked that. And she would've liked the dolce Franco served in the ramekins I rarely had an occasion to use. More like never.

Lemon verbena *panna cotta*, yum and double yum. As a rule custard did not rank high on my dessert preferences but I made an exception of Franco's simple yet elegant creation enhanced even more by cordials of Amaretto. After the first round he collected the bottle and glasses like a dutiful bartender, all the while ignoring Romaine's objections that finally stopped when I set the fourth ramekin in front of her.

Our dinner for three ended with tiny cups of strong espresso. No point in asking if the coffee was decaf, an abomination no Italian would've served, even in the home I still considered my personal domain.

Romaine placed one hand over mine, squeezing it in a way neither warm nor inviting. "Now I have a question for you, sweet Elena or Ellen or whatever. *When* did your mother speak to Winchester?"

"There were several interviews."

"I mean the last time. When did they last speak?" She squeezed again, harder than before. "Don't lie to me, girl."

Girl, really. I pulled my hand away from hers. "More coffee?"

"Only if I make a fresh pot," Franco said, shaking his head for my eyes only.

"Never mind." My cue to end the evening, at least in my role as resident hostess, started with me clearing away the tiny cups and saucers and brushing away non-existent crumbs from the table.

As for the elephant in the room, Franco resolved that problem by offering to drive the tipsy Romaine home instead of taking her to the room he currently occupied at my place. What he and Romaine did at her

Not Worth Dying For

place or elsewhere made no difference to me, as long as one of them didn't kill the other.

∞∞∞

The headache I'd been battling all evening disappeared as soon as Franco left with Romaine and I entered the sanctuary of my own room. Back propped against the cushioned headboard of my bed, I called Margo and gave her a blow-by-blow account of the dinner party.

"Brava!" Margo gushed. "We must approach Romaine again, hopefully without the alcohol clouding her memory."

"*We?*"

"You were terrific, El. How can you possibly expect me to top your performance?"

"Romaine Sloane will hate me in the morning when she sobers up."

"Get real. She won't remember shit." Margo said. "Do you think Franco will spend the night with her?"

"Hard to say. After all, what do we really know about Zio Franco?"

"Point taken. Although there is something to be said for newly discovered blood relatives who haven't been around long enough to piss off each other. So where do we stand with our other person of interest?"

I relayed the basic Internet information I'd gathered about Jet Gregson and how I'd checked out the Ritz Charity Auctions on Google Images.

"That's it?" Margo asked, obviously not aware of my nodding head. "That much I could've dug up myself."

"Amen. Which is why I encouraged you to contact Blake's private investigator."

"And why I wanted to wait before calling in one of those precious chips he owes me." Her voice switched from accusatory to authoritative, neither of which I wanted to hear. "Now, about this previous commitment

135

Loretta Giacoletto

you claim to have for Saturday morning …."

"No, Margo." My hand gripped the phone so tightly I christened it with a smear of perspiration. "I did my part tonight; it's your turn tomorrow."

"Easier said than done. I really need you with me. You know, to catch any verbal farts from Jet Gregson I might miss."

"Mouthing off is your specialty, not mine."

"Come on, El. What would it take for you to change your mind?"

Hmm, at last we were getting somewhere. I proceeded with caution. "Give me some time to think about this."

"Don't make me beg."

"Margo! You know me better than that. What did *you* have in mind?"

After a pregnant, God forbid, pause, she came back with, "Well … in order to give you a break from Franco, maybe I could invite him to spend some time with me. You know, as my houseguest."

"It's not enough to invite, Margo. Franco would have to agree."

136

17

Morning Jog

The dreaded Saturday morning arrived with the no nonsense of an about-to-be-discovered fall day that found Margo and me at the city's jewel in the crown—Forest Park, both of us testing unyielding muscles on the asphalt parking lot near the tennis courts.

"Maybe Jet forgot," I said, trying to hide the ambiguous hope in my voice. Think eighty-three degree weather at seven in the morning, the only nourishment filling my belly, a protein bar and Diet Coke. Shameful, I know, but not on the level of a serious nutritional sin. My dedication to the pursuit of our mother's presumed innocence extended only so far, as did the more likely possibility of her aiding and abetting a justifiable homicide committed in the heat of passion. Think Kat Dorchester. Not to mention Franco Rosina who'd actually believed me when I insisted he make himself at home. My home, what once had been my refuge from matters involving the inevitable controversy that explodes within any family, especially an Italian-American, female-only family. That is, until recently.

"Jet forget? With that toned bod, I don't think so," Margo said, as if she'd known the woman for years instead of two minutes max.

"But, if she does turn out to be a no-show …." I slid one arm down

137

my leg and lifted the other one overhead, my sun visor providing a bird's-eye view of filtered rays. Just as I suspected, not a single cloud in sight

"El, you're such a worrywart. How many times must I tell you not to sweat the small stuff? So what if Jet doesn't show, which I seriously doubt. There's nothing stopping the two of us from taking a nice jog through the park."

Having placed both hands on her toned right thigh, Margo bent that leg to a forty-five degree angle and extended the left leg further behind. Ever so slowly she stretched her left leg without moving her bent right knee, while I went through the motions of a few half-hearted arm and leg lifts. She reversed her stance to stretch the other leg, giving me the once-over before posing the one question I'd anticipated her asking. "New outfit?"

"Hardly, I've had it for years." I glanced down at my white t-shirt and loose-fitting green shorts. Non-descript and comfortable, just as I envisioned myself.

"Hmm." Margo narrowed her eyes to me. "Granted, you may've had that outfit for years but I'd bet my whole collection of Jimmy Choo shoes you've never worn it before."

"I could say the same about yours, if I cared but I don't." True, my outfit had been sitting in the bottom drawer, waiting for a non-compete day such as I hoped this would be.

Pushing down on her bent leg, Margo expelled a soft grunt. "No way will I have Jet Gregson outshine me."

"A no-show cannot outshine," I replied.

Margo straighten up, lifted her arms overhead, and bent them, hands gripping the opposite bent elbows. She held that stance, giving her a chance to notice me doing nothing other than watching her. "Better stretch those hamstrings," she said. "Otherwise you'll pay dearly during our run."

"Yes, Mother." I copied her bent-knee stance, one I'd learned back in high school but hadn't bothered with since. "Just so you know, Franco is looking forward to spending more time with you."

Not Worth Dying For

"And what if our Super Jet doesn't show?"

"She will."

"And you know this because?"

I straightened up, and did a quick scan of the parking area, unable to control the wide smile overtaking my face on locating our reason for being there, a formidable figure worthy of her own spread in a senior edition of *Sports Illustrated.* I waved and called out, "Over here, Jet!"

Jet Gregson returned my wave. She trotted over and explained she'd already loosened up with her daybreak swim. After jogging in place for a long minute, she moved toward the trail, gesturing for Margo and me to join her. We started out three abreast, giving me enough confidence to keep up the pace Jet had set, at the same time wondering if she'd lowered the bar to accommodate our obvious lack of athleticism. Okay, *my* obvious lack. A nice gesture, if that had been her intent. Even at the slow pace of a jog, it was all I could do to inhale a sufficient amount of oxygen, let alone engage in any chitchat, meaningful or otherwise. Still, I kept up as well as Margo did, an exemplary testament to all the casual walking we'd done in Italy plus those lengthy strides through numerous international airports.

The three of us crossed a wood-planked bridge. It spanned a stream of clear water that reflected the graceful branches of a weeping willow and other trees along the bank. At the first sign post we stayed to the right and headed into an open area, its seemingly endless trail venturing into parts unknown. After five minutes of jogging at what would've been considered a reasonable pace, my body started an all-out rebellion against my brain, in spite of the tolerance for discomfort I'd willed myself to accommodate. When my chest began to ache, I took a deep breath, only to gasp for the next and each one thereafter. From the far corner of my right eye, I saw Margo take a sip from her water bottle. Good idea, only that level of multi-tasking went beyond my Saturday jog description, one I expected never to repeat. *Enough, I've had enough, you idiot,* my brain screamed at me.

Evidently, Margo didn't share my inability to communicate. She tapped my shoulder and in a concerned voice, asked, "You okay?"

Like hell, I would've said if only I'd have had enough breath to expel

139

those two words from my gaping mouth. Instead, my feet stopped working, leaving me immobile and Margo aghast. Not what either of us needed. I motioned her to continue since our running partner seemed oblivious to my predicament.

As soon as Margo and Jet had distanced themselves into an accelerated pace, I bent over, head lowered to my knees. After taking in my fill of much needed air, I straightened up, shuffled to a grassy area, and leaned against the closest tree until I returned to a facsimile of the normal me.

Rather than hold up the tree any longer, I strolled back to the parking area, passing by a number of sweat-free joggers who'd just started on the trail. Little did they know or perhaps they did. To thine own self be true— yes, a tip of my visor to Shakespeare. Twenty minutes later Margo and Jet returned to the parking lot where I'd propped myself against the car trunk. Jet had barely worked up a sweat; Margo was dripping with it; her face flushed, not only from discomfort but even worse, undeniable embarrassment. I popped the trunk lid and she grabbed her towel.

"Anyone for coffee and … half a banana?" I asked. "How about that café on De Mun?"

"Sounds good to me," Margo replied, glancing in Jet's direction.

"Sorry, guys," Jet said as she turned to leave. "I have a full day but don't let me stop you from a nourishing breakfast."

Nourishing? Who said anything about nourishing? Nourishing I could get in Mom's kitchen.

"Shall we meet again next Saturday?" Margo called out to the jogging Jet's back. "Same time, same place?"

Jet responded with a lift of her arm and a finger wave.

"Okay, what happened?" I asked Margo.

"For starters, we're not talking shits and grins. Jet Gregson didn't buy my recent collapse in the locker room. She made some reference to me being a phony and you, my lackey."

"Oh, that's one I hadn't heard before," I said, rather disappointed in my failed performance. "Does this mean we won't be jogging with Jet anymore?"

"Hello, where have you been? She said as much with that middle finger wave."

"Oh, really? I hadn't noticed."

"Dammit, El! Wipe that shitty grin off your face."

"Only if you tell me what happened on the trail."

"Coffee first. You know I can't think straight without my morning caffeine."

∞∞∞

When it came to my daily dose—with or without caffeine—Margo didn't have to use extreme measures to get me on board. The drive from the city's western border of Forest Park to Clayton's historic district of De Mun took but a few minutes. After arriving at the number one coffee house, we selected a sidewalk umbrella table where Margo prepared to drown her humility with an order of Americano coffee and two buttery croissants filled with creamy dark chocolate. Shocking, especially for my oh-so disciplined sister so I made her, and myself, feel better by matching her order, the only exception being decaf instead of regular coffee.

The outdoor tables were filling up fast with people from the neighborhood and others, mostly sweat-soaked joggers determined to jump-start their Saturday morning. Last sidewalk table went to a young couple pushing their baby in a stroller. At this hour, good grief, the baby must've kept them up all night. But what did I know, having never experienced the ups and downs of true parenting.

"We could almost be in Italy," Margo said, her first spoken words since placing her order. Scary, you bet. Margo never ran out of words without good reason.

"Dream on," I said. "Cutting our trip short was a Mom necessity, just when we were getting used to the simple life." This was not the time to bring up Franco, our Italian uncle she'd soon be entertaining full-time. Instead, my thoughts wandered to another Italian who had fixed my breakfast a number of mornings and admonished me for preferring decaf coffee, an abomination in the eyes of most Italians.

"Do you ever think of him?" she asked.

Margo often read my mind; more often than I did hers. I tore off a piece of croissant, popped it into my mouth, and chewed until the macerated remains slid down my throat. "Lorenzo? Only recently and not for long. Why torture myself with a situation I cannot change."

"Nothing stays the same, El. It's a matter of time."

"And how long I'm willing to wait for the next phase of Lorenzo's life. But that's not why we're indulging ourselves this morning. What happened with Jet Gregson?"

"Oh, her. Well, we were on our way back, keeping up a nice pace when all of a sudden Jet stopped and leaned one hand against a tree. At first I thought the heat had gotten to her, which surprised me because I felt okay and she appeared to be in way better shape. But then when I stood next to her, she screwed up her face and went into this attack mode, saying she was on to me and my fake seizure in the locker room. She even threatened to report me to … you know."

"Abby at the front desk."

"Right, Abby."

"Report you for what? Dehydration?"

"No, supposedly for stalking Jet, of all people. Last month some woman developed a crush on her, or so Jet thought. Turned out to be something else."

"Such as?"

"She didn't say. I didn't ask. Too busy calling me a bitch and you my pathetic lackey."

Not Worth Dying For

"Ouch! Here we go again."

"So color me assertive," Margo said with a flip of her hair. "I ask you: what outspoken female in my shoes hasn't been called a bitch at one time or another. Name-calling comes with the territory."

"And how often have you been referred to as a pathetic lackey?"

"Oh, that." Margo laughed, as only she could in times of stress. "Come on, El. You're tougher than you look; suck it up."

"As if I had any other choice," I said. "Anyway, what else did Jet say?"

"She mentioned Mom by name, figured she'd sent us to spy on her, which I insisted wasn't true. After that, we started jogging again."

"Hmm, what am I missing here? If Jet's personal attack was so vicious, why did you suggest another run for next Saturday?"

"Well, in spite of the nastiness—or perhaps because of it—she came across as someone I'd like having for a friend. One can never have too many friends. Isn't that what Mom always tells us."

"Need I remind you about friendship being a two-way street? I seriously doubt Jet wants you for her friend."

"Then maybe a mere acquaintance, like Twitter. Amen to some give and take with people you'd never dream of bumming around with in real life."

18

Who's Got Mail

The manila envelope arrived with the afternoon mail. A mere six by nine inches, it contained a cardboard insert, Clarita figured, to keep important information from bending. Without a second glance she added the sturdy package to the pile of business envelopes sitting on the foyer table, all waiting for Toni's attention. This latest piece of manila must've acquired a mind of its own, slipping from the stack as if calling for Clarita to notice its foreign postmark and stamps, along with the European cursive style of writing she'd been taught as a child. Taking a second look, Clarita realized the package was meant for her rather than Toni.

But who would've sent her such a package, with a Pont Canavese return address she didn't recognize? Other than Clarita's mama, who'd been dead for years and the lawyer who'd handled the Fantino family estate, only one other person had ever sent personal mail from Italy, an annoying friend from her early years whose treacherous relationship Clarita had dismissed before coming to America.

Without acknowledging Stefano's presence, she sensed him standing behind her, the manly scent of his breath warming the back of her neck. He leaned in closer and ran his tongue over the rim of her ear, its tickling sensation prompting her to giggle like the schoolgirl she'd once been with him. While treasuring this day's loving moment, she tried blocking out thoughts of all the years lost, those precious moments that had not occurred, the pigheadedness both she and Stefano had embraced when life could've been so much more if only they'd acknowledged the honesty of their emotions.

"Something special?" he whispered with lips still brushing her ear.

"I won't know until I open it." She reached for the letter opener, only to have his hand cover hers.

"Whatever *it* is can wait," he said. "Come to bed with me."

"At this hour? Are you crazy? It's barely one o'clock in the afternoon."

"All the better to see you."

"That's what I was afraid of."

"I never tire of looking at you. In my eyes you will always be as bella as the first time I saw you."

She knew better but didn't argue with him. "I got the kitchen mess to clean up. You know how Toni feels about dirty dishes."

He nuzzled his nose into the back of her head. "Our daughter, anything out of place bothers her, especially me."

No point in arguing what they both knew to be true. "Give Toni time," Clarita said. "Right now she's got murder on her mind."

"Not mine I hope."

She wiggled her hand away from his. "First the envelope. Then we talk about the other stuff."

"Talk? No, we do. What you call other stuff, I call making love."

He separated himself from her, moved to the living room sofa, and patted the cushion for her to join him. She did, bringing along the package, which she opened with care. Just as she thought, two sturdy cardboard

145

pieces secured the contents.

Not what she had expected.

Nor what Stefano had expected, judging from the muffled sound erupting from his throat.

And then from Clarita's.

Three pictures—photos as Toni would've called them. Three images of Stefano, as she knew him now, and with him in each picture the same woman, every bit as old as Clarita. Happy times, one over raised glasses of wine. Another with the woman sitting on his lap, his hand around her waist. The third, the two of them kissing. In much the same way Stefano had kissed Clarita hours before.

Clarita narrowed her eyes to his, willing them to meet her gaze. They did, but only for the moment it took him to lower his lids.

"I thought your wife died long ago," Clarita said.

Stefano crossed himself. "God rest her soul."

"And who is this woman?" Clarita waved the kissing picture in Stefano's face.

He sat back, waiting until she stopped before he spoke. "How many years has it been, Clarita? Did you expect me to go without another woman for the rest of my life?"

"Of course not. I just thought …."

"Not a day passed that I did not think of you."

"Even when you held another woman in your arms?"

"Especially when I held another woman, kissed another woman."

"Stuck your *cazzo* in another woman?"

"Si. That was the hardest part—the most difficult, I mean—always with you on my mind. You must believe me, Clarita."

146

Not Worth Dying For

"Humph. Don't tell me what I must do."

"And what about you? After John Riva was there never another man?"

"No one who mattered."

"It was the same with me. Can we please go to bed now?"

"Not yet. I'm thinking."

Clarita lined up the photographs on the coffee table. She arranged and re-arranged them, always ending with Stefano kissing the slender woman. Her short hair, a mix of gray and white, was styled in a way that flattered her face. Attractive, yes, but no more so than Clarita. "What? No picture of you making love to this ... this ... *puttanesca.*"

Stefano blushed, surprising for a man of his years. Or perhaps a reflection of his dishonesty. "*La donna* is no whore. It's not what you think."

"Really? So, tell me: what is it?"

"Two lonely people holding on to the past," Stefano said. "Do you not recognize her?"

After gathering up the pictures, Clarita walked to the window. One by one she held them up to the afternoon light that afforded her a better perspective. "Nobody I ever knew."

"Look again, Clarita."

She did, her knees almost buckling from the realization. "Merda! Donata Abba, that lying, whiny, cry-baby bitch. Her of all people. How could you, Stefano?"

"How could I *not*, with no hope of ever seeing you again. That was *then.*"

"*Then* was what—two months ago?"

"Forget about *then,*" he said, having joined her at the window. "This is *now*, Clarita. This moment in time—our time. Did we not agree to forgive each other? For all *trasgressioni.*"

147

"Tell me about it. There's bad and then there's really bad. Seeing you with Donata goes beyond the worst kind of bad. I gotta think on this."

He took her in his arms and pulled her close. "After we make love, si? Everything will be better after the love."

Clarita jerked away and headed for the kitchen. "Not now, dammit."

She hadn't thought about Donata Abba in ages, that is, until recently when Ellen and Margo had called from Italy, insisting she give them Donata's address, which she'd long forgotten. By choice. No point in hanging onto broken friendships that didn't need fixing.

Stefano followed her into the kitchen and tried to make himself useful with the clean-up. "Sit down," she said, pushing him aside. "You're in my way."

The smile he started to project faded into half a frown. "Just as I was all those years ago in Italy, and later in St. Louis when I wanted you to go back with me."

"Back to what? Your mama, my mama. The same old same old. I'd made a new life in America. You could've been part of that life. But no-o, you were …."

"Too Old World … too proud … too *testardo*," Stefano said, a testament to his inability to yield. "Then, it was you for you and me for me. What fools we were. Now, time is no longer on our side, not like it once was, and even then we wasted what should've been our best years. Ah-h-h …." Stefano stifled a sneeze into the crook of his arm. "Damn allergies," he said, taking a tissue from the box Clarita held out.

"Welcome to St. Louis," she said.

After taking care of his nose, Stefano sat down. He leaned back, drumming his fingers on the table, a habit Clarita now recalled from their earlier life together—a time too brief to acknowledge petty annoyances. The drumming she would tolerate for now but not forever. Having bypassed the automatic dishwasher Toni preferred, Clarita started washing dishes the old-fashioned way, by hand in the sink. When clean dishes piled up in the draining basket, she whistled through clenched teeth and tossed a linen towel toward Stefano's waiting hand.

"The American way," she said.

"In Italy too. Franco washes, I dry."

They worked in the comfort of silence, all the while Clarita's thoughts centering on wartime Italy and Donata Abba. The silly girl and her big mouth had all but ruined Clarita's teenage romance with Stefano, Donata telling her mother who then told Clarita's mother. At first Clarita had denied the allegation and later refused to reveal Stefano's name, a defiant act for which she received a terrible beating, as did Donata, for lying when she tried to recant the allegation against Clarita.

And after her final break-up with Stefano, all those wasted years concerning herself with the woman he married on the rebound, the legal wife Clarita had never met but nevertheless resented as much as Donata, the friend who'd betrayed her. Betrayed Stefano too, not by name but by implication. Worse, yet their young friend Tommaso, the innocent victim of Donata's gossip and innuendo. As for Clarita's own papa ... she couldn't bear to think of him. Nor of Tommaso's papa. How different all of their lives would've been if only Donata had kept her mouth shut.

"Please, *cara mia*," she heard Stefano say. "Do not torture yourself over the past."

"As if you know what I'm thinking."

"What I know is this: war and the tragedies of war cannot be undone."

"Must you always be right," she said.

"I cannot help myself. Is a curse I must bear, si?" He finished drying the last plate and arranged the towel on the dishwasher handle, making sure it matched the two towels already hanging there. "So, what can I do to make you forget the long ago, at least for a while?"

"If you're thinking nookie, which I know you are, it can wait. We should move our legs, outside."

Loretta Giacoletto

Stefano sighed but did not object. Instead he leaned over, kissed each cheek, and then the tip of her nose.

"Sunglasses," she said, putting on hers and waiting while he did the same. She led the way out the back door, pausing to inspect a rose bush that needed attention.

"Tomorrow, I'll take care of it," Stefano said, "after I sharpen the pruners."

She liked that, having someone—not just anyone, but Stefano—to help with the yard work. After further inspection of the roses, they left her yard and started down the alley leading to a side street. Along the way, Stefano stooped down to pull out a stray dandelion, the only intruder visible in an otherwise well-kept area.

"You still eat dandelions in Italy?" Clarita asked.

"Only those covering the meadows in early spring."

"Tell me about it, a pain in the neck to pick and clean. But oh so good mixed with boiled eggs, vinegar and oil."

"Then you do miss Italy."

"Not enough to go back. Whatever I hunger for can be found in America." *Now that you're here*, she almost told Stefano; but instead added, "Even tender dandelion leaves."

One of the neighbors hurried out the back door and made her way to the alley where she stuffed a large plastic bag into the garbage container. After Clarita exchanged greetings with Alma, the woman turned to Stefano, offered a broad smile and in a pronounced Italian accent, asked if he was enjoying his visit to America.

"Si," he told Alma. "More than I ever dreamed possible. What about you? Do you ever think of returning to Italy?"

"Calabria?" she said, referring to her region in Southern Italy. "*Impossibile*, now that my heart belongs to America."

150

Not Worth Dying For

"Then listen to your heart," Stefano said with a smile.

"You must come over for coffee. Tomorrow morning around ten." She hesitated, shifting her attention. "You too, Clarita."

"Grazie, but I got things to do."

"Things can wait," Stefano said. "We will be there."

Clarita felt his hand on her elbow, pushing her to move along at a quicker pace. After they'd passed two garages, she stopped.

"What?" He made no effort to conceal the twitching corner of his mouth.

"Nobody speaks for me," she said in a low voice, "especially you."

"Is not the first time Alma invited me for coffee. If you come too, she will not ask again."

She brushed her lips against his cheek. "For you, I will go."

He responded with a kiss far more passionate, to which Clarita glanced around to make sure no one had seen the display of affection. No one except Alma, that is. Satisfied, she slipped her arm through his. After continuing to the end of the alley, they turned onto the side street and from there, strolled further into the neighborhood of Tudor-revivals and brick bungalows on the order of her house. Toni's house too, mustn't forget Toni. Not that Toni would've tolerated such an oversight, however unintentional.

"About Donata Abba, how should I begin?" Stefano said. "I thought *i nipoti* would have told you about Donata and me."

"My granddaughters? You mean *i nostri nipoti—our* granddaughters."

"Si, I keep forgetting, to my shame. Although I tried not to show it, Margo and Elena captured my heart in Italy."

"Yeah, Italy. They talked about Donata. They talked about you. They did not talk about you and Donata being a couple. Is that what you wanted them to do?"

151

"I wanted them to know how life had been between you and me, how I still thought about you, how I knew you still thought of me the same way." He pressed her hand to his lips. She pulled away.

"What you wanted was to make me jealous. But Ellen and Margo knew better."

"Did they? Because of them, I'm here. With you."

"So, when you and Donata were together, did the two of you ever talk about me?"

"Donata more so than me. She was—is still—jealous of you."

"And jealous of you—way back when and no doubt now. Does that surprise you?"

"Enough about Donata." He stopped and tugged on her elbow. "We can discuss this later, after I make love to you. Or, you make love to me. Whatever makes you happy makes me happy."

She jerked away. "I should send you packing, back to Ellen's."

A sound of annoyance erupted from his throat. "Ellen has Franco; that is enough. If I stay with Margo, her mouth will soon be fighting my mouth. Not a good thing for either of us." He stopped, bringing Clarita to a halt as well, and took her face between his calloused hands. "If you do not want me anymore, I go back to Italy."

A single tear trickled down her left cheek. "I still want you, more than ever if that's possible. God help me. God help us both."

He kissed the tear, making it disappear. "Good, then do not make me beg. When can we make love again?"

"You always had a way with words, Stefano."

"When it comes to love, words only go so far."

"You got that right. I guess we've walked long enough and talked long enough. Let's go home."

19

A Season for
Everything

"You'll need a new dress," Margo told me when she stopped by on Tuesday. "And, please, not one from a clearance rack. I will not have you embarrassing me."

Margo-induced acid reflux crept into my throat. I gulped, sending the sour taste back to my stomach where it would most likely inflict further damage.

"Well, don't just sit there." She folded her arms in a manner similar to the stance I often took with my students. "Ask me what for."

"Uh ... not sure I want to know?"

"Of course you do. On Saturday we, as in you and I, are going to The Ritz-Carlton. Blake got us tickets for the annual St. Louis Kids Auction."

"Blake Harrington, your boss?"

"Who else but. We'll be sitting at his table."

"Not me." As if on cue, one hand rushed to my eyes, thumb and forefinger ever so gently massaging lids on the verge of drooping. "I feel a dreadful migraine coming on."

"Good, consider it a step in the right direction. After we get you a decent outfit, take your meds and call in sick tomorrow morning. By Saturday you should be fine."

I shook my head, hard enough to bring on the potential migraine I'd been faking. "Get yourself a real date, Margo. Trust me, you'll have more fun. And so will I, that's for sure."

"Fun?" Margo raised her brow. "Who said anything about fun. This is strictly business, of an investigative nature. Among The Ritz-Carlton guests will be Jackson and Saradell Littlejohn. And don't tell me you never heard of them. They're the couple pictured on Google, along with Val Corrigan and Jet Gregson."

"Oh, sure, that Jackson and Saradell. With any luck Jet Gregson will be there too. She can hurl insults at you again, perhaps dump a bottle of wine on your dress. Or the new one I'm supposed to buy."

"Show some guts, El."

"Those would be on my early-stage bucket list, but currently not a top priority. That would be when Franco moves out of my life and into yours. As per our Forest-Park-morning-jog agreement."

"You had to bring up Franco."

"To do otherwise would be a huge failure on my part. No Franco move-in for you means no dress for me which means no me for you at The Ritz-Carlton."

∞∞∞∞

On my way home from Margo's I stopped at the Saint Louis Galleria, in particular Nordstrom whose upscale selection of formal wear would surely meet Margo's expectations, even if she wasn't there to give her thumbs up. Or down, God forbid.

I perused the racks, focusing on regular price not clearance, a project I preferred doing alone but Jillian the sales clerk felt compelled to earn her salary by helping me. I wanted to brush her off but would the woman allow me the courtesy of being me—no-o-o. She insisted on knowing my first name and where I planned on wearing *the outfit* that, in her opinion and with her years of expertise, would surely change my life forever. I did not go into the purpose of my Ritz-Carlton event. Nor did I share her enthusiasm for anything Ritz-related, especially after looking at the price tags of said formal wear.

Five try-ons later I stood in front of a full-length mirror, Jillian just out of view. Turning to the right and then to the left, I ended up with a posed view of my rear end, which didn't look half bad. Nor did the overall effect of the red strapless gown with its mermaid skirt flaring out at the knees. Jillian must've agreed, her eyes growing wide behind a pair of oversized black-rimmed glasses. She clasped one hand to her mouth and expelled a gasp worthy of any awestruck admirer.

"It is so you, Ellen. Or should I say Cinder Ellen? Prepare to make your grand entrance at the ball and to maybe … just maybe … meet your one and only Prince Charming."

"You think?"

"Would I lie to you?"

Wasn't that what sales people were paid to do? Key words: just maybe. Jillian unzipped the dress and helped me step out of it. Only then did my eyes zero in on the price tag, an amount that made me stagger to keep my balance. If only I'd brought Margo along. She possessed a certain knack for discovering retail flaws, however obscure or formerly non-existent, whatever it took to knock a hundred or so off the original price. Too late. Jillian was heading toward the register, sticker-shock in hand. If maintaining my independence from Margo meant paying full price to look stunning, who was I to object? At least I wouldn't have to worry about embarrassing her. Or myself, which would've been preferable to the wrath of Margo.

∞∞∞∞

Loretta Giacoletto

"You what?!" Margo said when I called the next morning to tell her I'd already bought my Ritz Carlton outfit.

"Give me some credit, Margo." I described the dress, omitting the part about how terrific I looked in it. "The Nordstrom clerk said it would be perfect for a ball."

"Except we're going to a charity auction for the disadvantaged. The objective is to look smashing but not to the point of extravagance."

"But you said—"

"To avoid the clearance racks, El. Were you not paying attention? Meet me at Nordstrom's at six this evening. And don't forget to bring the dress—we'll exchange it for something more suitable."

"Maybe I should keep the dress for another occasion."

"You have something coming up in the next two months?"

"You never know."

"Nor do you. The strapless red goes back. On the outside chance you need formal wear in January, look for your return in Clearance."

"But you said—"

"For everything there is a season, El. And a reason."

∞∞∞∞

I truly believe Franco was as ready to leave my condo as I was to see him move into Margo's. Bless her heart. She welcomed him with open arms and an already opened bottle of Barolo that I recognized as last year's Christmas gift from Blake Harrington. A fine wine too good to pass up, I stayed long enough for a single pouring. And no regrets. Margo had plastered a smile on her face to complement the state of euphoria Franco had adapted while inspecting the pristine gourmet kitchen she'd limited to morning coffee and dry toast.

"Will you allow me to cook for you?" he asked. "And perhaps a lady friend or two."

"Whatever blows your skirt up," Margo said, the smile fading from her face.

Franco's face went blank. He rubbed his chin, a gesture reminding me of Stefano. "This I do not comprehend. Only men in Scotland wear ... the skirt."

"Franco means kilt," I explained to Margo, who should've known better. "Keep the English simple, okay?" I mouthed the word *stupid* so as not to confuse Franco any further.

She rolled her eyes. "Simple I can handle."

20

Ellen at the Ritz

Saturday night found Margo and me putting on the ritz, in the main ballroom of The Ritz-Carlton, that is, after Margo had changed outfits three times, each one exceeding the other to make sure I didn't overshadow her. Fat chance of that ever happening although I did feel every bit her equal, me in a classic black sheath and her in a form-fitting royal blue bordering on extravagant. After leaving my car with valet parking, we hurried to the ballroom and made our splash as last to arrive at the Blake and Linda Harrington table of ten.

Blake was working hard at working the room, spreading good cheer from one table to another while Linda did her part by taking charge of the Harrington group, steering us in the direction of two mid-to-late-thirties men who'd come without partners, unless they considered each other as such. No, that didn't seem likely since I recognized one of them as an old boyfriend of Margo's, an architect who would've been a nice fit for me, had circumstances been different. Greg Lupino moved one seat to his left, opening up two adjacent chairs for Margo and me. Margo introduced me to Trey Millstone, who must have been her doing since she'd already positioned herself next to Greg, leaving me to make nice with Trey. Or,

158

Trey to make nice with me, judging from his engaging smile and warm handshake that negated any annoyance over Margo's version of a blind date. As in blindsided.

Linda continued her introductions, beginning with the couple sitting across the round table from us. On hearing the Littlejohn names, Saradell and Jackson Littlejohn looked up from their head-to-head whispering and gave synchronized nods before resuming their private exchange. Those two I recognized from my Google-stalking research, their photo taken with Val Corrigan and Jet Gregson during an earlier Ritz-Carlton event. And speaking of Jet, I glanced over to the next table and saw her chatting with … of all people, our own Auntie Kat Dorchester, both of them part of the now defunct Corrigan sisterhood. Talk about a small world, or as some people refer to St. Louis as a small town in a big city.

The last of Linda's introductions focused on Del Durante, an executive with Central Alliance Bancshares who brought an attractive blonde named Zoe Ponce. She kept playing with her hair, pulling out corkscrew ringlets, then letting them spring back like the Slinky of my childhood.

"Any relation to the appraiser Toni Savino?" Durante asked, directing his question to either Margo or me.

"Daughters," Margo replied with a smile, "but please don't hold that against us."

Durante chuckled. "On the contrary, your mother and I go back a long way. Count me as one of many loan officers who consider Toni Savino among the most reliable appraisers in St. Louis."

Margo nudged her foot against mine, igniting the dormant light bulb in my head. Zoe Ponce, hmm. Mom did mention running into Val at the Ritz with Zoe Somebody or Other. How many Zoes connected to Val could there possibly be in St. Louis?

This Zoe perked up with her own light bulb. "I might've met Toni Savino. Brunette with her nose in the air?"

Inwardly, I chuckled at Zoe's perceptive observation.

Loretta Giacoletto

Not Margo. She didn't even attempt a half-hearted smile. "Not sure our mother would agree. She considers herself salt-of-the-earth."

Zoe's cheeks flushed a bright pink. One hand covered her gaping mouth until she blurted out an apology. "Pardon my *fufu*. I didn't mean *nose-in-the-air* as an insult."

"None taken," Margo said through curled lips so chilling they made Zoe's upper lip twitch. "Where did the two of you meet?" Margo asked.

Zoe tugged on Durante's coat sleeve. "Doo, I forget where we met."

"At church, Baby. Margo wants to know where you and Toni Savino met."

Zoe clenched the twitching lip between her teeth. She closed her eyes, a moment later opening them wide. "Here maybe … or there. Every now and then my brain gets fuzzy but when it passes, I'm good as new. Well, almost."

"You'll have to excuse Zoe. She's still recuperating from a nasty accident," Durante explained, patting down her tousled hair with one hand.

"Yeah. Watch the head, Doo. Like I said, scrambled brains. Or did I say that? Did I thank you for saving us, Linda?"

"For *inviting* you," Linda blew her a kiss. "You most certainly did, Zoe."

"Thank you, again. In case you didn't hear me the first time."

"Really?" I said to Margo on our way to the ladies room. "Is there no end to your shameless scheming?"

"Excuse me," she said, her defensive manner making me doubt my own intuitive nature.

"Well, for starters, what's with this Zoe Ponce?"

"You know as much as I do. The woman has issues."

160

"And what about my so-called dinner companion. Talk about a less-than-spontaneous coincidence. Blake just happened to know your old boyfriend who just happened to be best buds with a city alderman who had nothing better to do than attend a charity auction?"

"Give me some credit, El. We're not talking Bachelorette 101. We're here to make connections. It's all about who we see and who sees us."

Whom we see, I refrained from saying. Putting our conversation on hold, we slipped into adjoining stalls and took care of business. After that, we stood side by side washing our hands, again in silence, out of respect for our mother who taught us not to discuss family business within earshot of anyone outside the family.

Back in the broad hallway congested with people on their way to and from the ballroom, Margo picked up the conversation from where we'd left off. "As for my shameless scheming, other than the Harringtons every person sitting at our table and the neighboring table has at least one common bond—the late Val Corrigan."

"Modesty will get you nowhere," I replied, still unconvinced.

"Nowhere without Blake's generosity."

No way could I let that comment pass without further elaboration. Taking Margo by one elbow, I backed her against a gigantic urn filled with greenery and went nose to nose with her. "How generous?"

She lifted her chin, Mom's defiant gene. "Seven hundred and fifty per head which includes food and drinks, but only for our table, not the other one."

"Margo!"

"Cool your chops. Blake's on the charity's board and needed to fill a table as much as he needed the tax write-off."

"Nevertheless, I hate taking advantage of him—hate *you* taking advantage of him. Speaking of, the least *you* could've done was to have given me some warning."

"What more did you need? I told you to avoid clearance racks, to get your hair and nails done professionally instead of doing them yourself. Did you think all the attention to personal appearance revolved around Blake and Linda, people we already know and don't need to impress? Sure, they're part of the St. Louis upper echelon but not an integral part of our investigation. More like a conduit to the ins and outs of it. Besides, had I gone into the specifics of our table mates, you would've considered yourself unworthy and chickened out."

"Excuse me. Since Cinque Terre, I now have a better opinion of myself."

"Well, it's about time you grew some balls."

"Speaking of balls, what am I supposed to do with this Trey Millstone?"

"Keep your hands off his, at least for now … sorry, couldn't help myself."

We resumed our stroll back to the banquet hall, slow but steady. "Okay, about Trey," Margo said. "Smile and don't act bored, even if you are. Who knows, engaging in small talk might lead to bigger things. After all, the man is an elected city alderman, one who lives in the Washington Avenue Loft District."

"And you want me to find out what?"

"How well he knew Val Corrigan since Val made a bundle of money developing the Loft District."

"Just because Trey lives there, doesn't mean he knows the district's history."

"Hello, he's a local politician."

"I hate this, Margo."

"*This* is not about you, El. Or me for that matter. Think about our misguided mother and her insurmountable troubles."

Not Worth Dying For

"That's all I've thought about since Italy."

"Well, think harder and longer. Did you see who's sitting at the other table?"

"Dearest Auntie Kat and not-so-dear Jet Gregson. Don't tell me you arranged that too."

Margo gave me her know-it-all grin. "Well, not the actual invitations, but I did make a few last-minutes suggestions regarding a compatible floor plan for a few select tables. Like I said, Blake's on the charity's board."

The auction began with a series of weekend retreats, the bidding far exceeding actual value. Trey Millstone raised his paddle a few times and eventually managed a long weekend at a Colorado ski resort. During the bidding, Trey and I quietly chatted, mostly about him which I preferred over making small talk about me. He turned out to be likeable enough, from a well-respected family in the black community's higher echelon. Divorced with two children living with their mother, he expressed zero interest in acquiring a special someone in his life.

"Amen to that," I said.

"Not the reaction I usually get," Trey said, straightening his tie.

"On the contrary, I couldn't be more pleased." Also relieved for the opportunity to relax and be myself instead of engaging in the mild flirtation Margo would've initiated had she been in my shoes. Actually her shoes, the four-inch black pumps she insisted I borrow. For now not a problem since I'd already kicked the damn things off, leaving my fashion sin to hide under the floor-length tablecloth.

"I sense a recent break-up." Trey lifted his wine goblet in my direction.

"Too recent to talk about." Or too painful. End of discussion.

Across from me Jackson Littlejohn raised his paddle for a fourth time, finally winning the bid for Tino's Trattoria on The Hill. "Dinner at Jackson's home," Trey whispered. "That should be some meal."

Jackson turned to shake hands with his bidding competitor—Blake Harrington, of all people.

"Just doing his duty," Margo said for my ears only.

At that point Saradell Littlejohn excused herself and headed toward the hallway. As did Margo, no doubt planning to corner Saradell in the ladies room. Better Margo than me; to repeat my sister had no shame. "Can Jackson afford it?" I asked Trey. "You know, the over-priced dinner for eight."

"Jackson Littlejohn? Where Jackson comes from, whatever he paid for that dinner is considered chump change. He and Saradell live on Lindell Boulevard, in one of those glorified mansions facing Forest Park."

"Really? What does Jackson do for a living?"

"For starters, he married well," Trey said. "The house came with Saradell; it's been in the family for generations. Ditto for St. Pierre Investments—Jackson now heads the firm."

"Should I be impressed?"

"Only if you're interested in what goes on behind the scenes in St. Louis."

"Absolutely. Those stories behind the stories fascinate me, more so than anything published in the *Riverfront Times* or *Ladue News*." I hadn't planned on opening up to Trey Millstone, but somehow found the courage to draw him into the periphery of our family drama. "By any chance are you familiar with the story behind the Creole Exchange renovation?"

"How could I not be," Trey said with a chuckle. "I live at the Creole. Been there since Day One, after putting up with a ton of delays before construction was completed. A bachelor when I bought; married with Baby One in the oven before we finally moved in." He wrinkled his brow and sighed. "After Baby Two, life took a different turn and started falling apart."

"I'm sorry, Trey."

Not Worth Dying For

"Hey, no need for a pity party. My ex and I have both moved on. We share custody of the kids and hope they'll turn out okay, which at this point is anybody's guess. Now, what's this about the Creole?"

I lowered my voice to one notch above a whisper. "How well did you know the developers, in particular, Val Corrigan?"

He gave some thought to my question before answering it. "The recently deceased Val Corrigan? Better than most, which isn't saying much. Val did like the ladies and they adored him. He had a knack for turning rags into riches—most of the time."

"And those other times?"

"Let's just say: shrewd ain't all it's cracked up to be."

"Any thoughts as to who might've wanted him dead?"

"Hmm." Trey pondered this for about twenty worthless seconds. "Not off the top of my head." After scrolling through his cell phone, he handed it to me. "Enter your name and number. I'll call if anything comes to mind."

By the time Margo and Saradell returned to their seats, the auction had moved into the serious phase of major bidding, what I considered a stretch for some at our table. For sure, Margo and me. She was leaning into Greg, the two of them engaged in a lengthy discussion with Saradell and Jackson Littlejohn who were sitting to Greg's left. I was getting more comfortable with Trey Millstone, who showed some class by including Zoe Ponce in our conversation. On the other hand, Del Durante had captured Blake's attention and had no intentions of letting go, in spite of Blake glancing around as if looking for a credible reason to excuse himself.

"So, you had a nasty accident," Trey said to Zoe.

"I did?" she asked, all wide-eyed in bewilderment.

"Del mentioned it earlier," I said. "Something about your head …."

"Oh that, yeah." Zoe ran the fingers of one hand through her hair. "I fell on my head, down a flight of stairs. It really hurt—my head. Not sure

165

about the stairs." She bent one elbow on the table, opened her palm, and rested her cheek on it. Zoe closing her eyes afforded me the perfect excuse for chit-chat with Trey.

"Are you and Greg Lupino long-time friends? "I asked.

"Since our days at SLUH," he said, referring to Saint Louis University High School. "God bless the Jesuits for making me the bastard I am today."

Refusing to play the game of *Where did you go to high school*, I said, "You do realize Greg and my sister were extremely close at one time."

"Like two sheets in a ream of paper. Greg does attract beautiful women."

"And Margo does attract handsome men."

With a lift of goblets, we clicked our Chardonnay together. "To meaningful relationships," Trey said.

"Amen again," I replied with my sister in mind. Neither Margo nor I needed another Margo on the rebound, not after the Jonathan from Iowa fiasco. Nor did I need the swiftness of her wrath should I fail to squeeze some useful information out of Trey. So far so good but with Margo enough was never enough.

From over my shoulder came the welcomed sight of a waiter's hand, delivering a plated arugula salad onto the gold-rimmed table charger sitting before me. "On a whole different topic," I said while Trey received a similar first course, "by any chance did you know the late Val Corrigan? I've been told he was quite the … man-about-town."

Trey raised his brow. "Val? I knew him well enough, though not in the biblical sense." Whatever look crossed my face prompted Trey to add, "No, I don't swing both ways; but yes, I'm well-acquainted with every aspect of life in St. Louis and the metropolitan area. Why do you ask?"

"My mother—that would be the Toni Savino—"

"So I heard."

Not Worth Dying For

"Er, right. Well, she was sort of involved with Val ... at the time of his death ... along with other female companions. How many, I can't say for sure. It's complicated."

"No more so than any other unsolved homicide in St. Louis. Still, I wouldn't want to be in your mother's shoes. Or yours." He grinned. "In particular, the one under the table that clobbered my foot when you kicked it off."

"Busted," I said. "But don't tell my sister."

He switched to his version of ghetto talk, a poor example from my limited experience. "Yeah, this dude's no snitch. Can't blame you for not wanting to tangle with the Margo I once knew—again not in the biblical sense." And back to the typical Midwest All-American accent. "As for Val Corrigan, we interacted a lot during the Creole renovation so if you have specific questions about that time frame, I'll do my best to enlighten you. For something more current, I suggest you talk with Jackson Littlejohn; Saradell too since Jackson doesn't wipe his ass without her okay. It's possible the firm invested in some of Val's real estate developments. None of which involves me but if there's anything I can do ...."

"Thanks. I'll keep that in mind."

Having focused my attention on Trey through the arugula salad and later the wild mushroom soup, I only became aware of our waiter during the main course when he brushed against my arm while serving what the menu written in cursive described as a surf and turf. What's not to like about petit filet mignon, mushrooms sautéed in butter, Maryland crab cake, and creamy whipped parsnips.

"Pardon me," the waiter said.

"No problem," I murmured, preoccupied with the conversation Trey and I were having about rumors of voter fraud during last year's primary election.

"That state representative got away with it once but she won't be so lucky the next time," Trey said.

"Maybe she learned her lesson," I said, to which Trey scoffed at my remark.

"Highly unlikely." He raised his wine goblet and added, "To justice and a much-deserved fall from grace."

A second, less subtle contact from the waiter prompted me to lift my head in his direction. My initial glance called for a double take that evolved into a thorough observation of the man's facial features. Those speckled blue eyes and high cheek bones did look familiar, perhaps a ghost from the past, not that my previous life in the convent had allowed much, make that zero, wiggle room when it came to the male species. Yes, indeed, a ghost from my high school years, one I never expected to re-enter my life. Yet, there he was, a grown man and better looking than the teenager who once betrayed and humiliated me in a cruel manner I didn't see coming. Blindsided, indeed.

Sisterly vibes came my way. Margo communicating as only she could, her foot kicking mine. If that wasn't enough, she snorted into her napkin. Most unladylike for Margo at the Ritz.

"Are you all right?" Greg asked her.

She dismissed his question with a wave of her hand. By then the ghost-server had moved on; but I knew he'd eventually return to pour more wine or remove soiled plates or to serve the *crème brûlée,* a dessert I didn't particularly relish. How many years had passed since I'd last seen Mike the Jerk? Eighteen. Mike ... Mike ... what was his last name? No surprise that I'd forgotten it, after erasing him like chalk from my virtual blackboard, then wiping the slate clean.

Trey speared a piece of tenderloin he'd cut with his steak knife. Fork poised in mid-air, he asked through half a smile, "Old boyfriend?"

I nodded before popping a bite of crab cake into my mouth.

"Been there," Trey said. "Nothing hurts like a broken heart."

I finished chewing and swallowed before answering. "Especially the first, I didn't see it coming."

"Get a grip, girl. There's no expiration date on getting even. But before using up your energy to plan the perfect payback, see what the guy wants. Better yet, what he can do for you."

"Spoken like a true politician," I said.

"Thanks, I'll take that as a compliment. By the way, it's been a while but I think I once knew your heartbreaker—our waiter. Not a bad sort, but definitely not in your league."

"You're saying he's in your league?"

"Any voter in my ward or for that matter, in all of St. Louis, is in my league."

"Er, right. That's politics."

How convenient, that nature should've been calling at that moment. Or perhaps I'd sent a subtle message to my bladder. In any case, for the second time that evening I excused myself and wandered through the maze of round tables before exiting the ballroom. Who should be standing out in the hallway but Mike, my long-ago teenage heartthrob. Make that heartbreaker.

He must've grown a few inches since his sixteenth year, putting him around five foot ten. The dark hair reflecting his part-Cherokee heritage had been pulled back into a man bun that no macho teenager would've worn back in the nineties when he hung out on the front porch of what Margo and I still considered our family home.

"I wasn't sure you'd remember me," he said.

"Not exactly." I stood there, searching his face for the teenager I once knew. "Mike ... or Matt ... drawing a blank."

"You're kidding, right?"

"Not ... sorry, help me out here."

Loretta Giacoletto

"Come on, Ellie. It's me, Mike Rutger."

"Oh, that Mike." Silence followed, awkward for him, satisfying for me. "Well, I won't keep you."

He shifted from one foot to the other. "I couldn't help overhearing your conversation at the table."

Damn, I tried using my whisper voice with Trey but evidently had not succeeded. "Is that what upscale waiters do? Listen in on other people's chitchat."

"Not unless that person happens to be an old friend."

"Friend, please. I beg to differ."

"You always had a way with words, Ellie. Not that I mind."

Another waiter hurried by, clearing his throat for Mike's benefit.

"Yeah, right behind you, Wyatt," Mike murmured before turning his attention back to me. "Look, duty calls so I gotta make this fast. You mentioned your mom and Val Corrigan. Just thought you'd like to know, I knew Val. His uncle too."

"You did?" I asked, unable to resist the virtual carrot he dangled for my benefit. "How well and when?"

"Can't talk now." He reached into his pants pocket and handed me a scrap of paper. "Here's my number."

Me call him? Maybe so, maybe never. And yet, after all these years I couldn't help feeling a sense of anticipation over the prospect.

Back at the Harrington table I found Jackson Littlejohn occupying my chair, engrossed in a conversation with Margo and Greg. Rather than intrude, I circled to the left of Greg and sat between Jackson's wife Saradell and our hostess Linda Harrington.

"Congratulations on winning the bid for that dinner party," I told

Saradell. "You can't go wrong with Tino catering it."

She projected a smile exuding the confidence of old money. "Linda and I were discussing whom to invite. Of course she and Blake will be there. I'd love to have you and your sister as well."

I stuttered and stammered. "I'm honored, as I feel sure Margo would be as well. But please don't feel obligated to do so because we happen to be sharing a table this evening."

"On the contrary, Ellen. Since we share a common interest in Val Corrigan's scandalous death, having the two of you join our party seems quite appropriate."

"If you don't mind my asking: What common interest?"

"That, you will have to find out elsewhere."

Memo to self:

1. *Dress for my success, not Margo's.*
2. *When it comes to table mates, keep an open mind.*
3. *Ignore intrusive waiters.*
4. *Do not undo erased relationships.*
5. *Free always comes with a price.*

21

Margo at the Ritz

El at the Ritz had done me proud, you bet. Little sis held up her end of an on-going conversation with Trey Millstone, one that hopefully would produce useful info on the St. Louis scene, in particular the Washington Avenue Loft District where Trey lived, an area Horace and Val Corrigan had played major roles in developing over a period of ten-plus years.

As for my date, Greg Lupino just happened to be an architect with Studio Alpha, and had designed a number of renovations in the Loft District, including the Corrigans' Creole Exchange Building. I'd dated Greg for a brief period some years back—nothing serious but always fun since Greg's rising star in the industry had earned him megabucks, making him generous to a fault. His fault not mine since I consider generosity a desirable quality in any man. I'm not sure which of us ended the affair first but probably me since I'd never have forgiven Greg otherwise.

Fast-forwarding to present day, Greg seemed over-the-top glad to hear from me when I called about the charity auction. Even better, he didn't hesitate about inviting his recently divorced buddy, Trey Millstone, to be El's table mate. Trey I sort of knew, having met him and his then-wife outside the New Cathedral on Lindell during my Greg period. Mom had

172

considered Greg Lupino ideal husband material, him being a practicing Catholic and all. Bringing him around again, as a friend and nothing more, seemed like a good idea, whatever it took to get her mind off the murder investigation.

After Linda Harrington introduced El and me to the other people at her table, we settled into our seats and like Ritz-Carlton magic, wine flowed into our goblets. Mild yet fruity white, a good choice to start off the evening with Greg, a self-proclaimed expert on such matters. Not that I doubted his knowledge which certainly surpassed mine. We shared a few minutes of chitchat with Saradell Littlejohn before Greg gave me his full attention, starting with the proverbial, "How long has it been?"

I put my brain to work calculating the question I'd considered earlier, pausing half-way through to finish counting with my fingers "Hmm, five years, two weeks ... four days and ... twenty-two hours."

Greg laughed, showing me the miracles of modern orthodontics available to our generation as children. El and I counted ourselves among a rare breed, having survived puberty without resorting to dental braces. Unlike our own dad who, as a twelve-year-old, had endured an elaborate contraption that wrapped around the back of his head to correct an impossible overbite. Good dental genes, Mom had insisted, acknowledging ours came from her side of the family. Make that Nonnie's side. John Riva may've been revered for nothing more than his posthumous contributions to the family finances, not that there's anything wrong with that. But one thing was for sure: the Riva DNA did not match our mother's, nor mine and El's. As for the newly discovered Rosina branch of the family, perhaps when Franco and I got better acquainted, I'd ask him to open wide and show me his molars. As for Stefano's mouth, what teeth I could see seemed decent enough for a man his age.

"Sassy as ever," I heard Greg say, interrupting the family drama that plagued my thoughts. "And twice as gorgeous," he went on, "if that's even possible."

"Flattery will get you everywhere." I circled my tongue over my lips, a not-so-subtle reminder of the intimacy we once shared.

173

Loretta Giacoletto

"That's what I was hoping for." He covered my hand with his, bony and sensitive yet warm and protective. More than I expected; more than I'd wanted or so I thought before that moment. "Refresh my memory, Margo. Why *did* we break up?"

"Too many distractions?" I asked, a question that could've applied to either of us.

"For that I take full responsibility," he said with the slight accent of his early years in Italy. "I should've been more attentive."

Spoken like a true gentleman. As I said before, Greg was generous to a fault. Not bad looking either, with reddish brown hair and amber eyes intent on capturing mine until I turned my attention to the River City Builders table next to ours. Kat Dorchester and I exchanged finger waves. Unlike my interaction with Jet Gregson who gave me a most unbecoming puckered scowl, to which I responded with a light pressing of fingertips to my lips. Little did Jet know I'd made sure our tables would be close enough to allow a virtual rubbing of elbows.

"I see you're acquainted with some of our neighbors," Greg said.

"Only a few. How about you introducing me to the others."

"What makes you think I know the *others*?"

"You do know everyone in the construction and real estate industry, don't you?"

"Wouldn't have gotten this far if I hadn't made more friends than enemies along the way." He stood, offering his hand to mine. "Your wish is my command."

We approached the River City table where Greg undertook the introductions, beginning with host Morgan Davisson and his wife Greta. Both stood to shake my hand; his big and beefy, hers lean and soft from a recent manicure.

"By any chance are you head of River City Builders?" I asked.

"One in the same," Greta Davisson replied, squeezing her husband's

174

forearm. "But forget about business this evening. Morgan's wearing his trousers with extra deep pockets and I have my eye on several choice items. Right, darling."

"Right as gold," Davisson said. "Greta won't take wrong for an answer."

Boyd and Eve Tennison jumped the gun on Greg, introducing themselves as with Tennison Insurance. "Don't worry," Eve said with a laugh. "We're not pushing personal life insurance or annuities. Tennison underwrites multi-million-dollar projects."

"That is so-o interesting," I said, tucking the Tennisons on the back burner of our rescue-Mom project.

Pierce Rendley I recognized as Mr. Big-Bucks Lender for Centennial Mid-America Bank. His current wife Beale needed no introduction, having preceded me as Blake Harrington's paralegal. She grabbed me by the shoulders, administering air kisses to each cheek. "Margo, you never cease to amaze me ... here with Greg Lupino of all people." Lips close to my ear, she whispered. "Hang on to him this time. You won't find another catch as good as Greg."

Before I could state my position as *just friends and nothing more*, Greg nudged my elbow, steering me on to the next couple. Jet Gregson nodded with daggers in her eyes, which didn't faze me because mine had moved on to her date, Boris Tainer, who'd already stood and was shaking hands with Greg.

"Boris and I go back a long way," Greg said.

"All the way to the Creole, as I recall," Boris added. "A project I still hold in high regard."

"Really, and why is that?" I asked.

"Not to brag but I made sure every environmental code was adhered to, quite an accomplishment for a building older than dirt, one that hadn't been modernized for years until Horace and Val Corrigan redeveloped the property."

Loretta Giacoletto

"Then you knew both of them," I said.

"Hell, yes, Horace more so than Val although Val and I hunted together from time to time—mostly deer in Missouri. And how did you know the Corrigans?"

"Val only and not personally," I said. "He was a friend of my mother, Toni Savino."

"Ah-h, that explains a lot." He turned to Jet, now standing, her arm linked with his, and asked, "You two know each other?"

"Sure do," I said. "As a matter of fact, we work out in the same gym." Sort of, in spite of my temporary suspension for reasons yet to be explained.

"Excellent … if that's your thing," Boris replied as Jet sat down, pulling him with her.

I would've continued the conversation had it not been for Greg pushing me to the next person who needed no introduction.

"Mogo," Auntie Kat said, giving me an actual hug instead of the fake variety. "I didn't expect to see you here. You should've brought Toni."

"Mogo?" Greg said with half a smile. "This is a first for me."

"Also a last. You remember Kat Dorchester, don't you?"

"Once a Kat fan, always a Kat fan," Greg said with a slight bow of his head. "As usual, you look stunning."

"Down boy." Kat pushed a long forefinger against his chest. "Greg Lupino, architect, say hello to Reavis Worden, surety agent."

"We've met before," both men replied as one.

Worden gripped my hand in his, pumping as he said, "We've never met. But I know your mother."

"I'll be sure to say hello," I said, for lack of anything better. Reavis Worden I wanted to remember, in case he'd ever connected with Val or

176

Not Worth Dying For

Horace Corrigan since surety agents were essential in the building industry, guaranteeing the payment and performance of a contract would be fulfilled.

With that, the ballroom lights were dimmed so Greg and I returned to our table. We evidently hadn't been missed, especially by El or by Trey Millstone. They were engaged in pleasantries and didn't bother looking up when a five-piece combo of tuxedo-attired musicians gave a rousing welcome to the master of ceremonies, a comedian of some national renown. After opening with a few St. Louis-related jokes, the emcee introduced the auctioneer. Let the bidding begin, and it did.

"If there's anything you'd like," Greg murmured in my ear, "say the word and I'll raise my paddle."

An opportunity such as this I couldn't pass up. It was my turn to cover his hand, the one holding the bidding paddle. "There is something I'd like and it won't cost you a thing."

"Nothing in life comes without a price, Margo. You know that as well as I do. But if it's help you want, count on me to do my best."

"No strings attached," I said.

"Depends on what you're asking of me."

I sat back, arms folded at my waist. "Never mind. That kind of help I can do without."

"Dammit, Margo. What do you take me for? You know I was kidding."

Of course, but before I could respond, excitement stirred within our table. Jackson Littlejohn had won the bid for a dinner catered at his home.

"Don't stop now," Saradell Littlejohn told her husband. "I won't be long." She got up, as did I, and walked several paces behind her to the ladies restroom. Vacant as a glossy hotel promotional piece, except for the two of us and an attendant who kept the hand bowls spotless and made sure the miniature amenities never ran out.

Having answered nature's call, Saradell and I stood side-by-side, washing our hands at the marble counter of basins while eyeing each other's reflections in the mirrored wall.

Can I be you when I grow up, I so wanted to say. Corny but true, Saradell at fifty-something represented the epitome of perfection, a prime example of how I pictured myself twenty years from that moment. Subtle make-up emphasizing flawless features, hair styled to accent the contours of a face yet to go under the knife. Or if it had, kudos to the cosmetic surgeon. Saradell's dress alone would've cost me a month's salary. Trust me, Blake Harrington was no cheapskate when it came to fair pay for those he employed, men or women.

"So, Toni Savino is your mother," Saradell said.

I shook water from my hands, reached for a nearby folded paper towel, and asked Saradell if she knew her.

"Mainly as a business acquaintance," Saradell said, "although we do go back a long way."

"Then you might know Mom's good friend Kat Dorchester as well."

"Kat, I've encountered on several occasions. No love lost between us. I make it a point to avoid her whenever possible."

"Really? Why, if you don't mind my asking."

Saradell turned on an endearing smile. "Oh, Margo, you sound just like your sister. I certainly don't mind your asking as long as you don't mind my not answering."

We continued making small talk during our return to the ballroom where the auctioneer was prodding wealthier participants to outbid each other on a shitload of luxury items, all for the sake of St. Louis Kids.

"I think we should have a serious chat," Saradell said as we neared our table. "Let me think on this." She did, much to my satisfaction. Before the evening came to an end, she'd invited El and me to one of the auctioned dinners her husband had secured. She also invited the other people at our table, making the count two more than Jackson's original bid had covered.

Not Worth Dying For

"Don't make this a problem," Saradell said when Jackson called the discrepancy to her attention. "Another thousand or two should cover the extras."

Hardly the ambiance for the private chat Saradell had suggested; but I'd make sure it happened before dining at the Littlejohn residence.

I could've gone home from the auction with a pricey gold watch but when the bidding exceeded ten thousand dollars, I told Greg to back off, that I really preferred the upcoming diamond hoop earrings described in the auction catalogue. He won that bid, adding three thousand dollars to the St. Louis Kids coffers and making me one happy recipient, having helped my former squeeze contribute to such a worthy cause. El and I did our bit as well, each of us donating five hundred dollars—that she could barely afford—toward the purchase of winter coats for the kids.

When the auction ended, El excused herself to queue up for valet service, leaving me to continue cheek-to-cheeks with Greg and Trey. "Thanks, guys," I said, holding hands in a three-way. "I really appreciate your coming."

"The pleasure was mine," Trey said. "Can't wait to tell my kids about the Colorado ski trip this winter."

Greg brushed my cheek a second time and whispered, "Is it okay if I stop by for a nightcap?"

"Only if you promise not to behave yourself."

"I'll do my damnedest."

If past performances were any indication of Greg's dependability, I knew he wouldn't disappoint. Nor would I, after making a quick phone call to Franco in which I asked him to spend the night at El's. An unavoidable emergency, I explained to him, and afterwards to El, who had no choice but to acquiesce.

∞∞∞∞

My drive home with El produced a drizzle of raindrops that spattered the

179

windshield until she turned on the wipers, their steady swish-swish all but putting me to sleep. After my second wind kicked in, we exchanged scraps of information gathered during the evening, both of us agreeing that Trey Millstone might be a valuable source since he first met the Corrigans during the early stages of the Creole renovation.

"As did Greg," I reminded El. "After all, he was the architect."

In fact, almost everyone sitting at those two tables had been involved in the Creole Exchange, from initial conception to eventual completion or somewhere in-between. How many enemies Val or Uncle Horace had made along the way was yet to be determined; but El and I agreed that we'd make sniffing out pertinent information our top priority. After all, when it came to unresolved issues, we'd learned a thing or three over the past few months.

Time for the nitty gritty elephant in the car. "Anything else, El?"

"You just had to ask, didn't you."

"Never mind, sorry I brought it up."

"No you're not. If you must know, Mike from high school wants to meet with me. He knew the Corrigans too. Or so he claims."

"For sure you're going."

"As if I can't decide for myself," El said. "The guy's bad news. He's like the return of my worst nightmare."

"Come on, it couldn't have been that bad. Take one for the team, El. For Mom to be more precise."

"I hate you."

"You won't after talking with him. I promise."

Although I'd been cheated on in the past, most recently in Italy, getting dumped was one humiliation I'd never had to face. Nor getting stood up,

Not Worth Dying For

which wouldn't have been nearly as bad but nevertheless a huge mortification. Neither happened that night after the auction. Greg Lupino, who must've forgotten I once dumped him, did show up at my condo, bringing with him a bottle of my favorite *vino rosso*.

"You remembered," I said, relieving him of the Barolo I opened with undeniable pleasure.

After drinking half the bottle and playing catch-up with the years since we last dated, Greg took the goblet from my hand and set it on the coffee table. "Love the dress," he said. "Would love to see what's under it."

"You first," I said, stretching my arms overhead.

He stood and taking his good old time, performed the same Chippendale routine I so loved watching in the past but had forgotten until that moment.

"Satisfied?" he asked, having stripped to nothing more than form-fitting boxer briefs.

"Evidently you're hoping to be, judging from the optimistic reaction I can't help but notice."

"Your turn," he said.

To which I responded with my version of a class-act striptease, Greg egging me on with a barrage of hoots and hollers.

"We really were meant for each other," he said when I had nothing left to dangle in his face. "So much so, we could take our act on the road."

"Not without a lot of practice," I said, taking him by the hand. "Shall we start in the bedroom?"

"Lead the way, Margo the Magnificent. Although I know my way around you, and love every nook and cranny, your current condo is new to me."

Loretta Giacoletto

What started out as a convenient auction date with an old boyfriend soon evolved into an all-night lovefest, the likes of which I'd never experienced before with Greg Lupino or any other man. Confusing, you bet, considering the number of times Greg and I had hooked up during our previous period of dating. But nothing could compare to this night, a combination of reckless passion linked with a level of maturity neither of us had expected.

The next morning after a wake-up-with-sex shower, I went the extra mile and fixed breakfast for two, my all-time favorite quickie: frozen toaster waffles smothered in sugar-free, maple-flavored syrup.

"We should do this more often," Greg said while stirring coffee straight from the microwave. Again, one of my specialties, although the desirability of this expedient brew had dampened considerably since my recent Italian holiday. "More often means at least every other night."

"If it also means here at my place, we might have to put that on hold." Talk about poor timing; if only I hadn't agreed to Franco becoming my house guest. "For now it's rather complicated. On the other hand ..."

"I wish. My place is undergoing a make-over. For now I'm camped out at my brother's."

"Your brother with the three kids?"

"Four and one more on the way. What more can I say."

182

22

Missing Link

The next morning I called Mom and asked her to meet El and me at Carondelet Park. "This afternoon at two," I said. "Just the three of us."

"Really, Margo? You do realize there's a storm in the forecast. Not that I'm concerned about melting, sweet as I may be."

Or not. Either way, Mom seemed to have regained a touch of her sarcastic humor. "If it's raining, stay put. We'll swing by and pick you up. Just you, okay?"

"Thank God for favors, however insignificant. These octogenarian lovebirds are driving me bananas. I'd move out if—"

"Save it for later but not later today."

"You're not going to make me eat, are you? Seems like that's all I've been doing since *he* came barging in."

"He as in Stefano?"

"Who else. I swear, if your nonna isn't cooking for him or walking

183

with him, she's doing you-know-what with him. Anything to get away from the madness, I'll be there."

The forecasted rain let up by the time El and I arrived at the park. We found Mom sitting under the only pavilion not reserved for a private event, her back resting against a picnic table, and dangling from one end, the umbrella I bought her eons ago. While I made room for my sturdy shopping bag next to the umbrella handle, she heaved a deep sigh confirming her current state of annoyance.

"Apparently you weren't listening when I told you no food," she said.

"As usual I obeyed, but you didn't say anything about alcohol."

"Margaritas, yay!" El said, looking inside. "I can tell by the glasses. If you don't want yours, Mom …"

"You know better than that. I don't suppose you brought salt."

Not only salt but lemon wedges too. After pouring a round we gathered around the table, elbows bent and between El and me, gave alternating versions of our auction at the Ritz.

"You might like this," I told Mom while circling one finger around the rim of my margarita glass. "Del Durante still regards you as a top real estate appraiser."

"Good for Del. To this day I regret fudging on that first Creole appraisal; but I must say, over the years he's brought me some serious business."

El sucked the lemony salt from her finger and spoke through puckered lips. "His date Zoe Ponce remembered you, well, sort of. She seemed a bit spacey, something about a recent fall. Could she be the same Zoe you once met at the Ritz with Val Corrigan? Attractive with dark curly hair?"

"Hmm, that would be Zoe. At the time I thought she might've been a high-class call girl. Just goes to show the unpredictability of first impressions."

Not Worth Dying For

Or the occasional spot-on accuracy of them. An oxymoron if ever there was, me occupying the same wavelength as Mom. "You'll never guess who was sitting at the table next to ours," I said. "Boris Tainer, the TEC environmental engineer."

"For the Creole Exchange among other projects," Mom said. "A bit weird but aren't we all. Did Boris have a date?"

"Jet Gregson," El said. "I don't like her."

"Nor would I expect otherwise of you."

"Thanks. I'll take that as a compliment."

"As for Jet and Boris—what an odd match."

"Temporary and for a good cause," I said. "On the order of El and Trey Millstone."

"The city alderman?"

"*Divorced* alderman. Not my type," El said. "Don't know his; nor do I care. Margo's idea, not mine. Of course, it's not like she spun the Wheel of Fortune to come up with any old table mate for herself, one who exceeded your wildest expectations, Mom. A certain someone from her past."

Our mother reflected on this for a long minute. "I can't imagine who, unless … Greg … Greg Lupino?"

"A date and nothing more," I said. "Don't get your hopes up, Mom."

Too late, from the look on Mom's face, those hopes were rising with each passing second.

"It's time you settled down, Margo. All I ask is you not lead the man on. Greg deserves better."

"I'll drink to that," El said with a lift of her glass.

As did Mom, following up with a resounding, "Amen."

Having already emptied my glass, I, on the other hand, abstained from

185

saluting Greg Lupino. Still, I promised myself to consider him as more than an occasional convenience. A welcomed lull in the conversation gave El a chance to refill our glasses.

"Oh, I almost forgot," she said. "Auntie Kat was sitting at the Boris and Jet table."

"With Reavis Worden," I added.

"The surety agent," Mom said. "Leave it to Kat. Anybody else I might know?"

I mentioned Boyd and Eve Tennison, to which Mom replied with her usual candor, "Mega-bucks insurance. They only deal with people who can bring them business."

"Speaking of, do you remember Beale who used to work for Blake before I came on board? She married Pierce Rendley."

"Second mortgage holder on the Creole," Mom said with a snap of two fingers. "A tough nut but I finally convinced him to let me re-appraise the property a third time and final go-around, in spite of my questionable first appraisal. We've had a great relationship ever since."

Forget any pretense of lady-like sipping, Mom finished her latest margarita in a single gulp while I braced myself for her next words. "You know, Margo, I really should've been there last night. Those people were, and still are, my business associates." She looked from El to me. "What? The two of you were ashamed of your own mother, a person of interest in a murder investigation? Through no fault of my own, I might add, in spite of any nonsense those prying detectives are determined to uncover."

"Nothing of the sort, in fact just the opposite. El and I were on a Val Corrigan fact-finding mission. We didn't want this particular group of people distracted by your presence."

"So, who else was there that I might've distracted?"

"Morgan and Greta Davisson, River City Builders."

"Him I know by reputation—highly regarded in the industry. Greta, I

Not Worth Dying For

met once years ago. That's it?"

"Well, except for Blake and Linda. Oh, I almost forgot—Jackson and Saradell Littlejohn too."

Mom poured another margarita with her next comment. "Head honchos for St. Pierre InvestmeOnts. Saradell I know better than Jackson."

"Yeah, she said you were business acquaintance," I said. "Kat's name came up too, in private I might add. Saradell can't stand her."

"Is it any wonder? Ellen, you may recall my telling you that years-ago story, the one about Kat slicing the face of a girl she caught with her boyfriend, a guy Kat later married. Well, the unfortunate girl was none other than Saradell St. Pierre, during her wild years."

23

The No-Show

Hello. Just color me incredibly stupid. Whatever had I been thinking, letting El talk me into taking Franco Rosina off her hands and into mine, however unwilling and ill-equipped we both knew those hands of mine were, and still are. Oh right, the idiotic trade-off in which I agreed to Franco moving into my spare bedroom if El agreed to accompany me on a morning jog with Jet Gregson, one-time squeeze to Val Corrigan.

Yes, El did agree to the anticipated sweat-friendly jog, although with considerable resistance on her part and a bit of arm twisting on mine. My little sis might've been short on the athletic genes; but without a doubt she did possess a thorough understanding of her physical limitations, which on that fateful Saturday meant conking out five minutes into a forty-minute run through Forest Park. A run, I might add, that left me to suffer the humiliation of a tongue lashing from Jet. I would not have given that self-appointed fitness snob the time of day had it not been for major crime bloodhounds Winchester and Reardan sniffing out the life and times of the late Val Corrigan.

Shortly before his murder, Val had been sleeping with my mother. And with Mom's unpredictable BFF, Kat Dorchester. During the same time frame. And before them, the rumored-to-be-suicidal Jet Gregson. And God only knows who else. Perhaps Zoe Ponce, who may or may not have been at one time a call girl, but could now be described as more than a little loopy. Talk about Soap Opera St. Louis. Give me a break.

All of these concerns went down prior to or during the charity auction, an unexpected eventful event for me due to rekindling of a long-ago romance with Greg Lupino. Common sense had since warned my impulsive heart to slow down to a manageable pace until I got my life back to some degree of what passed for normal. First things first—dealing with family issues squeezing me from more than one side, beginning with my private space. Or lack thereof.

Damn and double damn. Having honored my agreement with El, I'd welcomed Franco Rosina with a broad smile and warm hug when he moved his things into my place, a simple task requiring no more than ten minutes tops. On seeing his new bedroom, twice the size of the one he'd vacated at El's, he circled his right thumb and forefinger, declaring his approval in a single word, "*Perfetto!*"

Perfect for him. Not so perfect for me.

As for total imperfection, all this bullshit about Val's murder had taken its toll on Mom, as had her annoyance over Franco Rosina, her biological father who moved into Nonnie Clarita's bedroom, both now referring to it as *their* bedroom. Mom must've aged five years from the time El and I left for Italy to our return, cutting short our vacation to act as her advisers or, better yet, to lend our support to Detectives Winchester and Reardan who hadn't asked for it, yet. Of course, those hard-nosed detectives didn't know the real El or me. During our Italian holiday we'd learned a thing or two about mystery solving. More like unraveling. Not all mysteries are meant to be solved; or so we'd been told more than once in Italy. Here in America, those-in-the-know, not necessarily El or me, took a different approach to solving or unwinding or leaving up in the air. And don't get me started on the mysteries of life and love or just plain lust.

Still, in the comfortable confines of my former bachelorette pad one thing was for sure, Franco Rosina, our recently discovered though somewhat unacknowledged uncle, could cook as well as any imported

Italian chef working on The Hill. During my first ten days of hosting Franco, I'd already gained two pounds. At that rate I'd be needing an entirely new wardrobe before his imminent return to Italy. Four or five months max, I so wanted to believe, preferably no more than half of his remaining time spent crashing under my roof. Not that he was a bother, more like the company he kept, as in the obnoxious Romaine Sloane, who bothered me whenever she opened her mouth. Add to that the lack of company I'd been keeping with Greg Lupino, having resorted to several nights in luxury at the Ritz-Carlton. Room service including bubbly Champagne and caloric-ridden chocolates—naughty but nice. Yes, we are judged by the company we keep, or so my mother always told me. Too bad she hadn't followed her own advice.

∞∞∞∞

"More pasta?" Franco asked as he speared a serving fork into the oval platter sitting on the table between us.

"Not another bite." Using some restrain, I released an unladylike burp behind one hand.

Franco slid the remaining pasta onto his plate and twirled a generous amount onto his fork, leaving one short strand to dangle, all of which he shoved into his mouth. Talk about mysteries, how the man managed to eat with such gusto and not gain a pound remained a mystery to me.

"Nor do I have room for dessert," I said.

"What? But for you I made—"

"Maybe later." I pushed my chair away from the table and was preparing to get up when Franco motioned me to stay put.

"About tomorrow night," he said.

"*La mia casa è la tua casa,*" I said, telling him my house was his. "I plan to go out for the evening but don't let that stop you from inviting Romaine for dinner."

Franco stopped twirling his pasta and set the fork down. "Margo,

Margo, whatever I have done to offend you, please forgive." Head lowered, he pressed his palms and extended fingers together, creating a prayerful position.

"There is nothing to forgive, Franco." I hadn't told him about Greg Lupino. We'd already made plans for tomorrow night.

"But always you go out, stay out all night, after being gone all day."

"Not always, just on certain occasions," I said. "Just like in Italy."

"This is true. But the Americani live for their television and electronics, si?"

"Not all of us. Not all the time." Not with Greg occupying my every thought.

"Without you, my dinner will not be the same," Franco said.

"I'm sure you'll think of something." Not to be deterred, I stood up.

As did Franco, having forgone his questionable humility. He leaned across the table, kissed one of my cheeks and then the other. "*La tua casa, le tue regole*," he said, adding in English, "your house, your rules."

"Did I say that?"

"Actions speak louder than words, Margo. Is the same with Romaine. This woman plays the fool but is no fool. She knows more about Val Corrigan than she has told the police."

"And you know this because?"

"Did you ever wonder why Romaine does not have a job?"

"Well, now that you mention it, no. Who knows, she may've retired early to live off of her investments. Or perhaps she's a widow."

"Or perhaps, like in Italy, the mistress of a rich man who passes from this life to the other and has the decency to remember the mistress in his will."

"You have someone in mind?"

"Not for sure." He rocked his hand from side to side.

"Franco, I do not have time for games. Just tell me what you know."

"Nor do I have time for any more games with Romaine. She is not … how you say … not my type, always wanting something from me, threatening to make trouble for me. But for the sake of my sister Toni I will continue the masquerade for a few more days. Tomorrow night you stay for dinner and have Elena come too. With enough wine, Romaine should have plenty to say in front of witnesses. After that I will kiss her goodbye for the last time."

We Savino sisters—El and me—plus Franco and Romaine for dinner, thank you, four was my max entertainment limit during the week, even with Franco doing all the cooking. Although I considered adding Greg to the count, I hadn't told Franco about him yet. Better for all concerned to wait until Franco gave Romaine a final send-off.

The next day I came home from work to find Franco in what he referred to as *mia cucina*. Thanks to El, my kitchen had become his cucina, which I didn't mind since he'd been adamant about cleaning up any mess he and he alone made. Having already arranged a variety of ingredients on the counter, he continued prepping for the dinner I could just as easily have done without, Romaine or no Romaine revelations. I filled two goblets of wine, passed one to his expectant hand and kept the second for myself. Having walked into the open area of living space where we could still see each other, I sat down on the sofa and kicked off my pumps. I lifted my feet onto the coffee table, an abomination my mother never permitted when El and I were kids. Nonnie didn't mind but in the interest of keeping peace, usually kept her mouth shut about minor issues.

"You invited Elena?" Franco asked while piling five garlic cloves on the cutting board.

"She'll be here around six, give or take."

192

Bam! He pounded the side of his fist on the flat blade of his chef's knife, crushing the cloves underneath. "Give or take? *Non capisco.* This I do not understand."

"Give or take means *around*," I explained.

"But you already said *around* six."

"You're right, Franco. Next time I'll try not to repeat myself."

"I think you are annoyed with me, Margo. Again, I apologize for whatever I have done to offend you."

"Good grief. Don't you dare apologize for me being cranky ... er, irritable. I had a rough day at work."

"Then you desire a good meal. Tonight will be special. I promise."

Be careful what you promise, I so wanted to say. True, I was annoyed about postponing my time with Greg to the following evening. Even more annoyed with Franco for putting El and me in a position of having to entertain Romaine Sloane, a woman neither of us were interested in having as a friend. On the other hand, if Romaine knew more than she was telling about Val's murder, we could put up with her bullshit for a few disagreeable hours. To say nothing of Franco's never-ending culinary projects. Never did I think it possible to grow tired of upscale Italian food but a steady diet of it every day kept bringing me closer to that realization.

My internal tirade ended when the telephone rang. After answering the land line and getting nothing but the dial tone, I wiggled the pinky I'd stuck in my ear. Nada to the possibility of ear wax, at least from my ill-informed perspective.

"My phone," Franco yelled while sautéing chopped bacon. "On the coffee table ... can you answer for me?"

Well, duh. One more time. "Franco's phone," I said into the speaker.

A pause followed before the response. "Franco who?"

Games, don't waste my time with silly games. I made no effort to hide

Loretta Giacoletto

my annoyance. "Depends on who's calling."

A clearing of the throat came through, followed by an audible sigh. "This is Detective Winchester, Major Case Squad. To whom am I speaking?"

Damn, how embarrassing and what illegal activity had Franco been involved in while I was working my tail off for Blake Harrington. "Er ... uh ... Margo Savino here."

"Savino ... Savino ... by chance any relation to Antonia Savino?" the detective asked in a wary voice.

"She's my mother."

"Hmm, interesting. We—Detective Reardan and I—are tracking down the owner of the cell phone you answered."

"That would be Franco Rosina. He's a relative visiting from Italy."

"We'd like to speak to Mr. Rosina."

"Sorry, he's in the middle of cooking dinner right now. Would it be okay if he called you back?"

A pregnant pause followed before the detective answered my question. "Negative. Either we speak to him now or within the hour at the Fourth Precinct."

Naturally, Franco got on the phone, leaving me to stir bacon bits on a low flame. Although he'd stepped into the living area, I did manage to hear his exclamations of disbelief followed by a series of stuttered comments. "Si, si. Is okay. I will come tomorrow morning."

After the call ended, he returned to the kitchen with shoulders slumped, the usual cheeriness absent from his face. He turned off the flame under the skillet of sautéed bacon, and without looking at me, he said, "No special dinner tonight."

"Don't tell me Romaine wants you to bail her out of jail."

194

Not Worth Dying For

"Never will Romaine want anything from me again. She has left this world for the next. Police say murdered. They found my telephone number among the last she called."

"Oh, no, that's horrible. How?"

"Police did not say. I did not ask."

Although Franco insisted he didn't need help cleaning up, it didn't take a genius to see the poor guy was too rattled to tackle the project alone. No sooner had we finished than El walked in, a vision of goodness and mouth-watering hunger. After Franco gave her the brief run-down of Romaine's death, she made the sign of the cross and led us in a prayer for the departed soul, a nice gesture on El's part, one that came naturally to her but would've been super awkward for me.

Having ended with another sign of the cross, El paused and then glanced around the kitchen, a look of disappointment creeping across her face.

"We, that is, Franco, decided to abstain from dinner this evening," I explained.

"But not from the vino," he said while uncorking a bottle he'd brought from Italy.

"Maybe some crackers?" El asked, eyeing the cabinet where I kept them.

I opened an imported variety that came from The Hill and along with some cheese, arranged our substitute tray for supper-on-a-plate while defending myself to El. "Okay, I should've called, saved you the trip over here. But since Franco will be meeting with Detectives Winchester and Reardan tomorrow morning, I thought we could put our heads together and help him get his story straight."

"What story?" Franco said. "I do not weave tales. What I say will be the truth as I see it."

"Of course, as you see it," El said. "Have you ever been questioned by

195

the police before?"

"Si, but never about murder."

"And never in America," I added, setting three goblets on the counter in front of Franco.

"Nor as a foreigner," he said. "In Italy I am somebody, a *paesano*." He filled the goblets, turning the bottle after each pouring so as not to spill a single drop onto the table.

"Rest in peace, Romaine," I said with a raise of my glass.

"*Riposare in pace*," Franco repeated in Italian.

"Amen," El contributed and with a click of our goblets we took a sip to honor the memory of a woman none of us particularly liked or trusted, which may've been reason enough for someone—outside our family—to have killed her.

"One thing's for sure," El said. "Franco should not go to the station alone."

"So true. Can you take off work tomorrow?" I asked her.

"Sorry, Margo. You'll have to bite the bullet."

With one final gulp, Franco drained the wine from his glass and swiped the back of one hand across his mouth. All this in preparation of the "*Mio Dio!*" he muttered. "You would take a bullet for me, an innocent man you are ashamed to call *Zio*, your mama to call *Fratello*?"

"No, no," El said. "*Bite the bullet* doesn't mean the same as *take a bullet*."

"And we're not ashamed," I said, trying to come up with a plausible explanation that even I could understand. "More like still in shock."

"Basta!" He threw up his hands. "What good is any man without the respect of his family? Or an innocent man sitting in jail for nothing more than making nice with a lonely woman who died at the hands of a monster.

Not Worth Dying For

Get me on the first plane back to Italy, with or without Papa."

"Hold on," I told Franco. "Getting out on a moment's notice won't be that easy. You're in America now."

"Trapped in America, Margo."

"Not so. Every person accused of a serious crime is entitled to a fair trial."

"And then they die—this I see on the television again and again."

"But not in real life," I said, to which a disgruntled sound erupted from Franco's throat.

"Don't be offended but there's one question I feel compelled to ask," El said. "Did you have anything to do with the murder of Romaine Sloane?"

"I did not." Franco folded his arms in a defensive manner. "And, si, I am offended."

"All the more reason one of us should go with you," El said. "Of course, Margo is the logical choice. She's smart and sassy and works for a ... a."

"A lawyer, I've already explained my position to Franco."

"*Un avvocato*," he said with a nod of his head. "For knowing—having the carnal knowledge—of a woman who has since died, I need a lawyer?"

"Of course not," El said. "But trust me, you do need Margo."

197

24

Tit for Tat

With Margo at Franco's side, what could possibly go wrong? She was perfectly capable of handling Detectives Winchester and Reardan much better than I, especially on their own turf, which they preferred due to the number of scheduled interviews regarding Romaine's death. Besides, I had other plans first thing the following morning, having already arranged for a personal day off from school, time I expected my students to relish even though I couldn't say the same for myself. Several days after the St. Louis Kids Auction, I'd mustered the courage to call Mike Rutger, the heartbreaker I'd erased years ago only to have him resurface now, claiming to have information about the investigation that might prove helpful. We'd agreed to meet at the Saint Louis Zoo, around the same time Margo would be lending her support to Franco.

I saw Mike Rutger before he saw me, more like before I let him see me, having stationed myself behind a convenient post, one of many holding up the zoo's Living World. Dressed in skin-tight faded jeans and a navy blue sweatshirt, Mike was warming a park bench, legs stretched out and ankles crossed. Instead of the man bun he'd worn at The Ritz-Carlton, a grey headband now covered his forehead, keeping his face unobstructed but allowing the long hair to hang loose around his shoulders. Cherokee style, as if making a cultural statement. Not that there was anything wrong with honoring a person's heritage, however vague, as was the case with recent revelations regarding my Italian bloodline. Nor was anything at that zoo moment stopping me from walking away, except Mike throwing me that bone about knowing the late Val and Horace Corrigan.

My turn to bite the bullet could not be delayed any longer. One deep inhale followed by a satisfying exhale propelled me forward into the bright morning sun. While approaching Mike, I noticed his ankle-length leather boots, similar to a pricey pair I'd seen displayed in the men's department at Nordstrom. He looked up, uncrossed his ankles, and stood. Ignoring the open arms he'd positioned into a welcoming hug, I offered my hand instead. Two polite shakes and we sat down, Mike at one end of the bench and me at the other, my purse between us, creating a physical as well as an emotional barrier.

"I wasn't sure you'd come," he said.

"Don't make this about me. As you already know from eavesdropping on my private conversation—"

"It wasn't intentional, Ellie. I didn't even recognize you at first. But then you mentioned your mom and the Corrigans."

"Okay, I'll buy that. What do you know that I should know?"

He showed me his palm. "Whoa, slow down, will you. Before we get into the Corrigan stuff, can we just talk for a while?"

My heart told me no way and yet I gave him an opening. "Are you suggesting we play catch-up for the past fifteen years?"

"More like seventeen but who's counting." He leaned forward, elbows to knees, head lowered so as not to look at me. "About that long-ago day at the St. Louis Fair, I want to apologize."

I wrinkled my brow, a lame effort to look confused. "Apologize for what?"

"The shitty thing I did, dumping you with my cousin Yancy, my asshole way of letting you know it was over between us."

"Oh that. Let's see … I was almost fifteen. Your stinking cousin … seriously, he had an extreme case of halitosis … was nineteen, already married and a father according to the photo he showed me. You tried passing me off to him, as if … as if …"

"Jesus, Ellie, how could I have been such a jerk." He tilted his head in my direction, showing me those blue eyes I'd all but forgotten. "When I called to apologize, your sister read me the riot act. She told me never to call again. Then I went to your house and rang the bell. Your grandma opened the door. She seemed nice enough, even smiled. She told me to hold out one hand and show her my palm. Hell, I thought she was going to tell my fortune, her being a foreigner and all. Instead, she grabbed my hand and," he snapped two fingers, "quick as that, she sliced my palm with what looked to be an ordinary paring knife. Turned out, the damn thing was so sharp I didn't feel any pain, leastways not right away. Then, holy shit! While I stood there, trying to stop the bleeding, she threatened to cut off my dick if I ever came back."

"Nonnie Clarita? You've got to be kidding."

"Like hell, still got the scar to prove it."

He leaned back, opened his palm, and showed me a thin white line that went from the base of his thumb to above the wrist. Although seeing the scar gave me a strange satisfaction, I resisted the urge to touch it. The best I could manage was, "I guess she figured you had it coming."

"Can't argue with you there."

"Whatever happened to the girl you dumped me for?" I asked.

He scoffed at this. "After putting two and two together as to how I dumped you, she dumped me. I had that coming too."

"So that's when you stopped by my house to apologize."

"Not because of her, because of you."

Not Worth Dying For

Minutes passed with no words between us, then Mike spoke up. "Say something, will you. Hit me over the head with your purse if it'll make you feel better."

I turned to him and slung my arm over the top of the bench. "On the contrary, Mike. From the bottom of my heart, I want to thank you for humiliating me at the fair, for making sure I'd never want to see you again. It was a lesson well learned, the best I ever got."

"Weird, how we never crossed paths after that."

"I made sure we didn't."

"Right, you being in a Catholic school and all. I heard you went away to become a nun."

"Sure did, years later and not because of you. The religious life didn't work out so I left before my final vows. I'm a teacher and librarian now." Keep it vague and without emotion, I told myself. "Now what's this about Val Corrigan and his Uncle Horace?"

"Don't you want to know what I've been doing? Aside from waiting tables, which I only do now and then as a favor to my buddy, the banquet captain."

I glanced at the time on my cellphone, a non-issue for me, having taken off the entire day, but Mike didn't need to know that. "Fire away. I'm all ears."

He assumed his earlier position, outstretched legs and ankles crossed, before asking, "Cigarette?"

"No thanks."

"I ... uh ... mean, do you have any. Every so often the urge hits me even though I quit last year."

"Good for you. I never started. You were saying …."

"Oh, yeah. Well, in a nutshell, I almost got married once but she couldn't go through with it. Said I lacked commitment. What the fuck—

201

pardon my language. She had her place; I had mine. But on those days we didn't see each other, she expected me to call so she could tell me what she ate, where she went, who said what to her and what she said back. Then I was supposed to do the same with my day, from my first shit in the morning to the last one at night. Talk, talk, talk ... there's only so much talking two people should have to do, right?"

"To each his own," I said, trying not to think about the yawn I so wanted to stifle. Or of my first heartthrob taking care of private business on the john.

"More like to each *her* own," Mike said. "She married a guy who listened as much as he talked. They live in the burbs—St. Charles, with their three kids and a mortgage. Not that any of this bothers me. Don't knock what you haven't tried I always say."

"Amen," I replied.

He leaned back and closed his eyes, giving me the opportunity to turn my head and execute the much appreciated yawn before he sat up and lifted his eyelids. After a long sigh, he continued recapping his life. "For the most part, I work construction—a journeyman carpenter, which ain't bad for a guy who took five years to finish high school. At the bottom of the class, which I'm not bragging about other than to demonstrate my persistence." He showed me his broad hands, clenching them into a tight fist and then releasing in quick, repetitive motions. "Not that I'm comparing myself to Jesus, but did you know He was a carpenter. Or so the Bible says. Do you believe that?"

"No reason not to. Carpentry is a time-honored profession."

"Damn right, Ellie. Been with River City Builders since my apprentice days."

"Then you know Morgan Davisson."

"Morgan? You bet. He took a liking to me from the get-go. It's not like we exchange Christmas cards, but the man knows me by name and always speaks unless he's got more important things on his mind. Like the other night at the Ritz. His job was to schmooze; mine to be invisible."

"Except with me."

"Made you look, didn't I?"

"Against my better judgment," I said.

"You won't be sorry, I promise."

"Uh-huh. What about Val Corrigan?"

Mike squinched his eyes, then released them. "About ten years ago, after I became a journeyman, I started working on the Creole Exchange reno. That's when I first met Val Corrigan on one of his many walk-throughs. Bet you don't know what they used to make in that building."

"Haven't a clue."

"A century's worth of ladies underwear, everything from corsets and bloomers and petticoats to girdles and bras and panties."

"Who would've thought you an expert in lingerie," I said with a touch of sarcasm.

"Yeah, imagine that. See, my grandma used to work in that same building—piece work on an industrial-strength sewing machine. Talk about a weird feeling ... what's that Yogi word about all over again?"

"Déjà vu?"

"Right, sometimes I felt like Grannie's ghost was there with me."

"That's not really déjà vu."

"Close enough. For another weird thing, the Post-Dispatch ran a story on the Creole Exchange. Val had the article framed and when the building was done, he had me hang it in the lobby. Anyway, back to his uncle. Horace had bought his own personal condo for a song because it needed a makeover. Val asked if I knew a really good carpenter who might want to make some money on the side. Well, duh, I'd just moved up from apprentice and could've used the extra bucks so I offered myself. Turned out to be a win-win situation for me and the Corrigans since old man

203

Horace paid his nephew Val to jump whenever he snapped his fingers."

"Tell me about Horace," I said.

"A shitass if ever there was but not with me. Sorry about the language, Ellie. I keep forgetting you were almost a nun. What a waste that would've been. Any guy with half a brain would love to have a girl as pretty as you."

"Too late, Mike. That ship sailed long ago."

"I'm not kidding, Ellie. Back then you were pretty. Now you're just plain gorgeous."

"So I've been told." Or not, anything to keep him on track. "About Horace, you were saying?"

"Right, about Horace. Yeah, he was an SOB around some women, but not this one, Romaine … Romaine Sloane. Good-looking gal, used to be a dancer, I think. Anyway, Romaine came and went as if she owned the condo even though she didn't live there with Horace, leastways not when I was working there on weekends."

Evidently, Mike hadn't heard about the recent demise of Romaine Sloane, whatever the cause, which I figured Margo would tell me after she and Franco returned from the police station. Rather than distract Mike any further, I focused my efforts on the Corrigans. "Was Horace involved in renovating the Creole Exchange?"

"Yeah, from a distance. Like I said, Horace called the shots and Val made sure whatever Horace wanted, Horace got." He stood up, stretched his arms overhead, and plopped back down on the bench, closer to the middle, one thigh now pressed against my purse. "I don't know about you but I could use some coffee. What do you say, Ellie? My treat."

"Not today. I'd really like to move forward. Tell me about Val."

"If not today, some other day?" he asked. "I'm talking coffee."

"Uh … maybe. Right now I'm so worried about my mother and clearing her of any involvement that I can't think about anything else."

"Think again. What about finding Val's killer? And then there's Horace. Sure, the old fart had cancer but you never would've known by looking at him. Then all of a sudden he ups and dies from catching a lousy cold that went into pneumonia. Poof!" he said, gesturing with a wave of one hand. "Just like that, here today, gone tomorrow."

I shifted and looked into a pair blue eyes contrasting with a face weathered and lined, the same high cheekbones from long ago. His eyes held mine until I turned away to focus on a young mother and two kids walking across a nearby wooden bridge. He laid two fingers under my chin and turned my head in his direction.

"Look at me, Ellie. I'm not bullshitting you. Horace was too mean to die from a case of the sniffles that went haywire."

"People still die from pneumonia," I said, "even with the miracle drugs we have today."

"I got my own iPad, Ellie. I ain't stupid."

"Did I say you were?"

"The look on your face said enough."

"But not what I was thinking. Do you have proof there's more to his death than the medical report?"

"No, dammit. Just my gut feeling."

"Hmm. So, did you ever contact the police or did they contact you?"

"Not exactly, and not if I can help it. I got my own history with the cops and don't like reminding them of who I once was. Nothing serious, you understand, but when it comes to sit-downs with nosy detectives, less beats better any day of the week."

"Okay, forget about Horace for now. What about Val Corrigan. Any thoughts as to who would've wanted him dead?"

"I got a few ideas. Again, none I'd want to share with the cops. Sharing with you, on the other hand, I might consider." His phone rang and

205

he glanced at the screen. "Damn, I gotta take this." He got up, moved a few steps away from the bench, and listened more than he talked. After putting the phone back in his pocket, he said, "Problems on the job site that need me ASAP. Sorry, Ellie."

Not nearly as sorry as I was, having to ask my next question, one I'd hoped wouldn't be needed. "Would it be possible for us to meet again?"

Another annoying grin before he turned and from over his shoulder, called out, "Any time. Any place. You got my number, right?"

Memo to self:

1. *Yes, I have Mike's number.*
2. *I do not owe Mike a damn thing.*
3. *I will be nice to Mike for the sake of my mother.*
4. *Mike is not as dumb as he once was.*
5. *Mike is dumber than me and always will be.*

25

Franco and the Detectives

"Stay calm and show no fear," I told Franco. Practice what you preach, I should've told myself. We were walking across the parking area adjacent to the Fourth Precinct Station and I was trying to ignore the butterflies playing hell with my stomach, in particular the breakfast espresso and yogurt I'd inhaled moments before.

"Fear, Margo? What fear?" Franco asked. "First you say I have no reason to be afraid and now you tell me this."

"Forget about fear. Sorry I brought it up."

"Papa wanted to come with me. I told him not necessary."

"Hey, Franco. You got me, that's all you need."

"But Papa knows things you and I will never know. Did he not tell us about the war? How he was only seventeen when he killed a *paesano* who would've caused the death of more *paesani*? And how he killed those other men—German soldiers."

Franco opened the door and together we entered the police station.

207

Loretta Giacoletto

From there we were directed to a conference room where Detectives Sam Reardan and Guy Winchester were waiting.

Following a round of introductions, Reardan turned his attention to me. "And you're here because?"

"To lend moral support," I said with an inflated air of confidence.

"We'll get to that later." Reardan gestured for us to sit at the table, Franco and me across from him and Winchester. After a few preliminary questions regarding Franco's address in Italy and his visitor status here, he asked Franco about his relationship to me, Ms. Margo Savino.

"Margo? We live together. I live with her. She is my … my … *nipote*."

"Mr. Rosina means niece. He is my uncle."

Reardan raised one eyebrow. "Thank you Ms. Savino but in the future, please allow Mr. Rosina to answer all questions. That is, unless Detective Winchester or I should direct a question to you, in which case …."

"Yes, of course, my bad. It's just that sometimes I can't help myself."

"Unfortunately, should that inability to contain yourself persist, we will be obligated to help you out the door," Winchester said. "Do I make myself clear?"

"Clear as … as plastic wrap," I replied, my lame attempt at a bit of humor.

Winchester tightened his full lips into a thin, puckered line, his not-so-lame version of *knock it off*.

"So, Mr. Rosina, tell us," Winchester continued. "If Margo here is your niece, how are you and Antonia Savino related?"

"She is my sister."

"Really? You and Mrs. Savino were raised together in Italy or in America?"

Franco cleared his throat. "Me in Italy, Toni—Antonia—in America."

208

Not Worth Dying For

"Your parents divorced?"

"Never married … same papa, different mama."

"Who's older?" Reardan asked. "And by how many years?"

"Toni by four months."

Unable to take anymore, I found the courage to speak up. "Excuse me, Detective Reardan, is this interview about my mother or about my uncle and his interaction with the late Romaine Sloane? Whatever the reason, does my uncle need an attorney?"

"For a preliminary inquiry such as this, of course not," Reardan said. "Why would you think otherwise?"

"For starters, based on your line of questioning."

"Then you are representing Mr. Rosina?"

"Good grief, no. I'm not a lawyer although I do work for one, Blake Harrington. He specializes in personal injury."

"Enough, Ms. Savino," Winchester chimed in, showing me the palm of his huge hand. "Unless we invite further input from you, do not volunteer any."

I opened my mouth to protest and on hearing Franco suck in his breath, I swallowed my words so as not to jeopardize his chances for a non-eventful morning. He raised his hand for permission to speak, the simple gesture resulting in a sigh from Reardan and a nod from Winchester.

"Romaine Sloane, she was my friend," Franco said, "one of the first since my coming to America. Can I ask how she died?"

"Still waiting on the autopsy report," Winchester said. "Beyond that we prefer not to elaborate on the cause of death. However, this is what we've passed on to the news media. A passing motorist who stopped for a … personal business … discovered Ms. Sloane's body early yesterday morning outside East St. Louis—a deserted stretch along Interstate 70 in Illinois, a swamp-like haven for wild turkeys and other wildlife."

209

Loretta Giacoletto

Reardan cleared his throat. "As for a caveat we haven't shared the media yet, it is possible that Ms. Sloane died elsewhere and was brought there in the middle of the night. Happens all the time."

Silence filled the room, giving Franco and me a chance to absorb the detectives' words. I conjured up an image of the deceased Romaine Stone that sickened me to the core. Granted, the woman may've been a pain in the ass but she didn't deserve to end up like trash along the highway. No one did.

"Now that we've given you more information than the media got, what can you tell us about Ms. Sloane?" Reardan asked.

Franco cast a sideways glance in my direction.

"What? You need an okay from your niece before proceeding?"

"No okay but Margo and I met Romaine at same time. Same goes for Toni and Elena ... Ellen."

"Ellen Savino?" Winchester cleared his throat. "You're saying she knew the deceased as well."

"Si, we met at Rudi's, a nice bar although I have tasted better vino ... wine."

"Yeah, yeah, I know the place," Winchester said. "Go on."

Franco described our afternoon at Rudi's but omitted what had taken us there in the first place—allowing his Papa Stefano some long-overdue alone time with our Nonna Clarita. "Romaine gave me her telephone number, told me to call her," he said. "We talked about food, how she lived to eat and not the other way around."

"What way would that be?" Winchester asked.

"Eat to live, that's what Romaine said, which seemed odd for an American. But then I have only been in America for a short time. So, I cooked for her ... which made her very happy. I went to bed with her ... which made me very happy. Her too, if I am to believe what she told me. Not always did she tell the truth."

210

Not Worth Dying For

"How often and over what period of time?" Winchester asked.

"Is hard to say since every lie bears some truth, and every truth—"

"Forget the truth versus lies debate, at least for now. About the sex, how often and over what period of time."

"Ah-h, please forgive." Franco thought about the question, lips barely moving as he made some mental calculations. "In the three weeks since we first met, maybe seven or eight times. Maybe ten but no more than that. I'm not as young as I once was. Nothing serious. We—I mean Margo and me—were expecting her for dinner when you called last night."

"Nothing serious, you say." This from Reardan. "But was it headed in that direction?"

"No."

"That's it? Just no."

"Is no different here than in Italy, si? I was nice to Romaine because she knew things no one else knew, things about Val Corrigan. A Casanova pretender not worth dying for, that's what she told me and kept promising to tell me more the next time we made love, except she never did. As for my sister Toni Savino, she is innocent I tell you."

"And you know this because?"

I leaned over and whispered in Franco's ear. "Don't go there."

"Where?" he whispered back.

"Enough, Ms. Savino," Reardan said. "We are interested in hearing more about Romaine Sloane. Continue Mr. Rosina."

"Grazie, Detective Reardan. Romaine wanted to show me Horseshoe Lake, a car drive across the bridge into Illinois, where I'd not been before. We parked near a green area and walked to the place where this Val Corrigan's body was found. Romaine carried a single white rose, and cried as she tore off the petals one by one, letting them float to the ground. I felt sorry for the lady but feeling sorry didn't make me like her any better. What

211

I mean, want to have more sex with her. That's all I know."

Reardan drummed his sausage-like fingers on the table before turning to me, "Anything else you'd like to add, Ms. Savino?"

I took a deep breath, exhaled, and let the words spill from my mouth. "Well, Romaine told El the same thing—more to the point, that she and Val had engaged in their usual sex the night he died, and before then, on a regular basis for years. All hearsay, I get that, what with Romaine telling El and El telling me and me telling you. I do know that Franco considered Romaine a nice enough person."

He nodded. "Nice doesn't mean I wished to continue with the love."

"Nice may be somewhat of a stretch, if you ask me," I said. "As was Romaine's ability to stretch the truth. Her stories about her relationship with Val Corrigan and others kept changing every time she told them."

"Well, now," Reardan said. "Some people hesitate to speak ill of the dead. Doesn't seem to be a problem with you, Ms. Savino."

"You asked; I delivered. Not a condemnation of Romaine but rather the observations of a somewhat bitchy female, for which I make no apologies, at least not at the moment. So, unless you have any more questions, are we free to leave?"

"Not so fast," Winchester said. "We do have more, Mr. Rosina. Regarding these sexual encounters with Ms. Sloane, where did they take place?"

Franco blushed, rather charming for a man his age and unabashed sexual attitude. "At the home of my niece Elena or where Romaine lived."

Winchester flipped through his notebook, more for show than reconfirming what he most likely already knew. "That would be in the Central West End," he said, lifting his eyes to capture Franco's. "Coincidentally, the same building in which Kat Dorchester resides. Imagine that."

"Is *impossibile* for me to imagine," Franco said, "since I do not know

212

Kat Dorchester. Nor do I know where she lives, or what she looks like. The name I know, si, because she is a good friend to my sister Antonia Savino and to Antonia's family."

"What about you, Ms. Savino?"

"What about me, Detective Winchester. If you're referring to Romaine Sloane, I had no idea she lived in the same building as Kat Dorchester. Nor do I know if my mother knew where Romaine lived, although Romaine did mention something about a recent move. Now if you have no further questions for my uncle or for me …."

"Go," Reardan said with a wave of his hand. "If we need more information, we'll be in touch."

"I'm sure you will. In the meantime if either my sister and I, or both of us together, can be of any help to you, don't hesitate to call on us."

"Somehow that unlikely scenario escapes me."

"Quite understandable, Detective Reardan, since you weren't in Italy to observe El and me this past August. I'm not saying we actually solved several mysteries, but rather that we were instrumental in tying up a few loose ends."

Priceless, the look of disbelief plastered on Reardan's face.

26

Loud and Clear

"Where's Franco?" were the first words out of El's mouth when she opened her condo door. "Please don't tell me the police are holding him."

"Relax," I said, making a beeline for the sofa. "I dropped him off at Leonardo's. He's meeting somebody for lunch."

"He actually knows people on The Hill?"

"Including a few chefs imported from Italy, what can I say? The man gets around." Having kicked off my shoes, I propped my tootsies on a short stack of books displayed on the coffee table. "Speaking of lunch …."

"There's cottage cheese in the fridge. Help yourself."

"Thanks, but I'll pick something up later. So, you've given up food, how utterly courageous of you."

"To be quite honest," El confessed with remarkable candor, "not having to eat comes as a welcomed relief."

"Don't get me started. If Franco keeps up his quest for the perfect five-course meal, I may have to borrow some clothes from you. No way am

214

I springing for my own plus-size wardrobe."

"Tell me about it," she said. "I moved my larger sizes into the spare bedroom. The extra space Franco vacated was like a gift from the gods."

"That's right, rub salt in my open wound, little sis. You, the almost nun who—"

"Forget about my past life. We should be talking about your morning at the Fourth Precinct."

"So true. For starters, those smarmy detectives were more interested in Franco from a Savino family perspective than as a possible suspect in Romaine Sloane's death."

"What next. Perhaps we should consider a reality TV series."

El listened without further comment while I filled her in on the Franco meeting with Detectives Reardan and Winchester, including their sidestepping the cause of Romaine's death. After I'd covered Romaine's recent move to Kat's building, which came as a shock, plus every other detail, however minute, El took a deep breath and asked, "Should Franco be worried?"

"Not in my opinion, for what that's worth. Our zio did himself proud, so typical of the macho *Italiano*, justifying his amorous interest in Romaine, however short-lived. Pardon my morbid pun. Romaine expected sex in return for welcoming him to America and Franco was only too happy to oblige her."

"Until he wanted out," El said. "Not that I'm blaming him for what happened to her."

"That's for sure. Not everyone is as uptight as you."

"Nor as aggressive as you, Margo." One corner of her mouth curled up, reacquainting me with the El I knew so well. "Unless I'm mistaken, you've hooked up with Greg Lupino again," she said. "Mom will be so pleased, him being a practicing Catholic and all. If only he hailed from Northern Italy instead of the Calabria Region, Nonnie would be showering

215

you with hugs and kisses."

"Can't argue with you there. Although, aside from the religious angle, Greg does have some other fine qualities."

"Such as those fine diamond earrings you brought home the other night," El said. "They must've cost him a small fortune."

"Compared to other items on the auction block, I don't think so. Besides his money went for a good cause."

"You're right. Pardon me for being a jealous snot."

"I wouldn't have expected otherwise. After all, you are my little sister and I taught you well. So, how was your pow-wow with … with … Mike Somebody?"

"Rutger, Mike Rutger." She explained how Mike's occupation as a carpenter had led to his connecting with Val and Horace Corrigan. "Mike wanted to tell me more but he got an emergency call—work related—and had to leave."

"Sorry, El. Looks like you'll have to take one for the team again."

"I was hoping you'd come with me next time. You're much better at squeezing information out of unsuspecting people than I am."

I threw back my head and laughed. More like cackled, couldn't help myself. "Girl, you are so on your own now that I'm stuck with Zio Franco. Just thinking about how you outsmarted me hurts my teeth. You know, like brain freeze after biting into one of those Ted Drewes concretes. Cardinal Sin, wasn't that your fave?"

"Haven't touched that evil concoction since we got back from Italy," El said. "Nor do I intend to."

The discussion ended with me answering my phone. I listened more than I talked, and ended with a half-hearted promise to see what I could do.

"What now?" El asked, faint lines of worry already creasing her forehead.

"Kat called Mom to say she's been arrested for the murder of Val Corrigan."

"Why call Mom? Kat should've called her lawyer. Wait—don't tell me Kat didn't get a lawyer yet."

"Okay I won't but she didn't. Which means I now have to bother Blake right before his special time with Linda."

"The Harringtons go out on dates during the day, how … romantically efficient."

"Get real. Blake and Linda stay home and send the kids to her parents."

Enough with the procrastinating. I placed the dreaded call to my boss and explained Kat's inexcusable predicament. Although my phone wasn't set on speaker, I held it away from my ear so El could hear Blake sigh loud enough to make both of us wince. After giving him the pertinent information about Kat, I expressed my undying gratitude for his agreeing to contact a criminal lawyer friend. Another sigh came through loud and clear before our conversation ended.

27

Beggars and
Jailhouse Blues

Kat begged Mom to come so she did. Mom begged me to go with her so I did. To be fair, her version of begging consisted of a mere shrug when Nonnie Clarita insisted I go with my mama because that's what was expected of any God-fearing daughter who'd almost married Jesus.

After passing the jailhouse expectations, we were escorted to the visitation area and joined a mixed group of other visitors, some as ordinary as my condominium neighbors, others struggling to maintain a shred of dignity, the rest having given up the struggle.

"One more chair and Margo could've been here too," Mom said as we took our seats on the visitor side of the compartment assigned to us. "Not that we need Margo. Nor do I need you to hold my hand or to protect me from my best friend, the closest thing to a sister I'll ever have."

"How fortunate that you now have a brother as well," I reminded her.

"Half-brother I barely know."

Not Worth Dying For

"Franco's actually quite nice and a wonderful cook."

"Too wonderful. Margo tells me she's gained four pounds."

"Two of which she's already lost," I countered.

"Do you think he killed Romaine Sloane?"

"Good grief, no! True, the police questioned him about her death but they also questioned Margo—because she happened to be there with Franco."

"She's still reeling from all that police drama," Mom said, "a good excuse for not supporting Kat in her time of need."

"Two visitors per day, that's the maximum number allowed each prisoner."

"Prisoner, how utterly outrageous. Kat didn't kill Val any more than I did. Just because there's a videotape of Kat leaving her garage after I told police the two of us went to bed around midnight doesn't make her a killer."

"Maybe the detectives figured out who was Kat's passenger in the car that night."

"All I know is that passenger wasn't me."

A good answer whether true or not. After all, this was the county jail and what better area to bug. I didn't tell Mom what Margo had told me, that Romaine Sloane lived in the same building as Kat Dorchester. All in good time, I rationalized. A door swung open from the prisoner side and in walked a guard with Kat, tall and proud as any runway model, even in the same drab clothing the other incarcerated females were wearing, but lacking the panache Kat was able to pull off.

[She sat across from Mom and me, our compartment separated by a see-through acrylic window. Tears streamed down Mom's face, a stark contrast to the lack of emotion visible in Kat's. They both picked up the wall phone receivers and Mom shared hers with me.

219

Loretta Giacoletto

"What took you so long?" Kat asked. She ignored Mom's hand pressed against the window.

"Red tape, that's what," Mom said, letting her hand slip away. "Did you get a lawyer?"

Kat scoffed. "Not the best. You got the best—Fred Montgomery. Nor did I get the second best. Nor the third, fourth or fifth."

"How do you know he's not that good," Mom said. "Give him a chance."

"Her, Toni. Any *him* I could've handled. Any *him* could've handled me better."

"A female lawyer for a female client accused of killing her lover ... sorry." My voice trailed off. I'd said too much and not enough.

"Is she arranging for bail?" Mom asked.

"*She* has a name—Molly Billingsworth. Ever heard of her? Didn't think so. Looks to be a year or two out of high school, supposedly clerked for one of the best criminal lawyers in St. Louis. As for her performance so far—ain't gonna be no bail. Since the charge is murder, I've been remanded into custody. The least Molly could've done was bring me my own clothes as promised. Negative on that too."

"Oh, Kat, I'm so sorry," Mom said. "If only you'd called Blake Harrington like Margo suggested."

"Look who's talking, bitch!" Kat slammed the side of her fist on the counter.

The guard stepped forward and gave Kat a cautionary stare, to which Kat made a show of patting her heart before apologizing. After the guard retreated, Kat moved in closer to the window and continued her telephone tirade in a menacing whisper that made the hair on my arms quiver.

"Dearest Toni and former BFF. If only you'd stayed away from Val when I got sick ... if only you'd not given Val an excuse to fuck you ... if only the two of you hadn't fucked with me ... neither of us would be sitting

220

here now ... and maybe, just maybe, Val would still be alive. Until your precious Joe died, you had everything. After he died, you still had memories of the good times. But was that enough ... no-o-o. You had to take my guy too, the best fuck I ever had, bar none. I hate you, Toni, more than the turnips and collard greens my grandma forced down my throat when I was a kid. Be assured, if I go down for this, I am taking you down with me. All the way to hell if I have to."

By this time tears were spilling from Mom's eyes. I transferred the receiver from her hand to mine, and spoke in a whisper to keep my voice from shaking. "How can I help, Auntie Kat?"

She smiled, as if first aware of my being there. "Bless you, Ellen. First, get that simpering woman out of my face. Then, find out who killed Val and that bitch Romaine."

"Speaking of Romaine, the police know she lived in your building."

"She did?" Mom said. "I had no idea."

"What the fuck, Ellen. Tell me something I don't already know. That's why my ass is in here and your mom's is out there." She paused to spit in Mom's direction. Not a pretty site, watching that stream of saliva roll down the acrylic separating Kat from us. Mom walked away, but not me. Not after coming this far.

"Can we talk some more?" I asked. "I really do want to help."

"Sure, kiddo. Let's get this shit over with."

"The night Val died, that condo security shot of you pulling out of the garage—Romaine was sitting in the passenger seat?"

"Bingo! I barely knew the woman. But after Toni went to bed, Romaine came tapping at my door with this sob story about her car being in the shop. Said she needed a ride to the apartment of a friend. Coincidentally, a block from Val's, although I didn't make a connection at the time. What a dunce I was—delivering Romaine to my lover, not knowing my lover was also her lover."

221

Loretta Giacoletto

"I'm so sorry, Kat."

"I know, sweetie. Good thing you don't take after your mother."

Rather than going there, I took the high road. "Anything else?"

"Yeah, if you have time, maybe give Jet Gregson a call. Since I'm stuck in here, I might have her close on a few of my pending real estate deals."

"But I thought you and Jet didn't get along."

"You thought right. Jet can't stand me almost as much as I can't stand her. But when it comes to closing high-end real estate, Jet's almost as savvy as yours truly."

Memo to self:

1. *Never cross Auntie Kat.*
2. *Auntie Kat is meaner than Mom.*
3. *Mom is not as mean as she used to be.*
4. *Real estate makes strange bed fellows.*
5. *Dog-eat-dog has certain advantages.*

28

For Old Times Sake

I waited until the next afternoon before calling Mike Rutger. After vetoing his suggestions for dinner—local diner, fast food, or upscale casual—plus the possibility of a graphic horror movie, I convinced him that a walk after he got off work would be the best option. We agreed on Carondelet Park, our go-to place as teenagers although neither of us mentioned that. The September weather had turned cooler than its original forecast, making me glad I'd wrapped a hoodie around my shoulders. We practically bumped into each other on the walking trail and from there, we strolled at a comfortable pace for conversation.

"Seems like old times," Mike said. "You and me walking down this path like we used to."

"It was never just the two of us. You always had an entourage."

"Yeah, right, just like the guy on TV that made a name for himself. Unlike me, oh well. As for my buddies, they all had crushes on the Savino sisters."

"No, they had a crush on Margo."

He scoffed at this. "Lot of good that did. Miss High and Mighty couldn't be bothered with any of them. Not that I blame her. Billie wound up in prison; so did Joey Coconuts. The other guys got the hell out of Dodge as soon as they could make it on their own." He paused for a moment. "So, that was Margo sitting next to you the other night, her and the architect."

"You know Greg Lupino?"

"Anybody who ever worked on the Creole Exchange, I know. Some better than others. Lupino was a young pup starting out, same as me. He used to walk around the site carrying a set of construction documents."

"Greg came here from Italy as a child," I said. "He worked his way up the ladder."

"Well pardon me for being born in America and having Cherokee blood flowing through my veins. I worked my way up too, only on a different ladder. And pardon me for showing up today in my work clothes. If you hadn't been in such a hurry, I'd've cleaned up before coming here."

"Really, it's not a problem," I assured him. In fact, other than the work clothes, Mike looked about the same as when we got together at the zoo. Margo would've labeled him a stud but that was Margo. She had a thing for long-haired guys wearing tight jeans and steel-toed work boots; the only thing missing was his hard hat. I conjured up an image of him on a construction site, having found his niche in the work world. He would've been the only guy not to whistle when a pretty girl walked by; and the only guy the pretty girl would've given a second glance.

"You seeing anybody?" he asked, catching me off guard.

"Not at the moment."

"Me neither. I was wondering if—"

"Sorry, not now," I said, in my heart knowing *not now* meant *not ever.* "Too much on my plate, what with my mother and Val Corrigan. A huge misstep on her part; but one that cannot be undone. I suppose you heard about Romaine Sloane."

"Yeah, what a bummer. Romaine must've pissed off somebody, big time."

"How well did you know her?" I asked.

"Well enough that she put the make on me twice. Once in a display condo at the Creole and once at Horace's place, right before he came home from wherever he'd been making even more money. Jeez, it took some scrambling for me to put on a straight face. Romaine too. Good-looking or not, the woman had enough rings around her trunk to be my mother. Plus she couldn't stop blabbering about certain things better left unsaid."

"Such as?"

He slowed his pace and then stopped, taking a moment to reflect before answering. "The body of a homeless guy that turned up one morning at the Creole and within the hour disappeared forever."

"You mean the dead man?" We started walking again, a little faster than before.

"Who else, the guy who once was but ain't no more, along with every trace that he ever existed."

"Tell me more."

"Like I said, some things are better left unsaid, leastways for now."

The only sounds I heard for another minute or two were that of chirping birds and cicadas along with four feet hitting the asphalt-paved trail. Then Mike spoke up. "You must be in pretty good shape, Ellie. Keeping up with me and all."

"Just got back from Italy," I said, making an effort not to sound winded. "Over there everybody walks instead of jumping in the car for a five-minute drive."

"Is it true what they say about Italian men?" He paused, waiting for a response from me. When I didn't take the bite, he added, "Them being great lovers, I mean."

"I know what you mean. Now about Val and Horace ..."

"Okay, I get it. After me spilling my guts to you the other day, you're giving me squat in return."

I stopped without warning, causing Mike to bump into me. "Whoa," he said, one calloused hand grabbing me by the elbow. "Look, I'm sorry if I said the wrong thing. It's pretty much my M.O.—that's modus operandi. You know—"

"I know what it means." My voice felt distant and hollow while I felt my eyes growing wider, focusing on the elderly couple walking toward Mike and me. He let go of my elbow and I shifted to the left, putting a good six inches between us.

"Sweet Jesus," Mike said. "Don't tell me that's your grandma."

By this time Nonnie and Stefano were within spitting distance of us. "Remain calm," I said, using my school librarian voice although several decibels lower. "The woman can smell fear a mile away."

"Great," Mike said. "Just what I need, a senior citizen rumble, followed by another disorderly conduct charge. Not that I've had that many."

That many, really. Before I could respond with a smart-ass comment, Nonnie had me wrapped in her arms. "Ellen, fancy meeting you here." Squeezing tighter, she whispered in my ear, "Is that who I think it is?"

No point in answering the obvious. I released myself from her grip, stepped back, and hugged Stefano. He and I exchanged the cheek kisses Nonnie and I had omitted in keeping with our Americanized custom.

"Well, don't just stand there," she said. "Introduce us to your young man."

Tongue tied for a brief moment, I found my voice and in the course of introducing, described Stefano Rosina as family from Italy. Mike extended his hand and along with a warm smile, welcomed Stefano to America.

"Is not my first time," Stefano said. "Fifty-nine years ago I came to

St. Louis for a short visit."

Long enough for him to make a baby with Clarita, the love of his life—no need to go there. Or where Nonnie describes the heartbreaking hotel scene. No need to worry about a re-spilling of family secrets, at least for the moment. Not with Nonnie viewing Mike through suspicious eyes while gathering a few choice words to spill from her mouth.

"The last time we met, I gave you something to remember me by," she said.

"I still have it," Mike replied, holding up the palm of his right hand as a gesture of peace.

"Monti di venere," Nonnie said, obviously pleased with what she saw. "Mount of Venus, I learned that from a gypsy in Italy."

"A gypsy without the bloodline—in other words, a fake," Stefano said as he stepped forward for a close-up view. Holding Mike's hand in his, Stefano traced the thin white scar curving upward from the base of Mike's thumb to the web. "Clarita, you did this?"

"To protect *our* granddaughter." Nonnie's words made me flinch and Stefano stand a little taller. She stuck her face in Mike's "It worked, didn't it? You never came back."

"Until now," he said without flinching. "In hopes of clearing Mrs. Savino's good name."

"What're you saying? That my daughter's name is no longer good?"

One corner of Mike's mouth twitched, just barely. He shoved both hands in his pockets. I did the charitable thing and came to his rescue. "Nonnie, Mike used to work for ... with Val Corrigan. He knew him better than most."

"Ah-h, then maybe you know something the police don't know."

"More than one something, ma'am."

"We should talk. You'll come to our house then. Now, I mean."

227

Mike looked at me for approval. I shrugged, leaving the decision up to him.

"Soon will be dark," Stefano said. "No woman should be out here alone after dark."

"Ellie has me, sir," Mike said without looking in my direction. "Sort of, considering we're not exactly friends. Nor enemies, at least for the moment. On second thought, I'd be honored to step inside your home, Mrs. ... I'm sorry. I don't recall your last name."

"Mrs. R will do," she said, giving me a wink.

Leave it to Nonnie. Riva or Rosina, the letter R worked for either surname.

Enduring another hour or two, possibly more, with Mike Rutger was not how I'd planned on spending the remainder of an evening that might've translated to reading or watching TV had I been at home alone. Nor had I envisioned my evening as one quarter of a foursome that also included Nonnie and Stefano since Mom was getting ready to leave just as we walked through the kitchen door. Outwardly, she'd regained her composure since our recent jailhouse visit to Kat Dorchester. Inwardly was anybody's guess.

"Of course, I remember you," she said when I introduced Mike to her. "Nice to see you again, after so many years."

After so many years being the key to her polite demeanor. After Mike stopped coming around those many years ago, not once did she ask what had happened between us. In her defense, and mine to this day, ours— Mike and mine—was an innocent fling destined to run its course. More like, after my father put a stop to it. Thankfully, with none of the deadly repercussions Nonnie and Stefano had experienced with their passionate teenage romance in Italy.

"Mike worked on the Creole Exchange as a carpenter," I told Mom.

"With River City Builders, ma'am, from beginning to end," he added.

Not Worth Dying For

"I saw you there early on, twice, maybe more, with Horace Corrigan."

"How bizarre," she said with a raise of her brow. "I don't recall seeing you."

"Only because I didn't want you to, ma'am. Wasn't sure how you'd react and didn't want to get my ass fired. Pardon my language."

"It's not your language I find offensive but rather your low opinion of me. More to the point, my character as a professional."

"Mom, Mike. Please, could we just get on with the Creole skeletons?"

"Sounds good to me," Mike said, "beings I know where most of the skeletons are hidden. Or buried."

"Really, you've seen these skeletons?"

"Enough to rattle a few nasty walls and friable pipes—you know, lead-based paint and asphalt-wrapped pipes."

"I'm well acquainted with the environmental issues associated with renovating old buildings." She hesitated, hand still gripping the doorknob. "We should talk sometime soon."

"Any time, Mrs. Savino. I can still taste those cookies you used to send out to the front porch for me and my buddies."

"Nonnie made those," I said, beating Mom to a punch that would've been sharper than the one I delivered. "We call them biscotti."

"Either way, they sure were good."

"Damn right they were and still are," Nonnie said, plopping a bottle of wine on the table, along with the essential corkscrew. "Anybody who wants to help Toni out of the mess she got herself into, sit down. We got the biscotti. We got the vino. And Mike's got the skeletons."

"You still leaving, Antonia?" Stefano asked. "Not that I am telling you what you should do."

"Mom?" I said, hoping she'd decide to stay.

229

Loretta Giacoletto

The look on Mom's face screamed *don't bother me. Can't you see I have nothing better to do than this, whatever this is?* Nevertheless, her face softened and she removed her grip on the doorknob, making me feel better about giving up my nothing evening. Only Margo would've completed the picture, highly unlikely with Greg Lupino once again in her picture.

We sat down to Nonnie's biscotti, dunked in homemade wine supplied by Southern Illinois friends whose families two generations before had emigrated from the Italian alpine village of Pont Canavese. Just as Nonnie had done after World War II. The same Piemonte village where Margo and I recently met our up-until-then unacknowledged grandpa and uncle. Family skeletons too complicated for the likes of Mike Rutger, who'd somehow crept back into my life while I was still reeling from a disastrous affair in Italy. One thing was for sure. Any skeletons discussed that evening would be limited to Mom's so-called involvement in Val Corrigan's murder. And other issues, however relevant, since one thing often leads to another and another.

"You like?" Nonnie asked Mike while he wiped the back of one hand over dribbles of wine dotting his chin.

"You bet, Mrs. R, even better than when we used to dip those cookies … biscotti … in Mello Yello. From now on I'm calling this my all-time favorite way to a good night's sleep."

Mello Yello, I hadn't touched it in years, not since the Fourth of July afternoon before Mike broke my heart at the Riverfront Fair. After getting home that day, I went through the fridge and tossed out every can of Mello Yello, along with those in the pantry. That was then, when life at fourteen was simpler but no less painful than my now life at thirty-two.

"Not so fast," I said when Stefano made a pass at refilling the empty glasses.

"She means *basta*," Nonnie told Stefano.

"Then that's what she should say," he replied while continuing to add wine to each glass, including mine, which I'd already changed my mind about not needing.

230

Not Worth Dying For

"So, Mike," I said to get the long-awaited ball rolling. "You're here to tell us about the Creole skeletons. How about starting with the homeless man."

"You knew the homeless living in the Creole?" Mom asked.

"That I did, ma'am, some better than others. There was this one guy, Wilton Blue, a Vietnam vet I took to the VA hospital for some tests. Dropped him off during my lunch break and picked him up when my work day ended. Next morning Wilt's madder than hell, all worked up about a locket with his mother picture inside that went missing from his corner of the Creole's second floor. To make matters worse, he accused Horace Corrigan of stealing the locket, along with a moth-eaten army blanket, as if Horace needed anything belonging to the squatters. There was no consoling Wilt. I helped him look for his stuff, even went through the other squatters' stuff. At risk to my own life, I might add. Let me tell you, what little those folks had, no one else would've wanted; but to them, their rocks and newspaper clippings and wrinkled photos told the story of the life they once lived.

"Anyway, Wilt may've been down and out, but the man was no dummy. Supposedly, he studied environmental science before getting drafted into the army. That morning he stood outside the building going off about certain hazardous materials in the building not being disposed of properly and Horace conspiring with the environmental engineer to cover up the oversight. Wilt threatened to take his story to the newspaper and TV. Most folks—squatters—would've said: fat chance of that ever happening; what with him being homeless and all. On the other hand ..." Mike inadvertently showed his palm with the Mount of Venus scar, "don't ever underestimate an underdog who makes sense to anyone willing to listen. It's all about getting the right audience to hear that dog bark."

"So what happened to the *ciarlone?*" Nonnie asked.

"She means blabbermouth," Mom said.

"Hold your horses, ma'am. I'm getting there."

Stefano wrinkled his brow and nudged Nonnie. "Horses? Who said anything about horses?"

Loretta Giacoletto

"Mike means we should be patient," Mom said.

"*Scusami*," Stefano said. "From now on I will be patient and keep quiet." He leaned over and kissed Nonnie's cheek, prompting Mom to relax her pursed lips before draining the last drops of wine from her glass.

I gestured for Mike to continue.

"To make matters worse," Mike said, "Wilt's Bible disappeared. I offered to bring him a Gideon that belonged to my ma before she passed but Wilt wanted no part of it. What the hell, a Bible's a Bible, ain't it. Right, Ellie? You were almost a nun."

"Don't even think about going there," Nonnie said, arms folded across her chest.

"Elena, you a nun?" Stefano asked. "This I do not understand."

"*Almost a nun*, Stefano," Mom said.

"Stefano, bah! Nor do I understand why my only daughter cannot call me Papa."

"Good grief," Mom said. "Must we expose our family skeletons to … to Mike, a near stranger who couldn't care less one way or the other."

"No problem, Mrs. Savino. There's more than a few skeletons rattling my cage."

"Just get on with the story," I said.

"Uh … sure. Where was I? Oh yeah, the Bible I should never have brought up. Sorry about that. Anyway, the next morning when I go to work, what do I see but smoke belching from one of the second floor windows, same area Wilt called home. A trash fire he started. To keep warm, he said since the furnace hadn't kicked on yet for cold weather, which didn't surprise me since the building was getting a new heating system. Good thing me and some of the workers put the fire out, I mean before the firetruck showed up and created an even bigger mess that would've taken weeks to clean up.

Not Worth Dying For

"Couple days later Reliable Systems starts tearing out the old boiler. Wouldn't you know, about that same time Wilt goes the way of his Bible." Mike snapped two fingers. "Just like that, gone with the wind, never to be seen again, leastways to my knowledge. Hell, I even checked the VA hospital and got zero."

"Any idea what happened to him?" I asked.

"Not exactly, other than what Romaine Sloane said about a dead squatter disappearing from the Creole one night. It might've been Wilt or maybe some other guy in the wrong place at the wrong time. Can't speak for the squatters but if any of them knew, they weren't about to say."

"Anything else worth sharing?" I asked.

"Nothing I can think of at the moment," he said with a shrug. "About the squatters, I mean. Now the Corrigan duo, they're another story." The familiar sound of a vibrating phone erupted from Mike's shirt pocket. "Sorry," he said, checking the screen. "I'd better take this call." He excused himself and stepped out the back door, only to return moments later. "Gotta go but whenever you want my take on the Corrigans, just call. Ellie's got my number."

Memo to self:

1. *Yes, Mike, I still have your number.*
2. *Hey, Mike. I'm glad Nonnie gave you something to remember her by.*
3. *Mom likes you, Mike. Don't get any ideas about me.*
4. *I miss my dad but Stefano will do in a pinch.*

29

If Walls Could Talk

After a hectic day at the office of Blake Harrington, LLC, Attorney at Law, I dropped by El's place and let myself in with the extra key she'd given me, in case of an emergency. Fat chance of El ever encountering an emergency, other than the three times she saved my ass in Italy. But we were no longer in Italy.

Not one enticing fragrance floated from the kitchen to greet me. Not one offer of a good quality wine to wet my lips. Those temptations I could've gotten in my own home, courtesy of Franco Rosina. Or not. Our uncle had made a few friends on The Hill, among them a sous chef and his line cook—Southern Italians who had extended the hospitality of their short-handed trattoria kitchen, an offer that Northern Italian Franco had wisely accepted, in spite of the difference in their knowledge of regional dishes. Helping out, Franco had explained his new situation, which translated to unpaid labor, the only kind his visitor visa would allow.

I found El out on her postage-stamp balcony, relaxing in one of two canvas chairs, feet propped against the iron railing as she basked in the treasured solitude I disrupted without a single pang of guilt. I settled into the other chair and listened with a touch of annoyance while she filled me

234

Not Worth Dying For

in on her interactions with Mike Rutger. First, their stroll in the park and later, over wine and biscotti with our nonnie, our mother, and the biological papa she resented having around. I looked down my nose at El and asked why I'd not been included in the Corrigan discussion with Mike, who obviously knew more about the deceased than we first thought.

"Because, in your words," El said, "where Mike was concerned, you insisted I take one for the team. *Again,* being the keyword I take pleasure in adding for complete disclosure."

"Must you always be so ... so nun-appropriate?" I'd almost forgotten about my one-time hyphenated description of El and rather enjoyed resurrecting it. "Did he ... Mike ... ask about me?"

El narrowed her eyes, all the better to ponder my question. "Hmm, as a matter of fact he did. Miss High and Mighty he called you."

"What?! The nerve of him."

"Coming from Mike, it's more a compliment than an insult. Back then his buddies all had a crush on you. None of them turned out worth a damn although Mike must be doing okay for himself. Or not, depending on one's definition of okay. Either way, not my problem."

Did I detect a slight case of nostalgia on El's part? Please, any nobody but Mike Rutger who qualified as Jerk of the Year way back when. As for the here and now, one could only hope her real first love, the unavailable Italian who claimed her virginity, had resolved the personal issues keeping them apart, such as El not being her first love's first love. What a bummer, this thing called love. It's all about timing and El had crossed paths with her Italian at the wrong time.

"Wake up, Margo," I heard El say, her voice echoing from a distant chamber. "Have you even heard a single word I said?"

"Excuse me? Talk about calling the kettle black, where have you been these past thirty-two years? As you well know, I am perfectly capable of listening to you while thinking to myself at the same time and absorbing both perspectives with a spot-on degree of understanding."

235

"Your version of multi-tasking," El said. "I'm impressed."

As usual, we called a truce before our playful potshots got out of hand. I convinced El—okay, we decided together—that a walk through the Creole Exchange inner workings, the guts of the building, might provide some clues to the disappearance of one, Wilton Blue. And in the event of discovering foul play, if it might've tied into the death of Val Corrigan, and possibly Uncle Horace, plus that of Romaine Sloane. Mustn't forget Romaine, whose murder had been downgraded to a single paragraph in the Post-Dispatch Local Crime section. Since we needed to pick the brains of a few people in the Creole know, I told El to set up a time with Mike Rutger and I would do the same with Greg Lupino.

El all but stamped her foot, reminding me of our mother. Scary, since I tend to be more like Mom, not that I'm bragging about this annoying cross I must bear. Nevertheless, to appease El, I agreed to call both Greg and Mike, fully expecting she would change her mind about Mike and call him herself. Not a chance in hell. Good for El—she'd finally developed some backbone, even if it was at my expense.

Back in the privacy of my own condo—Franco was *volunteering* at Trattoria Tino—and after a series of back and forth phone calls that felt too much like working overtime, I managed to coordinate a Saturday afternoon group meet at the Loft District's Creole Exchange. And since my personal agenda included Saturday evening with Greg, I had El pick me up that afternoon. We found a parking spot on the street and began our two-block walk to the Creole.

"Do we have a plan?" El asked as we turned onto Washington Avenue and headed west.

I rocked one hand back and forth, a habit I'd picked up from Franco. "Maybe so, maybe not."

"Good grief, you sound just like our uncle," El said.

"Can't help myself. Perhaps it's time he moved back in with you."

"He's been staying with you how long?"

"Long enough for me to gain four pounds and with tremendous willpower—"

"Managed to lose two of those pounds," El said, "Or so you already told me. I take it Franco's still working at Tino's."

"The man's in hog heaven and eating like a king, even though he claims the food is too Americanized to be authentic Italian. Since he's gone most evenings, Greg and I have the place to ourselves."

"Then Greg knows why we invited him."

"Of course, as does Mike Rutger. It's not like they don't have anything better to do on a Saturday afternoon. Although in Mike's case, he jumped at the idea of spending another hour with you."

El scoffed at this but she didn't fool me. No way, no how. The girl needed a touch of romance in her life, something to tide her over until the real thing came along, or came back.

Over the years I'd driven through the Loft District countless times but until that afternoon had never viewed the Creole Exchange up close. Nor had a reason to venture inside. When El and I walked through the revolving door, I couldn't help but notice the wide expanse of terrazzo floor, a diamond-shaped pattern throughout the lobby and hallway leading to a coffee bar, beauty salon, nail salon, and real estate development office among other convenience shops. Directly ahead at the elevator bank, Greg and Mike were engaged in a lively conversation, non-confrontational or so it appeared from my vantage point. What an odd pairing—two guys from either end of a St. Louis spectrum, one clinging to mid-twentieth-century values and the other carving out his own niche.

"I told you they knew each other," El said, once again showing off her ability to read my thoughts, even those I preferred not to share.

"And your point is?" I asked.

"Nothing profound, other than keeping a lid on Mike Rutger," she said. "And don't even think about anything as unthinkable as our double dating with you and Greg. Mike is a means to an end, strictly business on my part."

Loretta Giacoletto

"You are so right. The very thought of that jerk slobbering on you makes me want to toss my cookies."

"Spare me the graphic insight, Margo."

I could've elaborated without the graphics but Greg was fast approaching as was the object of our distrust, Mike Rutger, a far cry from his Ritz-Carlton waiter image or the teenager I'd kicked out of El's life years ago. In today's light, not bad for a diamond in the rough but most definitely not in the same league with Greg Lupino. Greg kissed me on the cheek while El maintained her Sunday Mass routine, extending three unsure fingers for Mike to grasp for a brief moment before she pulled away as if he might infect her with a contagious disease. Paybacks were hell, no matter how often they stung or how trivial the offense. I almost felt sorry for the guy. After separating myself from Greg, I turned to Mike with an equal opportunity smile plastered on my face.

"Mike, you devil you!" I said. "How long has it been—other than auction night at the Ritz?"

Before he could say something clever, El answered on his behalf. "Seventeen years at least, although I could be wrong. It's not like I keep tabs on such trivial matters. Shall we get started?"

"Not before I give an old friend a proper greeting," he said, placing his hands on my shoulders. I took his cue and leaned forward, our lips but a few inches apart. I closed my eyes to avoid gazing into his, and waited. Mike's next move came as a total shocker, one laced with a touch of erotic humor. He actually licked the tip of my nose, leaving behind a trace of saliva before kissing the damn thing away, which left me wide-eyed and blushing like I hadn't in years. What started as a giggle between us soon erupted into a hardy laugh that ended with me doubled over. "Damn, you taste good," Mike said, taking my elbow to help me straighten up. "I've wanted to do that for as long as I can remember."

"Was *that* all you expected it would be?" I asked, having regained my composure.

"Oh, yeah. And more."

238

Mission accomplished. Between Mike and me, we'd managed to jerk El's chain, big time. I could feel the tension exploding in mid-air, its aftermath creeping into my bones. Greg, on the other hand, was more amused than annoyed, a plus benefit of knowing he and I belonged to each, at least for the moment; perhaps longer, depending on the sustainability of our relationship. He jiggled one of the Creole's utility keychains, signaling us to join him at the elevator and pressed the UP button.

"Can't leave home without that crutch?" I asked, referring to Greg's grip on the case containing his Notebook.

"Not today." He patted the pricey leather satchel. "I brought the Creole's original construction plans as well as other pertinent information."

The elevator door opened and we stepped aside, allowing the exit of two kids on a sugar-high and their exhausted dad. Not any run-of-the-mill dad but Trey Millstone, El's convenient date for the Ritz auction. The elevator doors closed, leaving us still in the lobby where we exchanged greetings with Trey and met his kids. Only then did I notice Trey's ex waiting off to one side. Her I recognized from the last time Greg and I had been dating. I caught her eye and we both waved before Trey passed the kids to her, a changing of the guard, so to speak, from one loving protector to the other. Choose wisely and only once, I reminded myself in deference to Kat Dorchester, which may've accounted for my still being single. Trey ended the exchange with a peck on his ex's cheek, followed by another round of hugs and kisses with the kids. In spite of the show of modern civility, his eyes were welled with tears when he strolled over to where we'd resumed our positions near the elevator.

"Hello again, one and all," he said, giving the four of us a collective once-over. "What brings you to the Creole on this fine Saturday afternoon?"

Using the minimalistic approach of a man anxious to move on, Greg explained our mission in as few words as possible. "Just trying to get a handle on some renovation issues that may've been passed over during the final inspection."

"Such as?" Trey asked with a raised brow.

239

Loretta Giacoletto

"Won't know 'til we see them," Mike chimed in, making me cringe at his brash attitude toward a well-respected city alderman.

As did Trey, or so I thought, until he took a closer look at Mike and smiled broadly. "I thought I recognized you from the Ritz—sure as the goblins will be out on Halloween and my kids'll be trick or treating, come hell or high water. Mike ... Mike Rutger, you ol' son of a ... you worked here during the renovation."

"From beginning to end," Mike said. "Never missed a workday."

"And supposedly knows where all the skeletons are hidden," El added, her first acknowledgment of Mike since he made a show of licking my nose.

"Skeletons?" Trey asked with a chuckle. "What makes you think there are skeletons?"

"Ghosts, trolls, skeletons—doesn't every building collect a few over the years?" I asked.

"Uh ... nope. Have yet to see a single ghost or detect any foul odors it would bring."

It was all I could do to keep myself from shaking Trey, anything to jar his memory. "By any chance do you recall a man named Wilton Blue who used to hang around here?"

Trey thought a minute. "Homeless Vietnam vet. One squatter among many, all forced to leave when construction got underway."

"Actually, Wilt disappeared weeks before the serious work began," Mike said. "About the same time Reliable installed the new heating and cooling system."

"Right." Trey rubbed his chin. "Wilt insisted there were environmental issues that would create health hazards if not addressed during the demolition process. Now that I think about it, I arranged for Channel 4 to interview him near the Soldiers Memorial. But when Wilt didn't show up, the story went bye-bye, flushed down the tubes, so to speak. Never saw the guy after that, figured he moved on."

240

Not Worth Dying For

"We should move on too," Greg said, one finger on the elevator button. "You're welcome to join us, Trey."

"Nah, thanks but I got things to do, places to be."

"One more question," I said. "Other than Channel 4, did you tell anyone about Wilt Blue's concerns?"

Again, as with El's question, Trey gave some thought to mine before answering. "I wasn't living here at the time, more like hanging out, as were a number of other owners, bugging the Corrigans to get Creole finished so we could move in. That said, I wasn't about to tackle polluted air or friable asbestos on my own."

"Friable asbestos?" El asked.

"Traces of asbestos dust left behind after removing ceilings, floors, roofs, and pipes containing asbestos," Greg said while we watched the elevator door open to admit one individual and then close, again leaving us to continue our conversation with Trey. "If the stripped area hadn't been sealed properly, dust would get tracked all over the building. An obvious turn-off for potential buyers and those already committed, but from a practical standpoint not likely to make people sick."

"Either way, who wants to take a chance on contacting mesothelioma," Trey said. "Not me, that's for sure. Damn right I went to Val Corrigan. Whatever needed doing, Val was the man who pulled the right strings to get it done."

"And did he get the asbestos dust resolved?" El asked.

"Hell, yes. At least to my knowledge. Val assured me he had, as did Boris Tainer."

"That would be the environmental engineer," Greg said, directing his next words to me. "You met him at the auction, Margo."

"Right, Jet Gregson's date. Small world, isn't it."

"Even smaller, considering Jet was property manager of the Creole in its early years."

241

Loretta Giacoletto

"Funny you didn't mention that at the Ritz," El said.

"Didn't seem important at the time," Trey said. "Nor does it now, unless you know something I don't."

"Not a thing," El said. "Just making an observation—Jet's connection with Boris Tainer."

"Even I know Boris," Mike said, obviously itching to contribute anything of value. "When it comes to developing commercial real estate and all the shit that goes with it, you better believe everybody involved knows each other, or knows about them, or, in my case, the head honchos."

"Well, Mike," El said, "since you know so much, what about Val's Uncle Horace?"

"Like I told you before, the old man delegated. Val executed. Not literally but you get my drift."

By this time the door to the elevator opened again. I took the lead and stepped inside, as did everyone else including Trey. When the door opened on the sixth floor, he said a quick goodbye and left. Not a word was spoken as we ascended two more floors and stepped out to the roof level where caterers were all abuzz, setting up for an evening event. Quite the party, I surmised, judging from the array of linens, china, and barware.

To my right I took in a distant view of picturesque church steeples dotting North St. Louis—a once proud area that over the years had fallen on hard times, into a domino effect of crime and poverty not visible from our perch high above. El had taken her place beside me; I grabbed her hand and squeezed it.

"Remember when you wanted nothing more than to serve the poor," I said. "Had you stuck with the religious vocation, you could've been down there serving God instead of up here thinking about it."

"She never belonged down there," Mike said, gesturing with his chin. "Take it from one who knows, being that close to God ain't all it's cracked up to be."

242

Not Worth Dying For

"Money isn't everything," El said, pulling her hand from mine and stepping away from Mike.

He scoffed. "Says those who have plenty. For the rest of us, it comes damn near close."

"Money can't buy good health," I said, thinking about my dad who'd carried enough insurance to cover his medical expenses. And funeral.

"You got me there," Mike said. "But when it comes to food and fun, money sure comes in handy."

"Over here, people," Greg called out from the other side. "Unless you're waiting for the stars to come out and sprinkle happy dust."

Enough about the haves and the have-nots. We hurried over to where Greg stood near the utilities section. He opened one door and ushered us inside. "The mechanical room," he explained and began pointing out the various aspects of it. Having removed his Notebook from the satchel, he opened it to the Creole's floor plan and matched up certain features from the drawings to the physical equipment before us. From there, we moved on to a second room that housed the elevator shaft.

"Okay to look inside?" Mike asked, his hand already on the slide.

"Be my guest," Greg said.

Mike pushed the slide open and the four of us peered down the shaft.

"It's a long way to the bottom," Mike said. "If the fall didn't kill you, the thought of splattering on impact most likely would."

"Must you be so graphic," El said.

"Must you be so uptight," Mike countered, confirming what I'd known about El for years.

"Must you both be so confrontational," Greg said. "Margo and I have better things to do on a Saturday afternoon than play referee."

"Amen," I said, squeezing his hand. "Carry on, please."

After Mike closed the shaft door, we waited for the next elevator and on entering it, Greg pressed the sixth floor button. "Don't tell me you're suggesting a potty break at Trey's condo," El said as we stepped out.

"Wouldn't dream of it," Greg said. "I want to give you some idea of the general layout on each floor." He stopped at a sideboard decorating the lobby, again opened his Notebook and pointed out a typical layout for various condos and how they lined up with those above and below. "Trey has one like this. In fact, this is his condo. Three bedrooms, three baths, a view facing the Arch."

"That must've cost him some bucks," I said.

"The guy's a city politician," Mike said. "He's got an image to uphold."

Greg pointed to a janitorial closet before closing his Notebook again. "Follow me," he said. "As long as we're here, we might as well take a look at one." Midway down the hall, he opened a door and we stepped inside to view an orderly display of cleaning supplies. "There's one of these on every floor."

We returned to the elevator, this time descending to the basement where electronic and fire protection equipment could be found as well as an intricate maze of pipes.

"So, Mike," El began while we were walking around the basement's perimeter, "as I recall from our earlier conversations, you mentioned first meeting the Corrigans during the early stages of construction. And that you renovated Horace's own condo—apart from your work at the Creole."

"Yeah, Val called the shots on Horace's reno but Romaine Sloane jumped in with her ideas from time to time. Not that I'm bragging—more like complaining—but there was a time when Romaine had the hots for me."

"Really?" I said, shifting my face into one of wide-eyed doubt disguised as wonderment. "Do you suppose Romaine having the hots had anything to do with her getting killed?"

"Hell, no, those hots cooled off before I let them get out of hand. Romaine wasn't my type. And even if she had been, I wasn't about to go

244

against Horace Corrigan. She took care of the old fart every which way imaginable. Talk about a chatterbox. With Romaine, nothing was off-limits, especially anything involving the Creole reno, most of which I already knew. Except for what she referred to as the *dead body*, which I never saw but Romaine insisted she did. She went on and on about seeing it and then poof—gone within the hour, making me think it might've been Wilt Blue, a guy Romaine claimed she never knew. Hell, everybody knew Wilt. Next time I saw her, I asked about the body and she brushed me off, said she'd had too much to drink and imagined the whole thing. Like hell. Horace must've told her to shut up about it.

"What's really weird is this: couple days before Romaine died, she called. Out of the blue—pardon my pun—just like that. Wanted to meet with me, said she had things to get off her chest—only she said, bazooms 'cause that's how she talked, leastways around me. Whatever she had to say, died with her. Damned if I know who did it."

"All the more reason you should talk to the police," El said.

"Not if I can help it," Mike said. "Not with my past run-ins with the cops. You know, how one thing leads to another and another. Next thing you know, I'd be cooling my heels in lockup while somebody on the outside got promoted to my job."

Our basement walk-around took us to a partitioned area in one corner. "What the hell, I don't recall the door being filled in," Greg said, rubbing his hand over concrete blocks covering the former entrance. "Not that I would've been informed of a last minute decision such as this. Let me check it out." He began scrolling his Notebook while humming a tune that eventually faded away. "Hmm, no mention of anything here." He lifted one eyebrow to Mike. "Unless I'm mistaken, this is something you might've worked on."

"Might've and did. Don't give me any shit about the sloppy workmanship. I'm a carpenter, not a mason."

"Why the blocked door?" I asked. "And what's behind it?"

"To conceal an unused room is the '*why*'," Mike said. "The '*what*' concerns out-of-date mechanicals and an abandoned sump pit."

Loretta Giacoletto

"Or a dead body," El said. "That never occurred to you at the time?"

Mike folded his arms and leaned against the wall. "My mother didn't raise no fool, Ellie, in spite of what you think of me. Yeah, it occurred to me as soon as Wilt Blue went missing. It also occurred to me when Romaine started blabbering about some dead guy, then quick as silver shut her trap. It also occurred to me when Val made sure I worked every day on the Creole and when he hired me to renovate Horace Corrigan's condo in my spare time, as if no out-of-work carpenter couldn't have done just as good. Or maybe better, although that I kind of doubt."

"As for Wilt Blue, no one gave a damn, except me, that he didn't show up at the VA hospital for more testing. Or that he didn't show up for the TV interview. You heard that fine, upstanding Trey Millstone. Shouldn't he have been worried, given a damn? Contacted the police? Hell, no. And what about Wilt's family, if he even had one. And what about the other squatters? Did any of them give a damn?

"And what about you, Ellie? How much of a damn are you willing to give. Maybe you should give Reardan and Winchester a call. Tell them there's a blocked section in the Creole basement that might be hiding the body of a squatter who disappeared ten years ago. Or, not. Maybe Wilt decided to move on, clean up his act and rejoin the world. Or maybe he died of natural causes and found his peace in the family plot.

"So what's it gonna be, Ellie? How 'bout you, Margo. And you, Greg?"

30

Touching Bases

I did care about Wilt Blue, enough to convince Margo that we should have a conversation with Detectives Reardan and Winchester—on Monday in the late afternoon, which meant she had to convince Blake about the need for her to leave work early, at the same time reminding him of the overtime and sick days she'd accrued over the years and never expected to recoup.

Fortunately, when we arrived at the Fourth Precinct without first calling, Detectives Reardan and Winchester happened to be there. After Margo requested a private exchange, they invited us into a small conference room.

"Now this is what I call respect," Margo whispered as we took seats next to each other at a rectangular table that took up most of the room.

"Coffee or sodie?" Winchester asked before settling next to Reardan.

"Neither," Margo said, speaking for both of us as if I had no say-so in the matter.

Although my dry mouth could've used a cold beverage—what Winchester referred to as sodie in St. Louis talk—a show of Savino loyalty

247

took precedence over any physical discomfort. As soon as Winchester sat down, Reardan checked his watch while Margo and I expressed our thanks for them seeing us on such short notice.

"You got fifteen minutes," Reardan said. "Don't waste in on polite chatter."

Music to my ears. Margo and I quickly explained the purpose of our visit, including Greg Lupino's behind-the-scenes tutorial, but omitting any direct reference to Mike Rutger.

"Let me see if I understand," Reardan began in his sarcastic tone. "While on a Creole Exchange exploratory mission, in hopes of finding clues regarding the murder of Val Corrigan, you came to the assumption that a disgruntled homeless vet who talked too much during the Creole renovation may've been murdered."

"And you think we should send in a crew to tear down a blocked door in the basement, with hopes of discovering the remains of Mr. Wilton Blue who went missing," Winchester added. "Because the late Romaine Sloane claimed to have seen a dead body around that same time and then changed her mind."

"Something like that," I said.

"Bullshit," Margo said. "No *ifs, ands, buts, or somethings*. That's exactly what we think."

"Not only the part about Wilt Blue," I said. "But there's a possibility that the death of Romaine Sloane may be tied-in as well."

"And why is that?" Reardan asked.

"Well," I started out, then paused, not wanting to bring Mike's name into the conversation. "Somebody—can't say for sure who—said Romaine wanted to come clean about what she actually saw those many years ago."

"Hearsay," Reardan said. "Unless this *can't-say-for-sure*, this unknown entity, comes forward with the details. And even then, it's more than a little iffy."

248

"Since we're on the subject of Romaine Sloane," Margo said, "did you ever get the autopsy report regarding her cause of death."

"We did, but at this time don't plan on making it public." Winchester stood up. "Thanks, both of you, for coming in to share your concerns with us. We wish more citizens were willing to bring forth any evidence, however useful or insignificant that evidence may be."

"You're most welcome, Detective Winchester," Margo said. "You too, Detective Reardan. "My sister and I have every intention of continuing our investigation of these unsolved murders—that of Val Corrigan and Romaine Sloane as well as the disappearance of Wilton Blue and the untimely death of Horace Corrigan."

Reardan jerked his head in my direction. "Horace Corrigan? You mean Val Corrigan's uncle?"

"Of course. I realize Mr. Corrigan was suffering from cancer but it was supposedly in remission. We—Margo and I—believe he may've been murdered as well, perhaps by the same person or persons who killed Val Corrigan or Romaine Sloane. Which, incidentally, we do not believe Kat Dorchester capable of committing murder. Nor, would she have been aided and abetted by our mother Toni Savino."

Winchester suppressed a know-it-all smirk. "Next time, before casting aspersions, get your facts straight, Ms. Savino and you too, Ms. Savino. Horace Corrigan cashed in his chips by way of self-imposed euthanasia with supported video documentation, in spite of whatever cause-of-death version his nephew Val gave to the public and how the media reported it. As for Kat Dorchester, having been charged with the murder of Val Corrigan, she will remain incarcerated until the Grand Jury meets and indicts her as charged. As for your mother's involvement, be glad she has a top-notch lawyer. It's only a matter of time … and of justice for all concerned."

Four days later Margo called. Having skipped the usual sisterly preliminaries, she got right to the point. "You do realize some paybacks are more hellish than others."

Loretta Giacoletto

"Okay, your point being?"

"We shouldn't have harassed Detectives Reardan and Winchester about Wilton Blue."

"Expressing our concerns about the disappearance of a homeless Vietnam vet would hardly be considered harassment."

"Tell that to the detectives. They stopped by Mom's again. With hardly any advance notice, knowing full well both of us would be at work. Thank God, Fred Montgomery arrived shortly after those yapping bloodhounds."

"So they sniffed around and reconfirmed—at least for now—that Mom is innocent of any wrong doing."

"In other words, a payback that turned out to be an expected blessing," I said. "Although-h ... never mind."

"Although what, El? Don't tell me you believe Kat actually killed Val."

"Kill may be a bit extreme. I do think Kat was more involved than she admitted to the police. You weren't at the county jail when Mom and I visited her. The way she spoke to Mom showed me a side of Auntie Kat I'd not seen before. Not only was it brutal but more than a little threatening."

31

More Tit for Tat

The invitation arrived via snail mail, hand-written calligraphy on linen paper I recognized as top-of-the-line. Saradell Littlejohn had stood by her word and invited me to the dinner Jackson had secured for her during the Ritz-Carlton auction. Within the hour El called and confirmed that she too had received an invitation for the same event.

"Pure insanity, that's what," I said. "It's little more than a week from now. Barely enough time to get the right outfit, the right shoes, and the perfect hair style. Not to mention the perfect pedicure and manicure. No way will I allow these washer-woman hands to be displayed at one of the Littlejohn tables."

"Tables, as in more than one?" El asked.

"That's what Saradell told me when we last talked."

"Getting a little chummy with the elite, aren't you."

"It's not only who you know," I said, "but who they know. And trust me, when it comes to the upper echelon of St. Louis, Saradell Littlejohn knows everybody who's anybody. And even some influential nobodies."

251

"How fortunate for us," El said. "As for me, I'm thinking about another trip to Nordstrom. With any luck the red dress you insisted I return might've been demoted to the Clearance Rack."

"Where it should stay. Had you read the invitation's fine print, you'd know the red number wouldn't work. Think casual elegant."

"Right, starting with the Clearance Rack."

"Leave it to you, El. Always on the lookout for a bargain."

"Can't help myself—it's in the genes."

"Not mine," I assured her as much as myself.

Several days passed before I got up enough nerve to call Saradell and ask if I could help with the dinner plans. Not that Saradell actually needed my help. More like me needing hers. That said, Saradell must've wanted something since she invited me to lunch on Saturday, eight days before the main event.

"Not that it matters one way or the other," she said, "but Jackson has other plans during lunch, which means we'll have the place to ourselves."

And what a place it was. Money can't buy happiness. Okay, I get that. But Old Money in St. Louis did make it possible to inherit an impressive turn-of-the-twentieth-century mansion. Saradell and Jackson resided in theirs on Lindell Boulevard, a tree-lined Central West End street bordering the north end of Forest Park, site of the 1904 World's Fair and modern hub of the city's most prestigious cultural institutions alongside shimmering man-made ponds and acres of meadows mixed with trees entering their autumnal phase.

The Littlejohn house had its own name—Cranmore, Saradell explained while ushering me through richly appointed rooms that seemed more *Architectural Digest* than *Family Circle*. "A tribute to my late grandmother," she explained. "The old gal never liked me."

"Aw-w, that's too bad. My nonna is still around and we get along just fine. Always have."

I was anticipating a fabulous lunch prepared by a cook who'd been with the family for years, and served in the sunny solarium filled with exotic plants and antique wicker furniture. Wrong on all counts. Having breezed past the solarium, we wound up in the kitchen where Saradell directed me to one of two stools pushed against a granite-topped island. Another culinary smarty pants, I figured, mentally loosening my waistband button. Instead, she gave me a three-minute lesson in the art of toasting cheese sandwiches to melted perfection.

"After removing your masterpiece from the cast iron skillet, place on a seasoned cutting board, and divide into four triangular sections," Saradell said, applying two diagonal whacks of a butcher's cleaver. "Wedges are much easier to attack than rounded corners, don't you agree?"

"Well, I hadn't given much thought to geometric appropriateness."

"Kudos for having the courage to express your own opinion without worrying about mine. That's what I like about you, Margo."

She plated the two sandwiches and after sliding one in my direction, started quizzing me on various culinary topics. After missing two questions, I confessed my ignorance of basic cooking skills.

"I do appreciate a good meal though, just not every day," I said, patting my stomach. "My uncle's visiting from Italy and he loves to cook more than I love to eat. Thank God, Franco found a new outlet for his talent. He's been helping out a chef on The Hill in exchange for good eats."

Saradell had one hand poised in mid-air as she prepared to attack the triangle between her thumb and forefinger. She let the triangle slip back to the plate, cleared her throat, and asked, "Franco Rosina from Trattoria Tino?"

"You know Franco?"

"Do I know Franco? He's my favorite new cook, just as Tino is my all-time favorite chef. Tino agreed to cater the auction dinner; but wouldn't you know, one of his cooks got his rotator cuff repaired, so-o, we—Tino and I—have been trying to recruit Franco to lend a hand. But Franco already has a family obligation that evening, his own special dinner that will hopefully mend the animosity between his papa and the sister he only recently discovered. Tell me, are all Italians obtuse to a fault. Oops, sorry for the faux pas. I keep forgetting you're one of them. Not that being *one of them* is a bad thing." Her voice drifted off before resurfacing. "Hmm, by any chance would Franco have been referring to his sister as the one and only Toni Savino?"

Mending the animosity—I was still trying to wrap my arms around her upper crust observation. Nevertheless, I responded with a generic, "It's complicated."

"If only the mending could be moved to another time. As you probably know, most restaurants on The Hill are closed Sunday, which is why Tino agreed to cater an auction dinner on his day off."

"Of course I can't speak for Franco. He is, after all, his own man. I doubt he would change the date for me ... although, on the other hand, if Mom were to have other plans ...."

Saradell put her hands together for a single clap. "How absolutely, wonderfully fortuitous of you! Zoe Ponce can't make the dinner—something about an electrode malfunction in her brain. What if Toni would agree to take Zoe's place?"

"Well, Del Durante and Mom have been friends for years. On the other hand, not to open old wounds, but from what Mom told me recently, the two of you share some negative history."

"Indeed we do, as Toni Riva and Saradell St. Pierre—two lost souls once headed down a wayward path. But that was eons and eons ago. No hard feelings from my end, at least where Toni is concerned." Saradell touched one cheek. Flawless, thanks to the miracles of cosmetic surgery. "As for that bitch Kat Dorchester, may she rot in jail until her teeth fall out and her hair turns white and her arthritic fingers can't hold a knife any more. Or a gun. Or the most intriguing part of a man's anatomy."

Ouch, that seemed a bit extreme although I understood Saradell's resentment, given the scar erased from her face might still have been lurking in her psyche. It was, however, loyalty on my part that prompted me to say, "I can't begin to rationalize Kat's past behavior, nor should I; but for what it's worth, I don't think she killed Val Corrigan."

Saradell blew a kiss from the fingertips of her right hand. "I find your position admirable, naïve but nevertheless admirable. However, when it comes to Kat Dorchester, we shall have to agree to disagree."

"Without rancor," I added.

"But of course, Margo. I'm not a vindictive person although my memory would put most elephants to shame. I also take pride in my ability to negotiate, which is why I leave the Franco and Toni issue to your discretion. Now, tell me: what can I do for you?"

32

The Big Night

Our special evening at the Littlejohn mansion smacked of déjà vu, a partial throwback to the Ritz-Carlton auction, but with a few changes in the line-up. Of course, Kat Dorchester was absent, still incarcerated in the county jail with no hopes of getting out in the near future. At my suggestion, Saradell had paired El with Kat's auction date, surety agent Reavis Worden, a harmless match I figured would allow El to focus her attention on the other Littlejohn guests. After all, delightful as the evening promised to be, El and I were there on our self-imposed mission, a sorting out of people who had at least one thing in common, the Loft District's Creole Exchange. Beyond that anything was possible. Or nothing, as El kept reminding me.

Prior to dinner, the Littlejohn's rent-a-butler ushered arriving guests through an open area on Cranmore's main level where the town's most sought-after musician performed his magic on a grand piano—selections I recognized as covering the past two decades. Using the solarium as a watering hole couldn't have been better, showing off an array of hibiscus, lilies, and ferns muted in the afterglow of an autumnal sunset. Two waiters clad in black pants and matching vests over white shirts carried trays of hors devours and flute glasses filled with sparkling wine. Make that Champagne, the real stuff from France, per Jackson Littlejohn's singular

256

contribution to the party plans. One of the waiters caught my eye and managed to wink without changing the expression on his face. Under different circumstances a return wink would've been my standard response but this time I merely helped myself to the bubblies.

After a quick sip, I turned to my current and best-ever squeeze, Greg Lupino. We'd arrived at Cranmore arm-in-arm and somewhat flushed, having engaged in a pre-party quickie the hour before while taking a shower. Without wetting a single strand of my seemingly casual hairdo, I might add, a feat which took an array of imaginative maneuvering.

"You seem way too relaxed," Greg said, placing his empty flute on a tray passing by. "Saradell must've been okay with your party suggestions."

"Only because she thought most of those suggestions were hers." Ever so gently I removed a tiny dollop of shaving cream clinging to his ear lobe. "You can thank me for getting both of us invited and seated next to each other."

He leaned over, aiming for the tip of my nose, but instead planted a kiss on my forehead. "*Grazie, amore mio.* Your attention to detail is much appreciated."

"It must be. You've never talked Italian to me before. Nor, for that matter, to anyone else. At least not when I've been around."

"A prelude to things to come," he said, adding a sexy growl. "Just make sure you behave yourself this evening."

"And what about later tonight?" I asked.

"That will depend on our alcoholic intake, so use some discretion."

Discretion, code word for the entire evening. I turned again, almost colliding with El, who'd been sipping her own glass of bubbly. A few drops spilled onto her lace tunic, causing me to issue an immediate apology.

"It must be the outfit," El said as she brushed away the droplets before they did any damage. "You're the third person to christen it in the past ten minutes."

"Are you sure it's the outfit—which by the way is stunning—and not a certain waiter serving the Champagne?"

"Oh, really? I hadn't noticed." Stretching her neck, she located the person in question, and gave me one of her exasperated looks. "Mike Rutger, of all people. Is there no end to your meddling in my past?"

"Wake up and smell the garlic, El. We need all the help we can get, unless you want your next visit to Mom taking place in the county jail. With any luck she can have the cell next to Kat."

"Fat chance of that happening—Mom neighboring with Kat, I mean, since there's no way the police will ever arrest her for aiding, abetting, concealing, manslaughter, or, God forbid, murder."

"My, you have been doing some research. I am truly impressed."

"As well you should be, now that I have all this alone time to do as I please in my own condo. Speaking of, how is Zio Franco?"

"Last time I checked, cooking his heart out in the Littlejohn kitchen."

"One can only hope our uncle stays out of trouble and out of sight. That's all we'd need, Franco making out with one of the guests."

"Give the man some breathing room," I said, "especially if he breathes on anyone who knows anything about the murder of Val Corrigan. Or Romaine Sloane. And if there's a connection between the two murders."

"Don't look now," El said, "but Cinderella has just entered the ballroom ... solarium."

Cinderella—our very own Antonia Riva Savino, the woman who gave life to El and me. And had been the proverbial thorn in our sides ever since; just as we, no doubt, had been in hers.

Talk about fabulous fifties, Mom upstaged every female in the room, including our hostess who must've spent thousands of dollars to come in second best. So much for elaborate casual, Mom had taken it to a new level in flowing yellow chiffon that contrasted with her dark hair. If only Dad could've seen her from his heavenly perch and if God is truly good, maybe

Dad did. In fairness to our hostess, Saradell Littlejohn went beyond gracious, grabbing Mom by the hand and guiding her through the small gathering, making sure everyone knew this evening's star had come out to light up the sky. Trailing behind Saradell and Mom was Del Durante, perfectly content to bask in the attention of a business associate whose career he'd helped boost years before. Granted, through means that were somewhat questionable.

Count me among those basking in Mom's glory, until I got this weird feeling of hateful vibes shooting daggers at the back of my head. "By any chance has a turbulent jet stream invaded our space?" I asked El.

She glanced over my shoulder for no more than a nano second, the expression on her face showing no emotion. "Hmm, Margo. Now it's my turn to be truly impressed. In addition to your many obvious talents, you have developed the instinct of an animal sensing danger. Or one about to be pissed on over a territorial spat. Either way, count to ten and make a quick turn to your left."

I did as El suggested, almost knocking the crystal flute from Jet Gregson's hand.

"Margo Savino!" Jet said. "Never in my wildest dreams did I expect to see you at such an auspicious gathering. How utterly democratic of Saradell to include you. Oh, and you too ... the younger sister. I keep forgetting ... Ellen, isn't it?"

"Er, right ... the pathetic lackey, as you referred to me not long ago."

"In the heat of a rather cranky moment," Jet said, directing her next words to me. "Shame on you, Margo, tattling on me to ... uh ... your sister."

"Ellen, e ... double l ... e ... n."

Forget about phony smiley faces among frenemies. And no way would we three have lowered ourselves to engage in an equally phony group hug. We did, however, manage a Hollywood-type, non-touchy, kiss-in-air acknowledgment of the existence of one another. To make matters worse, or better, depending on one's perspective, along came Saradell with her prized guest in tow plus the convenient escort.

"Jet, darling. Surely you remember Toni Savino. Now I ask you: what are the chances of one beautiful mother and her two gorgeous daughters showing up at the same Littlejohn party. And, of course, you know Del Durante. Boris, darling. Is that you, hiding behind Jet? Fat chance of your not being seen there, considering Jet's ultra-trim figure. Still working out, Jet?"

Amazing what a bit of honey can produce. Jet loosened up and projected a half smile that soon expanded into a full-fledged grin. Saradell had that effect on anyone hoping for a return invitation to Cranmore. El, on the other hand, couldn't have cared less, given her past history of self-denial and more recently, of guilty pleasures. Before things got any uglier, she wandered off in the direction of Reavis Worden, per my earlier instructions to make small talk with her table companion, in hopes of his shedding some light on the Creole Exchange's shady side. Greg moved on as well, after treating Mom like a long-lost relative—perhaps a precursor of things to come.

As for Mom, she'd already secured a spot on the Littlejohn's future guest list, given her willingness to postpone Franco's dinner to some obscure time in the never future. So while she and Jet commiserated over the sagging real estate market, I engaged Boris Tainer in generic chitchat, a preamble to the more serious discussion we'd be having later since I'd made sure he'd be sitting next to me. I couldn't help but wonder what Jet saw in Boris, given the paunchy midsection protruding from his ill-fitting suit and a leaky nose requiring the constant attention of his handkerchief. Another victim of the St. Louis allergy season, the man had my sympathy if not my confusion for his connection to Jet Gregson, who was still chatting with Mom. Odd, how the business of real estate development and sales creates a shitload of offbeat relationships. As does the legal profession.

Speaking of, my terrific lawyer boss Blake Harrington came wandering by and stopped long enough for an introduction to Boris Tainer, Jet Gregson's dinner partner.

"Linda and I will be sitting at Jackson's table," Blake said while shaking the puffy hand Boris had extended.

"Bummer," I said, tongue in cheek, having already filled Blake in on certain details, such as Saradell assigning Jackson to one table and herself to the other and which guest would be sitting where. "We'll be with Saradell. Not that I'm complaining, more like delighted," I quickly added in case the room had been bugged. Talk about paranoia. "Mom and Del Durante will be at your table."

"Your mother? Here tonight?" Blake swiveled his head and on seeing her, gave a slight wave. "Excellent. She and Linda should have lots to talk about."

"Only if you can get her out of the horrific mess she's gotten herself into," I said.

"Relax," Blake said. "As I told you before, she can't do any better than Fred Montgomery."

"Toni Savino in trouble," Boris said, having joined the conversation at last. "That sounds rather ominous. If ever there's anything I can do …"

"Thanks, I'll keep that in mind." Truer words were never spoken.

El returned to my side minus Reavis. "He's taking care of business, literally," she said, "answering Nature's call."

"Anything else about him worth sharing?" I asked.

"Well, let me think. He doesn't like insuring major projects that Boris Tainer has signed off on."

"Because …"

"Boris tends to overlook issues that might postpone deadlines and increase overall costs. He'd just as soon slit his old lady's throat than let any deal go south. Reavis's words, not mine."

"Hmm, interesting."

El stretched her neck for a fourth time that evening, lips moving as she counted heads before asking, "You're sure they're coming?"

Loretta Giacoletto

"Saradell promised," I assured my worry-wart sister. "She and the wife go all the way back to their grade school days at Cathedral. What's more, they've been involved in archdiocese charities for years, even served as co-chairs on multiple occasions, in spite of the obvious differences in their social and financial backgrounds."

"Sounds like this long-time friend owes Saradell big time."

"Doesn't everybody. Or maybe it's the other way around. I didn't ask and Saradell didn't elaborate."

"All of which counts for zero if the wife can't get her husband to show up."

"A moot point, little sis. No need to turn around but here comes Saradell, arm in arm with the childhood friend and the friend's husband who looks as if he'd rather be anywhere but where his wife has dragged him. Welcome to Cranmore on Lindell."

Of course, El knew one of the two final guests, having encountered him on several occasions. As had I. "Be still my beating heart," she said, tapping hers with two shaking fingers. "I haven't been this excited since ... Italy ... Cinque Terre."

Halleluiah and then some. Saradell Littlejohn had fulfilled her end of our tit for tat—the quid quo pro I'd only dreamed of achieving.

Before I could take a much deserved internal bow, I felt the familiar grip of fingers circling my wrist. "Watch the merchandise," I told Mom. "I need it for keyboarding come Monday morning."

"Is this your doing, Margo?" she said in an accusatory voice. "Or yours, Ellen. You of all people I would've thought had better sense. Had I known that sly fox would be here, I would never have accepted Saradell's invitation."

"Sly fox or not, Saradell thinks the world of his wife Jessa," El whispered. "Please don't do or say anything that would further embarrass the family."

262

"Yeah, Mom. Think about your career, your reputation."

"My what? Why I never ..."

Hold that thought or forget it forever. Saradell was but a single breath away, exuding a whiff of the pricey perfume that served as her protective armor.

"How perfectly delicious," Saradell cooed. "The Savino women together again, for the second time this hour. I know the three of you are well acquainted with my dear friend Sam Reardan." She paused, allowing time for an exchange of handshakes. "But I'd be willing to bet than none of you have met his lovely wife, my dearest friend, Jessa Reardan. Where would the St. Louis Archdiocese be without us? Right, Jessa?"

Jessa and Sam Reardan—in no way what I'd expected. Whereas the Sam I knew as Detective Sam Reardan always looked as if he'd just climbed out of an alley recycle bin, Civilian Sam Reardan looked quite comfortable in the toney Central West End, him and his lightweight sports jacket over blue oxford shirt and dark trousers with knife-sharp creases. Jessa Reardan stood shoulder to shoulder with our either-way, chunky Sam. She wore her auburn hair in a page-boy and a casual outfit so elegant it must've come from Saradell's collection since both women appeared to be about the same size. Jessa smiled with the warmth of her handshake, making it difficult not to like her. From where I stood, she had the same effect on El and Mom. All we needed was the likes of Detective Guy Winchester. Not. No point in pushing my luck with their good-cop-bad-cop routine.

Saradell led Mom and Jessa back into the gathering, leaving Sam to scowl at El and me. El returned his scowl with the modest smile of her convent years and with words undeniably less than truthful. "What a delightful surprise, Detective Reardan."

"Hardly delightful," he said. "Had I known the Savino family would be here, I'd have declined the invitation."

"And no doubt disappointed your wife," I said, "and Saradell. They're such good friends."

"Who lunch together at least once a month so this dinner party is not

263

the rare treat for Jessa you'd have me believe. Friend or no friend, I don't appreciate my wife being exploited under the guise of a special event. Nor having my evening turned into a fucking practice game for the benefit of two wannabe sleuths who haven't a clue as to what they're doing."

"Before the evening ends," El said, "you may have to eat those words."

"Is that a promise, Ms. Savino, or a threat?"

"Neither, I hope, but please hear us out. Among the guest assigned to our table will be Reavis Worden, surety agent during the Creole Exchange renovation, and Boris Tainer, the engineer who signed off on the Creole's inspections."

"And Jet Gregson, the broker who made a bundle of money from the initial and subsequent sale," I added.

"As did your friend Kat Dorchester," Reardan said. "Both of whom were screwing Val Corrigan, as was your mother. Imagine that. No, I don't blame you for wanting to downplay the awful truth. None of this is pretty but that's how it goes when murder's involved. Aside from that, my being here better not compromise this case in any way whatsoever, or the two of you will need your own lawyers. Let me assure you: that's not a threat—it's a promise."

No sooner had Reardan walked away than the tinkling of hammered chimes announced dinner. Greg appeared at my side and together we walked across the grand piano area and into the dining room where two round tables awaited the Littlejohn guests. Mom and Del Durante joined Blake and Linda Harrington at Jackson's table, as did the banker Pierce Rendley and his wife Beale, who used to work for Blake, along with Boyd and Eve Tennison, whose big league company had insured the Creole during its renovation and still carried the policy. Next to Jackson sat Jessa54 Reardan, who had no problem being separated from her husband during dinner—as a favor to Saradell who was doing me a favor. One of many, I should add.

Saradell welcomed us to her table and casually motioned to name cards located at each place setting. As prearranged with our hostess, I sat next to

Greg, who sat next to Saradell. On my right was Boris Tainer and to his right, Jet Gregson. Next to the pouty Jet sat our illustrious but equally pouty Sam Reardan and next to Sam, El and surety agent Reavis Worden. River City Builder Morgan Davisson and his wife Greta rounded out our group of casual acquaintances. I caught El's eye from across the table and gave a slight nod which she returned. We were determined to make the most of this night, as long as our mother didn't suffer the consequences of anything we might provoke.

How can a seven-course dinner be eventually digested without the aid of two or three antacid tablets? That's how El and I prepared ourselves before ever leaving home. Greg poo-pooed the idea but he did chugalug milk from the carton in my fridge. Ugh, disgusting but in a sexy way I otherwise wouldn't have tolerated had it been anybody but Greg. What a guy—so far. He'd better be worth the time I'd invested in him this second time around.

Mike Rutger, who winked at me earlier, would be serving our table. Wyatt, who'd also worked the Ritz auction, was responsible for Jackson's table. Again, both assignments due to my intervention. Mike placed the antipasto in front of El, brushing against her arm as he turned the plate of three prosciutto-wrapped figs and gorgonzola to maximize eye appeal. El moved her arm ever so slightly, more in recognition than revulsion. Good for her and for him. She needed a casual distraction in her American life, not the guy across the sea who was too honorable to cut the loyalty strings binding him to an impossible situation.

I turned to Boris Tainer, who'd cleaned his plate in three quick bites, and offered him the two delicacies I hadn't touched. To my surprise and Jet's, he reached over and with his fork plucked both from my plate. He opened wide, popped one into his mouth, and savored every chew before tackling the other. A good choice on my part, not letting those calories go to waste.

Next came the soup, a golden butternut squash topped with wild mushrooms. Again, I only consumed a few mouthfuls that exceeded my expectations before passing the bowl to Boris. Never had I seen a man eat with such gusto. Nor Sam Reardan with such vehemence. Good grief, the man needed to get over himself. Offering him several of the antacid supply

I carried in my purse was an option I considered. But not for long. Letting Sam endure a bit of stomach distress better suited my self-serving interests.

One glance in the direction of Jackson's table relieved me of any personal heartburn, at least for the moment. Jackson had the entire table laughing, including Jessa Reardan and Mom, who until that moment, had barely cracked a smile since my return from Italy. Diversion, yes, that's what we needed at our table—a good dose of unadulterated diversion. I cleared my throat and was about to take the plunge when El beat me to it.

"If you don't mind my asking, Detective Reardan, are there any new developments in the Corrigan case?"

The soup spoon gripped in Reardan's hand froze, inches from his mouth as he narrowed his eyes to El. If looks could kill, my sis would've been swinging her sweet ass from a heavenly cloud. The entire table went silent, waiting for him to answer her question, which he did in a manner so succinct it spoke volumes. "Nothing I care to discuss at a private dinner party."

"Ellen!" The well-practiced admonition spewed from my mouth in a tone similar to what our mother would've used. "This is hardly the time or place to ask Sam about an ongoing investigation." El opened her mouth to speak, reconsidered, and closed it, allowing me to continue. "Is it okay to call you Sam? After all, this is a private party."

"Oh, dear." Saradell experienced an unplanned oops moment, fingertips patting her pursed lips. "My apologies, Sam. How inexcusable of me. It was not my intention to put you in such an awkward position. However you wish to be addressed, I leave to your discretion."

Reardan's gaze moved to the other table where his wife Jessa had taken over from Jackson and was regaling her new friends with a humorous tale. No husband in his right mind would've interrupted his wife's moment to shine and Reardan was no exception. "In private life I answer to either Sam or Detective Reardan, but to avoid any further misunderstanding, there's never a time when I consider myself off-duty. It's one of many non-perks that comes with the territory."

El's voice was shaking when she spoke. "My apologies ... Sam." She addressed her next comment to Reavis Worden. "You mentioned being a surety agent, whatever that is. Would you mind enlightening me and anyone else outside the industry?"

Reavis's face turned a weird shade of yellowish pink, reminiscent of the prosciutto and squash from our first two courses. "Well, uh ... most people here have worked with surety agents," he paused, looking from El to me, "but for those of you who've never had the pleasure, I represent Eckridge Security, a type of insurance that covers the cost to finish a project if the contractor fails to perform. You know, fulfill the terms of the contract. We work directly with the contractor but it's the developer who pays for the insurance."

"Like Horace and Val Corrigan did for River City Builders," Morgan Davisson said, "when we renovated the Creole Exchange."

"Who would've thought," I said. "Reavis, were you also the surety agent for other projects developed by the Corrigans?"

"More for Val than Horace," Reavis said. "Horace stepped back from the business after Creole."

"Oh really? A problem between Horace and Val?"

"Not that I'm aware of; but as a rule I don't make other people's business my business."

"Nor do we—my sister and I—unless other people's business somehow becomes our business."

"Is there a point to this?" Reavis asked. "If not, I would like to finish my soup."

After Reavis woofed down the last of his soup, Mike circled the table again and removed the remaining settings from the second course. Next came the fish, a roasted amberjack with almonds and leeks. I closed my eyes and breathed in its intoxicating aroma. After three bites I didn't want to stop but needed to pace myself for what was yet to come. Boris had been scooting his last bite around the plate, waiting for me to offer the rest of mine. Damn, I did not want him depending on my leftovers. Nor did I

Loretta Giacoletto

want to risk offending him. My dilemma was soon resolved when Greg initiated a whispered conversation in my ear.

"If you're not planning on eating all that fish, I'd like first dibs on it."

"What's in it for me?"

"You won't be disappointed. That's not a threat; it's a promise."

"Be my guest," I said aloud, passing my plate to Greg before giving Boris a virtual crumb to gnaw on. "Next course has your name on it."

One glance across the table told me El had been enjoying her every bite instead of following my example of self-denial. Oh, well, there was only so much I could do without ruffling her sensitive feathers. Having cleaned my plate of telltale morsels, I picked up where El left off.

"Your turn, Boris. Talk to me about environmental engineering. That is what you do, isn't it?"

Before Boris could answer my question, Jet came to his rescue, as if the man needed rescuing from anything other than his appetite. "Really, Margo, must you persist in all this tedious job talk. It's not like we're neophytes or we need to impress each other."

"Well, I for one am certainly interested and happy to put in a plug for the family business," Saradell said. "For those of you who don't know, Jackson and I run St. Pierre Investments. We provided a large chunk of funding for the Creole Exchange." Without pausing, Saradell made the sign of the cross to accompany her next words. "Rest in peace, Val. You too, Horace, wherever the two of you may've landed, which I hope wasn't developing property too hot to handle." At this, she giggled into her oversized linen napkin, as did most of her guests. "Sorry, couldn't help myself, although knowing Val as I did, he would've love the touch of humor." She passed a salt shaker to the left, as if it were a wireless mike. "Your turn, Greg."

Taking Saradell's cue, Greg tapped the shaker's lid and continued. "I have a connection with the Creole too. It was my first major project though not as the primary architect. I was physically there most days and learned

268

more than I ever could have sitting at my Studio Alpha desk." He paused and offered the pseudo mike to his neighbor. "You were one of the brokers, weren't you, Jet?"

Ignoring the shaker, Jet spoke from anywhere but what passed for her heart. "Not that it matters but yes, I did represent the seller when Horace bought the Creole and later worked with Kat Dorchester when it sold again."

"You also managed the Creole Exchange for a while," I said, as if she needed a reminder.

Jet bit her lower lip before answering. "During its start-up phase to get all the units sold, which took forever after the economy tanked. None of which is here or there; or perhaps it is since I'm here and Kat's there—in jail, as we all know, for the murder of Val Corrigan." She leaned over for a better view of Detective Reardan. "Sorry, Sam. Close your ears if shop talk such as this cuts into your private life. Mine too, as if I have any choice, other than leaving early—a sacrilege for those of us who not only appreciate good manners but make every effort to practice them as well."

Sam responded by emptying the wine from his goblet. Talk about manners, however phony, or lack thereof, I couldn't help but think of Jet's behavior during our Forest Park run.

"For the record, I have no connection with the Creole Exchange," El said with a laugh. "I'm a middle school librarian who also teaches literature appreciation."

"I'm a paralegal for Blake Harrington," I said, raising my goblet to where he sat at the other table.

"But both of you *do* have a connection with the Creole Exchange," Jet said, raising her goblet in the same direction towards Mom.

"Which brings us back to you, Boris," El said without missing a beat. "Exactly what is it you did for the Creole Exchange?"

Boris wiped his mouth, first with a swish of the tongue and then with his napkin. When he spoke, his words reminded me of a rehearsed job

269

interview. "As an environmental specialist I was involved in every phase of the renovation, from taking measures to ensure the building was free of contamination to removing all asbestos from the interior and associated dust particles to making sure the air was clean and met all the required standards. I take great pride in my work, as does everyone sitting here."

During the discussion of our various occupations, Mike had been serving the second half of our main course—veal cheek in a red wine sauce on pureed potato, in deference to Franco, who'd refused to accommodate Saradell unless allowed to make the Piemonte specialty. I'd been saving myself for this one, and wished I hadn't promised a portion of it to Boris.

"Speaking as a total novice in such matters, Boris, I find environmental concerns utterly fascinating," El said, all but fluttering her eyelashes. "Social issues too. It must've been heart-wrenching, dealing with all those homeless."

"We had a job to do and got it done, all of us."

He shoved a piece of veal in his mouth and chewed with obvious relish. Before he could spear his next bite, El eased into a casual question. "By any chance, during those days at the Creole, did you know one of the homeless people sleeping there, a Vietnam vet named Wilton Blue?"

Boris furrowed his brow, as if digging deep into his memory bank. "Wilton Blue ... Wilton Blue ... doesn't ring a bell. Back then there were so many squatters, none of which were pleased to see us revitalize the Garment District."

"That's understandable given the circumstances," El said. "Getting all those homeless relocated must've been a huge inconvenience when it came to construction deadlines."

"Tell me about it. And Reavis." Morgan Davisson nodded in Reavis Worden's direction. "Eckridge Security would've had to pay out the difference, which in the case of the Creole wasn't a problem since all concerned met the conditions of their contract."

Unable to speak due to the buttered roll stuffed in his mouth, Reavis Worden managed an enthusiastic nod.

Not Worth Dying For

"Refresh my memory," I said to Boris Tainer. "What's the name of your company?"

"My company?" Boris rolled his eyes. "Hardly, more like my uncle's. Tainer Environmental Consultants—TEC."

"I think I've heard of TEC," El said. "As I recall, the press has been giving TEC a rough time lately."

"Don't believe everything you read in the newspaper," Boris said.

"How true," I said. "A picture's worth a thousand words and film even more. For example, those photos and videos of that new North St. Louis residential community making the rounds on the Internet and local TV news." I paused for an appropriate tsk. "All those environmental issues such as undetected mold and asbestos dust that TEC supposedly overlooked must be keeping you awake at night."

Boris puffed up his barrel chest. "Not me, because I followed all the guidelines, just like I always do." Sweat beads were forming on his upper lip and he licked them away. "Now, about that veal cheek you left on your plate ...."

"Help yourself," I said, ignoring Greg's knee banging against mine while Boris pounced on my leftovers with the enthusiasm of a condemned man making the most of his last meal. No sooner had he shoveled the last bite into his mouth than Mike whisked away the plate, leaving a few morsels to fall from Boris's mouth onto the tablecloth. Not one crumb went to waste; Boris made sure of that, using two fingers to tidy up the miniscule mess.

He noticed me looking at him and grinned in a sheepish way. "Mother would have a fit if I didn't clean up after myself."

"Been there, done that," I said without snatching a glance in my mother's direction.

During the lull before our next course, the conversation shifted to Morgan Davisson of River City Builders, and his latest project: the new construction of a mid-town office building, a welcomed relief that allowed

271

me time to collect my thoughts. In the meantime, Mike and Wyatt began serving the salads, ladies first in keeping with the established routine.

Boris glanced up, as if seeing Mike for the first time, and said, "You look familiar."

Before answering, Mike took his next cue from Saradell. "We're not that formal," she said with a sweet smile. "Feel free to answer a direct question unrelated to food."

"You might know me from the Ritz-Carlton," Mike told Boris. "Both Wyatt and I worked the Kids Auction but not your table."

Boris cocked his head, still searching his memory. "Not the Ritz. I'm thinking someplace else, years ago."

Mike continued around his half of the table, and after ending with Sam Reardan, he answered Boris's question. "That would've been the Creole Exchange renovation where I worked as a carpenter. Don't you remember? You had me block off that abandoned mechanical room in the basement."

"You're confusing me with somebody else," Boris said. "I'm an environmental specialist."

"That's right. The owner of the building told me to fill in the door. He said due to safety issues. But it was just you and me down there when I started laying the blocks."

"Liar!" Boris sputtered and then started coughing in his napkin, more for show than for need.

Feeling not only victorious but surprisingly virtuous, I attempted to catch El's eye. She, however, had focused her attention on Sam Reardan. As did Franco, who'd been standing in the hallway, his apron stained with the makings of our meal.

Having wiped his mouth, Reardan folded his napkin, and placed it over his half-eaten salad. He scooted his chair back and stood. Nodding to Mike Rutger and the now-recovered Boris Tainer, he said in a low voice, "Stop, not another word from either of you. I've heard enough for one night."

Not Worth Dying For

Reardan wasn't through yet. He looked from El to me in a menacing way that canceled out the fortifying antacid I'd been so diligent about taking earlier. "Savino Sisters One and Two, same goes for both of you. Be assured, you will be hearing from me."

After apologizing to Saradell and then to Jackson, who assured Reardan he'd make sure Jessa got home safely, Sam kissed Jessa's cheek and she patted his. But did it end there? No. He returned to our table, issuing a single word to me that spoke volumes. "Satisfied?"

Well, yes and no. Thanks to Mike Rutger, El and I had made progress in the Corrigan case but I did feel terrible about putting a damper on the dessert course—chocolate cake layered with chocolate mouse and topped with shaved chocolate, followed by coffee, then Frangelico and Limoncello. None of which sweetened the mood at Saradell's table although Jackson managed to keep his table entertained until the dinner came to an end, at which point I apologized to Jessa Reardan.

"Not to worry, it comes with the territory," she said, squeezing my hand. "It's not the first time Sam has been forced to bail on me. Nor do I expect it will be the last."

Boris Tainer left with a smile on his face and an oversized doggy bag. For his widowed mother, who appreciated fine dining, Boris explained, even though she rarely ventured out anymore.

As for Saradell, she initiated a group hug with El and me. "I can't remember when I've had so much fun at one of my own parties," she said with a chuckle. "Should a similar occasion ever arise in the future, don't hesitate to call on me again."

33

Family Matters

Monday morning brought me back to life with my head still spinning from the Littlejohn dinner. While I was eating breakfast, Detective Reardan called to schedule an eleven o'clock interview for the following day. His place, not mine. "My sister too?" I asked, trying to ignore the bagel turning flip-flops in my stomach.

"Wouldn't have it any other way," Reardan said, "nor would my partner."

Winchester, of course. I could help wondering if the Detectives from Hell felt the same way about Margo and me as we did about them.

Going to the station with all my ducks in a row, plus dealing with the possible aftermath of subsequent interviews, would require my requesting a personal day. For me, not a problem since prior to what had started as Mom's problem, I'd rarely asked for time off. Check and double check, with Margo at my side, I knew we'd have everything under control.

That is, until she called during lunch period with her own directive. "We're meeting at Mom's this evening, seven o'clock."

Having already taken a bite of my tuna salad sandwich, I spoke with a mouthful of celery crunching. "We as in who besides those who currently live there?"

"You, me, and Franco," Margo said. "What's that noise?"

"Must be a bad connection." I swallowed the evidence and using my tongue, pushed the remains to one side of my mouth. "Seven seems kind of late for dinner, don't you think? Not that I mind, but what about Nonnie and Stefano?"

"Really, El, must everything revolve around food?"

"If Franco has any say-so, yes."

"Not this time. Actually, Franco suggested the bare-bones get-together, which I wholeheartedly support."

"You want him out," I said, suppressing a giggle. "He's cramping your style."

"True, but that's not the only reason. It's time for certain warring factions to make peace."

"That would be Mom against the rest of us."

"I'm talking intervention, El, as in family matters."

That evening before the family gathering, I was going through a stack of book reports written by my seventh graders when the phone rang. Having recognized the number, I answered with mixed feelings.

"Sorry to bother you," Mike Rutger said. "Just thought you'd like to know I got a meeting with Reardan and Winchester, tomorrow afternoon at one."

"A meeting you requested?" I asked.

"Hell, no. You know how I feel about police precincts."

Loretta Giacoletto

"You've got nothing to worry about."

"Says you, Ellie."

"I'm sorry if—"

"No need to apologize, Ellie. If I can pull this off, you're gonna owe me big time."

∞∞∞∞

Count me as last to arrive in Nonnie Clarita's kitchen. At one end of the table sat Mom; at the other end, Nonnie. To Nonnie's right, Stefano. To her left, Margo and to Margo's left, Franco. I sat to Mom's left, across from Franco. Not one crumb of food graced the table although it had been blessed with two bottles of red wine, uncorked and allowed to breathe until we hopefully resolved certain issues. Discombobulated issues, as Mom often referred to them while trying to guide Margo and me through our rebellious era.

"Is this really necessary?" Mom asked, arms folded on the table.

"Only if you love me as much as I do you." For Nonnie quite a reach, considering she rarely got personal about mother-daughter love. "Only if you care about my final days ending in some kind of happiness."

"Now we're playing the death card," Mom said. "What next?"

"Stop it!" Franco said. "Both of you. I brought my papa to America so he could spend time with his first love—the woman he loved more than my mama, much as it hurts to say what I only recently learned to be true. Had he been unfaithful to my mama, I would not have been so forgiving, but as far as I know he stayed true to her until she took her last breath. Si, Papa?"

Stefano tapped two rows of fingers to his chest. "Much as it shames me to say, your mama deserved better than me but never did I lay with another woman while Monica was alive."

"Which is not to say you didn't after she died," Nonnie said with a lift of her defiant chin.

276

Not Worth Dying For

"Do you really want to go there?" I asked, thinking of her long-time nemesis, Donata Abba.

"No," she said, reaching for Stefano's hand. "I want to spend every minute of every day with the man I married sixty-six years ago."

Stefano opened her hand and kissed the palm.

Mom's eyebrows shot up. "Married, since when? You never told me."

"I tried," Nonnie said. "But would you listen? No. Too much a *testa dura*, a hard head just like your papa, the one who gave you life."

"As opposed to the one who gave us a monthly income for life," Mom said.

"Show some respect," Franco said, "for both your papas. Neither one of them got to see you as a baby. Or watch you grow from a little girl into the beautiful woman you are today."

Thank you, Franco, I wanted to say, as did Margo, judging from the expression of her face. Instead, we both took a back seat to our elders.

"I'm all ears now," Mom said. "Tell me about the marriage."

"We were so young," Stefano said. "Me, eighteen. Your mama, sixteen."

"Sixteen, Mama! You were a baby."

"Maybe in today's world but not then," Nonnie said, squeezing Stefano's hand. "I knew what I wanted. Damn the so-called gypsy who made a mockery of our wedding."

"It was my fault," Stefano said. "When I went to register our marriage to make it legal, only then did I learn Clarita had to be at least eighteen to marry without her mama's permission."

"An impossible situation," Nonnie said. "My mama hated Stefano as much I loved him. But three people died because of our love."

277

"For which I take responsibility," Stefano said.

"Me too," Nonna said. "To punish the both of us, I left him and started a new life in America, for which I have no regrets. Five years later, Stefano was among a group of Resistance fighters being honored in America for their Second World War service. He and I renewed our love during a single weekend here in St. Louis. Any more than that was not in the cards. Not with me weeks away from marrying John Riva … God rest his soul. No way could I go back to the life I'd left in Italy."

"So, I went back alone," Stefano said, "not knowing I'd planted my seed inside Clarita. Nor did I know when I married Monica shortly afterwards—legally."

Stefano got up and went to Mom. He knelt beside her chair, suppressing the grunt that showed on his face. "Please, Antonia, forgive me for the grief I have caused you all these many years. Allow me to be part of your life, to live here as husband to your mama. I want to marry her again, in church before God and a priest."

Talk about tears, not one eye was dry, including Mom's. She leaned over, hugged Stefano, and spoke with a catch in her voice. "Welcome to the family, Papa. I think I love you."

We were on our third bottle of wine when Franco brought up the subject of Romaine. "I was so worried about making trouble for Toni, I did not tell the police everything I knew about Romaine. But from what I heard last night at Saradell's party, maybe I should talk to them again."

"About what, if you don't mind my asking," Margo said.

"Remember when I talked about *i benefattori*, dead men in Italy leaving money to their mistresses? Since Romaine never worried about money, is there any way to find out if this was the case with her?"

"And Horace Corrigan," Margo said. "Wills are a matter of public record. I'll check with the probate court tomorrow morning before our eleven o'clock with Reardan and Winchester."

Not Worth Dying For

"Anything else?" I asked, wishing Franco hadn't waited so long to come clean with Margo and me, yet thankful that he did.

"Just this," Franco said, reaching into his pants pocket. He held up the item, a battered locket dangling from a gold chain. "Why Romaine gave it to me, I don't know; but she did say it once belonged to a man without a home."

34

Precinct 4

I pride myself on being prompt, which is why we walked through the door of the South County Precinct 4 at precisely eleven o'clock on Tuesday morning. *We* being the key word, since both Margo and I had convinced Franco to come with us.

"What if they put me in jail for not telling the whole truth before?" he asked, wiping his brow while we stood in the foyer.

"It's not like you were under oath," I reminded him.

"Put the blame on Detectives Reardan and Winchester for not asking the right questions," Margo added, unaware our group of three had increased to four.

"What questions?" Reardan asked. He directed his next question to Franco. "And why are you here? It better be good; I'm in no mood for another play date."

By this time Winchester had joined us and after further discussion about there now being a total of five, he and Reardan decided to use the same conference room we'd occupied before. After drinks were offered and

280

Not Worth Dying For

declined, Reardan leaned back from the table and said, "Okay, let's get this show on the road. What's your story, Mr. Rosina?"

Franco cleared his throat, then cleared it again. "After my last time here, I remembered this." He handed the chain and locket to Reardan.

Reardan glanced at the jewelry before passing it on to Winchester, who then motioned Franco to continue.

"Romaine Sloane gave the locket to me. She said it was cursed, not that I believe in curses ... unless they come from the Evil Eye." He made a sign of the horn with his forefinger and pinky, holding the two middle fingers down with his thumb, a gesture I'd seen more than once in Italy.

Winchester had his own gesture—a no-nonsense show of his open palm, long fingers pointing upward. "Stop with the Evil Eye shit, we've heard that excuse one too many times from anybody whose last name ends in a vowel. As for the aforementioned, why'd she think the locket was cursed?"

"What four?" Franco gave me a quizzical look.

"*Aforementioned*, he means Romaine."

"Ah, si." Franco nodded. "Romaine believed the two most important men in her life had died because of it—the curse I am not supposed to talk about."

"That would be Horace and Val Corrigan," I explained.

"Then let him tell us and not you," Reardan said. "Unless you have pertinent information to add."

"As a matter of fact, I do. The locket belonged to Wilton Blue, the homeless vet who went missing during the Creole Exchange renovation. As you can see, his initials are engraved on the back—WB."

"Dear God, are we back to the Creole again," Winchester said.

"Only if you're willing to go there," I said. "Ask Mike Rutger this afternoon."

"The mouthy waiter from Sunday night," Reardan said for Winchester's benefit. And to me he added, "So much for confidentially, Ms. Savino. Don't tell me Rutger posted our upcoming meeting on that damn Facebook."

"Not his thing. Nor mine. On the other hand, it's not like I twisted Mike's arm. He told me. Mike and I go back a long way. As do Mike and Boris Tainer the environmental specialist."

"No need for a reminder of what I already know and passed on to Detective Winchester," Reardan said. "Anything else, Mr. Rosina?"

Having removed a small envelope from his shirt pocket, Franco took out a photo and handed it to Winchester. "A picture of the same locket," Franco said, "also given to me by Romaine."

"Stamped with an October 2003 date," Winchester said, tapping the photo. "Anything else?"

Margo, who rarely is at a loss for words, finally raised her hand.

"I take it you wish to speak on Mr. Rosina's behalf," Reardan said.

"Only to confirm what Franco ... my uncle ... asked me to investigate." Margo slid the folder she'd been carrying across to Reardan and continued, "As you can see from this copy of Horace Corrigan's will, he left Romaine Sloane a monthly income for life. A modest annuity, I might add, that would've required additional funding to maintain the lifestyle she appeared to enjoy without working a regular job."

After both detectives reviewed the document without comment, Reardan refocused his attention to Franco. "On another topic, more or less related, didn't I see you Sunday at the Littlejohn party?"

"I was helping out in the kitchen."

"Our uncle is too modest," I said. "He prepared the veal cheek in wine sauce. It's one of his Northern Italy specialties."

"Not bad," Reardan said "Not bad at all. You work at Tino's?"

282

Not Worth Dying For

"No work visa, no paycheck. Again, helping out until the sous chef's shoulder gets better."

Reardan checked his wristwatch. "In that case you should go, in case Tino needs you."

"Er ... uh, please don't take this the wrong way, but after we drop Franco off at the trattoria, my sister and I would be willing to come back," Margo said. "Both of us took a personal day from work."

"If you have more pertinent information, speak up now," Reardan said. "It's not like Tino's going to fire his star volunteer help for showing up late."

"Thank you, Detective Reardan. We—El and I—thought we could maybe help ... offer our personal insights into Mike Rutger's recollections."

"We promise not to get in your way," El said, crossing her heart.

Reardan thought a minute. He looked at Winchester who nodded with a blink of his eyes. "Yeah," Reardan said. "Might as well since you already got the time off."

"Park around the back of the station," Winchester said. "I'll meet you there at 12:45."

∞∞∞∞∞

Never did I expect to find myself sitting behind one of the precinct's two-way windows. Yet there I was, along with Margo and Guy Winchester watching Sam Reardan and Mike Rutger on the other side. Mike was unaware we were inches away, our presence totally obscured. I was comfortable in my role as an observer, primed as I felt sure Margo was as well, to offer any insights that might prove helpful. We half-way listened to Reardan recite his list of dos and don'ts regarding the interview process while Winchester flipped through his little black book, I figured to be prepared for the actual Mike Rutger interview. I was not, however, prepared for Winchester's comments on our eleven o'clock meeting.

"I gather you and Mike Rutger go back a long way," Winchester said

283

Loretta Giacoletto

without looking up from a notebook page containing miniscule scribbles.

"As teenagers, nothing serious," I replied.

"Lucky for you. Rutger was never in your league. In case you're wondering how I know, he used to be a regular around here before I made detective."

"He may've alluded to some minor issues." None of which concerned me, I wanted to say.

"Lucky for him they never got too far out of hand before he wised up. Nevertheless, he's still not in your league."

"And what league would that be, Detective Winchester?"

"The same as your mother's, Ms. Savino."

"Take that as a compliment, El," Margo finally chimed in and about time. How very un-Margo she'd been up until then, staying quiet while Winchester badgered me like I was guilty of some wrongdoing, before or after the fact.

Nor was Winchester through casting subtle aspersions. "Both of you seem pretty savvy. By any chance did you prep Rutger prior to this interview? Be honest now."

"Mike? Please," Margo said before I had a chance to respond. "The guy doesn't need any prepping, not with his line of never-ending bullshit. He'll wear Sam down before Sam wears him down."

"Sam is it. That must've been some party on Lindell Boulevard."

"My apologies for taking liberties with Detective Reardan's given name," Margo said with her sweetest of smiles. "And for not including you on the Sunday evening guest list."

"Shh," Winchester said, touching a forefinger to his lips. "This is a new day and another party's about to begin.

After a preliminary discussion of Mike's employment during the Creole Exchange renovation, Reardan asked him to elaborate on comments he'd made during the Littlejohn dinner, starting with Wilton Blue.

"Sure thing," Mike said. "Wilt was an okay guy who'd lost his way after Vietnam. He'd been hunkering down in a deserted section of the Creole's second floor, along with other squatters who knew a good thing when they saw it. Not a single person had any intentions of leaving until the Corrigans forced them out, a deadline that was fast approaching, what with owners like Alderman Trey Millstone threatening to take away the city's incentives if their condos weren't move-in ready by the promised date. All of which might've worked out, what with that nearby homeless shelter providing breakfast and dinner plus a place to sleep at night."

"Provided there were enough beds," Reardan said.

"You got that right. On the other hand Wilt Blue was not a man to go quietly. Before his post-traumatic stress flared up, he'd taken some college classes in environmental issues and thought the asbestos clean-up guys had done a piss-poor job at the Creole. After bending Trey Millstone's ear one too many times, Millstone threw him a bone, the chance to air his complaints on one of the local TV stations—Channel 4, I think. Wilt practiced what he planned on saying with me. It wasn't half bad, except I did tell him to slow down and leave out the cuss words if he was serious about making a splash—you know, get results."

"Yeah, I get it."

"That afternoon in the Creole basement what do I hear but Horace Corrigan calling out Boris Tainer for approving the asbestos clean-up too soon, before everything was considered *a go*. Boris may've been a mama's boy but that didn't make him an automatic pushover. He blamed Horace for pressuring him on the environmental approval, whatever it took to keep that damn surety agent from having to pay out the insurance claim for not meeting the contract agreement. Not my problem, that's for sure. I got the hell out before either of them saw me.

"Early the next morning I'm searching the second floor for Wilt so he can practice one more time before his big break on TV. Damned if his corner wasn't clean as a whistle. The blanket I gave him in place of the stolen one, gone like the wind. I figured he chickened out and took a hike. Maybe caught a ride south before the weather turned cold."

"Uh-huh," Reardan said. "Moving right along, you mentioned something about closing off a door in the basement."

"It's a something I regret to this day, not speaking up when I should've."

"Yeah, I hear that a lot. Rarely do people talk about their own accomplishments unless it's to cover up their failures."

Mike sat back and blew out air through his teeth. "It happened before I realized Wilt might've got himself in trouble. That same morning Horace Corrigan called my cellphone—something his nephew Val usually did, but not this time. Anyway Horace told me to meet Boris Tainer in the basement, near the old storage room. I'd been there before and knew it contained a lot of junk plus an abandoned mechanical pit. Traffic was crazy that morning, making me a couple minutes later than usual but still on time."

"What about Boris Tainer?" Reardan asked.

"Ready to pounce on me until I told him to knock it off. That didn't stop him from being all nervous and fidgety while I checked out the room before starting on the door. The mechanical pit had been filled with some debris from the basement and under that debris I could see patches of black plastic. The room smelled like chemicals, I figured to help cover up the odor of decaying debris and foul water."

"Did you mention the chemical smell to Mr. Tainer?" Reardan asked.

"Not my problem, leastways I didn't think so. Boris said due to environmental concerns the doorway needed to be filled in with concrete blocks—ASAP. And that Horace wanted me to take care of it. I felt honored that the head honcho trusted me to get the job done the right way. So I did."

"You never thought to look in the pit," Reardan said.

Not Worth Dying For

"At the time, no. I was more concerned about closing in the door so I could get back to my regular job. After Wilt didn't show up for the TV interview or in his second floor corner, I got to wondering what happened to him. I even checked at the VA hospital where I brought him for tests."

"What about Horace Corrigan?"

"Back to business as usual, with Val making the phone calls and issuing Horace's orders. It was Val who hired me to renovate Horace's condo during my off hours."

"To earn extra money you kept your mouth shut?"

"It wasn't just the money. I saw a chance to make something of myself. Val told Morgan Davisson how valuable I was to the Creole project and likewise, River City Builders. Next thing I know, Morgan moves me up to lead carpenter. I ain't looked back since."

"Obviously," Reardan said. "I still recall those pre-carpenter days when we were hauling your ass in here every couple of weeks."

"Working fulltime and making decent money goes a long way toward rehabilitation without incarceration."

"Can't argue with you there." Reardan showed him the evidence Franco had offered, letting the locket dangle from its chain. "What about this?"

Mike grabbed the swinging piece. He turned the locket over several times, rubbing his thumb into the engraved initials on the backside. "It could've been the one Wilt swore somebody stole from him. Sure as hell don't know why anyone would want it, or the Bible he claimed got stolen, other than to upset Wilt so much he'd decide to give up his corner. Where'd you get it, from Romaine Sloane?"

"You knew Ms. Sloane?"

"Better than most. She hung out at Horace's condo while I was working there weekends, always putting in her two cents. We got along okay but I never trusted her. And, no, I didn't have sex with her. Nor did I

287

kill her. Or Val Corrigan or Horace Corrigan. What the hell. Why bite the hand that feeds."

"Including Ms. Sloane's?"

"No way. Her hand was always open, waiting to be fed." Mike looked toward the window, one corner of his mouth turned into a slight smile. "Anything else, Detective Reardan?"

"Since you asked, any thoughts on who killed Val Corrigan or Romaine Sloane?"

"If you're asking if I think Boris Tainer had something to do with either murder, I don't know."

"In other words: See no evil. Hear no evil. Speak no evil."

"Not quite. I told you what I saw and what I heard. The rest I leave up to you."

"Time will tell," Reardan said.

"Speaking of, I gotta get back to work—if that's okay with you."

"Yeah, 'til next time," Reardan said, gesturing one fat thumb toward the door.

Reardan waited for Mike to leave before he entered the room where we'd been observing his interview. He sat in the only remaining chair, next to Winchester who didn't bother looking up—too busy writing in his little black book.

"Any thoughts?" Reardan asked, looking from Margo to me.

"You first, El," Margo said, "After all you know Mike better than I do."

"That's debatable," I said. "Considering the wet greeting he gave you the other day."

Not Worth Dying For

Our usual give and take got Winchester's attention but not in a good way. He closed his little book and slammed it on the table. "What the shit. Unless the two of you two have something worthwhile to contribute, take a hike and let Detective Reardan and me do our job."

As much as I hated to admit it, Winchester had every reason to be annoyed with Margo and me. This was not the time for our being coy or self-deprecating. After we practically groveled in our subsequent apologies, I motioned for Margo to go first, as with all things we did as a team.

"Mike may be a bit rough around the edges," she said with thoughtful candor, "but I believe what he said to be true, at least from his perspective. Although ... I do have to wonder how this street-smart guy could've been so naïve about the junk room. He sees the pit filled with debris, smells the chemicals that might've been covering the odor of a decaying body, and after Wilt goes missing, doesn't make a possible head-scratching connection. "Talk about biting the hand that feeds. Mike practically licked the sweat off of Val's and Horace's."

"The Corrigans were no dummies," I added. "They fed Mike's ambition, gave him opportunities he wouldn't have otherwise had, in exchange for his silence and loyalty. Does that make him an accomplice, Detective Winchester?"

Winchester hesitated before answering. "To what and with whom? At this point, too early for me or Detective Reardan to make any determinations."

"Break-time," Reardan said, checking his watch. "Avoid the precinct's front entrance and come back here no later than 2:45. That is, if you're still interested in hearing Boris Tainer's version of the storage room and whatever followed."

Lunch consisted of coffee down the street, consumed while we silently pondered the Rutger interview and then took care of business in the ladies room.

"Your thoughts," I asked Margo while we leaned over two

neighboring basins, rinsing soapy lather from our hands.

Margo dried her hands. She checked out her image in the mirror, not one strand of hair out of place. Not one eyelash caked with mascara. Only then did she speak. "Hard to say since I don't know Mike Rutger that well. And the Mike I knew as a teenager is more than a whistle stop from the Mike I've now reacquainted myself with."

"True, although I didn't realize you paid that much attention to Mike back then. Or now. " A bit of jealousy had reared its ugly head within me, so obscure I doubt Margo noticed. But I had, enough to make me uncomfortable. "I did notice that today's Mike and yesterday's Mike still have one common denominator—vulnerability."

"Rather charming, wouldn't you say?"

More like cheesy, Margo's lame attempt to bait me. "Rather insecure would be my take," I countered, a reminder of my own shortcomings.

"Let's not forget those ambitious balls Mike has grown over the years," Margo said.

"Not big enough to kill a man he befriended, one who trusted him."

"Like the Corrigans trusted Mike." Margo made a show of sending one hand to her surprised mouth. "Oops, that didn't come out the way I meant it to."

"Maybe a Freudian slip."

Having returned to our same seats facing the two-way window, Margo and I watched Sam Reardan go through the same preliminaries with Boris Tainer that he'd done with Mike Rutger a short time before, creating a basic profile of the man's existence. Unlike Mike who lived in St. Louis, Tainer lived across the river in Granite City, a working-class Illinois town that once thrived on the steel mill industry.

"Will this be a case of *he said, he said?*" I asked Guy Winchester.

290

Not Worth Dying For

He leaned back, covered his mouth, and yawned before answering. "Highly unlikely."

"Then you already have an idea who the killer is," Margo said.

"We're good but not that good. Not yet anyway. Besides, we're talking two, possibly three deaths. Whatever gave you the idea there's only one perp?"

"Nothing in particular. Just thinking out loud."

"Better you should listen first," Winchester said, "before coming to conclusions that don't pan out."

"Shh," I said, mimicking Winchester's previous finger to the lips. "Detective Reardan has loosened his tie. He's unbuttoning his shirt collar."

"Good observation." Winchester sat back and bent one long leg, resting his ankle on the opposite knee. "Let the games begin."

"There's more than one?" I asked.

"Always, Ms. Savino, always."

Boris Tainer took a long gulp of soda from the 12-ounce bottle Reardan had given him during the warm-up and then wiped his mouth with the back of one hand. "Whatever you think I might've done, think again because I sure as hell didn't."

"Whoa," Reardan said. "This is a basic interview, one of many we've conducted in the past few months, mostly regarding the death of Val Corrigan and more recently that of Romaine Sloane. The two victims may've had a mutual connection or simply been the result of an unfortunate coincidence."

"That's not the impression I got Sunday evening," Tainer said, "the way you jumped all over me."

Reardan leaned forward. He settled his forearms on the table and

291

interlaced his fingers. "You mean certain accusations made by the waiter Michael Rutger—an incident that supposedly occurred some ten years ago. Totally out of line during a private dinner party, which is why I invited you in for a civilized one-on-one."

"Thanks, I appreciate that."

"Would you mind giving me your version of the Creole incident?" Reardan asked. "Or, to simplify matters would it be okay if I asked you a few questions?"

"Ask away. I got nothing to hide."

Tainer drained the remaining soda while Reardan skimmed over the first page of typewritten notes he taken from his folder. "Going back those ten years, whose idea was it to close off that Creole Exchange storeroom?"

"Horace Corrigan's," Tainer said without hesitation. "He called me one morning during my drive to work, wanted me to meet him in the Creole basement, at the old store room used as a catch-all for construction scrap, dilapidated furniture, junk and more junk. By the time I got there, Horace, who considered himself above any form of manual labor, had just finished shoveling filler into the old mechanical pit. Seems he was worried about a possible lawsuit in the event some idiot stumbled into the hole and broke a leg or worse. The more we talked, the more we—make that Horace—decided it would be easier to block in the door instead of hauling out the useless crap. Having Rutger take care of the door instead of a stone mason was Horace's idea—to save a few bucks in labor costs. He made the phone call and told Rutger to meet me, that I'd tell him what needed to be done. End of story—no big deal."

"Any idea what was in the pit?" Reardan asked.

"Building scrap, dead rats and mice that stunk to high heaven, according to Horace. I had no reason to doubt the man's word. Just so happened there was a shelf in the maintenance closet that contained the ideal chemicals for dissolving waste and eliminating odors, so I poured some in the pit."

"Thank you, Mr. Tainer. That's very helpful."

Not Worth Dying For

Tainer scooted his chair back and started to get up, only to have Reardan stop him with his next words. "Just a few more questions, if you don't mind." Reardan got a bottled water for himself and another soda for Tainer.

"That's my cue to get in there," Winchester said from our side of the glass. He untangled his legs and stood up. "Pay attention, Savino Sisters."

As soon as Winchester entered the interview room, he introduced himself to Boris Tainer. After Reardan briefed Winchester on his conversation with Tainer—as if Winchester didn't already know—the three men assumed some level of comfort at the table.

As did Margo and I in the observation room. "I suppose we should take notes," Margo whispered to me.

"No need to whisper. Use your cellphone for notes."

"Well, duh," Margo said. "Where have you been for the past ten years? Never mind."

"No need to backpedal. I got it the first time. This works for both of us, having Winchester out there, away from you and me."

Tainer drank half the contents of his second soda before taking a breath to ask, "You have more questions?"

"A few," Winchester said. "According to the State of Illinois Gun Registration, you own a Walther PPK .380 handgun. Is that correct?"

"Yes and no." Tainer paused to lick his upper lip. "I did own a Walther PPK semi-automatic, which I used for target practice. Unfortunately, it's gone."

"Gone, as in misplaced, lost, or stolen?"

"Well, I didn't misplace it. And I didn't lose it. So, I guess that leaves stolen, sort of."

293

"From your house in Granite City," Winchester said.

"My mother's house. I live there with her. Kept the gun for protection among other things. Last time I looked, back in June, the damn thing was gone."

"Did you report this to the police?"

"Nope. I figured it would turn up sooner or later. Mother sometimes goes through my things and takes what she thinks might be a danger to me. She's not quite right anymore."

"Yeah, that would be a tough row to hoe for the both of you," Winchester said as he reached for a bottle of water. After opening it and taking a swallow, he continued. "So what happened after Mike Rutger closed in the door?"

"Nothing. He went back to his carpenter job. I went back to my job as an environmental engineer, not only at the Creole but elsewhere. Eventually, the Creole project got completed—on time and to everyone's satisfaction."

"Horace Corrigan made a bundle of money on that project," Reardan said. "As did his nephew and partner, Val Corrigan."

"God bless the American way," Tainer said. "I got no objection to people making money, as long as they don't take unfair advantage of me in the process."

"Ain't that the truth," Winchester said. "How well did you know Val Corrigan?"

"Well enough to know he took care of Horace's dirty work."

"Comes with the territory, I guess," Winchester said. "Like you taking care of closing off that storage room. Better yet, having Rutger take care of it."

"A no-big-deal that happened years ago."

"Whereas the murder of Val Corrigan is still a Major Case on-going investigation."

Not Worth Dying For

"You don't say. I almost lost track of it, what with barely a mention in the newspapers or TV anymore."

"Considering all those years you did business with Mr. Corrigan, any thoughts on who might've killed him?"

"Isn't that why Kat Dorchester is sitting in jail?"

"In all probability, not much longer," Reardan said. "We're considering other possible suspects."

Tainer took another swig of soda and smacked his lips. "Maybe one of those many women Val had been stringing along for years."

"You knew about them."

"Just rumors, no names. I ain't into kinky gossip. If there's nothing else, can I go? Otherwise, I need to call my mother. She'll be worried if I don't come home for supper."

"Not a problem," Reardan said, pushing back his chair. "You've been most helpful. I hope we can call on you again, should the need arise."

Kat Dorchester getting out of jail, halleluiah! What a nice surprise and affirmation of our justice system, in spite of Auntie Kat's wretched attack on our mother that in all probability would end their Best Friends Forever status. As for Margo and me, having already engaged in a running commentary during the Tainer interview, we could barely contain ourselves while waiting for Reardan and Winchester to put in an appearance. Within a matter of minutes they walked into the observation room and sat down. Winchester placed a folder on the table but didn't bother opening it.

"Thanks for allowing us to observe," Margo said.

"It wasn't from the goodness of my heart," Reardan said, his way of letting us know he outranked his partner. "With Kat Dorchester set to be released, Detective Winchester and I would like the perspective of an unbiased layperson." Having transferred his attention from Margo to me, he added as an afterthought, "Make that two."

295

"Well, for the most part El and I tend to agree. Right El?" Without waiting for my positive response, Margo continued. "First off, we think Wilton Blue is buried in the mechanical pit. And that Horace Corrigan killed Wilton."

"Horace Corrigan, really?" Winchester said. "Why Horace and not Tainer?"

"Human nature," Margo said. "In Horace's case, not wanting to do the grunt work. Had Tainer killed Wilt, he would've buried the body without involving Horace, other than to insist the store room door be filled in, as a safety precaution, which happened anyway—regardless of who issued the order."

Reardan cleared his throat. "So, Horace eventually dies via self-induced euthanasia. No *ifs*, *ands*, or *buts*. No way am I budging on the medical examiner's report or Horace's own words in an after-the-fact videotape sent to this precinct."

"We'll take your word for that," Margo said. "Fast forward to August of this year. Consider the possibility of Val Corrigan being murdered for the wrong reason. Suppose, just suppose, that after Horace died, a yet-to-be-determined individual starts blackmailing Boris Tainer for the murder of Wilt Blue, a crime Tainer didn't actually commit but in all likelihood, helped cover up."

I picked up on El's theory from there. "Tainer figures the blackmailer must be Val Corrigan since he and Horace pretty much shared everything, including Romaine Sloane. After years of paying out, Tainer decides he's had enough and kills Val. But the blackmail demands continue. I'm going back to a comment Mike Rutger made to me, about Romaine being privy to all of Horace's dealings. She tells Mike she saw the body of a dead man at the Creole, a body that disappeared shortly thereafter. It could've been that of Wilton Blue, who went missing around the same time. But then Horace orders Romaine to shut up about the body, so she does."

"Think Daddy Warbucks," Margo said, rubbing the fingers and thumb of one hand together.

My turn again to add my two cents. "After Horace dies, the generous allowance he'd been giving her gets reduced to a modest monthly annuity—a pittance compared to the lifestyle she'd been enjoying. What does she do? Blackmail Boris Tainer, forcing him to either move on or continue living with his elderly mother because that's all he can afford."

"And what about this," Margo said. She held up one forefinger while glancing at the notes on her cell phone. "Tainer admitted having a Walther PPK revolver. Was that the kind of gun used to kill Val Corrigan?"

"Still considered confidential," Reardan said without revealing any expression in his voice or general demeanor.

"But why didn't Tainer question your interest in his gun? He didn't even break a sweat. And what about Romaine Sloane? How did she die?"

"Ms. Sloane was beaten to death with a blunt instrument."

"How horrible," I said, conjuring up a picture of Romaine's bloody corpse.

"Murder under any circumstances is an inexcusable way to die," Winchester said.

I looked at Margo and we both nodded in unison. "Please understand," Margo said. "This is not out of morbid curiosity, but would it be possible for us to see photos of the crime scenes?"

"For what purpose?" Reardan asked.

"As the saying goes, a picture is worth a thousand words," Margo said. "Both El and I knew Romaine and to a lesser degree, Val. Picturing how they lived is one thing; picturing how they died is quite another. I would hope those images would provide some clues as to why Romaine and Val were brutally murdered."

There are times when Margo amazes me with her subtle sensitivity. This was one of those times.

Reardan nodded to Winchester, who stretched his long arm to a folder sitting at one end of the counter. He opened the folder and pulled out two sets of photographs. One set he gave to Margo, the other to me. Had I not known I was viewing the corpse of Val Corrigan, I would never have recognized him from the photo Mom had shown me or the Ritz-Carlton photo displayed on the Internet. Val was laying on his side, clothes disheveled, and a look of disbelief clouding his bloodied face. There were two gunshot wounds—one to his bleeding heart, the other between his eyes. "A perfect bullseye," I murmured. "That must've taken some practice."

"Hmm," Reardan said, followed by an indistinguishable sound that may've been a grunt. Margo hadn't said a word about her set but was chewing on her lower lip when we exchanged photos. Nothing could've prepared me for Romaine Sloane, her once attractive face crushed into a gaping skull, brains spilling out onto her high forehead, blood woven into dark hair splayed out on the ground. A dislocated shoulder, the bones most likely smashed, along with her collarbone.

"Romaine must've put up quite a fight," I said, "judging from her fingernails. How she loved showing off her pricey manicures and pedicures."

"This would've taken a very strong man," Margo said.

"Or a deranged woman," I added. "An unexpected first blow, violent enough to knock Romaine off her feet. After that, repeated blows from a very angry attacker."

"You think Tainer was capable of that kind of anger?" Reardan asked.

"Hard to say. I don't really know the man."

"And yet you think he's guilty of two murders," Reardan said. "Val Corrigan's death appears to be planned somewhat in advance ... although it may've started over an argument. Romaine Sloane's death—the killer definitely had anger management issues."

"Are you suggesting a test of the waters—so to speak," Margo said. "That we do something to provoke Boris Tainer."

"Are you out of your mind," Winchester said, waving her off in obvious annoyance. "We asked for some civilian input, not advice from Wonder Women wannabes."

Not Worth Dying For

"End of session," Reardan said as he got to his feet. "Do not, I repeat, Savino Sisters, do not attempt some lame-brained scheme on your own. You're not trained. You're not qualified. And in the event you get yourself bogged down in a pile of deep shit, you are not to expect the Major Case squad to rush in and bail you out. That kind of pipedream scenario represents made-for-TV crapola."

Memo to self:

1. *Reardan and Winchester don't play good cop, bad cop.*
2. *Margo and I are smarter than they think we are.*
3. *Crapola has certain advantages.*
4. *Still consider Mike as ho-hum.*
5. *Not sure he's that far out of my league but Winchester may be right.*

35

Mother's Day

What better way to introduce a somewhat sticky topic than after an incredible romp in the hay, or to be more precise, in the more realistic venue of my bedroom, especially with Zio Franco otherwise occupied that evening, volunteering his culinary services at Trattoria Tino.

My latest and best-ever squeeze rolled over to face me. He propped himself up on one elbow and in no uncertain terms, asked, "Are you out of your obscenely misguided mind? No, don't answer that because nothing you'd say would make an ounce of sense." Cupping my chin in his hand, he planted an endearing kiss on my lips, bold enough to make my toes tingle for a second time in less than ten minutes.

Obscenely misguided, really? Had those words been regurgitated from the mouth of any man other than Greg Lupino, I would've shoved him out of my bed and out of my life with no regrets whatsoever. But not Greg; Greg was different and hopefully pliable enough to reconsider the off-hand request I'd casually made of him.

"Let me explain," I said with reasonable restrain. "El and I think—"

"Not just you but also El," he countered, as if El couldn't possibly be part of what he considered a hair-brained scheme.

"Both of us, and don't interrupt me again."

He listened and after a bit of naughty persuasion on my part, agreed to lend his support—provided El wasn't directly involved. Little did he know, my sister was far gutsier than the milquetoast she often passed herself off as being.

But then, after a private reevaluation of our options by phone, El and I decided that since Greg was an important part of the plan we'd devised together, we'd let him think he was in charge. Sort of.

"You made the phone call?" I asked, having called Greg at work the next day.

"For the third time, yes. The man was so excited he could barely contain himself. This evening, his house, seven-thirty. After supper, his words not mine."

"After supper, of course. Why am I not surprised."

"What? You would've preferred sharing a meal with him?"

"Please, that meal at the Ritz auction was one share too many. Don't forget to pick up El before you stop by for me."

"Two people was our agreement, Margo—you and I."

"It's still the two of us. El stays in the backseat, unless you prefer she drive her own car."

"Hell, no. Dealing with one car is bad enough, in the event a violent reaction triggers the need for a quick getaway."

"Triggers, really," I said. "You watch too many cop shows."

Loretta Giacoletto

"More like horror movies."

Our going-no-where discussion closed with an abrupt click of the receiver from Greg's end, which I interpreted as an okay to proceed.

I was no stranger to Granite City, having been there a number of times during the day with Blake Harrington when he was handling depositions for his injury clients. But on a cold November evening the Illinois side of the Mississippi seemed even more dismal and foreboding than its industrial Missouri counterpart. Our trek began with Greg behind the wheel of his Lexus, me riding shotgun, and spread out behind me, El. After crossing the McKinley Bridge into Illinois, we followed Route 3 as it led to the village of Venice, where boarded-up buildings stood side by side with well-maintained structures housing the village offices.

"Did you have to come this way," I said, looking down from the overpass we were crossing to countless railroad tracks below that were weaving through an industrial area as we entered the village of Madison.

"Now that you mention it, the area does seem kind of creepy," El said, shifting her butt into a more comfortable position.

"Only after dark," Greg said from over his shoulder. "Trust me, I designed two warehouses in the area and could travel this route with my eyes closed.

"No need to demonstrate," El said. "I won't say another word unless an emergency should arise, which I seriously doubt would happen, especially since there's three of us and who would be foolish enough—"

"We get it, El," I assured her while ignoring the flapping of butterflies disrupting my stomach.

After passing old warehouses, some dilapidated, others still in use, we entered Granite City, what had once been the thriving home of numerous steel mills. Now those mills had been reduced to an essential few, more important than ever to an economy extending beyond the immediate city. Eventually we reached the area known as West Granite, in particular, 23rd

Street, where block after block of modest homes led westward toward the looming silhouettes of nearby mills.

Gesturing to a long fenced-in stretch of vacant ground across from the houses, El asked, "Any idea what used to be there?"

"You got me," Greg said. He pointed up ahead to a series of large plumes belching into the atmosphere. "Those I do know about. Steam coming from ovens at the coke plant."

"And the smell?" I asked, pressing the already tight window button even tighter to keep out the distinctive odor.

"Burning rubber or maybe coal," Greg said, impressing me with his knowledge that went beyond the field of architecture. "Get a load of that endless stream of trucks delivery coal to the coke plant. That'll go on for hours on end."

"A pain in the neck for the unfortunate homeowners," El said.

"But one that translates to low-cost housing and property taxes for this old part of Granite," I countered, based on my experience with some of Blake's personal injury clients. "Slow down, Greg, we're almost there."

Having arrived on the wide street leading to our destination, Greg parked in front of an inconspicuous frame house. As planned, El stayed behind to cool her heels in the back seat while Greg and I headed up the sidewalk. Two large pots of faded chrysanthemums flanked the front entrance, a nice touch that lessened the anxiety I tried to ignore. After several unanswered rings of the doorbell, Greg decided it wasn't working and instead knocked with commanding authority. His personal touch made all the difference. The door opened partway, revealing a tall, buxom woman who might've been this side of eighty. Most of her dark hair had turned into a cloud of white, a mushrooming bomb that had exploded on top on her head.

"Do I know you?" the woman asked with a slight curl of her upper lip.

Greg gave her our names, then followed up with a warmhearted explanation. "We're friends of your son, Mrs. Tainer. He's expecting Margo

303

and me but traffic was on the light side so we got here early. My apologies for any inconvenience."

"You know my name," she said in a voice betraying no emotion.

"Boris frequently talks about you," I said.

"You don't say—good or bad?"

"Good, of course. Having now met you, I can't imagine otherwise." A bit of a stretch if ever there was but we had a limited amount of time to complete our mission.

"I guess it would be okay for you to come in." She opened the door halfway and gestured for us to enter. "Just don't get any airs of familiarity by referring to me by my first name. In case you're wondering, it used to be Milena before I changed it to Mercy."

"What a lovely name," I said, hoping it reflected a similar personality.

Greg tapped his jacket pocket. "I brought Boris some tickets to next week's Blues Hockey game. He's quite the fan, same as me. I'm also a gun collector, same as Boris." Having gotten no response from Mrs. Tainer, Greg took advantage of her silence to check his cell phone. "Time appears to be slipping away from me—my apologies." He placed the ticket envelope in Mrs. Tainer's outstretched palm and she shoved the envelope into her sweatshirt pocket, her eyes never leaving Greg's face. "Uh … Boris mentioned something about his Walther PPK, a firearm of special interest to me. Would it be possible for me to take a look at it before I leave?"

Pursing her lips, she gave some thought to his request before giving him an answer. "Well, I'm betwixt and between, what with Boris not knowing I took possession of the damn thing. Had to take it away from him after the last mishap."

"Mishap?"

"Damn near shot his toe off. Good thing I patched him up, me being a retired practical nurse. Anyways, he's all better now."

"That's good to know," I said. "The gun—could we see it?"

304

"I suppose seeing wouldn't cause any harm. Wait here."

While Mercy Tainer went down to the basement, Greg and I checked out the vast display of living room photos, most of which focused on Mercy from her childhood years as a first communicant to that of a baton-twirling teenager with the high school marching band. Weird, the realization that this woman once lived a care-free existence filled with the usual excitement of growing up. There was one photo of an immigrant couple, most likely her parents. Also a wedding photo of Mercy and her husband but no others of them as a couple. Boris Tainer had his share of photos as well, the usual yearbook pose and a few more recent, including one that might've been taken to commemorate the Ritz Carlton auction, those familiar shirt buttons straining to hold in his abundant belly.

Having checked the time on his cell phone, Greg asked, "What's taking her so long?"

"Maybe she forgot where she hid the gun."

"Oh brother." Greg went to the basement door and called down. "Everything okay, Mrs. Tainer?"

Mercy didn't answer right away but when she did, it was in a barely audible voice conveying pain. "I fell and hurt my ankle. My knee too. I might need help getting up."

Greg was ready to head down the stairs until I grabbed his arm and whispered, "Not so fast. I'm texting El so she'll know what's happening. You make sure the front door is unlocked, just in case."

Details, it's those little things that make a difference, plus the loud groan from Mercy Tainer. I followed Greg down the stairs, expecting to find Mercy at the bottom. She was nowhere to be seen, although most of the lower level was illuminated with overhead lighting, a nice touch for the ornate pool table occupying one section. "Boris's man cave," I whispered to Greg.

"You got that right," Mercy bellowed as she came out of a shadowy area, her right hand gripping what appeared to be the Walther PPK. The gun wavered back and forth between Greg and me until her forefinger finally settled on the trigger, its barrel aimed directly at me.

305

"You idiots must think I just fell off the turnip truck," Mercy said. "I'll show you his gun all right. Where would you like to see it? Between the eyes or in your heart. Either way, you'll be dead before you hit the floor. You there, Ms. Smarty Pants. Step onto the concrete now."

"Why the concrete?" I asked.

"Silly girl, concrete's way easier to clean than having to deal with blood soaked into my new carpeting." She paused, gesturing with her free hand to encompass the entire area. "As you can see, I'm a stickler for cleanliness, a trait I consider next to godliness."

God bless Greg, my human shield and defender of immobilized terror. He stepped in front of me and appealed to her gullible side, "I'm so sorry, Mrs. Tainer. It was never my intention to offend you."

"Like hell it wasn't." Again, she waved the gun in our direction. "You and that Val Corrigan fella must've been cut from the same cloth. Mealy-mouthed, hypocritical do-gooders with no conscience. Too bad smartass Corrigan didn't share my views on the virtues of honesty, justice, and morality. All those years, letting us think it was him bleeding us dry on nothing more than hearsay and ... and ..."

"Innuendo," I said.

"That too. Forcing us to exist in the near poverty of my parental home. And for what? Giving some homeless guy a final place to rest his head."

"You mean Wilton Blue," I said. "Did Boris kill him?"

"Hell no, all my boy did was cover up for the real killer, Horace Corrigan. But that didn't stop his nephew Val.

"Only it wasn't Val Corrigan who did those things, was it, Mrs. Tainer?" I said for the sake of argument and a possible extension of minutes on my life.

The woman I no longer thought of as Mercy, expelled a disgusted grunt. "The damn fool came to our house, insulting Boris with Cardinal baseball tickets in one hand and the other itching for more money by challenging my boy to a game of pool. Doesn't matter how fair the game was, or if either man cheated. But when Corrigan won, I showed him the barrel of Boris's gun and told him we'd had enough of his bloodsucking, year after year. Corrigan should've spoke up, then and there. Instead, he started advancing on me, claiming his innocence like some red-faced schoolboy. Saying he just wanted a favorable environmental report on his latest project, as if Boris could be bought with some lousy baseball tickets. That's when I shot him. Once between the eyes, once in the heart. I could do that again without batting an eye. What a bloody mess!"

"Which explains the new carpet," I said, squeezing Greg's hand. "Nice color."

"Just so you know, I ain't no monster. Boris and I waited until the middle of the night before transporting Corrigan to his final resting place. We laid him out at Horseshoe Lake, nice and peaceful it was. I used to fish there for bluegill with my pa. He came from Bulgaria and never stopped working until the day he dropped dead, shoveling coal into the steel mill furnace."

"You have my belated sympathy," I said in a voice I didn't recognize as my own.

"Hmph, don't try buttering me up." Using her left hand to steady her right arm, Mrs. Tainer aimed the gun at Greg. "I might not be fast enough to do both of you but one wouldn't be a problem. Most likely Mr. Blues Hockey tickets since Margo here wouldn't move fast enough to save him. Right, Margo?"

"Of course, Mrs. Tainer, but we still have questions before we meet our Maker. What about the woman—Romaine Sloane. Did she come here too?"

She relaxed her position. "That greedy bitch? Hell, no. After Corrigan made me kill him, we expected the blackmail to end. Instead it went on. At a higher price, I might add, until we decided to find out who else we were dealing with. Missing one payment was all it took. The real bloodsucker told Boris to meet her on the Illinois riverfront one night. So I invited myself to the party. What a numbskull Romaine Sloane was, bouncing out of the Cadillac we helped paid for, not a care in the world, and not a soul around except the three of us. Boris tried to reason with her, get the monthly payments reduced by half. The bitch wouldn't hear of it. In fact, she added on an extra hundred per month for what she called insolence. That's when I knew we had to end it, then and there."

"You hit her?" I asked.

She nodded. "With my twirling baton 'cause Boris couldn't abide my bringing the gun, as if it was my fault Corrigan got out of line."

"Didn't Romaine try to defend herself," Greg asked.

"Too late for that. While she was shaking her head no to everything Boris suggested, I whopped her a good one behind both knees. Down she went like crumpled cardboard. I turned her pretty face into a bloody mess, again and again until she quit fighting me and gave up the ghost. For good measure I whopped her some more because the sound of bone crunching made me feel good. She didn't get a decent send-off like Corrigan. From car trunk to side of the road was good enough for that unrepentant bitch."

As soon as Mrs. Tainer started to resume her firing position, Greg pushed me to one side and he zigzagged in another direction. I rolled behind a chair, squeezed my eyes shut, and waited for the sound of death, but instead heard a sudden yelp of surprise. I opened my eyes in time to see the soles of Mrs. Tainer's shoes airborne as was Mrs. Tainer herself, having slipped on a rag rug covering the concrete part of the floor. The gun went off, a bullet whizzing past my ear and in all probability embedding itself in the paneled wall.

"Damn you," she said, gun in hand and on her knees while attempting to regain her standing position. "Hold still while I get myself resituated. Hold still, I tell you!"

Not me. I backed off in time to see El running down the stairs, phone to her ear while giving the 911 operator our location. She tripped over Mrs. Tainer, causing both of them to fall and a second bullet to barely miss Greg before finding its way into the sofa. Mrs. Tainer wound up in a tangle with El, her weight pinning El to the hard concrete. Thank God Greg was able

308

Not Worth Dying For

to remove the gun from Mrs. Tainer's hand. I pushed the half-dazed woman away from El, who immediately scrambled to her feet.

"Did you contact Reardan?" I asked between gulps of breath.

"Before I called 911," she said, giving me her smile along with a thumbs up.

Within minutes the local police arrived. After helping Mrs. Tainer up the stairs, they listened to a blubbering account of her perceived justifiable homicides while I stood off to one side with Greg and El, making ourselves as inconspicuous as possible. Outside, the evening was lit up like early Christmas, what with the flashing lights of two police cars, which may've explained Boris Tainer's level of high anxiety when he came crashing through the front door.

"Mother, Mother! Are you okay?" he yelled, his head swiveling around the living room in search of her.

"Over here, son," 1she said from her position on the sofa. "Don't be worrying about me, you hear. I got everything under control, including the hockey tickets."

Mercy Tainer was still patting her sweatshirt pocket when Sam Reardan and Guy Winchester walked in. The detectives looked from El to me and back to El, all the while shaking their heads.

"Anytime, Detectives Reardan and Winchester," I said, breaking the spell of disbelief surrounding the two of them. "As you may recall, I did tell you to never underestimate the crime-solving ability of the Savino Sisters."

36

La Famiglia Rosina

On Saturday after the Tainer incident in Granite City, Margo and I were seated in the kitchen of our Holly Hills family home. Greg was there too, charming our mother and nonnie as only an Italian can do—Italian-American to be more precise.

"Is it too soon to open the wine?" asked Stefano—my nonno as I now thought of him, even before he and Nonnie Clarita made it official.

"I'll get it, Papa," Mom said, putting a smile on his face that traveled from one to another around the table like a contagious wildfire.

Franco puffed up his chest, tapping the fingers of his right hand to his heart. "Papa, she said. Does this now make me your official brother? Not in secret but for all the world to know?"

"If you'll have me," Mom said, passing the bottle for Greg to open. "I've behaved like a spoiled brat far too long and for that I apologize most profusely." She walked around the table, stopping where each of us had stood for an exchange of hugs and kisses.

While Mom was making her family apology tour, Greg poured the first

310

round. We *saluted*, we drank, and then repeated with more enthusiasm than the first round. Never did I dream our recent adventure in Italy would come full circle and end up back in St. Louis. Nonnie with her first love she planned on marrying as soon as possible. Franco hoping for a work permit that would allow him to stay longer than he originally planned. Mom with the family she never knew as a child. Margo leaning toward a more lasting relationship with Greg Lupino, a match approved by everyone in the family. A few miles away Kat Dorchester might've been relaxing in the comfort of her home, reassembling her life and real estate career. As for her relationship with Mom, I didn't know if their BFF status would ever be what it once was.

Under lock and key were Mercy Tainer, who proudly confessed to the murders of Val Corrigan and Romaine Sloane, along with her son Boris Tainer, who confessed to covering up Horace Corrigan's murder of Wilton Blue, and would've happily thrown his mother under the bus had she not gone into such explicit detail outlining his involvement in her horrific crimes.

Having checked the time on my cell phone, I got up and made a show of hurrying to the door while mumbling something about being late for an appointment.

"Your old friend-new friend?" Mom asked.

"Later," I called out, as good a way as any to avoid answering her question.

I drove the short distance to Carondelet Park, parked my car along the street, and got out. From there it was a short walk to the park bench where I'd agreed to meet Mike Rutger. I stopped fifty feet short of the object of my destination. Legs stretched out, one arm across the top of the bench back, eyes closed, a slight smile on his face. He looked at peace with himself, no doubt proud of his role in helping to resolve Val Corrigan's murder as well as tying it into the murder of Romaine Sloane. Mustn't forget the death of Wilton Blue, the details of his murder still unresolved since Boris Tainer's version had not been substantiated, but at least the Vietnam vet had been laid to rest with his parents in Arkansas.

I couldn't help but think back to that summer day long ago, the Riverfront Fair at which Mike had dumped me for an older and much wiser girl, who then dumped him after learning how he'd dumped me. From dumper to dumpee—ah the angst of teenage love and all loves thereafter.

I stood there at Carondelet Park for a long minute, trying to decide if I wanted to resume that long-ago romance by taking it to a more adult level. Or whether I should move on, a wiser and more confident new me. The decision didn't prove to be as difficult as I'd anticipated earlier that day. Having made up my mind, I turned and walked away without looking back to what might've been, secure in the knowledge that I'd found peace within myself.

Memo to self:

    1. I will always be smarter than Mike Rutger.
    2. Paybacks are more precious to give than to receive.
    3. The ultimate payback is happiness.
    4. I am happy.

Not Worth Dying For: From The Savino Sisters Mystery Series is a work of fiction. Names, characters, places, and incidents are either products of the author's imagination or used fictitiously. Any resemblance to actual events, locales, or persons, living or dead, is entirely coincidental. All rights reserved. No part of this publication can be reproduced or transmitted in any form or by any means, electronic or mechanical, without permission in writing from Loretta Giacoletto.

314

BY
LORETTA GIACOLETTO

Mysteries

From The Savino Sisters Mystery Series:
ITALY TO DIE FOR (Book 1)
REGRETS TO DIE FOR (Book 2)
NOT WORTH DYING FOR (Book 3)

LETHAL PLAY

Family Sagas

CHICAGO'S HEADMISTRESS
THE FAMILY ANGEL
FAMILY DECEPTIONS

Coming of Age

FREE DANNER

Short Fiction
A COLLECTION OF GIVERS AND TAKERS

316

ABOUT THE AUTHOR

Loretta Giacoletto divides her time between the St. Louis Metropolitan area of Southern Illinois and Missouri's Lake of the Ozarks where she writes fiction and essays for her blog Loretta on Life while her husband Dominic cruises the waters for bass and crappie. An avid traveler, Loretta has written Italian-American historical sagas inspired by her frequent visits to the Piedmont region of Italy, a mystery series featuring two thirty-something sisters, a St. Louis soccer mom mystery, and an edgy New Adult novel about a young drifter searching for the father who doesn't know he exists. She has been named a finalist in the 2015 and 2014 "Soon to be Famous Illinois Author Project" for her sagas, Family Deceptions and Chicago's Headmistress. Her short fiction has appeared in numerous publications including **Literary Mama, which nominated her story "Tom" for Dzanc's 2010 Best of the Web.**

Made in the USA
Columbia, SC
18 April 2018